Ruins

ALAINA T. LEE

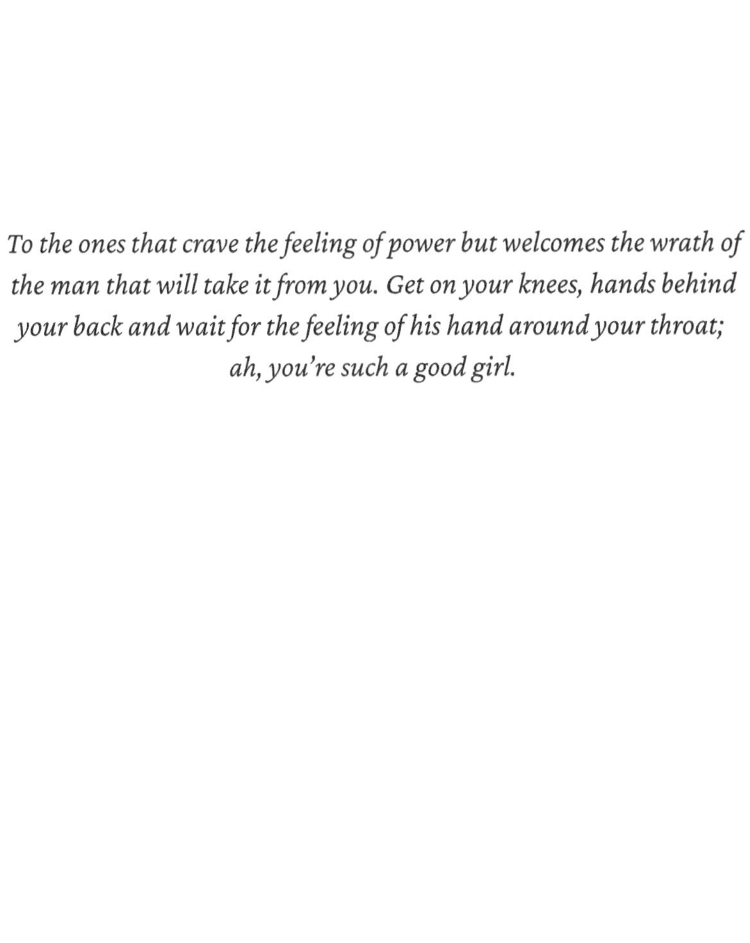

To the ones that crave the feeling of power but welcomes the wrath of the man that will take it from you. Get on your knees, hands behind your back and wait for the feeling of his hand around your throat; ah, you're such a good girl.

CONTENTS

PLAYLIST

Go F**k Yourself x Two Feet
Love Me Harder x Steven Rodriguez
Dive x Luke Combs
Wicked Games x The Weeknd
Heartless x The Weeknd
You broke me first x Tate McRae
Save me x Jelly Roll & Lainey Wilson
Apologize x OneRepublic
What Was I Made For x Billie Eilish
Gonna Love You x Parmalee
Pretty Little Poison x Warren Zeiders
Love in the Dark x Adele
I See Red x Everybody Loves an Outlaw
when the party's over x Billie Eilish
Pointless x Lewis Capaldi
PLEASE x Omido & Ex Habit
Tear It Down x Michael Sanzone
The Door x Teddy Swims
All That Really Matters x ILLENIUM & Teddy Swims

Cold x Paddy Ryan
Trading Places x USHER
Psycho Killer x Talking Heads
Misery Business x Paramore
The Only Exception x Paramore
Kill of the Night x Gin Wigmore

CONTENT WARNINGS

It is important to know and understand that this book contains, BDSM, breath play, suicide (in mention), rape of minor, murder, knife play, blood play, bondage(rope and chains), abduction, CNC, torture, PTSD, drugged drink, forced marriage, death of parent, amnesia memory loss/ repressive memory. If any of these could be triggering to you, I strongly recommend you do not move forward with reading this. Your mental health is important to me and I trust you know your limits. Read at your own risk.

Xoxo,
Alaina T. Lee

CHAPTER ONE

ALESSIA

Fuck, I should've checked the weather before I pulled this stunt of mine. These stupid fucking *family* dinners are driving me insane—especially when I have mountains of other things I need to be doing, like studying for finals. So I decided to ditch my dad's driver that's waiting for me and sneak out of class early to avoid him. I look up at the angry sky as the booming sounds off around me. *Why didn't I just drive myself?* Because that would be too easy, and I can never do easy things. Shaking my head at myself, I start walking towards my apartment that's not too far from my classes.

The rain picks up, and at this point, I'm soaked. My long, chestnut hair is sticking to my face and my vision is turning blurry. I turn when I hear a car approach, rolling my eyes when I spot the black Maserati. *Not today.* I ignore it and keep walking when he rolls the window down and blares his horn at me. I groan and turn toward the rolled-down window, clashing eyes with the devil himself.

Astor.

It must be a cruel fucking world for someone so ruthless

and cold to look so *attractive*. His hair just brushes his dark gray eyes and he has on that stupid fucking white dress shirt again, the one that hugs onto his muscles so tight I think they'll rip through his shirt. He has the sleeves rolled up and the first two buttons undone, allowing me to see pieces of his tattoo seeping out across his chest. The tattoo that continues onto his back. The one that makes me want to drool anytime we're at our family swimming parties. The one that makes me forget that I absolutely hate the fucker that I'm looking at. He watches me ogle him and flashes me that incoherent, annoyed look.

"Get in." It rolls off his tongue as an order and I tilt my head to the side.

He should know by now that if I'm ordered to do it, it doesn't happen. We've known each other our whole lives, our families bonded at the hip, practically. You'd think that since I'd been around him for twenty-two years, that I'd build a tolerance for his tyrant ways—think again. I shake my head and continue walking when he blares the horn again.

"Last chance, *malyshka*. I could give a fuck if you drown out here. Get in or don't, but you're not missing that fucking meeting." I glare at him and push my hands on my hip.

I hated when he called me that. I am not his baby anything.

"Fuck. You," I spit back to him.

At that moment, the weather decides to add onto my spiciness and the thunder makes me shudder. He smirks at me as I look up at the sky and growl. He pushes open the door and I slide in, slamming the door behind me. He raises his eyebrow and I refuse to meet his stare.

"Fucking brat." He pulls off and I groan, realizing I'll have to actually talk to him.

"Take me home. I'm soaked." He ignores me. I turn to face him. "And don't call me a brat...or your baby girl."

"Someone's been brushing up on their Russian," he says sarcastically. I roll my eyes, folding my arms and facing the window.

"Just take me home." He gives me nothing in return, instead he ignores me and keeps his eyes on the road.

The tension is always so thick when we're around each other.

We hate each other, well, at least he acts like he hates me. He avoids me like the black plague, never wanting to be in the same room as me, but yet is still always around. It's...torture. I love his sister, Elsi, and we're pretty close. But us? We can't seem to become friends, no matter how hard I've tried over the years. I finally stopped and just attempted to be a ghost around him. Elsi thinks it's because we're sexually tense with each other. She says that her brother's eyes always linger over me when I walk in a room, that he always pays attention to what I'm doing. I told her she's insane, even though she's right.

We weren't always like this, but I can't remember why he pulled away from me. When we finally *did* talk to each other again, he was so distant and nonchalant that I just avoided any conversation with him. I'll never know what I did to make him go from being one of my closest friends to someone I barely speak to. I asked him once and he ignored me, as usual, as if it was a stupid question. He seems to know why, but also seems to enjoy me scraping my brain to figure out what the fuck I did to deserve it.

"WHY AREN'T YOU WITH YOUR DRIVER?" I ALMOST DON'T REALIZE he's talking because I'm so caught up in my own mind. "Alessia."

"Hmm? Oh sorry."

"Why aren't you with your driver?"

"Why aren't you in class?" I dish back as he shakes his head, turning into my apartment building. He whips into a parking spot, watching two girls that are walking into the building and I roll my eyes. "Always thinking with your dick…" I mumble, reaching for the door handle. He grabs my wrist and stops me.

"Jealous, *malyshka?*" I yank away from him, glancing over my shoulder.

"Thanks for driving me."

"I'll wait for you to get changed." He cuts off his car and pushes the door open. I look at him and shake my head.

"Not a chance. Leave." He rounds the car over to me and wraps his hand around my neck, yanking me to him. He looks me straight in my eyes, his usually dark gray eyes are almost black.

Why is he touching me? We don't touch. Ever.

We avoid each other's presence, we ignore each other's existence most of the time. So why am I so affected by his touch? I don't miss the tightening between my legs as he squeezes harder.

"You are not exempt from family dinners. If I have to sit through the torture, so do you. Now, show me your apartment, *malyshka.*" He lets go and I grab my neck, rubbing where he just squeezed. I narrow my eyes on his and brush pass him, ensuring to bump him as hard as I fucking can.

"Dick," I mumble as I walk through the doors of my building. I smile at the doorman as he opens it for me. "Hi, Beau, they still have you here?"

"I'm here all night, Ms. Ballerini." Giving him a small nod and smile, I head for the elevator. Astor has a blank look on his face that shows little to any emotion. He's looking around and I tilt my head at him.

"Looking for those two girls?"

"Shut up," he says to me.

I glare at him, stepping to him so we're face to face. Well, more like face to chest, because at 5'5 compared to his 6'3, I look like a shrimp.

"Do *not* tell me to shut up." He pushes forward more, and I'm sure he can practically hear my heart beating out of my chest, showing how much this bravery is a charade.

"Or what?" he challenges.

I bite my lip and snarl at him in disgust.

"Why are you even here? *Willingly*, I might add."

"Because I saw you sneaking out of class to avoid your driver. You know they said this is an important dinner, but you were going to miss it anyway. And who would have had to sit and listen to our parents' bitch about it for three hours? *Me*. Not to mention, this is the only time Els gets to see you. You're not upsetting my baby sister."

The elevator dings and he tilts his head towards the exit. I roll my eyes as I pull my keys out of my bag. This is the most he's ever talked to me. I'm not sure why this dinner is so fucking important; he's never cared if I missed them before.

I glance over my shoulder and he crowds my living room. This is a big apartment. One of the biggest in this expensive fucking building, the building where everyone who comes from money hides their precious, piece of shit kids. But for some reason with Astor in here, it suddenly seems small, too fucking small.

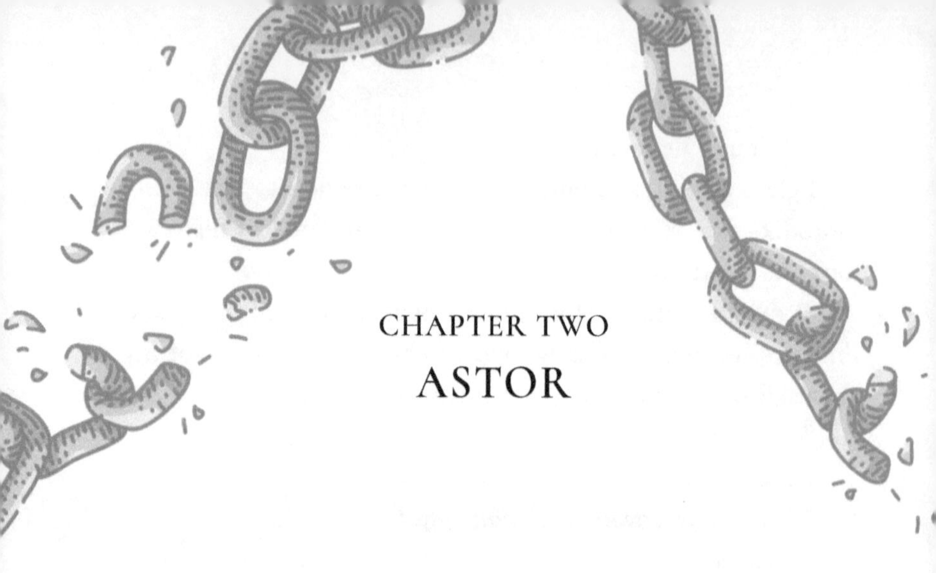

CHAPTER TWO
ASTOR

As expensive as this place is, the fucking lack of security has me on guard. There were two girls that walked in completely unaware of their surroundings. Alessia thought I was watching for sexual purposes, and I don't know why it makes me happy that it pissed her off. It shows how naïve she is. Anyone could take her from this building and no one would know. There are only two cameras in the whole fucking place, and the one out front barely catches anything. I know because I hacked into the system to see for myself. There's no way she should be living here, and alone, at that.

She's been changing for the last fifteen minutes and waiting for her is starting to irritate the shit out of me. I should've let her skip the fucking dinner. She's done it before, and while our parents bitched about it, the one that was most upset was Els. My eighteen-year-old sister, who gets no freedom between my dad, his guards, and me. It's not that I don't think she's capable of handling herself, it's the fact that our family is a part of the Bratva. In the last three years, there have been four attempted kidnappings of her and two attempted murders on me. So, for the last two months, she hasn't been allowed to do anything. Her only time to have conversation and *fun* is at these family dinners.

I look at the closed door and throw my head back, looking around her apartment. It's neat and everything is perfectly placed. I walk over to her door and push it open.

She glares at me from her bathroom. "Can I help you with something? Get the fuck out."

"I'll get out when you're done." I look her up and down. She curled her hair and applied a little makeup. I sit on her bed and she puts her hands on her hips.

"You know what? Just leave. I'm capable of driving myself, I have a car." She turns back to the mirror and applies her lip gloss. I stride over to her bathroom, hovering behind her. Her breath quickens and I tilt my head, watching her.

"What?" she asks, looking at me through the mirror.

"Hurry up." That's the only response I can force out. I turn around and walk out, because there's no way I can be in a confined space with her right now. Or ever, for that fucking matter.

I wish I could hate her. It would make everything so much easier, but I can't. I can't because it's not her fault that she lost her memory. And it's not her fault that *she still doesn't know that.* From the moment we met, I knew she'd be the death of me. I knew she'd be the reason I wanted to set the world on fire. For years, I've chased off every boyfriend, every fucker who thought they'd get a piece of her. Why? Because it felt like my job. She's close with my sister, she's her best friend. It's a role I stepped into without thinking twice about it. It was something that I just knew to do, even when it became gut wrenching. Our fathers instilled in my mind that her and my sister were my responsibility.

*Take care of them, Astor. Protect them, especially Lessia. She's
yours.*

Mine, except I was too young to know what the fuck that
meant. Now that I know what it means, I want to hate her even
more. Because I'll have to spend the rest of my life fighting off
the entire fucking world and I'm already up to my fucking ears
in bodies because of her.

There's so many things she has no idea about. So many
people who have been a threat to her and she just allows them
in her life.

"I NEED TO LOOK MY BEST, MAYBE I'LL ACTUALLY GET FUCKED
tonight. I might go out with Caroline." She pushes her head up
and continues to apply her lip gloss. I grind my teeth and push
against her. She gasps and looks at me with hooded eyes in the
mirror. "What are you—"

"No one will be fucking you. You're going to dinner and
then you're coming straight back home. So, you can tell *Caroline* that someone else will have to take your spot at *my bar* you
seem to love to hang out at."

"How did you..." She gulps and turns to face me, pushing
me backwards. "You don't tell me what to do. And I *am* going
to *your* bar tonight." She steps around me and grabs her purse,
looking back at me.

Her dress is four inches too fucking short, and the front
cuts so low I'm afraid her fucking tits will fall out if she moves
wrong, She's showing every tattoo she has, some in places that
shouldn't be seen, like the one that's on her upper thigh that's
currently taunting me. You can only see a slither of her
shoulder tattoo while her wrist tattoo and full sleeve is on
display. I follow behind her, shaking my head, reminding
myself that she is not my fucking problem. *Yet.*

WHEN WE GET TO HER FATHER'S MANSION, OUR PARENTS ARE AT THE door waiting for us, as usual. The rain has stopped and the weather is cool. Alessia shivers a little as we step out into the air and I chuckle. She glares at me and I raise an eyebrow. "Cold, *malyshka?*"

"Fuck you," she says as we approach the front door.

"Alessia Catalina!" I smirk at her as her mother scolds her.

"Sorry, Mom…" she mumbles. "Hi, Papa." She smiles at her father and he pulls her into his arms.

"That dress is too goddamn short, *figlia.*" Ander looks over his daughter and then glances at me in question. I shrug and walk into the house. She's not my fucking responsibility. She's twenty-two-years-old.

"Fuck, finally. What took you so long?" Elsi asks, wandering over to me. I ruffle her hair and smirk at her.

"Your beloved Alessia. She took forever getting dressed."

"Wait, you came *together?*" She smirks at me and I shake my head, ignoring her. I walk to the bar and pour myself a drink, quickly downing it as our families start to gather in the dining room. This conversation is about to set off a very strong-willed, emotional girl. I can't tell if it'll push me over the edge, I've fought so hard to not step over.

"SHE'S GOING TO BE PISSED, SO I HOPE YOU'RE PREPARED," MY FATHER says behind me. I turn to him and grunt.

I stare at the man who has raised me to be strong, to not be afraid of anyone or anything. To always put my family first and never blink when it's a life-or-death situation. He doesn't look any older, it's like he doesn't fucking age. If it weren't for the crow's feet around his eyes, you'd never know his years.

Xavier Pavlov, the man who would burn the entire world down and not show an ounce of remorse for it. He puts his hand on my shoulder and grins. This was their plan ever since Alessia was born and I only recently became aware of it. Their plan to put the two most powerful families together. Their plan to make me the most powerful man and her the most powerful woman to take over their business when the time came.

My father and Ander grew up together. They both have no problem eliminating problems nor do they have problems showing their Achilles' heel, being their wives and children. They are known for being cutthroat and not giving second chances—especially when it comes to their family.

"Yeah, well, I'm not too excited, either."

"Ah, you can do this. This is exactly what you both need."

He's lost his fucking mind if he thinks I can handle this, if I can deal with this on top of everything else they've thrown at me.

No, he hasn't.

"I don't understand why you all are so adamant on this. Why are you all making me do this? You want me to marry her after everything that's happened?" He pats my back and gives me a knowing look as we take our seats.

CHAPTER THREE
ALESSIA

I'm staring, dumbfounded at the words coming out of my father's mouth. I look at my mom and she won't meet my stare. The room is quiet and I'm sure my jaw is on the fucking floor.

"Papa…"

"Alessia, it's what's best for you."

"I will not marry *Astor*."

"Yes, yes you will."

I look at Astor and he's grinding his teeth; he does that when he's pissed. And I'm sure he's so pissed that if he grinds any harder, he's going to crack his tooth.

"I haven't even graduated college. You promised me you'd let me find love. You promised me I wouldn't have to marry someone I hate." I glare at Astor when I say that and he raises his eyebrow at me.

"You two know each other inside and out. You say you hate each other, but neither of you can keep your eyes off each other when you're in the same fucking room. Astor has ran every goddamn boyfriend off you've had. Every time you think you're getting an inch; he takes a mile and you haven't even realized it. What happened to your last boyfriend, *figlia*?"

I frown at him bringing Zander up.

"He moved...he didn't want to do long distance." He shakes his head and smirks, looking at Xavier.

"He didn't move, Alessia. Astor beat the poor fucker to a pulp when he found him kissing another girl at Redcrest," Xavier tells me.

I shake my head and tears well in my eyes as Xavier continues to speak. I don't hear anything he's saying. I stand up and the world starts spinning. I reach out for the chair to steady myself, but the next thing I know I'm on the floor and the world is black.

I THINK ABOUT ALL THE INFORMATION I JUST LEARNED. WHY WOULD Astor hurt Zander if he was cheating on me? He can't stand to be around me. If anything, I would've thought it brought him joy to see someone I loved, or thought I loved, betraying me. Then I'm flooded with the realization of what my father said to me. *"Figlia, you're going to marry Astor."* Yeah, like fuck I am. Thank God I fainted, because there was no way I could bear hearing anymore shit.

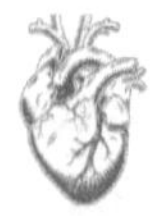

"SHE'S WAKING UP. GIVE ME THE WATER."

Astor.

I know it's his voice before I open my eyes completely. Except it's not cold, it's almost nurturing, warm and laced with worry.

"She didn't fucking eat. You were just letting her get hammered without shoving food down her throat. What did you expect?" he asks. I groan as I feel arms pulling me up. I try to yank away from him, but he tightens his hold on my arm.

"I'm fine."

"You're not fine. You fucking fainted."

Thanks, Captain Obvious.

"Yeah, because my family is insane and thinks I'm marrying a dick of a human being, who has no feelings and lives to make me feel like a blip in his life." I look up at him and he smirks down at me. He scoops me up in his arms and I frown. "I can walk, put me down."

He ignores me as usual and sits me on the couch, pushing a glass of water in my face.

"Drink," he orders. I open my mouth to protest until I see him grinding his teeth again. I slowly grab the water out of his hand and tilt it to my mouth. "Good girl," he says, crouching in front of me. My breath hitches and I bite the inside of my cheek. *Why is my stomach suddenly feeling warm in the bottom after hearing that?* I should not be affected by two words coming out this devil's mouth, but fuck if I'm not.

My dad clears his throat behind us and I look up at him, scowling. Behind him is my drop-dead gorgeous mother, Eleanor Ballerini, her long hair and bright green eyes full of unshed tears, looking at me. She puts her hand on my father's shoulder and his eyes immediately soften as they find hers. They're the epitome of love, so is Xavier and Astrid. They all love each other so hard, so it's unbelievable to me that they won't allow me to search for the same love.

"Let me talk to her," my mom says.

"I don't want to talk," I protest.

"She's your mother. And you *will talk* to her," my papa says with that same glare again. I roll my eyes, looking down at the water in my hand and a still crouching Astor. He looks at my father who raises an eyebrow in challenge.

"Don't fucking speak to her like that, Ander. If she doesn't want to fucking talk, you aren't going to make her," Astor says. My father opens his mouth when my mother speaks over him.

"*Figlia,* please," my mom says as Astor turns to face me.

"Talk to her, then I'll take you home," he whispers to me. I'm dumbfounded, yet again. Why is he being nice to me? He doesn't like talking to me, yet alone touching me. And he's done all those things today.

"Fine," I say leaning back into the couch. He and my father leave me and my mother alone. I see Elsi peeking around the corner and Astor yanks her away with him. I'm sure if anyone is happy about this shitshow of an arrangement, it's her. Now that I think about it, no one at the table seemed surprised besides me. It was like everyone knew except me. Everyone knew my fucking future except me.

"Sweetheart..." My mom reaches for my hand, but I slide it away from her. She sighs and turns towards me. "Please look at me." Tears well in my eyes as I turn to her as her tears already spill down her face. "I know this is a lot and I know you have questions. But we are doing this because we love you."

"You're making me marry someone who barely can stand the sight of my face. We don't want this. Why are you making me do this?"

"We all see what you and Astor are too stupid or proud to admit and see yourselves. Look me in my eyes and tell me that you don't want to do this with him."

I open my mouth to say words that I thought I believed, but nothing comes out. What the fuck is happening here? I hate him. I hate how cold he is. I hate how distant he is. I hate how he ignores my presence. I hate how he doesn't *care* about me. Fuck, I hate that he doesn't *see* me.

"*Figlia*, listen to me. You both have two months to figure out if you truly hate each other or if you have spent your whole lives running away from the one person who understands you inside and out. If you aren't happy at the end, I'll make sure you are free of him. I promise."

"Don't make me marry him, Mama, please. I'll do it, I'll do the two-month trial, but please don't make me get married just to get divorced. Don't take that from me." She pats my leg and pulls me into her side as I silently cry.

How the hell did my night turn into this? Why am I so angry that Astor was nice to me? Why am I so angry that he didn't get as upset as I did? And why am I suddenly so anxious to ask him those exact questions?

My parents' house has always been a serene place. My mother made sure to decorate it to feel at home regardless of how big it was. My favorite place to come was the balcony in my room. It's decorated with white lights and has a small reading nook with a lounge chair in the corner, overlooking the backyard. I let out a sigh and sank into the chair, tucking my legs underneath me and tugging a blanket over my lap. The night is chilly, but I don't mind the breeze right now. I don't understand what everyone is trying to accomplish—we're going to rip each other apart.

"Les? You, ok?" I look over my shoulder and see Elsi standing in the door frame. I give her a small smile and nod. "Can I sit with you?"

"Of course, you can." She slowly sits down and I chuckle at her. "I take it that you knew about this, judging by how apprehensive you are right now?"

Elsi lets out a deep breath and plays with her fingers in

her lap, something that we have in common. We'll both fiddle our fingers when we're uncomfortable.

"I overheard the conversation before dinner, but I didn't know before tonight. I promise, don't be mad at—"

"Elsi, I'm not mad at you. Even if you did know, I know your father and brother well enough to know that you would've had no say in it, either. Even though I know you're secretly happy as shit right now." She bites her lip to hide her smirk before she turns to me.

"Look, I know this is insane and I'm sure I'll have my turn in a few years. But just give it a chance. I know you two don't get along, but he needs you. More than you know. He needs someone who has his back, someone that will support him and be there for him. I mean *really* be there for him. And even though it's forced, I know at the end of the day, you'd never turn your back on him. Please, Les, try. Just try."

For only being eighteen, she sure as fuck knows how to manipulate someone. I glance away from her and she pulls my hands into hers as my eyes fill with tears, knowing that I have no choice in the matter. That at the end of the day, I always do what my father tells me to do. I thought I'd be able to rely on my mother for help in this, but for some reason it's the same story with her, despite the two-month trial. I don't understand why everyone is so caught up on this forced marriage. I'm just hoping my father will agree to the two-month trial my mom proposed instead of the real thing.

Elsi's voice wrenches me out of my own sorrow. I smile at her and she tilts her head at me.

"It'll be a blast, we'll probably even see each other more. So, please, just promise me you'll give it a chance?"

I tuck a piece of hair behind her ear and playfully nudge her.

"Elsi, I don't have a choice."

CHAPTER FOUR

ASTOR

"She wants a two-month trial. She's begging not to make her say *I do*, just to end up divorced," Eleanor says. We're sitting at the table discussing the *details* of this fucked up arrangement, and the more I hear about it, the more I'm thinking it's the stupidest shit I've ever agreed to.

"She says that we're making her marry someone who doesn't like her. That we promised we wouldn't do that." Eleanor and my mother look at me and I raise an eyebrow.

"What? This arrangement is dangerous. Why are you all making me do this? Why are you putting me through this torture, after everything that has happened? This is going to blow up in our faces. It's not a good idea and I don't want to do it. You see how I struggle being around her as is, and you want me to fucking marry her now?" I push the chair back and down the rest of my bourbon, pushing my hand through my hair. I glare at my father and Ander. "It's sickening. She's going to find out what she forgot six years ago. We all know what happened when she realized I was there, the threat she made, what the fuck are we going to do if she makes good on that fucking threat because she's not strong enough to handle it. I'll be the target of her anger, and that's *my* goddamn heart that's going to be ripped to shreds again."

Alessia had an *accident* when she was sixteen, and lucky for her, she doesn't fucking remember it.

But we do.

I do, and wish like hell I didn't.

I walk outside when my phone rings and my best friend's name pops up. *Justin.*

"What?" I groan.

"Fuck you, too, then asshole. Let's go out."

"Don't you have an 8:00 a.m. tomorrow?"

"So the fuck what? You do, too."

It's almost finals week then it's time for Christmas break, a month of me having to do duties for the mafia. As the next one to take over for my father, he always makes sure to remind me how important it is for me to show up and do the work when I have the time. He says that it's *imperative* for the Bratva to know they should fear me as they do him.

"Fuck it, I'll meet you in an hour. But I'm not alone."

"Who are you fucking now?"

"I'm hanging up." He laughs as I hit the end button. I look up to the sky and let out a long, low groan when I hear the door open behind me.

"Some dinner, huh?" Alessia says, standing beside me. I look down at her and nod slowly. "I'm not marrying you, Astor."

"It's funny that you think you have a choice in the matter."

"I do have a choice. If they force me, I just won't show up, I'll—" I turn to her, looking down at her. Her breath catches as I wrap my hand around her little throat.

"You'll what? Run away? Run, *malyshka,* I dare you. It'll be fun to catch you." I push her backward and head for the door. "Get your stuff, we're leaving."

I grab my dress coat and throw it on as Els walks down the stairs. She frowns when she sees me and I tilt my head at her. "Something wrong?"

"Why wouldn't you tell me this was the plan?" she asks.

"Because it doesn't concern you."

"Spare me the bullshit. She's one of my best friends, of course it concerns me. How are you ok with this?" I step closer to her and pull her into a small room next to the kitchen.

"Elsi, listen, there are things that you do not know. Things that I couldn't tell you because I couldn't dare ask you to keep it from her. Just understand that this is bigger than anything you can imagine and I don't have a choice, either. It may seem like I do, but trust me, I'm just as fucked."

"So that's it? You're going to marry her?" I shrug and the door opens. We both catch a glimpse of Alessia sagging through the door, her arms wrapped around her. "Be nice to her, please. And try to really make it work," Elsi whispers. I ruffle her hair like I always do and pull her into a hug, thinking to myself if being nice is a good idea. I know I'll have to talk to Alessia, so I guess tonight is when the ice breaks.

"We're leaving, I'm going to meet Justin." Elsi scrunches her nose up at his name and I shake my head. Seven years of us being friends she still despises him. "Hey, be nice." She rolls her eyes and walks back into the room with our parents.

Alessia is saying something to her mom as she grabs her stuff. I can't make out the words, but they look to be in deep conversation. She looks at her dad and he nods at whatever Eleanor said to him. The confirmation makes Alessia give a small, subtle smile to her parents before she marches away from them, brushing past me towards the door.

After saying goodbye to my parents and promising my

mother to be on my *best behavior*, I find Alessia standing next to the car door, her arms wrapped around her again. This time she's shivering, her perfect, red plumped lips chattering against each other. The sight of it shouldn't bring me the feeling of enjoyment that it does, but it's there anyway.

"Cold, *malyshka?*"

"Open the fucking door."

"First off, don't curse at me. Secondly, say please." She twists her mouth up in refusal and I lean against the hood of the car. "I have a jacket on, I can sit out here for hours."

"I could always just go back inside and make someone else drive me home. My *driver* is here, after all, and I'm sure he'd *love* to take me for a ride. He always was eager to pick me up from class on family dinner nights."

"You could, but you won't."

She unfolds her arms and starts to stalk back towards the house as I wrap my arm around her waist, yanking her to me. "Don't *ever* ask another man to take you home, unless they are instructed to do so by me. Understood?"

She fights against my hold and I tighten my grip on her waist, enough to leave my marks there.

"You do not own me. I won't just do what you say."

"Oh, *malyshka,* you have so much to learn. Now get in the fucking car." I let go of her, unlocking the car as I slide inside. She stands there for a moment and I wonder if she's really going to make me drag her out of the house in front of our families. I tap my finger on the steering wheel as I watch her weigh her options. The strength deflates from her as she rounds the car and slides into the passenger side.

"Good girl," I praise as I pull out into the road.

Even though it's a Wednesday night, Redcrest University is still crawling with students out on campus even at 10:00 p.m. This University is where any and every one with money and a powerful last name sends their fuck ups for kids. It's where their parents went and it's where their kids will come when they reach college, too. The social scene here is full of drugs, bad decisions, and no consequences for actions. Even off campus housing is a fucking shitshow.

The ride back to Alessia's apartment was deathly silent, just how I like it. She refused to look at me the entire drive, keeping her arms folded like the fucking brat she is.

I don't miss the sigh of relief she lets out when we pull into the parking lot. I can't wait to piss her off more.

I kill the engine and round the car, yanking the door open. She blinks up at me in confusion.

"I can walk myself up," she mumbles.

"You're coming out with me tonight."

"No, I have finals coming up. I need to study."

"You can study tomorrow. You don't have class."

She climbs out of the car and brushes past me as I follow behind her, ignoring her death stare. When we get into the elevator, she glares at the floor, her hands tapping away on her thigh. *She's uncomfortable. Good.* When the elevator dings for her floor, she can barely wait for the doors to open before she's slipping through them.

"Ok, I made it home safely. You can go now," she says, sticking her key into the door as a group of guys walk by.

"Hey, Lessia! Are you coming to Addie's tonight? She promised not to do truth or dare this time," one of the guys call out.

She laughs and waves him off. "Not tonight. I've gotta study, but I'll be at the next one." I raise my eyebrow at her and she shrugs.

"I'll text you the details in case you change your mind," he says.

I turn to him when I realize I'm grinding my teeth so hard that Alessia stares at my jaw.

"You won't text her. Matter of fact, you'll lose her number."

He looks at me and his eyes widen when he realizes who I am. That's how it is on this campus; everyone runs away from me once they learn my last name. They hear the stories and don't bother asking me if they're true, which most of them are. But still, the only people who aren't afraid of me are the small group of four friends I have, which I'm sure is because they're just as fucked up as I am.

He glances at Alessia, who I'm sure is giving me her best death stare, then back at me as his friend yanks him away, mumbling to him that it's not worth it.

I push Alessia into her apartment, slamming the door behind me. When I face her, her face is flushed and her breathing is visibly quickened. Her fist is balled up as she fists the side of her dress. I stride over to her couch, leaning back with my leg over my knee.

"Go ahead, let me have it." She opens her mouth and I hold up my hand. "But remember, before you yell, we are going out tonight. How well your night will go is depending on this conversation...now proceed."

"Fuck. You." She storms into her room and I chuckle to myself, following her. She's pulling her dress over her head when she spots me watching her in her door frame. "Turn around."

"Don't flatter yourself, *malyshka*."

Get it together, Astor. You have to learn how to be around her again.

She rolls her eyes at me and yanks out an oversized t-shirt.

"I told you we're going out—you're not wearing that." She stops and curses under her breath, reaching for the dress she had on earlier. "Fuck no, you're not wearing that, either. Pick something else."

"Why do I have to go? I've had enough of your energy sucking presence for a day. I want to study and go to bed."

"Too fucking bad. Get dressed and get out here in the next ten minutes, or I'll drag you out."

Goddamn brat.

CHAPTER FIVE

ALESSIA

After rejecting my outfit four times, we finally left my apartment after I put on a pair of jeans and a low-cut shirt with black pumps. He complained that my shirt was too low, but when I told him to fuck off, he surprisingly just yanked me out the door. Regardless of how many times I said I didn't want to go, he ignored every objection. My parents agreed to making this a two-month trial marriage. They promised me that if it ended in divorce, they'd do it quietly and no one would find out. While I'm not happy that I still have to marry the fucker, I am happy that they are agreeing to let me out of it in the end. I never wanted to get married just to get divorced, but for some reason, Astor and I marrying each other seems to be life or death to our parents.

I turn to him and he glances at me. "What?"

"You know my parents agreed to my two-month trial proposal, right?"

"Hm."

"They said that after two months of dealing with you and

your shitty ways, they'll let me go free of you. I'm not happy I'll have to add *divorced* on my impressive fucking resume, but at least I won't have to deal with you anymore."

He pulls the car over to the side of the road and I lean back against the glass as he turns his dark eyes to me. A chill runs down my spine and I unintentionally hold my breath. Astor has this darkness with him, this power that radiates off him. And right now he looks like he just snapped. It's a power that demands attention, a power that shows that you don't want to fuck with him. Too bad I'm just as powerful.

"Listen up, *Alessia*, since you're so set on this two-month agreement, let me promise you something. I promise that when I'm done with you, you won't remember who the fuck you are. I'll spend every day making you wish that your father made you marry someone fifteen years older than you to use as their whore. I'll spend every day making you wish that you were fucking dead instead of married to me. You think you hate me now? Oh, *malyshka,* you just wait. Now, shut the fuck up, your voice is giving me a headache."

I'm completely dumbfounded. My body tenses at his words as they roll off his tongue. He doesn't even give me a chance to respond before he's jerking us back on the road. He thinks he's won this one, but he has no idea that he's met his fucking match.

Instead of going to the bar I wanted to earlier in the night, even if it *was* Astor's bar, we went to his choice. The club we're at is one of the most elite clubs around Redcrest. It takes knowing a lot of important people to get in here, so it doesn't surprise me when Astor walks right to the front and is welcomed in. The bouncer looks at me and gives me a nod as I walk in behind Astor. Astor grabs my hand and the surprise doesn't give me a chance to yank away before he's pulling me deep into the club to the staircase that leads to the VIP section. I look around and note the bar at the end of the staircase. *I'll definitely be needing that.* When we get to the top, we're met with another security guard. Astor gives him a nod and he lifts the rope as I turn around and look at the bar again. Astor pulls me to the couch and all but throws me down onto it. I glare at him, but he ignores me. I haven't said a word to him since he told me my voice was giving him a headache. *Prick.*

"Ast! Fucking finally, what the fuck took you so long?" He glances over at me and I push my head up, ignoring his stare. "Is that Alessia? Fuck, when'd she get so hot?" Astor punches Justin in his stomach and he laughs as he grabs his midsection.

"Fuck! It was a joke. Why is she here?" I zone in on their conversation, acting uninterested, when really I want to know why the fuck I'm here, too.

Astor pulls Justin close and whispers something in his ear. I take the opportunity to beeline for the bar. If he thinks I'm going to sit here and deal with him sober, he's fucking stupid. The security guard glances at me and then to Astor, who still hasn't noticed I've left.

"Lift the fucking rope before I knee you in the balls."

He chuckles and shakes his head, lifting the rope. I glance over my shoulder and see Astor as he catches my backside walking down the steps. Justin hits his shoulder before he throws his head back and laughs.

I find a spot at the bar and wave down the bartender. "What can I get you?" he asks.

"Gin and tonic, please." He nods at me and I turn around,

placing my elbows on the counter as I watch everyone around me dancing to the beat.

"Here you go." I grab the drink, taking a long swig of it. It burns my throat and I welcome the sensation when I feel a shadow hovering over me. I know it's not Astor, because it doesn't smell like him.

How pathetic is that, to know the scent of the man you *claim* to want nothing to do with? I turn around and face a tall man that I would probably be into if I weren't so hung up on Astor, who I'm shocked hasn't run after me yet.

"Now tell me, what is something as good looking as you doing at this bar alone?" I tilt my chin up and look past him towards the balcony. I make eye contact with Astor and grin when I see him gripping the railing so tight, that even in the darkness of the club I can see the strain.

"Who says I'm alone?" I retort. He chuckles and looks at the bartender with a nod.

"Let me get you a drink." I open my mouth to object when a dark voice cuts in. "She already has a drink."

I roll my eyes and turn towards the bar as Astor and the man sizes each other up.

"*Astor.* I should've known," the tall man replies.

"Yeah, Rex, you should've." Astor grinds his teeth and looks at me as I throw the rest of my drink back, waving to the bartender for another. *Rex* walks off and Astor slides next to me, ordering himself a vodka. "Getting drunk, *malyshka?*"

"Will you stop calling me that?" He glares at me before leaning in and whispering into my ear. His lips run across the bottom of my earlobe and a shiver crawls down my back.

"I'll call you whatever the fuck I want to call you, get your drink and bring your ass back up the stairs, if I see you talking to anyone else—what I do to them will be on you." He throws back his vodka and slams the glass down, as he walks away from me.

Game. Fucking. On.

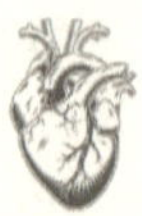

"Did you see Astor tonight? Fuck, that's a tree I still have yet to climb."

"Oh, I climbed it and trust me, it's worth every fucking splinter you'll get."

"He came with someone tonight, though; I think she's the mafia princess. He was holding her fucking hand....what's she got that I don't?"

The girls in the bathroom start laughing and I inwardly roll my eyes. I can't understand how he can tell me who I can and can't talk to when he's fucked half of the girls at Redcrest. I can't even use the bathroom in the club without hearing about his dick.

I exit when I hear them leave, not wanting to show my face that I'm sure is a deep shade of red after hearing that. Looking at myself in the mirror, I'm confused about who's looking back at me. There's no way I'm letting Astor push me around like he's the ruler of me. I am my own person and always have been. I've made my own rules since I knew what rules were. And there's no way that at twenty-two I'm going to let him push me into a corner.

The music is intoxicating and my hips start to move to the beat as I wander onto the dance floor. Even though I can't see him, I can feel his eyes on me. I know he's probably grinding his teeth down into his gums at this point. He probably can't believe I didn't follow his *orders*.

The beat changes and I expertly move my hips side to side, throwing my hands up as I sway. I've always been a good dancer, and today, I've never been happier to be able to show that. I'm in my zone when a set of hands wrap around my waist.

I smile to myself, because I know it's game time.

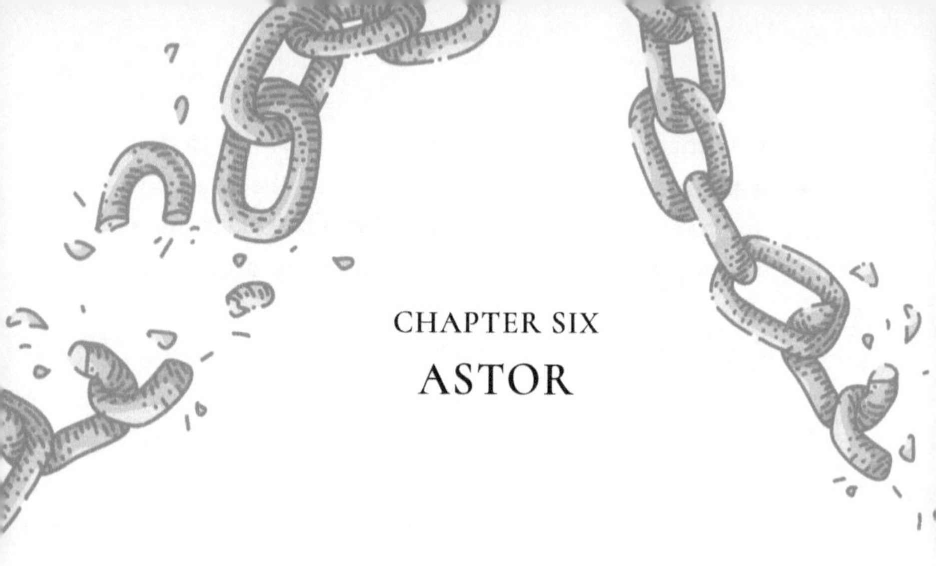

CHAPTER SIX

ASTOR

I don't know what she thinks she's doing, but this isn't a game she wants to play with me. She's swaying and bucking those fucking hips, like the pro she is, and I can't rip my eyes away from her. Justin chuckles behind me. "You just gonna let her dance like that? Only a matter of time before someone joins her."

"Yeah, and that'll be their death sentence."

"No one knows she's yours, Ast," he says matter-of-factly. "Well, would you look at that. Little miss pretty has a friend." I whip my head from him and back to the dance floor in time to see Alessia wrapping her hands around some prick's neck. *A very dead prick*, once I get ahold of him. I'm heading for the dance floor before I can fucking blink when Justin grabs my arm.

"It'll be easier if you don't care. Besides, you can't have her, remember?" I yank my arm out of his grip and practically fly down the stairs. He's right, I shouldn't care, but fuck if I don't.

I push my way through the crowd to where they are when

he pushes his hands through her hair. She struggles against his hold as he tries to force his lips on her.

I can hear her saying no to him, but he continues his quest. I yank her out of his reach and push her behind me.

"Go upstairs with Justin and wait for me." She doesn't move, so I push her more forcefully. She bites her lip while retreating upstairs.

"Is there a problem?" the prick has the audacity to ask.

"You have no fucking idea." I look at Tez, one of the security guards that work the club, and nod at him. He pulls the prick of a man out into the back of the club and I follow. I can't figure out why I'm so fucking mad, I just know that I am. Can I have her in the way that I want? No. But does that mean that anyone else will have her?

Fuck. No.

"What the fuck are you—" I punch him in the face and blood spurts all over as he groans and grabs his nose.

"I saw her pushing you away. I heard her say *no* and did you let her go? Or did you continue trying to put your filthy fucking lips on what's mine?"

"Dude, dude she was asking for it. You saw how she was danc— " I punch him again and look at Tez.

"Stand this stupid fuck up." I pull out the knife my dad gifted to me for my birthday last year and smile at the thought of what I'll be using it on. "I don't give a fuck if she was naked, dancing with a fucking sign on her body that said *fuck me*. When she said no, all bets were off."

He opens his mouth to talk before I walk behind him, pulling his neck back by his hair as I run the blade across his throat. Tez tilts his head at the guy as he falls to the ground and throws me a cloth. I wipe my blade off as gurgling sounds flood my ears. "Get rid of this piece of shit."

I text my father to tell him to send the clean up crew to the club as I ascend up the stairs. Alessia is chewing her nails and her leg is tapping rapidly. She looks up at me and her mouth freezes in place. "We're leaving," I say, barely looking at her.

"Jus, I'll see you tomorrow." He leans into me and glances at her.

"Did you kill him?" I raise my eyebrow at him and he nods his head. "Good." That's one of the reasons we're so close: he doesn't judge and he doesn't take any shit. Especially when it comes to a woman. He's just as possessive and protective. I have to say I do expect him to grill the fuck out of me with questions about Alessia later, but he knows this isn't the time. He knows the deal my father and Ander told us, and as unconventional as it is, he thinks it's something I should do and never look back from. When I asked him why earlier, he said, "Because every bitch we're ever with only wants us for our money or our name. She already has both."

Alessia waves at him and he gives her a quick nod. I stand next to her and wait for her to walk ahead of me. This is the last time I'll be letting her have her freedom.

When we get outside, the cool air gives me the breath I need to get myself back together before I get into a small, enclosed space with her. This woman is making it her mission to piss me off, anyway she can. What's worse is that I'm letting her. I can hear her heels picking up as she tries to keep up with me.

"Can you slow down?" she pleads. I halt and she runs into the back of me. I face her and she gasps as she looks at my shirt. "You're hurt!" She reaches for my stomach and I grab her hands before she touches me.

"You don't get to touch me."

"But—"

"Get in the fucking car." She puts her head down and climbs in the car without her normal arguing and I'm grateful for it. I don't like resulting to violence, despite my reputation. I'm used to it when I have to, but tonight I shouldn't have had to. I *wouldn't* have had to if she had just fucking *listened.*

My phone dings with a text as I'm opening the car door.

DAD:

Handled. Do I want to know what happened?

ASTOR:

No. You really fucking don't.

I think the ride will be silent as it usually is, until she whispers, "I'm...sorry." I tighten my hand on the steering wheel and she continues. "Say something..." I continue to ignore her and she pushes herself further into the seat, crossing her arms. She frowns as we pass the way to her apartment.

"Where are we going?"

"You'll stay with me tonight." I expect her to argue, but she doesn't. She just glares out the window while she plays with her fingers.

"I don't have clothes."

"I packed you a bag earlier."

"Unbelievable."

Ten minutes later, we're pushing through the gate of my house. The guard nods at me as we drive through and she raises her eyebrows.

"Who lives here with you?" I ignore her again and she huffs. "Ok, guess I'll talk to my fucking self."

I'm so fucking pissed with her that I'm afraid if I talk to her, I'll rip her fucking head off. When I walk in the house, she stands there with her arms wrapped around herself. She looks around as I remove my jacket and lay it across the back of the kitchen stool.

"Why'd you bring me here?" Her voice is small and almost a whisper as I glare at her. She meets my stare and I think for a moment that she'll drop her gaze, but she doesn't. "Answer me." I lean against the countertop and watch her as her breath quickens. She's getting pissed. I know there's only a matter of time before she starts yelling. "Fucking answer me. We aren't married, we don't even *like* each other. We hate being around each other. And apparently my voice gives you a fucking headache. Why am I here?" she screams. I take a deep breath and crook my finger at her.

"Come here."

"No."

"Alessia. Come here." She shakes her head and I realize at that moment that I have met my fucking match.

CHAPTER SEVEN
ALESSIA

He tilts his head at me and I swallow my spit. I refuse to back down; I'm going to stand my ground. He takes a step towards me and I take a step back. His eyes are dark, so dark that I'm sure they're black right now. He looks lethal, pissed, and like he's fed up with me for the night.

"*Malyshka,* you want to know why you're here? It's because even though I can't stand being close to you, you are *mine.* I have to start getting used to that and I'm starting tonight."

"What do you mean?"

"You'll be staying with me starting tonight."

"I have my own place and we aren't married. I'm not—" He advances on me and wraps his hand around my neck.

"Did I give you the impression that you had a choice?" I glance down at his bloody shirt and the words are out of my mouth before I can stop them.

"If you hate being around me so much, why'd you hurt that guy at the club? And why can't you seem to keep your fucking hands off me?" I pull at his fingers, but he tightens them.

"Fight me all you want; it'll make it a lot more fun ruining you. And I didn't hurt him, I killed him, Alessia." He pushes me away from him and I stand there in shock.

"Wh-why?"

"I was very clear that it wouldn't be my fault what I did if you decided to *talk* to someone else, yet alone *dance* with someone else. Someone who fucking tried to kiss you, at that."

"So you took someone's life because they almost kissed a woman who you've ignored for *years*? That's a crock of shit." I brush past him and head for the stairs. "Where am I sleeping? We're done here." He's on my heels seconds later, pushing me against the wall of the staircase.

"Tell me, what would you have done if I hadn't ripped you out of his arms? Would you have let him kiss you?" I turn my nose up at him and look him dead in his eyes. I give a small smirk and he raises his eyebrow.

"Maybe. Maybe I wanted him just as bad as he wanted me." He pushes his fingers through my hair and yanks it, forcing me to look at him.

"Do not play games with me, Alessia. Remember, once we say *I do,* your life belongs to me. And I'm telling you, I'm itching with desire to ruin that perfect little life you have conjured in that brain of yours." My eyes well up with tears and his lip tilts up in disgust as he climbs up the stairs.

"Pick a room. I don't give a shit which one," he says over his shoulder. The moment he's out of sight, I crumble. I cry as silent as I can, my knees drawn underneath me.

Two months. Two months. Two months.

Two months, then I'm free. I square my shoulders and wipe my tears. I can do this. I'm strong, and there's no way Astor fucking Pavlov is going to bring me to my knees.

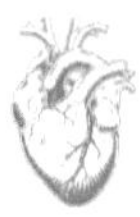

I PICK THE ROOM THAT'S NEXT TO HIS, BECAUSE AS MUCH AS I HATE TO admit it, I don't want to be alone. If he wasn't so fucking rude to me, and if he didn't hate me so much, I'd gather the courage to tell him I'm sleeping in his room with him. This house is too fucking big for just one person, yet alone a fucking college student.

I turn the water on and watch the tub fill up when I look for bath salts and luck out to find a tub of lavender salts. I remove my clothes and tie my hair up into a bun on the crown of my head. I didn't wear much makeup today, so taking it off was easy.

I climb into the tub, easing my way down, letting the suds and the scent of lavender take over. I chose to make the best out of this situation. I chose to continue with my life like he hasn't changed. I chose to be nice to the dickhole I'll have to call my husband. Even if it kills me.

MY PHONE RINGS, SHOWING MY MOTHER'S NAME. I REACH OVER AND accept the call.

"Hi, Mom."

"Sweetheart, how is everything?"

"It's fine, I'm having a bath."

"In that tiny little tub at your apartment?" She chuckles and I give her a small laugh.

"No..." I sigh, I wish I was in my tiny bath at my apartment. "I'm at Astor's."

"Oh..."

"Oh?"

"He mentioned to your father that he didn't think your building was safe and that he thought you should stay with him. Your father told him that it was your choice since you weren't married yet. I didn't think he'd get you to agree to it."

I laugh, I actually *laugh* because my mother must really not know me if she thinks I agreed to this shit.

"I didn't agree to *anything*, he practically kidnapped me." She's silent on the other end and I let out a sigh. "Why'd you call, Mom?"

"Because we need to speak to you and Astor about the wedding."

My stomach turns and I suddenly feel sick at the thought of actually having to do this. "Mom, there won't be a wedding."

"Honey, we talked about this. There will be a wedding. You will give it your best shot. And if you fail at it, we'll deal with it. But you *are* getting married."

"Why are you doing this? Are the families in some sort of trouble?"

"Let's just say that we have to get our affairs in order in case a storm comes that we aren't exactly prepared for."

"What does that mean?"

"Nothing to worry your little head about. I know you think this doesn't benefit you, but it does. Now, meet me at the house tomorrow so we can plan this wedding. Two weeks is not a lot of time."

I almost jump out of the tub. I'm hunched over hyperventilating when the door opens. Astor crouches at my side, wrapping a towel around my naked body. I'm so shocked that I can't even be embarrassed or pissed that he's in here right now. I hear my mother shouting my name on the phone, but I can't respond to her. Two weeks.

She wants me to sign my life over to this man in two fucking weeks.

"Jesus Christ, hold on to me." He lifts me out of the tub and I shamelessly wrap my arms around him, burying my face into his chest. He fists my phone in one hand while he effortlessly carries me to another room, which I'm assuming is his.

"What happened?" he asks into the phone, moments later grinding his teeth. "What time?" I look up at him and tuck my face further into his chest. "Don't call her again. We'll be there." He hangs the phone up and throws it on the bed next to us. He rubs the top of my head and the tears fall uncontrollably. "I don't like seeing you cry," he mumbles, tucking my hair behind my ear.

I am completely confused by his behavior; he's being *nice* to me. He hasn't been this close to me since my fifteenth birthday party. I don't know how or why I suddenly remember that, but I do.

"Why are you suddenly treating me differently?"

"Because believe it or not, I'm not a monster." I look up at him and he wipes the tears from under my eyes.

"They want us to get married in two weeks..."

"I know."

"I think they're in some kind of trouble and we're the key to getting them out of it." He adjusts us and grinds his teeth, his signature move. I narrow my eyes at him, sitting up and crawling out of his lap.

"Astor, what do you know?"

CHAPTER EIGHT

ASTOR

She looks at me with those hunter green eyes, her cheeks still wet from her tears. Seeing her cry is tugging at the black hole in my fucking chest. She has no idea just how much of the solution to this problem we are.

"Tell me. I'm so tired of everyone making decisions for me and keeping me out of the loop."

"I have nothing to tell you, Alessia. But if it were something like that, then you know the life we live: we were both taught kill or be killed. You know that."

"Yes, but I don't choose to live by it."

She's so naïve, that's always been the problem. As strong as she is, she likes to let people think she's weak. She likes to let people think that she's clueless and helpless. But I know her, I went through the same training as her. The difference is, I don't hide who I am or who I was raised to be. She, on the other hand, despises what her true identity is supposed to be. Before the day that changed all of our lives forever, she was just as ruthless as me. After it, though, she turned into this saint.

Someone who tried so hard to fight her anger and see the bright side of everything.

She looks down at herself, wrapped in just a towel, and tightens it around herself.

"Do you have my bag?" I nod to the bag sitting in the chair in the corner of my room. She strides over to it and turns to me.

"Sorry for crying. See you in the morning." I nod at her and she stops at the door. "I need to study. Did you happen to bring my books, too?"

"You need to sleep. It's 2:00 a.m."

"I can't sleep in...strange places."

"This isn't a strange place." She looks around and raises her eyebrows.

"It is to me. I can't sleep when I'm alone in new places." She shrugs her shoulder and catches my gaze as she looks around my room.

"You can sleep in here." She turns her lip up in disgust and I chuckle. "Or not. You're the one looking fucking pitiful because you're scared to sleep alone."

"I am not scared; I'm just I don't have my pillow."

"Pillow?"

"Yes, my body pillow. It...never mind—" She turns on her heels and I stop her in her tracks.

"Alessia...finish your sentence."

"It's stupid..."

"Don't make me repeat myself. I'm tired and I'm not a nice person when I'm tired."

"Oh, so I take it you're tired all the time, then?" I narrow my eyes at her and she picks at the side of the towel. "I don't like sleeping alone, so when I got my own apartment, I bought an extremely oversized pillow to wrap myself around."

"Hm, interesting."

"See, now you'll add that onto your list of shit to bug me about."

I raise my hands up in innocence as she retreats into her bedroom. I shake my head at the confession she revealed. She was vulnerable tonight, but I'm sure that by morning she'll be back to not speaking to me.

My phone dings moments later and I smirk at the message.

ALESSIA:

Tell anyone that and I'll kill you.

ASTOR:

Your faith in yourself is astounding.

ALESSIA:

I could take you. I've wanted to bring you to your knees for years.

ASTOR:

Bring it, malyshka. And if you want me on my knees, all you have to do is ask.

ALESSIA:

I'm not your baby girl. And gross.

ASTOR:

Soon you'll be my wife. Mine to torture. Mine to make cry. Mine to hurt. Fuck, I can't wait.

ALESSIA:

How romantic.

ASTOR:

Go to bed.

ALESSIA:

I can't. I told you that, already. So, keep the hate to a minimum in the morning because I'm destined to be in a God-awful mood.

I look at the phone, waiting for the three dots to appear. When they don't, I realize that I won the battle. She's too fucking scared of what I'll do to her if she sleeps in here. She probably thinks I'll suffocate her in her sleep. I laugh at the thought of what's going through her head right now. I climb out of bed and head into the bathroom to brush my teeth. I pull my shirt over my head and slide my sweats off. Usually, sleep doesn't claim me so easily, but I'm fucking exhausted from this goddamn day.

When I step back into my room, I see a small brunette with a messy bun piled on top of her head under my covers, staring at me. I tilt my head at her and she shrinks.

"What? Is this your side?" she asks, starting to slide over. I raise my hand to stop her and round the bed, cutting the lights off.

I crawl under the covers, hyper aware of her body next to mine. She's close. Not close enough to where I could touch her, but I can definitely smell her. The scent of lavender fills my nostrils and I groan. I feel her eyes on me as I turn to face her, the moonlight hovering over her skin. "What?" I ask.

"You groaned...not me."

"Go to sleep, Alessia." She shrugs and rolls over, giving me her back. I shake my head and close my eyes. There's no fucking way she can sleep in my bed again after this.

I wake up to the sound of soft, deep breathing and a leg thrown over my thigh. Alessia is snuggled up to me and has her hand wrapped around my midsection. I usually cringe at the thought of a woman touching me, but Alessia's touch is *different.* She groans when I move her off me and tap my phone to see the time.

4:42 a.m.

I shoot Justin a quick text, letting him know to go to class without me.

JUSTIN:

Fuck that class, I'm not going either. I'm fucking exhausted.

ASTOR:

Long night?

JUSTIN:

Let's just say my dick hates me right now.

ASTOR:

What'd I tell you about oversharing?

JUSTIN:

Not my fault you won't have hate sex with Lessia. Hate sex is the best sex.

ASTOR:

Says who?

JUSTIN:

Trust me, fuck her. Thank me later. Night, fucker.

CHAPTER NINE
ALESSIA

I wake up to the smell of coffee and an empty bed. I know it's early because the sunlight hasn't began to push through the curtains. I hit my phone to see that it's 5:00 a.m. *What the ever-loving fuck.* I roll out of bed and slug downstairs. Astor is standing in the kitchen, shirtless, with a pair of dark gray sweatpants and a coffee mug in his hand. He looks up when he hears me entering.

"Why the fuck are you awake at 5:00 a.m., when we just went to bed at 2:00 a.m.?"

"What'd I say about cursing at me?"

I roll my eyes at him and climb on the bar stool, to which he raises his eyebrow at me. I raise one back and he sips his coffee. "Go back to bed, Alessia. I'm going for a run." He slams the coffee mug down, a little too hard, and brushes past me, giving me a whiff of his woodsy, smoky scent. I groan inwardly and throw my head back. I follow behind him and climb back into his bed as he puts his running clothes on.

"What time did my mom say the meeting was?"

"She's your mom, call her."

"Nice to see you back to your normal, grumpy self." He ignores me while he slides his shoes on. "Can I ask you something?" I press.

"Even if I say no, you're still going to ask, so go ahead."

I take a quick deep breath and twiddle my fingers. He looks up at me and sighs. "Whatever it is, just say it."

"What did I do that made you start hating me? I remember we used to be friends, we used to be nice to each other. But then one summer, you just changed. You stopped being nice to me. Did I do something?"

He stills for a moment before quickly regaining his composure. "Why does it matter?"

"Because if I'm going to be forced to marry you, I'd at least like to know if our relationship is doomed because of something I did."

"There is no relationship. This is a business deal that our fathers made." He marches over to the side of the bed and gets in my face. "We will *never* be anything more than a piece of paper. And that's because of *you*. Be ready at 12:00 p.m."

"I hate you," I whisper.

He smirks. "Good. Hating me will make it easier."

I hear the door shut and I throw the covers back, pulling my phone out. He's dumber than I thought if he thinks I'll be here when he gets back.

ALESSIA:

Come get me? I'll love you forever.

CAROLINE:

Bitch, it's 5am..

ALESSIA:

I'm at Astor's.

Caroline immediately calls and I answer.

"What the fuck do you mean you're at Astor's? Why are you at Astor's?"

I sigh as I pull my clothes on, putting the phone on speaker.

"I didn't have a choice in the matter. Our parents are making us get married."

"What?!" she screams, making me roll my eyes. "Bitch, tell me you're fucking kidding me."

"I wish. But in two weeks, I'll be Mrs. Astor Pavlov. Woo fucking hoo."

"Two weeks?! What the fuck is this shit? He can't stand to be near you! I mean, I secretly think he pushes you away because he loves you. And I secretly think you hate him because you want to fuck him. But I mean *marrying each other*? That's pure fucking insanity."

"Yeah, well, you can't tell anyone. We have to make it seem real for the Bratva."

"Jesus Christ. Ok, whatever. Drop a pin and I'm on my way."

"Love you, Caro."

"Yeah, bitch, you better."

We hang up and I grab my things, stopping when I'm about to walk out of his room. I quickly make his bed and head downstairs.

Fuck Astor and his brutish ways.

True to her word, Caroline's Audi arrives at the gate twenty minutes later. I slam the door shut and run towards the gate. I'm too afraid that if she comes in, Astor will return and we won't be able to get out. The guard sees me and opens the gate, grabbing my arm as I run past.

"He's going to come after you, you know."

"Did he tell you to keep me here?" I look down at his grip on my arm and he lets go, shaking his head.

"He didn't say to let you leave, either." I take my knee and ram it into his junk, making him drop.

"Well, now you have an excuse as to how I left...you're welcome." I climb into the car and Caro is full blown laughing at the sight of a grown man on his knees. She backs the car up just as I see Astor and two of his bodyguards running into view.

"Caro, go. He's back from his run." She looks over her shoulder and shrugs as she steps on the gas. We both laugh as she takes the first corner, but when my phone rings, she glances at me with a smirk.

"Is that him?" I nod and hit decline. Fuck him. "He's just going to call you back. Why am I kidnapping you, anyway?

"Because he already thinks he owns me. I can't take his demeaning conversation skills any longer."

"It's been *one day*, Lessia."

"Yeah, and that was long enough." I look down at my vibrating phone and see his name and I decline again. She sighs and I turn to her. "Something on your mind, Caro?" I say sarcastically.

"I just think that maybe you should give it a chance." *Doesn't everyone?*

"You were just saying how bat shit crazy this was. Now you're saying to give it a chance?"

"Oh no, the marriage thing is absolutely fucking crazy, but being together might not be so bad if you two just stop being so fucking cold to each other."

"He started it."

"Alessia, you're my best fucking friend and you know I'll

always have your back and support you. But do you honestly hate him? Or do you hate the idea of him?"

I sigh and look out the window, mulling over her question.

"I hate that he made me hate him, when all I ever wanted to do was love him."

"That's what I thought."

I pull at my fingers, remembering how close we were as kids. He always protected me and took no shit from anyone that tried to mess with me. The first time he was mean to me, I was twelve. He felt so bad for making me cry that he let me punch him anywhere I wanted for payback. When I was about to turn sixteen, he cut me off. I don't remember much about it, honestly, which in itself is weird. It's like I blocked that part of my childhood out. The part where I lost the one person I could run to for anything. But why? What the fuck did I do?

I need to remember what happened.

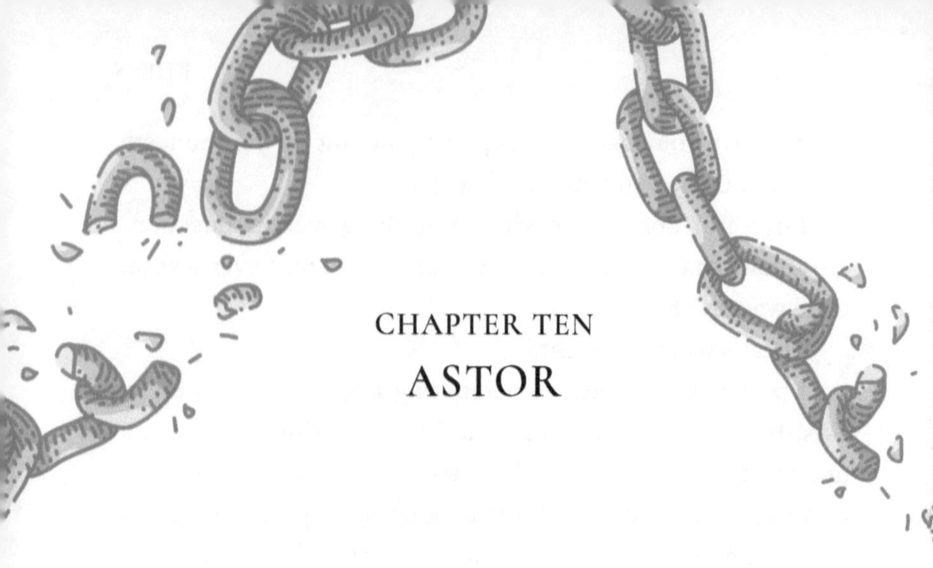

CHAPTER TEN
ASTOR

I put the phone on speaker as I start the shower, calling Alessia for the third time.

"What do you want, Astor?" she asks so low I barely hear her. I pick the phone up and slam it against my ear.

"Why'd you leave?"

"What, you wanted me to stay so you could insult me some more, and how exactly is *anything* because of me?"

"Awh, you sound hurt. Are you hurt, little devil?" A huge part of me, the darkest part of me, hopes she is hurt so she can feel what I've felt for the last six years. Hurt. Anger. Torment. Every time I look at her, I see the old Alessia. I wish I could forget that night, but I can't. I don't get the luxury of a fucking memory block.

She's silent on the phone for a few moments and I can hear Caroline in the background talking.

"Answer me, Alessia."

"I'm not hurt, I'm disgusted. With you, how you treat me, how you've been treating me. I don't know what I'll have to do

to get out of this marriage deal with you, but I'm getting out of it. I refuse to let you make me feel so insignificant." She hangs up and I'm momentarily dumbfounded.

Again, I've met my fucking match.

CHAPTER ELEVEN
ALESSIA

"Wear the jeans, they make your ass look like a peach; he'll drop to his knees so goddamn quick he won't know what hit him." I roll my eyes at Caroline as she lounges on my bed while I get dressed for this stupid meeting. A meeting to talk about a wedding that is *not* fucking happening. "So, what are you going to do?"

That's a loaded question. I push through my clothes, grabbing the jeans she told me to put on. I'm going to do whatever I can to stop this wedding from happening. And if that fails, I'm going to do whatever I can to make Astor tell me what the fuck happened when I was sixteen.

I tug the jeans up my legs and grab an off the shoulder sweater with a pair of heeled boots. I throw my hair into a messy bun on top of my head and put my glasses on. I'm not trying to impress this asshole, so why do I look at myself a little longer in the mirror? I shake my head and walk into the living room when I hear a knock at the door.

"You think it's him?" she asks, laying back on the couch with a smirk on her face. I roll my eyes and storm for the door.

If he thinks he can just start showing up, he truly is a mad man. I don't miss the way Caroline sits up so she can have a front row seat to this shit show.

"Astor, I don't feel lik—" I'm looking at the one person I never thought I'd lay eyes on again. My mouth goes dry and I can't force myself to swallow to moisten it again.

"Astor? He my competition, princess?" *Princess*. I haven't been called that since he called me, saying he didn't want to do long distance. Zander Castillo and his charming half smile stares at me as I hear Caroline gasp.

"What...what are you doing here?" He smiles brighter at me and raises his hand to my face to push a piece of my fly away back. I flinch at the touch. I always have. I don't know why, but being touched makes me uncomfortable sometimes. Certain movements, certain grasps. I lean away from his hand and he frowns.

"Oh, he really *is* my competition."

"There is no competition, because I'm not some prize to win. What do you want?"

We didn't end on completely bad terms, but that was before I learned he cheated on me. He left me and Astor made sure of that. He didn't fight for me, but claimed he loved me. It's funny, because in the back of my mind, I always knew it was something more to it. I found it hard to believe that one moment you're asking to take my virginity and the next you don't want to do long distance. In my defense, I honestly thought it was because I wouldn't sleep with him.

"Princess..." I raise my hand at him and step out into the hallway, closing the door behind me. Caroline widens her eyes and flips me the finger for shutting her out. Nosy bitch.

"Stop calling me that. I'm not your princess...why'd you break up with me two years ago?" He glances down at the floor and I can tell he's battling with the truth or a lie, so I save him the effort. "Leave, Zan…"

"You don't understand, I had no choice."

"You did have a choice, you could have chosen me." He backs me into the wall and steps into me. My breath quickens and I can feel my fight or flight instincts kicking in. There's a twist in the pit of my stomach and I know that if he kisses me, I'll probably vomit all over him.

"You're right, I'm stupid. I should've never left you. I miss you. I want you. Let me fix it." He cups my cheek and I flush. I place my hands on his chest and shake my head.

"Please don't touch me. That relationship, that was a long time ago. I'm not the same person, and quite frankly, it wasn't a healthy relationship." He cuts me off and smashes his lips against mine. My eyes widened as he tries to plunge his tongue in my mouth. I push against his chest, but he doesn't move.

This is the part of the relationship I remember being in: when I tell him no, he keeps going. Going and going until I think he really won't stop. The part in our relationship where he'd make me feel guilty for not spending every moment with him. The part where he'd make me cancel dates with Caro because he *didn't trust her.*

I throw my head back against the wall, hoping it'll alert Caroline, and moments later the door is flying open. He turns his head and I ram my knee into his dick.

"I told you *not* to touch me." He's lying on the floor, groaning when the elevator dings and Astor steps off. I physically see what little color is left drain from Zander's face when he sees him. I crouch down and tap his cheek. "I wonder if he'd kick your ass again if he knew you touched his *fiancée.* But don't worry, I won't tell him."

"But I will," Caroline says, tilting her head at Zander as he scrambles to stand up. He looks at me in disgust and then back to Astor as he approaches. I honestly didn't want Astor to beat him into oblivion. I'm sure I could've made up some story as to why the bastard was on the floor, but he *had* to open his mouth. He had to do the stupidest thing he could possibly do in front of the one person you do not want to piss off.

"I always knew you had feelings for him. The way you looked at him and swore you hated him. The way you perked up whenever he walked into a room even though he wouldn't give you the time of day, not even a fucking glance. He never saw you. Even as you practically threw yourself at him when you were a kid. He never fucking wanted you. I knew you were a fucking lying *slu*—"

Zander barely gets the last word out before Astor grabs him by his neck and cuts off his breath supply. Caro glances at me, but I can't take my eyes off how angry Astor looks. And hot, definitely fucking *hot*.

"You know, I really didn't plan on killing anyone today. But when life gives you lemons..." He tightens his grip around Zander's neck. I put my hand on Astor's arms when I notice the blue tint starting to surround Zander's mouth. He's dying.

"Please, don't. He's not worth it. I don't want anyone else getting hurt because of me." He doesn't acknowledge me for a moment. I start to think that he's really going to kill Zander in front of me, with no remorse and no shame. He loosens his grip, and the color starts returning to Zander's face, but he doesn't let go.

"Did you touch her?" Zander doesn't respond, he looks at me and I shake my head, giving him what I hope is the clue to keeping him alive. "Don't fucking look at her, look at me."

He shakes his head and chokes out, "No, no I didn't." Caroline rolls her eyes and glares at me. I glance at her and silently plead with her to keep her mouth shut.

"You were wrong about one thing, Zander," Astor says,

getting close to his ear. "I've always seen her, and guess what? She's mine. Take this as your warning. Touch her again, I'll fucking kill you."

He throws him down onto the ground and grabs my hand, yanking me towards the elevator. Caroline yells my name and I turn to see her running down the hall with my keys and phone in her hand.

"Astor, can you just wait a second!" I rip my hand out of his and put my hand on the elevator door to stop it from closing.

"Here. I'll lock up for you." I nod, taking my things from her as she narrows her eyes at me. "You, ok?" I give her a small smile and nod. She looks to Astor and squints her eyes at him. "Thanks for defending her. I mean, I could've done it myself, but the whole angry macho man thing helped, I guess."

"Caroline, it's not your job to defend her. It's mine. Please move. We have somewhere to be." I mouth, *I'm sorry*, to her as the elevator doors close.

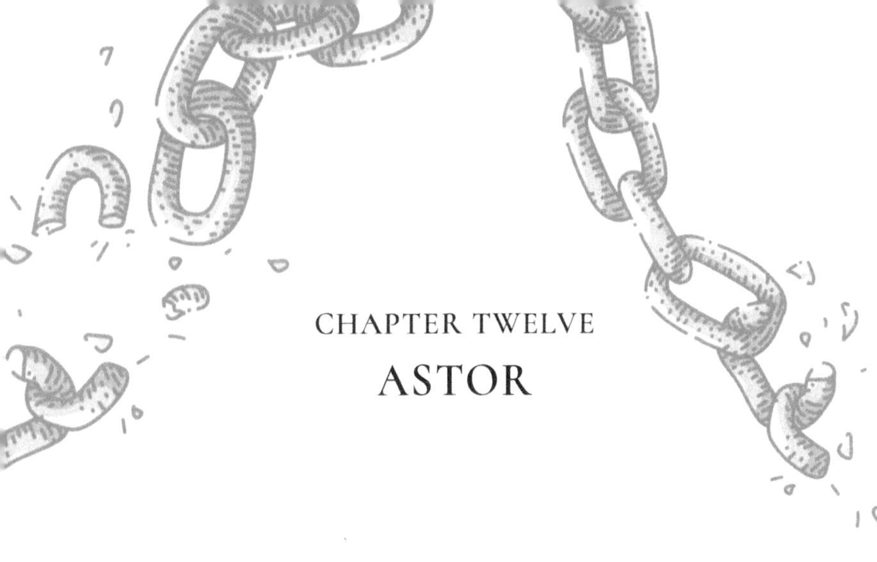

CHAPTER TWELVE

ASTOR

I'm gripping the steering wheel so tight that I'm afraid I'll rip the fucking thing off. I want to turn around and find that slithering piece of a man and kill him.

"You're grinding your teeth." I am. She's right, but I don't care. "Do you get headaches often? I would."

"Stop talking."

"Actually, I don't think I will. Why'd you say those things to Zander?"

"What things, Alessia?" She sighs and looks out the window as we near my parents' house. Her parents are already here and I'm hoping this will be quick. I'm fucking tired of talking. I need to work out. I'm so fucking tense I feel like I'll break whatever I touch. The gates open and I pull in. She pulls on her fingers and looks at me.

"You said that you see me and that I'm yours. I'm *not* yours and you *don't* see me."

I turn to her, startling her when I cup her face in my hands. I can't stop myself even if I wanted to at this point, so I don't even try. I'll give myself this moment, but only this moment.

Maybe my touch will bring her memory back or some shit. I'm getting desperate.

"Alessia, you're all I've ever seen. And I hate how true that is, just like you hate the fact that you are mine and you always have been." She opens her mouth, but nothing comes out. My gaze drops to her lips as she runs her tongue over them. I can't help myself as I pull her to me, planting a soft kiss on them. It's everything I'm not: gentle, soft and comforting. When I pull away, she runs her fingers over her lips, staring at me.

"You kissed me..." She's confused and I can't blame her. I've fought these feelings against her for years. But no matter what, I can't allow myself to love her any harder than I already do. Loving her is what's leading me to wish I hated her instead.

I could never hate her, but she can't know that yet.

"It won't happen again." I climb out of the car and she's right behind me, grabbing my arm.

"But what if I want it to happen again?"

"Then I'd tell you that you have no idea what you're asking for." She doesn't. She doesn't know how rough I am, how the idea of inflicting pain on her *arouses* me.

"If I'm going to be your wife, I'm not dying a virgin. So, unless you plan on letting me—" I cut her off, completely confused on what's coming out of her mouth.

"You and Zander never had sex?" She bites her lip and shakes her head.

"You know I thought that was why he broke up with me, because I wouldn't put out."

"Why wouldn't you?"

"I don't know...every time he'd get close to me or touch me, hell even when he kissed me, it made me feel sick. Honestly, it's like that with *any* man. The guy in the club, even. Maybe I'm broken." She shrugs her shoulders.

"Did you feel like that with me just now?" She pulls on her

fingers again and looks at the pavement, avoiding my stare. I tilt her chin up to look at me. "Did you?"

"No...I didn't. Which is why I think we should use this to our advantage." I chuckle at the wheels starting to spin in her head. I know her and I know her thought process. I fully expect what comes out of her mouth next, so I show zero emotion when she says it. "I hear that sex is better when you're mad, so I'm curious how it would be for two people who hate each other..."

I crowd her, backing her against the front door. She steadies herself by grabbing onto my shirt. "You want me to fuck you, *malyshka*?" She nods, but I shake my head. "Gestures won't work for me; I need to hear it. I need to hear you say that you want me to fuck that tight little cunt until you're screaming my name and your blood coats my cock."

"Astor..." Even with growing up around the mafia, she's still pure as ever. Well, as pure as she can be. But she's reckless, too. I've seen it.

"I tell you what. We're going to sit through this meeting and agree with everything they say so we can get the fuck out of here. Then I'm going to take you home and take the one thing I've wanted for so long. Understood?" She nods and I turn her around, walking her through the front door to greet our parents.

This is a bad idea. But bad ideas never stopped me before and I won't start now.

But first, I need to tell her that she isn't a virgin.

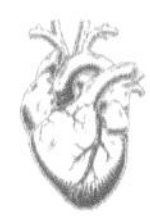

"Astor, honey. How's classes?"

"They're fine, Mom. Finals are next week, so just been studying before the semester ends."

"And you, Alessia?"

"Pretty much the same." She's shifting in her seat and I give her a quick glance, whispering in a voice low enough for only us to hear.

"Relax, *malyshka*." She tightens the grip she has on her fingers and I mindlessly think about reaching for them before stopping myself. I can feel my mother's eyes on me, but I can't tear mine away from Alessia. "You're going to hurt yourself," I growl, making her glare at me.

"I just want this to be fucking over. Leave me alone." I'm stuck between the battle of being my normal dick self or just letting her have this one when my father clears his throat.

We're all sitting in the family room, and despite it being noon, each of our parents have drinks in their hands as if we're celebrating something.

"Alessia, Astor. We know that you both are against this marriage and we know that you two seem to believe that you *hate* each other." He chuckles as he says that, and before I know it, my teeth are grinding again. "Alessia asked for a two-month trial marriage, and while we all think it's you both fighting the inevitable, we are obliging. But the conditions are that the wedding will be here in two weeks, and if you decide to end your marriage at the end of this two-month *trial*, you cannot file for divorce until you've been married for a year."

"You can't be serious," she says, putting her head down. I take a deep breath, containing my anger before it spills over.

"What in the fuck have you gotten yourselves into? And how are we the solution? Tell us now, or I promise a tempted runaway bride won't be your only worry."

My father raises his eyebrow at me, questioning my words.

"Astor, I'm not sure you want me or Ander to answer that."

"Answer it."

"I tell you what, how about I just tell you in private. Walk with me, son." I stand, not giving Alessia a second glance as I follow my father into his study.

He always brought me in here as a kid for our *man to man* talks, even though I was only ten or eleven at the time. They were the highlights of my day back then. I couldn't wait to be that big, to feel that powerful.

He closes the door to his study and gestures toward the chair. "I'll stand. What's going on?"

"Miles…"

One word. One word and my vision goes red, just at the mention of his name. My fists automatically ball at my sides.

"Don't say his fucking name."

"His family is a part of the Bratva, as you know, and for years, they've battled with trying to punish you for what you did to him."

"Do they know *why* I did it?" He nods.

"They were appalled to hear what you walked in on; however, his father is having quite a hard time accepting the fact that you almost killed his son. His heir."

He pours himself another scotch, quickly shooting it back. "He has been trying to turn the Bratva against us, exile us out. Obviously, their loyalty lies with me, so they're giving me the opportunity to *expunge* him how I see fit. The only way I can do that without going against the code, is if I have more power."

"Our name is already powerful, more powerful than his. And I am not going to use Alessia at the expense of Miles."

"Yes, that's true, but you know who is also powerful? The Ballerini's. A Pavlov and Ballerini together cannot be stopped. No one would second guess what we say and everyone would fall at our fucking feet. And if this shit goes south, we need to know that it wasn't for nothing. So I'm sorry, but it's time to get over the fact that she lost her memory and time to help her start getting back."

"What do you mean if it goes south?"

"I mean that Miles' dad may not be as powerful, but the fucker is just as crazy. And if he doesn't decide to leave quietly, I have a feeling a lot of blood will be shed in New York."

CHAPTER THIRTEEN

ALESSIA

Astor is quiet for the remainder of the meeting; he doesn't look at me or talk to me. He's completely in his own head. My mother and Astrid are showing me wedding dresses in a catalog, but I can't seem to focus on anything other than what his father told him that has him so upset.

My mother is grinning from ear to ear as she gets off the phone with the bridal boutique to set my appointment.

"They said they can get us in this Sunday at 11:00 a.m. and I'm already meeting with the florist tomorrow." I cut her off and stand as she looks at me in confusion.

"Sorry, just give me a...Astor, a moment please." He glares at me, but follows as I leave the room. "What the fuck did your dad say?"

"Cursing at me again?"

"Just tell me." He shifts on his feet, shoving his hands into his pockets. He looks nervous, almost scared in a way of my response.

"Do you remember Miles?" The name sounds oddly famil-iar, but I can't remember why I know him or how. I also don't understand the tightness that appears in my chest from hearing his name. I shake my head and he lets out a sigh. "When you do, come back and ask me that question. When you remember him, you'll be ready for the truth. But I can't give it to you any sooner."

"What does that mean?"

"You'll figure it out."

"Can we leave? I need to study and I'm wedding talked out."

"Thought you were going to do everything you could to get out of this?"

He's right, I did say that. And I meant it, and I kind of still do. But when I think about all of the people my father could have forced me to marry, I feel a little more grateful that it's Astor. Yes, we don't get along, but he also doesn't have feelings or emotions, so at least I can probably get decent sex out of this. Caroline swears that the sex will be over the top since there's so much history behind it. And I'm no longer being scared to find that out.

"Maybe I'm realizing this won't be so bad." He smirks at me and I think my knees are going to buckle.

"Is that a smile? Did I seriously get a smile? It's a fucking—"

"*Alessia*," he groans. Honestly, he might as well get used to it, because I curse. A lot. That's probably not going to change.

"Oh, yeah sorry." He shakes his head, looking at my mother as she approaches.

"Honey, what colors would you two like?" I shrug my shoulders and look at Astor.

"It's not like it's a real wedding..." He grinds his teeth at my response and I turn my gaze to the floor. *Oops.* "Black."

"It's not a funeral, Alessia."

"Ok, well let's do red and cream. It's a Christmas wedding, after all."

She smiles at me as she types away on her phone.

"We're actually going to head out, I have a lot of studying to do before finals next week." She kisses my cheek, followed by Astor's. He says something to his father before he opens the front door. I watch him as he glances over his shoulder and says my name.

"Alessia."

"Coming." I quickly hug my father and Xavier, giving Astrid a kiss on her cheek.

"See you Sunday, sweetheart," my mom calls.

Astor is already in the car when I get outside. His face is stone and I can already tell that the little moment we had earlier has dissipated.

"Are you going to let me go home now?" He glances at me, but doesn't answer. "Ok...I guess we're back to hating each other from a distance."

"How would you prefer this goes?" he questions.

"Honestly?" He raises his eyebrow at me and I pull my fingers together before whispering, "I'd prefer you not to hate me at all..." He doesn't respond and I secretly hope that he didn't hear the confession.

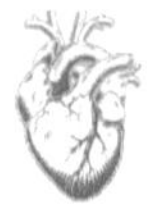

When he pulls up to my apartment complex, I quickly reach for the door handle and step out when he grabs my wrist. "Malyshka..." he says. I sigh and bend down to make eye contact with him.

"Yeah?"

"I don't want to hate you. But if I don't make myself, I'll love you too fucking hard."

My mouth goes dry at his words and I stand there frozen for a second. I nod because for the first time, I am fucking speechless. I shut the car door and walk to my apartment on auto pilot. What does he mean he'll love me too hard? He thinks he could love me? What the fuck is happening?

I know Caroline is here, because she texted me to ask if she could borrow one of my shirts. I shut the door and throw my purse on the counter. I flop onto the couch and replay his words over and over.

"I thought he said you were staying with him from now on?" she asks, stepping into the living room with me. I barely register her words until she snaps her fingers at me. "Bitch, what the fuck is happening?" I tell her the entire story, but I'm not sure how much she understood considering I was talking like I was running a marathon.

"Ok, so let me get this straight. He basically told you that he only hates you to not love you?" I nod my head and push my fingernail in between my mouth. She smacks my hand down. "Why the fuck are you here? Go fucking talk to him! Or don't talk, just fuck."

"I don't think that's a good idea. Feelings are going to change and it's fine how it is."

"Lessia, do you hear yourself? This is going to be your husband. You could make this work, like *really* work. He basically just confessed that his *hate* is not truly hate. That's your window. Don't be a scared bitch. Go."

I know she's right, but I can't bring myself to get off the couch. I am scared. I'm scared because I saw how quick he switched after he kissed me. I know how cold he can be, but I also know how warm and secure he can be, too. How he can make me feel like *I am* important, like I'm *not* a burden.

Just like he did when we were younger.

CHAPTER FOURTEEN
ASTOR

I'm starting to lose my strength, the strength I've held onto and had for the last six years. I've kept her away for a reason. I knew that if I got close to her, I'd fucking forget that I should never be with her. She brings out the feral animal in me. My need to protect her from any and everything. Now, I have to marry her. And the feelings I fought so hard to put away are busting through the bullshit wall I built, that she *made* me build.

The moment my father brought that piece of shit up, the only feeling I was filled with was regret. Regret that I didn't kill him when I had the chance. Regret that my father walked in when he did. Regret that he took every piece of Alessia and her memories. Her memories of us. She shut down completely that day. She didn't speak, she didn't eat, and the next day she didn't fucking remember. Miles had tormented her to the point of dissociation. She mentally placed herself somewhere else while she was in the process of being raped, and when she came back, she didn't remember fucking anything. What's even worse is that instead of just blocking out that *day*, she

blocked out every emotion and feeling she'd ever had that entire goddamn *year*, including for me. Including *us*.

I CHANGE INTO MY RUNNING JOGGERS AND A BLACK T-SHIRT. TIMES like this, I need to run to clear my head. How am I supposed to marry her without telling her what she forgot? She's said so many times to me how she is tired of everyone keeping things from her, how she hates that she always feels out of the loop. Our already doomed marriage is starting out with me keeping one of the biggest secrets ever from her. I want to tell her, but I can't. I'm not fucking allowed.

I'm pulling my shoes on when I hear footsteps nearing the stairs.

"I can find him—I don't need you walking me everywhere." I smirk at the sound of Alessia giving Todd hell.

"Miss, just let me tell him you're—"

"Will you stop fucking calling me *miss*? Astor!" she bellows. I stand at the top of the stairs as her eyes pierce through mine.

"Todd, she's good. Leave her." She rolls her eyes at him and crosses her arms as she stalks up the stairs towards me.

"What are you doing?" I ask her, eyeing the bag she's holding when she reaches the top of the stairs.

"You said I had to stay with you from now on." She shrugs as she drops her bag at our feet. I try my best to hide my surprise, but I can tell I failed when the side of her mouth tilts up in a smirk. She looks me over and raises her eyebrow. "Going for a run?"

"I was." I'm towering over her as she looks up at me. She's always been short, but today she seems extremely short.

"Was?" I can't stop myself when I reach my hand out and tuck her hair behind her ear. She flinches for a second and it makes me want to kill Miles all over again. Her body even knows what she doesn't. She steps closer to me, our bodies practically molded together. The scent of her fills my nose and I inhale her as much as possible before dropping my hand and taking a step back. She shakes her head and takes a step forward, making me take another back.

"Don't do that. You can still hate me, but at least hate me while you fuck me."

"You don't know what you're asking. You aren't ready. And I do not hate you, stop saying it."

She isn't ready...or maybe it's me. Maybe I'm not ready to admit that the moment I fuck her, all bets are off. I'm losing this battle, and if I don't regain myself quickly, I'm going to fuck her against this wall. The look she's giving me, the way she's pulling her shirt because she's nervous. And if she bites that lip one more time, I'm done for.

"Astor...please."

"Come for a run with me." She frowns briefly and then sighs, picking up her bag and chugging into the bathroom to change.

I attempt to adjust my cock that is now painfully hard against these fucking joggers. Leaning my head back against the wall, I mentally battle with myself and what to do. If I tell her, her parents will hate me. If I don't tell her, she'll hate me —more than she already does.

She doesn't hate you.

"Ok, ready." She's wearing a pair of leggings and a sports bra.

"*Little devil*, it's December and you're not wearing that."

"Of course not, I'm putting a jacket over it!" She gestures to the flimsy, light, black windbreaker she has in her hand as I shake my head. She sneaks past me and jogs down the stairs, giving me a view of her perfect fucking ass.

Reminder: Burn all of her fucking leggings.

WE'RE A MILE INTO OUR RUN AND I PEEK OVER TO HER. "DOING OK?"

"I'm fine, I run two miles every morning." I know she does, because I've run her same route for the last six years to keep an eye on her.

"When did you start doing that?" I ask.

"Uhm, six years ago. I don't know why, actually. It's just something I started doing one day."

Wrong. It's something your therapist told you to do.

"I can feel you staring, *malyshka*." She grins, slowing down and taking a sip of her water. "Need a break?"

"Nope, I'm good. How long do you usually run?"

"I usually do six miles." Her eyes almost double in size and I chuckle.

"SIX?! Fuck. Me. I'm screwed." She takes a deep breath and kicks her feet into gear again. The run is always beautiful here. There's a lake on my property that runs along the trail; it's always my rest point, to remind myself to take it all in.

The next three miles go by painfully slow. I'm hyperaware of the woman running next to me and how she's fighting so hard to make it to the end. She has unzipped her jacket and it's blowing in the wind as she runs.

She sees the hill and groans. I actually laugh, making her frown at me as I push up the hill. "We can break up here."

"Oh no! Don't stop on my account, I'm doing just fine."

"You look like you've ran twenty miles instead of four. That we practically could've walked with how slow we were *running*." She drops her hands on her knees when we get to the top of the hill, her chest rising and falling so fast that I think for a moment she'll actually hyperventilate.

"I'm never running with you again. I know you hate me, but I still thought you'd be a little nicer to me." I smirk at her as she stands up with her hands on her hips, looking at the lake in front of her. "This is beautiful."

"It is..." I want to touch her. I want to touch her so fucking bad that my hands physically feel like they're burning. She's a fucking vision and she knows it. I'm sure of it when she throws her hair over and pulls it into a bun on top of her head.

My chest constricts as I watch her. This woman is everything. And I can no longer make myself believe that there was ever going to be a time where I could move on without her.

CHAPTER FIFTEEN

ALESSIA

He's looking at me weird, like *extremely weird*, and the only thing worse than not having Astor's attention, oddly, is *having* his attention. His stare is overwhelming, is non-forgiving, and is brutal. He stares at me for what feels like hours before I clear my throat, willing myself to speak.

"Why are you staring at me?" I ask.

"Why not?" he retorts.

"It makes me uncomfortable, like you can see straight through me or something."

"*Little devil,* I know every piece of you." I pull at my jacket and he yanks me to him. "Like I know you do that when you're nervous or uncomfortable." I drop my hand from the jacket and glance up at him.

"I do not…"

"Lying isn't becoming of you."

"Don't analyze me."

"You're not hard to read, *malyshka.*"

See, that's the thing. I am hard to read—everyone thinks

so. My mother would always get so upset with me growing up because she said she couldn't figure me out. She always said that she wished I'd open up more, that I'd wear a little more feelings on my sleeve. But Astor has always been able to read me, for as long as I can remember. I never had to hide things from him because he always knew.

"What did you mean earlier? When you dropped me off?"

It's been taunting me since he said it, I have to know what he meant. I can't read him as well as he can read me, and I'm tired of acting like I don't want him. Of acting like I'm strong enough to continue to deal with the hate he gives me.

"Nothing," he says, rubbing his finger across my cheek. My body shivers at his touch and I don't know if it's from the cold or him.

"Astor...tell me, please." He closes his eyes and I take the moment to lean into him more, wrapping my arms around his waist. "Open your eyes, Astor." He groans and tilts his head back, looking towards the sky. I urge him to look at me, staring at him, knowing he can feel my gaze. "If you won't tell me, at least stop treating me so vile, like you hate me. It's ripping me apart when I know there was a time that we were inseparable. Acting like I hate you is exhaus—" He cuts me off gripping my face and planting a searing kiss on my lips. A kiss that is so good my goddamn knees buckle. And I'm not being funny; they actually fucking buckle. He wraps his hand around my waist, holding me up.

"Ok?" he asks as I nod, leaning back into him, not wanting the kiss to be over. He lifts me and pushes me against a tree that sits right off the trail. I wrap my legs around him and welcome the pain shooting through my back as the tree bark digs into my jacket. "I can't give you the answers right now. You have to figure those out for yourself, but I *can* fuck you.

Because I can't stop myself anymore. And I don't fucking hate you. I never have."

"Astor...."

"Shut up, Alessia. You need to understand that I am going to *ruin* you. Ruin you for any other man. You'll want no one but me, regardless of how much you *hate* me. I'll be all you fucking want."

Fuck. Me.

I must be insane, *certifiably* insane, because I believe every word he says and yet I still nod my head yes. He growls as he rips open my jacket, practically yanking it off me. His eyes are hungry and the way he licks his lips heightens the feeling of wetness that's starting to gather between my legs. As if he's reading my mind, he digs his hands in the front of my leggings. My breath hitches and I honestly think I'll faint when he pushes his fingers into my embarrassingly wet pussy.

"No underwear? Hmm...bad fucking girl, *malyshka*."

If not wearing panties makes me bad, then I'm the baddest fucking woman alive because I hate wearing them. They're uncomfortable and can mess up a perfect outfit with those horrendous lines.

He pushes his fingers in and out of me, and I let out a tiny whimper. His fingers feel like they belong to a giant at this moment. When he adds a third in, I think I'll explode right here and now.

"So fucking tight around my fingers. I can't wait to see how this pussy will strangle my cock." If I wasn't into dirty talk before, I am now because *holy fucking shit*. This man.

I push myself against his fingers, forcing him to push inside deeper, and he groans. He pushes me harder against the tree and runs his hand through my hair, tugging me to look at him. If this is what his fingers feel like, I have no fucking idea how

I'll be able to take his cock. He speeds up his pace and I feel my body tensing.

"Astor...Astor," I moan as he gently bites my ear.

"There you go, ride my fingers. Come all over them." And I do, I come so hard, fisting his shirt as I do. "*Goddamn*, you are beautiful when you come, *malyshka*."

"That was...I've never...*fuck* I can't even talk." He chuckles and I groan as he pulls his fingers out of me and shoves them in his mouth. He's giving me a piercing stare as he licks his fingers clean. He tilts my face up to his stare and I swallow uncomfortably.

"You've never what? You've never made yourself come?"

I shake my head. "I have toys, but they just never did the job. And I don't know what I like because I've never had sex before." He flinches at me mentioning my virginity; he seems to be on edge anytime I bring it up. I'm suddenly feeling in over my head. I know I can't amount to the girls he's probably been with. Girls who are experienced and know how to please him. "Sorry, I know you're used to girls who know what they're doing." He ignores me as he slowly pulls my leggings up and lowers my legs on the ground. I bite my lip and look past him.

"Do you see any other woman here?" he asks. I continue my gaze past him and he cups my cheek. "Look at me." He turns my face to him, but I can't because I'll want more and I also don't want him to elaborate on any other person he's been with. But fuck, that just wasn't enough. I close my eyes and he chuckles. I press my legs together as I feel his gaze raking over me. I peek an eye open and he raises his eyebrow at me. "You want more, *malyshka*?"

"Yes..."

"Hmm..." He runs his finger over the bottom of my lip and I shiver. "Run," he whispers. "And when I catch you, I'll fuck you."

ASTOR

She stares at me in shock and I raise my eyebrow at her. She searches my face and when she sees no hint of a joke, she takes off running towards the house. I chuckle to myself, knowing that she'll never reach it before me. I watch her run, her pace picking up when she hears me behind her. It wouldn't take much to catch her, but the chase is too much fun. Watching her look over her shoulder with fear and lust in her eyes, making sure I'm behind her. I fought it as long as I could, my feelings for her. My need for her. Our parents fucked up any progress I had when they told me I was to marry her. I did well only having to face her during the family dinners, I avoided her any other time. I watched her from a distance to make sure she stayed safe, but I never talked to her. Now, I have to marry her. I'll have to see her every day. I'll have to look at her, knowing she will have my last name. Knowing that she doesn't remember. Yet.

I watch her as she almost reaches the house. She stops and turns to look at me, making me stop in my tracks to watch her.

She looks at the house, then looks away to the lake. I follow

her gaze and watch her toy with what she wants to do. She rips her jacket off and I growl when she reaches for her bra.

"*Malyshka,* watch it."

"Why? Afraid I'll give your bodyguards a show?" She's right, I have guards posted all throughout these woods. But they're paid to see what I tell them to see, otherwise they know when the fuck to look away. For their sakes, I hope they remember that.

I take a step towards her and she raises her hand towards her bra strap.

"Another step and I'll take it off."

"Trying to call the shots?" I ask.

She purses her lips up in confidence and I lunge for her as she tries to run, quickly tossing her over my shoulder and marching for the house.

"Too bad I'm the one that calls them, sweet *Alessia.*" She claws at my back and I swat her ass as she yelps.

We make our way past the two guards at the front of the gate. I give them a nod and she laughs as we pass them. "Wait, is that the one I hit in the dick?"

I stop to glare at him and he puts his head down as she squirms, trying to get out of my hold.

"Oh yeah, you're fired. She touched your dick." I continue walking toward the house and she bellows out, "He's just kidding! I'm sorry about your di—"

I swat her ass before she can get the rest of the sentence out, slamming the door shut. I take the steps two at a time, tightening my hold around her waist.

"The *next* dick you touch will be the *last* dick you touch. Understand?" I ask, throwing her on the bed. She twists her mouth to the side and I see her fingers reach for the blanket that's laying under her. I chuckle at her tell and yank her by her feet toward me.

"Maybe we should..."

"Should what?" I ask as I pull her shoes off, one by one.

"Put a towel down, I don't want to ruin your bed..."

Fuck.

Fuck. Fuck. Fuck.

"I want to see the evidence of you on my bed, my sheets, and my cock." She swallows as I crawl over top of her, wrapping my hand around her neck and pulling her face to mine. "I can't wait to ruin you."

She grins at me as she bites her lips, but tenses a little when I run my tongue over her stomach.

"Are you sure about this?" I ask.

"Yes," she says without hesitation.

"You're stiff as a board, Alessia. If you're not ready—"

"I'm ready, don't stop...Please." I search her eyes and they fill with unshed tears. I run my thumb across her cheek and kiss her.

"Why are you crying?" I ask.

"I've always wanted it to be you...that I did this with." Guilt strikes me right in the fucking chest. This isn't fair to her; I have to tell her. I just can't form the words.

"Astor?" I turn my gaze back to her and she pulls my face down to her lips as she opens for me. "Please, I want you. Don't make me beg." The sight of her begging me to fuck her enters my mind. It's enough to make me forget about the guilt and let my dick think for me.

I pull her sports bra off and stuff one of her breasts in my mouth. She tilts her head back and lets out a small moan. I gently bite and tug while playing with the other in my hand.

She bites her lip as she watches me suck on her. I expect her to tense when my hand travels lower and I push her leggings down, but she doesn't. She watches my every move, her breathing increasing and lust filling her eyes.

"Mmm. Tell me why there's no panties?"

"I...don't like them." Fuck. Of course, she doesn't. I shake my head while

I push her legs apart. I run my fingers through her folds, checking her wetness, and fuck me, she's drenched. I groan when I slide a finger inside of her, watching how her mouth drops open. I slowly push my fingers in and out of her, adding another when she starts moaning.

"More...please, more." I'm milking her for everything she can give me at this point and she's taking it like a good fucking girl. Her body is tensing and I know this is just the beginning for the amount of orgasms I plan to give her. She pushes her feet into the bed and starts inching her body away, I follow her movements, increasing the speed of my fingers. "I...oh my God."

"Come on my fingers, let it fucking happen," I growl in her ear. She explodes over my fingers, yelling out my name as she comes. I drop to my knees in front of her. "We're not done." Burying my face into her pussy, I feast as if it'll be my last meal. I taste her, and I mean really *taste her*. The taste I've been craving since I was a fucking teenager. The taste that I will never get out of my fucking head now that I've sampled it. I devour her and she pushes her hands into my hair, yanking hard.

"Astor...Astor." My name rolls off her lips as she comes again. I lap and lap every ounce of come that squirts out of her pussy. It's the sweetest taste I've had.

"That's two," I say, standing over top of her. She's out of breath, but gives me a smirk.

"Actually, that's *three*. Remember? The tree?" I tilt my head as she speaks and pull my shorts down, taking my briefs with them.

"How about we go for four?"

She spreads her legs wider, giving me the perfect view of her pussy. My cock hardens and I lick my bottom lip as I fist my cock. Her eyes widen and I grin as she takes in all of my length.

"I'm not going to be gentle."

"I didn't ask you to be," she responds. I yank her to me by her ankles and she looks around. "Wait...when was the last time you were, umm...checked?"

"I've never fucked anyone without a condom. But I was checked last month."

"But you aren't wearing one with me?"

I line my cock up with her entrance, sliding it up and down, letting her juices coat me as a lubricant. She groans and I take the time to push inside of her.

"I'll never use a condom with my wife, *malyshka*." She claws my back as I move in and out of her again, tears prick her eyes as I kiss them away. "Take it, Alessia. You wanted it, remember?" She bites her lip as I plunge in and out of her, harder each time.

I look down and watch as my cock moves in and out her. I smile when I see it coated in red. "Look how well you bleed for me, *little devil*. I love seeing your blood coating my cock." She looks down and her face turns a shade redder as she grasps the covers.

"Ahh, don't be embarrassed. It's a fucking sight to see." I push myself deeper into her, fucking her relentlessly when she wraps her legs around me.

"Astor...fuck..." I pull out of her and flip her over, pulling her up on all fours. I wrap her hair around my hand and yank her head back when I force myself into her again.

She lets out a moan, arching her back more as I plow inside of her.

"You take my cock so well, Alessia. It's like you were fucking made for me." I slap her ass and she yelps. I do it again, but harder, watching her ass turn a deep red.

"Oh God..."

"That's right, I am your fucking god. I'm your devil, too, *malyshka*."

CHAPTER SEVENTEEN
ALESSIA

He's right. He is my devil and fuck me if I'm not going to worship him. He doesn't care that it's my first time, he fucks me just like I knew he would; like he hates me. This is the first time I think I'm happy that he does or doesn't, I don't know anymore. He pulls me out of my thoughts as his hand wraps around my neck, cutting off my air supply.

"Eyes. On. Me, *little devil*." He tightens his hold around my neck and I start to struggle for breath, but I don't stop him. "Did you know that the harder I fuck you and the more I cut off your breath supply, your body will only focus on the pleasure?" He's right. All I can think as I start to see stars is how close I am to coming. Just when I think I'll either pass out or fucking die, my body shivers and he loosen his hold around my neck. "Mmm, do you want to breathe or come? Tell me."

"I...want...to...come," I say in between catching my breath. He gives me a wicked grin and crushes my air supply again as he pushes in and out of me, harder and harder. My body comes alive and I come so hard my body physically feels like it's dead weight. I can't move, I can't scream, so I claw his back. I dig so deep as I come all over him. He grunts in my ear, finding his release. I feel warmth shoot inside of me and I'm so focused on how good it feels that I don't even realize his hand is gone from my neck.

"Now you can breathe, *malyshka*." I gasp in for air and he kisses me, slow and deep. "Good girl."

It's been thirty-five minutes and I honestly don't know if I'm alive, or if I'm in the afterlife. My body is sore and my pussy feels like it's been split open. Astor is mindlessly playing in my hair as I'm sprawled out on top of him.

"Can I tell you something?" I ask.

"Mhm."

"I liked you...when we were kids..." His hand stops briefly and his heart starts beating a bit faster.

"I liked you, too," he admits.

"Why didn't you ever tell me?"

"I did, Alessia. You told me then, too, when you were sixteen. You just don't remember." I sit up and look at him, my brow furrowed.

"What do you mean?" I'm confused, completely fucking confused. He sits up and leans his head against the bedpost.

"Ask your fath—" The sound of the doorbell ringing interrupts us and I swear I can hear the relief in Astor's breathing. He climbs out of the bed and throws his shirt and shorts on, opening his drawer next to the bed and pulling out a Glock. He shoves it in the back of his shorts and looks at me. "Get dressed and wait for me. I don't know who the fuck is at my house in the middle of the afternoon, unannounced."

I try to get up and fail miserably when my legs decide to give out on me. He wasn't joking about me not being able to walk. Fuck.

I drag my legs to a standing position as I get dressed, opting for one of his shirts and my leggings.

I'm in the bathroom fixing my hair, that clearly tells anyone what I just did, when I hear the voice of a woman. What the *fuck*?

I'm down the stairs before I can even process that my feet are moving.

"How the fuck did you get past the guards, Anna?" The woman leans into Astor and lays her hand on his chest. Neither of them has seen me yet and I stay quiet.

"You know me, persuasive." She's a little taller than me and is a slender redhead, with mid length nails that are currently running down Astor's arm. The feeling that creeps up my stomach is gut-wrenching. It's anger. It's fucking *jealousy*.

He grabs her arm away from him. "Stop touching me and get the fuck out of my house."

"Don't you wanna play tonight? It's been so long, I miss you."

That's it. I step forward, trying to get myself to relax. Because Astor and I both know how un-fucking-hinged I can become. I'm nice for a *reason*, I stay clear from the mafia stuff for a *reason*.

"Trust me, you'll want to leave. And quickly." My voice is clear, crisp, and deadly. She whips her head around to me and snatches out of the hold Astor has on her arm.

"Who the fuck are—"

"Watch it," he says to her. She tilts her head at me and takes in my appearance.

"You just got done fucking *her*. Interesting, she doesn't seem like she likes it rough. She can't give you what you need."

I march up to her, yanking her by her hair towards the door. She screams as I tighten on my hold on the roots of her scalp. "Fucking bitch. Let go of me! What is wrong with you!!" Astor stands by and watches as I lose control, the control I've always hidden for this exact reason. I become a loose fucking canon when I'm mad.

"Come back and I'll slit your fucking throat." I turn to Astor and glare at him. "*Baby*, please take the fucking trash out. Before I do it myself." I brush by him, briefly catching the glimpse of a smirk on his face before I head back for his room and start a bath.

I want to go back and fuck her up. I want so badly to suck every piece of life out of her for daring to touch what's *mine*.

Mine. He's mine. And I don't care how that makes me sound. I don't care if it makes me seem clingy all because we had sex. He's been mine since the moment I was fucking born. I've always been his, too, and he knows that. Tonight is the last fucking night I'll act like I hate him. And it's the last night he'll fucking hate me, too.

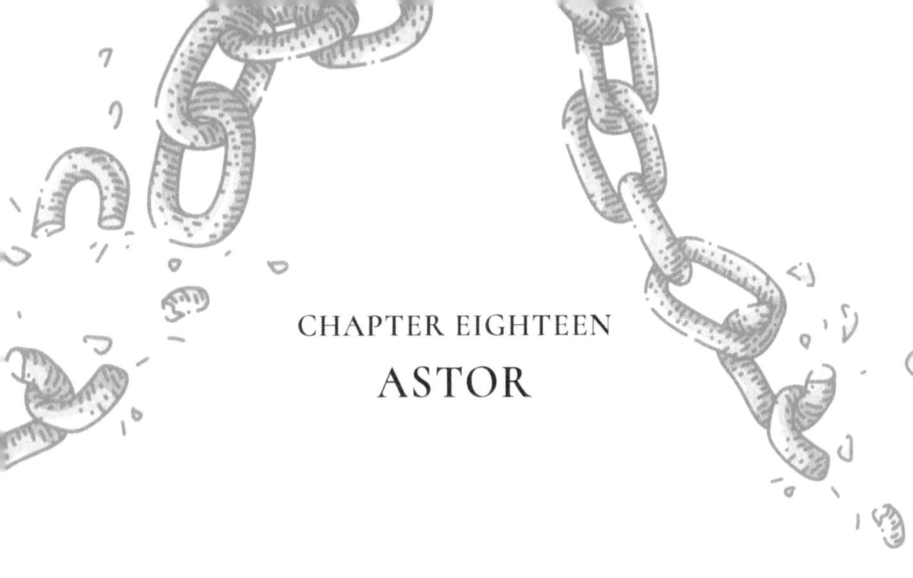

CHAPTER EIGHTEEN

ASTOR

I'm mesmerized at what I'm seeing in front of me. There she is. The Alessia I know, the one I remember. The one I fell in love with when we were teenagers. She's always been that way, ruthless when someone pisses her off. She's worked so hard putting out a fire that isn't meant to be contained. I watch her when she walks up the stairs, only turning to Anna when I hear the water turn on.

 think I'm fucked up? You have no idea with the monster that's upstairs."

"Fuck...her..." she says, catching her breath. I close in on her, stepping outside of the door and wrapping my hand around her throat. I pull until her feet are no longer touching the ground.

"Hear me, loud and clear. Do not speak about her that way. I can promise you she's probably upstairs, right now, talking herself out of making good on her threat. Go home." I push her

backwards and slam the door in her face before I beeline for the stairs.

She sits in the tub, bubbles covering her body with her eyes closed. Her face is in a frown and she slowly taps her finger over her knee. A trait she picked up after our training when we were kids. I sit on the edge of the tub, but she doesn't acknowledge me, keeping her eyes shut.

"Any more girlfriends stopping by tonight?"

"Not that I'm aware of. No."

"*Lovely.*"

"You almost lost control." Her eyes pop open at my words and she narrows her eyes at me.

"Fuck *you*. You should have kicked her out the moment she reached out to fucking touch you."

"*Alessia.*" My voice is low and deadly. She sits up and water splashes around her.

"No, don't *Alessia* me. You better get all of that shit out of your system before you say *I do*, because if you let *anyone* touch you—"

"Stop talking."

"Excuse me?"

"I said to stop talking. Let's get something straight, you don't make any rules in this fucking relationship. Next, if you curse at me again, I swear I'll shove you on your knees and stuff my cock so far down your throat you'll choke on it. Lastly, if I want to fuck the entire fucking city of New York, I'll do it. Just because I fucked you doesn't mean a happily ever after."

I don't mean the last part. There isn't anyone in the world that I would rather be with than her. It's just that I'm not used to taking orders from anyone and I feel like I need to make a point.

Her eyes fill with tears. She tries so hard to keep them in, but the moment one falls, she wipes it and closes her eyes. I watch her as she regulates her breathing before responding.

"And just because I *let* you fuck me doesn't mean I won't fuck who I want now, too." *Fuck. No.* I move closer to her, leaning down next to her ear. I drop my voice to a whisper.

"Then their lives will be on you." She nonchalantly shrugs her shoulders, dipping her head back in the water.

"Just...get out." Her tears are flowing uncontrollably now and she dunks her head under the water to hide from me.

Fuck.

I turn for the bedroom, forcing myself to breathe. What the fuck was that? We were *fine*.

I finally fucked her; I took what always belonged to me. I was ready to let that change the years of built up anger I've had. I was ready to cave and give it my all. To give her my all, *again*.

Her reaction to Anna turned me on, made me want her even more. Showed me that she wanted me, that I was hers. But when I saw how angry she was and realized that anger was towards *me*, all bets were off.

I wanted to hurt her, and if I didn't, my words did.

CHAPTER NINETEEN
ALESSIA

After the shitshow that happened hours ago, I retreated into the room next to his. Unable to face him after the way we talked to each other. You'd think I'd be used to it, but I'm not. Hearing him say he'd fuck someone else physically made me sick to my stomach. So much that I've been vomiting the last fifteen minutes. My head is hurting and I truly don't think I have anything left to throw up.

My phone rings in the midst of my vomit session. I groan and rest my head on the toilet seat.

"Hello?"

"Honey? You sound awful, are you alright?"

"Hi, Mom, I'm fine. What do you need?"

"Well, the bridal shop called and said they have an opening in an hour, we're on our way to Astor's to pick you up." My eyes spring open and I swallow the vomit that's threatening to creep up my throat.

"No, don't come here. I'll ride with Caro there."

"Are you sure? We're not far."

"Mom, I said not to come here. I'll see you there."

I hang up just in time for the vomit to eject from my mouth. Fuck me. Not only did we take two steps forward and then five back, but now I have to deal with both of our mothers on top of whatever the fuck I'm starting to come down with. Lucky me.

I place my phone on speaker as it dials Caro's number.

"Hey, what's up?"

"Wedding dress shopping is happening today, apparently, can you come?"

"Of course, bitch, like I'd miss it."

"Can you come get me? I don't want to stomach both mothers in a car today."

"On my way."

"Thanks, Caro." I hang up and shove my foot into a pair of jeans, sliding my Louboutin boots on. I look at myself in the mirror and almost vomit just from the sight of myself. I look like fucking death. I dabble some mascara on and do my best to conceal the red brims around my eyes from crying.

I haven't seen Astor since the argument and I'm hoping it stays that way. The last thing I need is him questioning me.

I grab my bag and head downstairs, grabbing a bottle of water and taking two Advil in hopes it'll deplete my headache. Todd is coming out of what I think is the control room when he stops and gives me a nod.

"Where's Astor?"

"I believe he is in the gym room, ma'am. Would you like me to walk you there?"

"No, no, that's alright. I'm heading out for some errands, if you'd be so kind to let him know."

"Of course."

The water is a welcome feeling down my extremely dry

throat. I practically drink the entire bottle before I feel it rising back up. I run to the bathroom, making it just in time before throwing it up.

I hear the door slam and then harsh breathing. *Fuck.*

I quickly rinse out my mouth and wash my hands before meeting an extremely sweaty Astor. He has a water in his hand, his chest is rising and falling so hard as he tries to catch his breath.

"Todd said you're running errands?" I don't look at him as I grab my phone when it goes off.

"Wedding stuff."

A text from Caro pops up.

CARO:

Outside, coming in for a second I have to pee.

"Were you just going to leave?"

"Does it matter?"

"If it didn't, I wouldn't fucking ask you."

"Honestly, Astor, let's just cut the shit. You don't care about me, and you've made that blatantly obvious. So, let's get this two-month trial over. We can go back to only speaking when we're insulting each other at family meetings while you fuck your way through New York." I brush past him when the doorbell rings.

"Hey, Caro, bathroom is right there." She steps in and frowns. I shake my head at her and she takes the hint, retreating into the bathroom. I grab my purse and jacket, feeling like I'll catch on fire from the heat of his stare.

"*Malyshka,*" he says behind me, closer this time. My hand tightens on my purse as he turns me towards him. I close my eyes, refusing to look at him because I know the moment I do, I'll be lost. Lost in his presence, in his aura. "Open your eyes."

"I don't want to. I don't want to *see* you, Astor." I look down at the floor and he grabs my chin between his thumb, forcing me to his gaze.

He takes me in for a moment and something shifts. "I'm *sorry*." I'm sure that my eyes double in fucking size. Because the last thing I expected was him to say he was sorry about anything. "I shouldn't have said those things to you."

"But you did. And you meant them."

"I didn't."

"It's not a secret, Astor, I know you didn't choose this, choose me. That I'm not *enough*. I know I'm just filling their space until this is ov—" He silences me with his finger over my lips as I fight the urge to open my mouth and suck them.

"Wrong. *They* were filling the space."

"For what?" I whisper.

"For you." He pulls me to him and I gasp in surprise, surprised at his words and his actions. This isn't the Astor I know. This isn't the Astor that has made me feel mute for the last six years, as if I was nothing but a blip and inconvenience in his life. His lips brutally attack mine. I'm stunned, too stunned to respond to his kiss. "Don't fight me, let me in," he murmurs against me. I relax into his hold, running my arms up his back and snaking them around his neck.

"I don't think you should kiss me...I think I'm getting sick." He leans back, breaking our kiss and frowns as he rests his hand on my forehead.

"So, stay home."

Home.

"I can't. I have to go find my wedding dress, for my very *first* wedding," I say with a devilish grin.

"You mean for your *only* wedding."

Caro clears her throat and I jump out of Astor's embrace. Well, I try to at least and fail miserably, because he just tightens his hold on my waist.

"Well, at least it'll make marrying him easier," she says with a smirk as she watches him kisses my cheek with a knowing look on her face.

"Don't be long, I've got some making up to do." My cheeks flush and I can feel the heat rising in my stomach.

I'm a weak, pathetic woman. All he said was he was *sorry* for me to move past how he declared he'd fuck anyone he wanted while I couldn't do the same. Because he's *sorry*, none of that matters anymore. What a joke I am.

"Get out of your head and go find a dress. I'll see you later," he says. I look up at him and tilt my chin up a bit.

"Ast...don't ever tell me you'll fuck someone else again. Understand?" He kisses my cheek and nods.

"Yes, ma'am."

THE FIRST FEW MINUTES OF THE DRIVE I CAN FEEL CARO SEARING A hole into my face. I tuck my lip in my mouth and mindlessly play with the hem of my shirt.

"You little fucking whore. You fucked him! Didn't you?"

"Caroline!"

"You did! And you weren't going to tell me?"

"I...I just..."

"Ah, you wound me. So how was it? And also, don't leave out the part where you went from hating each other's fucking guts to kissing goodbye practically overnight."

"We just, I don't know. Ok? I'm still wrapping my head around it. He's so hot and cold, Caro. Like, we had sex and it was fucking crazy hot sex. Rough, demanding, literally fucking brutal. Then we cuddled and he was sweet, and caring, and present. But then some bitch showed up at his house and I *lost* it. Told her if she came back, I'd slit her throat. I haven't gotten that mad in *years*, Caro. Years. Then I told him how pissed I was that he let her touch him and then he told me he'd fuck whoever he wanted. That just because we fucked, didn't mean we'd have a happy ever after. So then I told him I'd fuck who I wanted and then he basically said he'd kill anyone I fucked." I gather in a big breath, because I don't think I breathed at all during the entire time I talked just now.

"Ok umm, bitch."

"Oh! And then he comes back from working out and is this caring fucking asshole again. So, I'm sure when I get back, he'll be back to his brutish ways."

She turns the radio completely down and glances at me as she drives.

"You love him…already."

"Caro…I don't remember a time that I didn't love him."

"My advice…milk this shit for all you can. Force him to see that whatever the fuck happened all those years ago, doesn't matter. Show him that you are just as possessive as he is. That you aren't just his, but he's *yours,* too. I guarantee, seeing you get all worked up over that girl turned him on. That's probably why he went to work out. Was the girl scared? " I nod and she looks at me, the side of her mouth twitching. We break out into laughter.

"Atta girl."

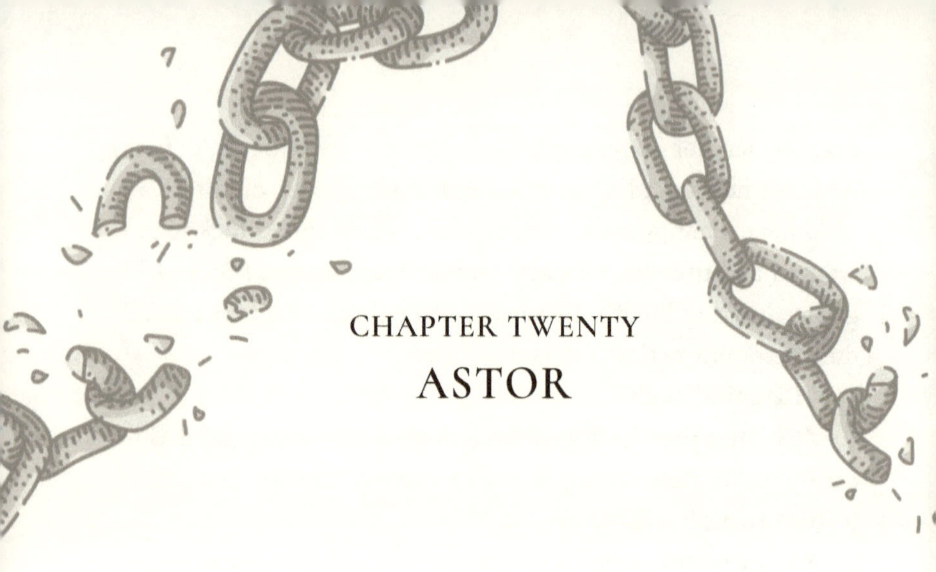

CHAPTER TWENTY
ASTOR

"So, explain this to me again. You fucked and now you don't hate her anymore? I mean, I know hate sex is good, but goddamn was it that good?"

I'm at the bar with Justin and his mouth is hanging on by a thread.

"First, I'm not discussing my sex life with you. Second, I never hated her. I hated that she fucking erased me in the first place."

Justin knew the history with Alessia. He knew what happened to her and was there to put the falling fucking pieces back together when I was a slither of myself.

"Are you going to tell her about Miles?"

"I want to. It's eating me alive, hiding it from her, and last night changed everything. I know you think I'm fucking whipped, but it wasn't about the sex. It's how she reacted to Anna, how she stood her ground to me. I know she wanted to leave, but she didn't. She fucking stuck it out. You know for a fact that *no one* can handle my wrath, but she fucking takes it and dishes it right back."

The more I think about her words to Anna, the more I get turned on.

I'll slit your fucking throat.

I hadn't heard that voice or seen that side of her since she was fucking sixteen.

"What about her father? He'll lose his shit if you tell her."

"Do you think I give a *fuck* about her father?"

I don't, and the more I'm around him lately, the more irritated I've become with him. The way he's been treating her, talking to her; it hasn't been sitting right with me. He usually holds her close and coddles her, but that hasn't been happening.

"Fair enough. Tell me, by chance, is she with a friend with blonde hair?"

My brow furrows at the mention of Caroline.

"And a body that should be goddamn illegal?" I follow his gaze, my blood boiling when I see her and Alessia sauntering over to us with every fucking man breaking their necks to watch them. I'm out of my chair before they reach me and Alessia walks straight into my arms.

"Fix your face, they're just looking," she whispers as I close my arms around her.

"If they value their sight, they'll look elsewhere. What are you doing here?"

"Caro wanted to get some drinks. I guess we like the same places." She sits next to me and Caroline sits next to Justin, who hasn't taken his eyes off her. I shake my head at him.

"Justin," Alessia says, leaning over the bar, "she's batshit crazy, so don't get too attached."

"Crazy is just my type," he says with a sly smile as Caroline raises her eyebrow.

"Doesn't she have a boyfriend?" I ask as Alessia chuckles.

"They broke up. He couldn't handle her. Some girl tried to talk to him, so she hauled off and hit her."

"Hmm, now I understand why you two are friends. You have that whole jealous thing in common." She bumps against my shoulder.

"I'm not jealous."

"Could've fooled me."

"I don't even like you."

"Right...keep telling yourself that, *malyshka*."

"*Malyshka, little devil*...any other names for me?" she asks, smirking at me.

"They're both so fitting, don't you think?"

"Justin and I are going outside. We'll be right back," Caroline says, approaching Alessia. She grabs her arm and gives her a look. I quickly eye Justin and he grins.

"We're just going to be a second," she continues, slowly releasing herself from Alessia's grip.

We watch them as they leave the bar and Justin puts his hand around the back of Caroline's neck. I know what they're going to do.

"She's going to fuck him," she says in disbelief.

"Not our business," I say, because it's not.

She downs the rest of her drink and turns to me.

"Tell me something," she starts.

"Hm?"

"Are you going to go back to being cold with me?"

"Cold?" I question.

"Yes. I never know what to expect with you. I don't want to seem naïve, and I don't expect things to be different just because we had sex, but..."

"But what, Alessia?" She tucks her hair behind her ear, looking at the ice in her glass.

"Nothing, never mind. It's stupid, I'm being ridiculous." I

turn her body towards me. Her green eyes quickly find mine and she tucks her lip.

"If you're asking me if you matter to me, you do. If you're asking if you have the option of getting away from me, you no longer do."

"I had the choice before?" She chuckles.

"Not really." She hides her smile and I'm a goner, a fucking goner. I tilt her chin up to me. "Bathroom. Now."

Her eyes widen, but she does as I say. I watch her walk to the bathroom and I wait a moment before I follow her.

I lock the door behind me and I'm on her in a second.

"I've been thinking of how good your pussy feels around my cock all fucking day," I growl.

"Yeah?" she breathes.

I yank her pants and panties down, turning her around. She grasps the side of the sink and looks at me through the mirror. I nibble her ear, running my tongue over it.

"Mhm. And now I'm going to fuck this pretty little cunt while you watch me." My jeans are down and I'm pushing myself in her before I realize what the fuck I'm doing. All I see is her, those fucking eyes and the look that's in them. I don't know how I went so long without this. Without this side of her.

"Astor..." she moans as I stretch her. Her grip tightens on the sink, her knuckles white from the pressure. I wrap my hand around her neck as I sink into her with so much force she jolts forward. I tighten my hand on her hip, holding her in place. My thrust is violent, rushed, and brutal. I know I'm probably hurting her, but I can't make myself slow down.

I'm angry. I'm angry that she thinks she doesn't matter. That she thinks she doesn't matter to *me*. I'm angry that she doesn't remember me or remember *us*. I'm angry that I let her get under my skin and I'm fucking angry with myself for not giving a fuck about it.

She's mine. And if I have to fuck the sense into her, I will.

"You can't..."

"I can't what? Hmm?" She throws her head back, her hand slapping against the mirror as I continue my assault.

"Fuck anyone else," she says, her voice breaking. Her words hit me in my chest, and hard. I reach around and push two fingers into her pussy. She gasps and moans, pushing herself back on my cock.

"Baby, this pussy is the only pussy I'll be fucking." She practically screams as I increase my speed, closing her eyes before I grab her chin. "Open them, watch us come together." Her eyes snap open and she comes with a force so fucking strong it gyrates through my fucking body.

Yeah. I'm completely fucked.

CHAPTER TWENTY-ONE
ALESSIA

Caro texted me after we silently did the walk of shame out of the bathroom and to Astor's car.

"Text her and tell her we're going home. If she isn't back yet, he's taken her hostage by now, I'm sure," Astor says with his hand on my lower back.

"She just texted me...looks like you're right." I hold the phone up and show it to him.

CARO:

Holy shit. There's no way one time will be enough—I'm going home with him. See you tomorrow. Love you, bitch!

"Tell her if she happens to call you a bitch again, I'll block her number from your phone."

"It's a friendly bitch, not a mean bitch." I shrug, but he doesn't acknowledge me as he opens the door to his car. I climb in and text her back.

ALESSIA:

> Astor said you aren't allowed to call me a bitch anymore. HAHAAHHA.

CARO:

> Bitch, does your man know I'm a part of the mafia, too?

ALESSIA:

> Be nice. Have fun tonight, lunch tomorrow to tell me about it?

CARO:

> Fuck yeah.

I watch him as he drives us home, his hand resting on my thigh. He tightens it and I raise my eyebrow.

"Tell me about your wedding dress."

"Ehh, I picked the first one I could find. Since it's not a *real* wedding," I say jokingly.

"Funny, tell me about it."

"I can't. It's bad luck. All I'll tell you is that our mothers wasted no expense."

I'm not exaggerating. When we walked into the bridal shop, we were worshiped, shown the best of every designer. The dress I chose was gorgeous, it even made me cry. It was a fitted type, with see-through sides, and a deep, low cut V neckline. It was covered in diamonds and made me feel as beautiful as it looked. It also cost $42,000, and my mother and Astrid didn't blink a fucking eye when they agreed to split the cost.

"That doesn't surprise me. They spent $15,000 on fucking flowers, so I'm sure they went double that on your dress."

"When are you going for your tux?"

"Tomorrow. How are you feeling? You look pale." He's right, I'm starting to feel lightheaded and nauseous again.

"I'm ok."

"You're lying. When we get home, I want you in bed."

"Bossy." He gives me a side eye and I sink into the seat, closing my eyes when another wave of nausea comes. "Can you pull over?"

"Are we back to you not wanting to be around me?"

"No, I just—" I cover my mouth and he quickly rears the car to the side of the road. I push the door open before the car comes to a stop.

"Alessia, wait until I've stopped!"

I lean over, not being able to wait. Vomit goes everywhere and I barely miss Astor's car. I climb out and drop to my knees as it comes out uncontrollably. He's at my side in a second, pulling my hair back out of my face.

"I didn't want to...mess up your car."

"It's just a fucking car. Are you ok?" I run my hand over my mouth and try to stand up. He's there, helping me and rubbing my back.

"Yes. I'm ok. I'm sorry."

"Don't apologize. Let's just get you home." I take a deep breath, mentally telling myself that we're only a few minutes away. He secures me in the car and zips us home as fast as he can.

WHEN WE WALK THROUGH THE DOORS, I'M HIT WITH A WAVE OF relief. I did manage to not vomit in his precious fucking car; even though he said he wouldn't care, he was driving like a psychopath. And I know it was in fear of me not being able to hold it in.

Astor's hands circle around me and he scoops me up in his arms.

"What are you doing?"

"Putting you to bed." He eases his way up the stairs, glancing at me when he feels my stare. "What?"

"You're just...nothing." He doesn't push me on it, he lays me down in the bed and helps me out of my clothes. He grabs one of his shirts and pulls it over my head, tucking me tightly under the comforter.

He feels my forehead and takes a deep breath. "You're burning up." He rises and retreats into the bathroom, coming back a moment later with a thermometer. "Under your tongue. If it's higher than 101, we're calling a doctor." I open my mouth and wait patiently for what I already know.

"What's the verdict, boss?" I ask as he stares at the numbers.

"Doctor. 102.8." He pulls out his phone. "I need the doctor here as soon as possible. Alessia is sick or something, I don't fucking know."

I start to shiver and I turn on my side. My body feels weaker and weaker as the minutes pass and my headache is coming back. I can hear Astor talking, calling my name, but I can't open my eyes or mouth to answer him.

I just need rest.

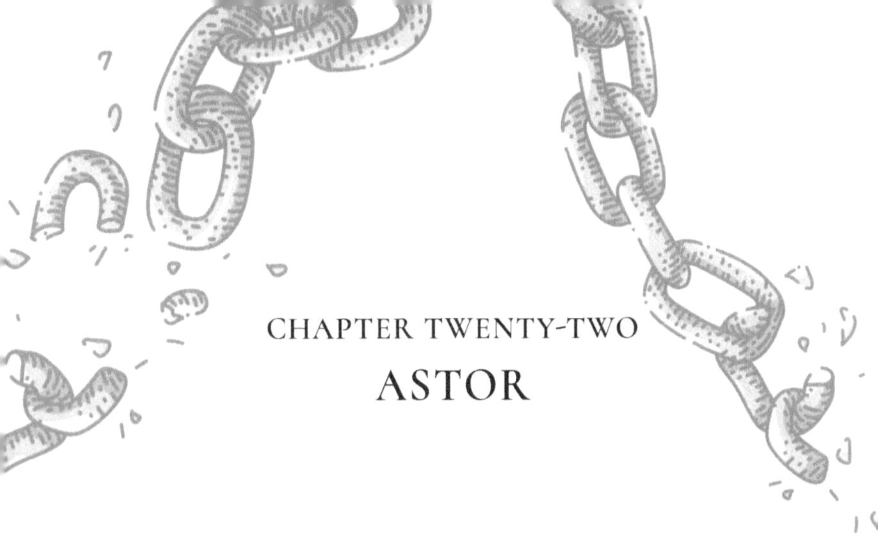

CHAPTER TWENTY-TWO

ASTOR

"I drew some blood, too, and my team is working on that now. I should have those results in the next hour or so. I'll call you with those. Her blood pressure was also a little elevated, which could be from the stress, but she definitely has the flu." He puts his stethoscope away and looks in his bag to retrieve some medications. "Give her this, the flu isn't something we can really treat, but she can try the Tamiflu. If she has any more dizzy spells call me, but make sure she gets plenty of rest and fluids."

"Thanks, Doc."

"Of course, call me if you need me. In the meantime, I'll call you with the blood work." I show him out and go into the kitchen to call my dad.

"Son, everything ok?"

"Alessia has the flu, I'm not going tomorrow."

"Tomorrow's the only day and you get married in two weeks. She'll be fine."

"I said I am not going. Figure it out, send me pictures."

"Yes, you are. I'm fine." I turn around and Alessia is walking towards me with a blanket wrapped around her. I hang up the phone and engulf her in my arms.

"*Malyshka*, why are you out of bed? You need to rest."

"I'm fine, it's just the flu. You're not missing your tux appointment. Caro can come over while you're gone."

"No," I say, peering down at her. "I can take care of you."

"I'm fine, Astor, I promise." I kiss the tip of her nose and she lays her head on my chest, or more like my stomach. She's so fucking small.

"Are you hungry?" I ask

"Yes," she replies.

"Go lay on the couch; I'll make you something."

"I can help."

"Lay." I push her toward the couch and busy myself in the kitchen, remembering her favorite thing to eat when she was sick growing up.

"How long was I out?" she asks, resting her elbows on the couch, staring at me.

"Four hours maybe. It's late." She yawns and turns back to the TV. I watch her and try to remember a time that I didn't think she was the center of my fucking universe. Even when that piece of shit took her from me, she was still wrapped around me like a fucking anaconda.

Twenty minutes later, I'm waking her up again.

"*Malyshka*, eat something." She groans and sits up, her eyes settling when she sees the tray in front of her.

She sees the tomato and cheese sandwich with cheddar soup.

"You remembered?"

"Mhm. Eat." I sit next to her, blowing the soup as I feed her a spoon full. I watch as she swallows and I fight the bulge that pushes against my shorts. She takes a bite of the sandwich and leans into me. Groaning.

"Good?"

"Yes, thank you." She pushes the sandwich up to my mouth and I take a bite. She wipes a crumb from the side of my lip and I catch her thumb in my mouth, giving it a soft bite. "More?"

"No, you eat."

"What time are you leaving tomorrow?"

"Noon. Why?"

"Caro is coming over; I need to study for finals. And I woke up to a million texts from our mothers about wedding food." I lean over and grab my phone, putting it on speaker as it rings.

"Astor! My sweetheart!"

"Alessia is sick, do *not* text her until she's well." Alessia elbows me and tries to take the phone from me. "And pass the word to Eleanor, or I will."

"Sorry, honey, I hope she feels better. We'll figure it out when she's all rested."

I've barely put the phone down before a fist lands in my chest.

"And you're keen on breaking your hand why?" I ask.

"I didn't tell you that for you to tell them to leave me alone. I can handle it."

"Well, now you don't have to handle it."

"Now my mom is going to think I want nothing to do with the wedding planning."

She's made it extremely clear that she doesn't want this wedding, so I'm not sure why she cares what her mother thinks about it at this point. She flips the blankets back and carries the dishes into the kitchen. I watch her, but stay silent. She has a crease in between her eyebrows. She's washing the plate for what seems like the fifth time when I wrap my arms around her waist.

"There's a dishwasher, you know."

"Cleaning helps me think...I guess I could just tell them to pick two of everything, that way there's a variety of food options. Then it won't seem like I'm blowing them off."

"*Malyshka*, you're *sick*. You're not blowing them off. And you seem a lot more invested in a wedding that you *don't* want." She dries the plate and faces me while she dries her hands.

"I didn't want it. I'm still not sure if I do, but it doesn't sound like the worst thing anymore."

I lean down and kiss the top of her nose.

"Good."

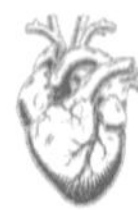

"Son, when you take over, there will be plenty of times where you have to choose to let someone else do the dirty work. Let someone else get rid of your problems. Maybe this is the time to learn that lesson."

I'm trying on tuxedos while my father badgers me about not going after Miles again. Last night, my guards said that they saw a black SUV one too many times near the house. I also kept getting unknown phone calls and texts threatening me. The threats are nothing new, it comes with the territory. No one is stupid enough to actually try to make good on it; *usually*.

"Dad, he raped her. I *am* going to fucking kill him. And if his piece of shit father or their little fucking minions want to get in the way of that, I'll kill them, too."

"What I'm saying is that you can't do it by yourself. We are one of the most *powerful* mafia families out there. Use your resources."

"Xavier, if you don't help him, I will. You know how angry I was with you for stopping him that day. You gave him more mercy than he deserved. He raped my daughter; Astor I'll give you whatever the fuck you need to wipe that fucking twat off this earth," Ander seethes. He was belligerent that day. I'd never seen him that angry, that out of wits. He's always in control, but that day, when he saw his daughter being ripped from her body, day by day, it was enough to make him pick off half of Miles' family for hiding him.

"Ander."

"No, Dad, he's right. You're worried I'll get myself killed. I won't. Don't worry, your *heir* will be just fine."

Justin pats my back and I know he's silently telling me he's there for whatever I need. I never have to question him, nor will I ever do it.

"Now, if we're done here. I need to go get my fiancée a wedding ring."

CHAPTER TWENTY-THREE
ALESSIA

MOM:

Family dinner tonight, 6:00 p.m. Can't wait to see you.

ALESSIA:

See you then.

I walk into my last final before Christmas break will officially begin, before I have one week left of freedom.

This last week, Astor has been missing more. Every time I ask him what he's doing, he tells me he's just been "busy". I know it's bullshit, but I've been finding the time to get used to the fact that this will be my new normal soon. He took his last final two days ago and I haven't seen him since then. He calls every morning and sends texts throughout the day, but when I ask where he is, he'll tell me our father's favorite line they used to tell us when we were kids: *when the mafia calls.* That just gives me anxiety, because they always come back either hurt or on edge.

"Once you're finished with your exam, you are free to go. Enjoy your last Christmas break! Oh, and Alessia, I hear congratulations are in order."

I try to avoid ducking under my desk when my professor says it, instead I smile and nod. How the fuck did he know about that, and why did he announce it?

"Good luck, and you can begin. Please put all phones on silent."

I glance at my phone to check the volume and notice a text from Astor.

ASTOR:

Make that exam your bitch. I'll be home late tonight, stay with Caroline.

ALESSIA:

No. I'll see you at home.

Stay with Caroline? What the fuck was that about? I tuck my phone back into my pocket and start the exam. It should have probably felt way more difficult than it was. I was studying business, just like my father. Not many women took over mafia gangs and those who did had to work way harder for respect. My father always wanted me to understand how business works and how to run one—*successfully*. By the time I got to college to study it, he had already taught me basically everything, so it was mostly repeated information.

I smile as I hit submit and close my laptop for the exam that I know I probably passed with flying colors.

When I get outside of the door, I feel my phone vibrate. Checking it, I find myself immediately rolling my eyes.

ASTOR:

Little devil...

"Hey bitch! How was your exam?" Caroline asks, linking her hands through mine as we walk towards the parking lot.

"Easy. Yours?"

"Fucking killed it. Let's go out tonight." I groan and she elbows me. "Come on.."

"My missing in action fiancé is kindly blessing me with his presence tonight." I suddenly stop and roll my lips, my finger tapping mindlessly.

"What is it? That's your thinking face."

"He told me he'd be home *late*...and to stay with you."

She tilts her head and pushes her hip out. "With me?"

"Yes. I haven't seen him in two days, he hasn't touched me in two days, and the day he can, he tells me to stay with you?"

"That's...interesting."

"Fuck him. We're going out."

"Hell yeah, we are!"

He thinks he's the only one that can go missing doing whatever he wants? He's got another thing coming.

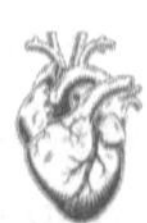

THE DRIVE TO ASTOR'S HOUSE FEELS LIKE IT'S TAKING FOREVER. I NEED to pack some stuff to take to my apartment. When I finally arrive, I'm hit with annoyance. I'm annoyed that I can still smell him everywhere, even though he hasn't been here in two days. I'm annoyed that a part of me still wants to stay here tonight because I miss him. And I'm annoyed that Todd is following me around like a fucking puppy.

"Ms. Ballerini, how are you? Can I get you anything?"

"Todd, if you Ms. Ballerini me again, I'm going to lose my fucking mind. And today, of all days, is not the day you want me to lose it. I've got it, please *go away*."

"Of course, I apologize." He practically runs to the other side of the house and I take the stairs two steps at a time.

I'm stuffing things to possibly wear in my bag when my phone starts ringing for the sixth time since I ignored his message.

"Yes?" I answer, holding back my annoyance.

"*Malyshka*, what are you doing?"

"No, Astor. What are *you* doing?" Silence. Complete silence. "I'm hanging up."

"If you hang up this phone, I'll lose my shit. And we both know we don't want me to lose my fucking shit."

"Lose it, *baby*."

Click.

"WHAT ARE YOU WEARING? I BOUGHT A BUNCH OF SHIT HERE," Caroline says, scrolling on her phone as she lounges in my bed.

"I don't know, maybe this dress?" I hold it up and her eyebrows shoot up, an evil grin spreading across her face.

"You know he's going to be pissed when he finds out we went out. Even madder when he sees that dress," she says, standing to stretch.

"Oh bitch, I'm counting on it."

Game on.

CHAPTER TWENTY-FOUR

ASTOR

Two days. Two days I've been torturing four men until they either die or give me the information I want before I kill them. I'm currently on the last one, and if he dies, or I snap and kill him before I get what I need, then I'm back to square one. That's good for him, but not good for my patience that's diminishing fucking quickly.

"You know…I expected more information from your friends over there. Hopefully, you'll be a better sport than them." I take my fist and drive it into his face, repeatedly. I hear a crack and another; blood spurts all over me and him. I admit, I'm being a bit rougher because I'm pissed that Alessia hung up on me. Not only did she hang up, but she's ignored every fucking call since then.

Twelve, to be exact.

Justin is sitting in the chair next to the door, his elbows resting on the back, shaking his head as I plummet him again. I don't know his name—I don't know any of their names. Nor do I give a fuck.

I take my knife and slice it across his chest as he bellows out in pain.

"Where is Miles?" My voice is dark, low, full of threat. I don't have time to waste on this. He shakes his head and I run my knife across his chest again, this time deeper.

"Boss," my head security, Benny, says, tapping my shoulder. I raise my eyebrow at him in question. "You might want to see this." He holds his phone up to me and I'm raging in anger. Not because this piece of shit in front of me won't give me any information, but because I'm watching a live fucking video of my *fiancée* standing on top of a bar, in a tiny, black piece of fabric that's a pathetic excuse for a dress, swaying her hips back and fucking forth.

Justin is out of his seat in a second, watching the madness unfold. He's fine until he sees who's next to Alessia. He snatches the phone out of Benny's hand, his eyes landing on Caroline. She has one arm around Alessia and the other in the air as she tosses her hair back and forth.

I knew they had a little thing since the bar, but by the way he's looking right now, it's obviously more than a *thing* now.

"Ast, finish this the fuck up..." he grits out, pushing the phone back towards me. A man approaches the bar and taps Alessia's leg. I push the phone away and turn back to the last man.

"Change of plans, buddy. Can I call you buddy?" I say, gently tapping his face. "My fiancée has decided to make a statement, an extremely bold one, might I add, and it's pertinent that I get to her quickly. You understand that, right?"

He groans and Justin pulls his chair to sit in front of him.

"Look, he's really obsessed with his girl, if you can't tell. I'd tell him what he wants to know. He's not nice when something, or in your case, *someone,* gets in the way of getting to her," Justin states with a grin on his face.

"I'll give you to the count of six to tell me where he is." I circle around him and he shifts back and forth, trying to break the ropes that are wrapped tightly around his body.

"One...Two...Three...Four...Five..."

"Stop! Stop! He's in Reno! He has a house there!"

"When is he coming to New York?"

"Next week, for a meeting with his father!"

"See, that wasn't so hard, was it?" I lean down close to his ear and chuckle. "But guess what? *Six*." I jab my knife into his jugular. I grab my extra shirt from Benny's hand. Justin and I quickly get to my car, not bothering to stay to watch the last man bleed out.

THE DRIVE TO THE CLUB WILL TAKE ABOUT FIFTEEN MINUTES. OF course they choose to go to one of my clubs. Alessia is a lot of things, but stupid isn't one of them. She knew someone would alert Benny; she knew I'd see her. Justin hasn't said a word since we left the house my father owns in the city. His knee is bouncing up and down and I can't help but wonder why he looks so murderous right now.

"How deep is this shit with Caroline?" I ask him. He huffs and turns his gaze to the window. "Fuck, Jus."

"I haven't spent a night without her since the bar," he mumbles.

"So, when you were ducking off these last two days, it was to see Caro?"

"You know how you met your match with Lessia? Well, I can promise you she's giving me a run for my fucking money. I've met mine, too."

"Then let's go get them, shall we?" I ask as we pull up to the front of the club. The bouncer waves us in and pushes people back for us to get through. My phone vibrates and I glance at it, seeing a text from Benny. He's been watching them on the live feed cameras.

BENNY:

Boss, I can't see her on the cameras anymore.
She was at the bar.

I shove my phone in my pocket and beeline it for the bar. The bartender sees me and his eyes widen. I yank him across the bar and Justin leans against it.

"Where the fuck did she go?" I ask him.

"I-I don't know. I thought she went to the bathroom!" I push him backwards and Justin taps him.

"The blonde with her, where'd she go?"

"With her. She went with her!" he screams over the music, his hands up. Justin nods and tussles the bartender's hair.

"Thanks," Justin leans down and reads his name tag, "Trent. We do appreciate it." I glare at him, unable to stop the thoughts of wanting to hurt him. The vibration of my phone is the only thing that takes me from that thought. Benny is calling me. Not texting, calling. Fuck.

"Yeah," I bark out.

"She went to the back. The best friend followed her. But boss."

"Spit it out, Benny."

"She took that guy with her."

"Call my father, tell him to have the clean-up crew on standby. Someone's about to die."

Alessia, sweet Alessia, I surely hope you aren't as dumb as you're sounding right now.

Justin and I push through the back of the club, everyone sidestepping to let us through. When I open the first door and there's no sign of her, I walk down the hall to the other abandoned offices.

"Alessia!" I bellow, stopping when I see the light illuminating the basement door. Justin elbows me and I nod. We both pull out our guns, silently opening the door to the basement. The voice we hear stops us both in our tracks.

"WHAT LESSON DID WE LEARN TONIGHT? HMM?"

Alessia.

I hear a groan, one that I know way too well after the last two days. It's a groan of pain.

"She asked you a question. Answer her," Caroline adds.

"You both are crazy fucking bitches," a male voice says, before I hear a feral scream.

"Last chance, what did we learn? Tell us and we'll let you go. Easy peasy," Alessia says, smiling at him. They have him hanging with arms tied behind his back, a rope wrapped what appears to be tight around his dick. *Ouch.*

"Not to touch without permission! That's what I fucking learned! Fuck, let me go!"

"And who exactly did you fucking touch?" I ask in an almost growl.

I step into view and Justin clears his throat, causing three pairs of eyes to turn onto us.

"Oh! Hi, Justin!" Caroline says. She smiles and licks her lips.

"Caro, what the *fuck* are you doing?" She shrugs her shoulders and starts untying the man.

"Nothing, just letting this nice guy here go ho—"

I'm in Alessia's face before Caroline finishes her sentence, my hand wrapped tightly around her throat.

"Who the *fuck* did he touch?" I grit out, tightening my hold on her neck. She does nothing but raise her eyebrow at my question. Justin and Caroline are saying something, but I can't take my eyes off the woman who lives to fucking defy me. "Alessia, answer the question."

"Does it matter?" I grind my teeth, and this time, I'm grinding so hard I actually *do* have a headache.

"*Malyshka*," I groan.

She sighs. "Both of us," she says quickly. I drop my hand from her neck and she rolls her lips between her teeth.

"Jus. Stop him." He moves with quickness and grabs him by his arm.

"No, leave me alone, man," the man groans, holding his dick.

"I already taught him a lesson," Alessia says, grabbing my arm. I yank away from her, my eyes dark.

"Go home. *Now*."

Someone is definitely dying.

CHAPTER TWENTY-FIVE

ALESSIA

"He was fucking pissed!" Caroline says as we pull into her driveway. I'm still fuming at how he came in acting like he fucking owned me. I'm also fuming at how my body betrayed me and was on fire the moment he wrapped his fucking hand around my neck.

Slut.

She nudges me and I snap out of my daze, looking at her. "What?"

"Text me when you get to your apartment."

"Ehh, I'm going to my parents. I skipped family dinner."

"Oh shit...that's not good."

"Caro...what's going on with you and Justin? He looked just as mad as Astor, if not more."

"Ehh, we're just feeling things out."

"Lie."

"I know. Text me when you get home." She gives me a mischievous smile as she walks to her apartment.

I want to go back to the club and see what Astor did to that guy. I'd say it was my fault that he grabbed me, but it wasn't.

Caro and I were just dancing, and he invited himself into it. The next thing I know, he was trying to plunge his tongue down my throat. When I pushed him off, he immediately went to Caro. I know Astor probably killed him. Honestly, I probably would've, too, if he had tried anything else.

Go home. Now.

I roll my eyes at the memory of Astor telling me to go home. I decide that I'm going home, but not the home he thinks.

When I get to my parent's, it's about 10:30 p.m. I try my best to be quiet when I open the door, just in case my parents are sleeping.

"Hi, honey! What are you doing here?"

"Oh. Hi, Mama. I thought you'd be sleeping."

She laughs and kisses my cheek.

"And you weren't at dinner tonight, why?" my father says coolly as he strides towards me with a glass of amber liquid in his hand.

"I went out with Caro to celebrate finals. I'm sorry."

"Your mother is going through every hoop to make sure your *wedding*, that's happening in seven days, in case you forgot, is perfect. The least you can do is pick up the fucking phone and let her know you won't make it. She sat here waiting for you, while you were out doing God knows what, in a fucking dress that I'm sure no one's daughter, especially *my daughter,* should be wearing."

I open my mouth to argue, but my mom pulls me towards her, looking over her shoulder at my father.

"It's fine, honey, did you and Caro have fun? And you look beautiful, ignore him."

"Yes, Mama, I'm sorry I didn't call."

"Are you staying the night?" I nod and she smiles, directing me towards the stairs.

"Great. We can iron out the last bit tomorrow. Don't you worry about it."

When I get into my room, I head straight for my balcony; the whole reason I came here tonight. My balcony is the only thing that makes me feel like the world is quiet around me. It's the only place I feel like no one can shake me. Most of all, it's my place. When I'm out here, no one bothers me. They let me have my time.

I look over and wave at the bodyguard who's placed outside of my house and he gives me a curt nod.

The sigh that comes out of me is long and deep. I miss Astor, and as pissed as I am that I hadn't seen him in two days, I was happy to see him in one piece. I didn't, however, expect how my body reacted to his touch. I don't know what I was expecting, but I did not expect him to grab me like that in front of Caro and Justin.

Not knowing what, or *who*, had his attention these last couple of days is starting to taunt me.

I lean my head back and inhale the smell of the pool water as the light breeze washes over me. I close my eyes and let myself drift off. It's cold out, but the alcohol from earlier is doing its job of keeping me warm enough.

I don't know if it's because I've been asleep or if it's because my nostrils are no longer filled with chlorine, but replaced with the masculine smell of smokey citrus. My body has come alive and sleep is no longer what is on my mind. I keep my eyes closed, even though my body is screaming to see him.

I take another deep breath, annoyed that he'd even bother me out here. He was the only one when we were younger who would come out here with me, but that stopped a long time ago.

"I told you to go home." His voice slices through the cold air and the hairs on my neck stand to attention. I keep my eyes closed and I fucking ignore him. "Come here," he continues.

"Leave me alone."

"Last chance, Alessia. Come *here*."

"No—" He yanks me by my arm and pushes me onto his lap.

"Your first mistake was thinking you had a choice. Your second mistake was letting someone else touch you. And the icing on the fucking cake was coming here instead of home." He kisses the side of my neck and I move away from him. I don't get far before his hand is around my neck. I can't fight the lethal groan that comes out of my mouth.

"I haven't seen you in two days, Alessia. And when I do, you're wearing something that I for sure plan on burning tomorrow." He tightens his grip and I tuck my lip in my mouth. "Why'd you go to my club? Was it to make sure I saw you?"

Yes.

"I don't care about you."

"Lies. You could've gone to any club you wanted, but instead you went to the club you know I own. You did it to make a statement, you did it to piss me off."

"I don't *care* about you," I repeat. He chuckles, loosening his hold around my neck.

"So, you *don't* care about what I was doing these last two days?"

"Or *who* you were doing," I spit out. He raises his eyebrow and I know when he starts rolling up his sleeves I've fucked up.

Good.

CHAPTER TWENTY-SIX

ASTOR

I watch her as she tries her best to maintain her breathing. She has no idea how torturous these last two days have been. But she's about to find out, that's for fucking sure.

"For your sake, I'm going to choose to ignore the blatant disrespect of that comment."

"Don't do me any favors," she says through her teeth. I tilt my head to the side.

I yank her by her feet towards me, our eyes locked on each other. We shouldn't be doing this right now, we're both so angry with each other. But that doesn't stop me from yanking her dress up and ripping her panties without an effort.

"Those were my favorite panties!"

"Shut the fuck up."

I push her against the railing of her balcony, quickly pushing my pants down and forcing myself into her. She screams and wraps her legs around me as I plunge deeper into her. She looks behind her at the ground under us and throws her head back as I go harder and harder.

"I'll tell you this once, and once only. Do not ever, and I

mean *ever* insinuate that I've fucked anyone other than *you*. And the next time you decide you want to go to the club, you go with me and *only* me. I'm tired of killing people. I'm tired of you testing every limit I have. And I'm tired of you acting like you do not belong to *me*."

I pick up my speed as I fuck her pussy harder and she lets out a louder scream when I tilt her over the balcony. At this point, I don't know if it's from pleasure or the fear that I'll drop her. I push her legs wider and she digs her nails into my skin. She's practically upside down as I fuck her, releasing the anger in me.

"Shut your fucking mouth unless you want your parents and everyone else on this property to see you getting fucked with your life dangling from my hands."

"Fuck. You. Astor."

I plunge my fingers inside of her to bring her over the edge.

"No, fuck you, Alessia...fuck you for making me lose my mind over you. Fuck you for bringing me to my fucking knees. And fuck you for running from me."

She moans as I yank her up the balcony and smash my lips against hers. Her pussy sucks me in and I can't last any longer. I fill her with my cum and she bites my lip until my mouth is full of the taste of copper. "Get your shit, we're going home."

"I don't have anything here. I came for the balcony..." I yank her dress down and shake my head. "I told my mom I was staying."

"*Malyshka*, I'm hanging on by a thread. We are leaving. Don't say another fucking word unless you want me to fuck you again and this time, I'll make sure you're loud enough for everyone to hear."

There's a knock at her door and she breaks out in laughter. "Too late."

She throws the door open and Eleanor is standing on the other side.

"Sweetheart, what in the world are you doing in here? I thought you were dying."

"Sorry, Mama, I was just—" I wrap my arm around her and step into view.

"Eleanor. Sorry, we were just leaving."

"Oh! Nonsense, we were going to have brunch tomorrow to iron out the last bit of wedding details."

"We'll be sure to come back for brunch, but I haven't seen my fiancée in two days. I apologize, but I'd like her to myself." Alessia turns into a statue next to me and Eleanor smiles from ear to ear.

"Of course."

"*Little devil*, I'll be downstairs." I kiss her cheek and she rolls her eyes, so I give her a quick pinch on her side.

When I get downstairs, I run straight into Ander, his face stone and his expression full of disgust.

"Let's not make it a habit of you fucking my daughter where anyone could see, sound good?"

I clear my throat and step towards him.

"And let's not make it a habit of you talking to my fucking wife like she's a child. Don't ever speak to her that way again."

I was already on the phone with Ander when Alessia arrived, and the way I heard him speak to her pissed me off more than the thought of someone touching her. He disrespected her, and that's not fucking allowed. I don't care if she is his daughter.

"She's not your wife yet," he says, raising his eyebrow.

"I'm *choosing* to ignore that. And if you're wondering, I found Miles. He's in Reno, he has a meeting with his father next week. You wanted the information, I got it. I'm going after him with or without you."

He opens his mouth to respond when Alessia comes barreling down the stairs.

"Doesn't anyone fucking—"

"*Alessia*," I growl. She rolls her eyes and secures her hair in a bun on top of her head.

"Clearly no one sleeps around here. See you tomorrow," she says to her father before we both practically run out of the house.

She's not your wife yet.

Seven fucking days and no one will say that shit to me again.

CHAPTER TWENTY-SEVEN
ALESSIA

When we get back to Astor's, I shoot up the stairs and to the guest bathroom, shutting the door behind me. I don't know why, because if he wants to come in, he will. Even if he has to break it down, he will.

I check my phone to see it's midnight. I'm exhausted and just want to sleep. I don't even know if I want to know what he was doing these last two days or if I just want to forget it. He's right—I'm tired of him hurting people because of me.

What I didn't understand is why he said *I'm* running from *him.* He's the one who left me for two days. I wash and rinse my hair, able to hear him on the phone when I get out.

I pull on an oversized t-shirt and pad my way down to his room. If I thought for a second that there was a chance he'd let me sleep in the guest room I would, but I'm not stupid enough to try it.

I climb into bed and text Caro.

ALESSIA:

How mad was Justin?

CARO:

Pissed enough to tie me up and spank me
until I begged him to fuck me.

ALESSIA:

Bitch.

CARO:

How's things there?

ALESSIA:

He fucked me on my balcony, like literally,
hanging from my balcony. I think my parents
heard us and pretty sure one of the
guards saw.

CARO:

Kinky. I guess Justin is like my boyfriend or
something now.

ALESSIA:

Oh, he's definitely your boyfriend. I think
they're on the phone with each other.

CARO:

They are. Are you still mad at him?

I STARE AT HER MESSAGE AND THINK ABOUT MY RESPONSE.

ALESSIA:

I'm tired of being mad. I'm going to bed,
meeting with parents tomorrow. Dad was a
dick to me tonight for missing dinner.

CARO:

Yikes. Love you.

I'm putting my phone on the nightstand when I hear his
feet knocking against the floor. He stops in the doorway and
leans against the frame, his arms folded. I raise my eyebrow at

him. He has a pair of sweats on and his chest bare. His hair is wet from what I'm assuming was a shower.

"I thought you'd sleep in the guest room."

"I thought about it, but I knew you'd just drag me out. I'm too tired to put up a fight, so."

I shrug and pull the covers up to my neck as he walks over to the bed and climbs in next to me. I reach to turn off the lamp, but he grabs my arm. I sigh and look at him.

"You've been mad for an entire day. That's enough."

I gently tug my arm out of his hold and he moves closer to me.

"Tell me what you were doing," I urge, taking a more soothing approach. I feel his hands as they run up my arm and glances away from me.

"I want to, but I can't tell you yet. So, I'll tell you this: I needed to get information on the whereabouts of someone. Someone who wants to cause a lot of problems for our families."

"And did you? Find them?" I ask.

He nods. "*Him*...and yes I did." I don't respond, instead I just tap my finger on my thigh over the covers and he grabs my hand. "I'm *sorry*."

The last thing I expected was him to apologize. Again. I push myself even closer to him, running my hand down his chest.

"I'm sorry, too." He watches my hand as it hovers over his cock and I pull at his sweats. "Take them off," I tell him. He groans when I push my hand inside and fist his cock with one hand, tugging his sweats down with the other. I don't know why him telling me *something,* even if it was vague, made things feel less important. I slide my body down and position myself between his legs, his cock in my hands as I stroke it up and down. He pushes his fingers through my hair and tightens his grip when I run my tongue over the tip of his cock, licking up the clear drop that sits on top of it.

"Fuck, *little devil*," he says. It fuels me—I'll show him a devil. I open my mouth and try my best to fit his entire cock inside. My head moves up and down as the sounds of slurping mixed with his labored breathing and groans fill the room. He matches my pace, shoving his cock further down my throat. This is the one time where I'm glad a gag reflex doesn't kick in. Instead, I take it. I take every thrust he gives my mouth, rolling his balls in my hand.

"I'm going to come in your mouth and you're going to swallow every drop. Understand?" he growls, his eyes hyper focused on me. I acknowledge with a yank of his cock and pick up my speed as I suck. His head falls against the headboard and my mouth is invaded with salty warmness. The more I swallow, the more that comes. And I do exactly what he said: swallow every drop.

I crawl up next to him, a grin of confidence on my face.

"Feeling good about yourself?" he asks, climbing onto me. He stops when he runs his hand over my panties.

"Don't you dare," I warn. He chuckles, and within a second, I hear the sound of my panties tearing. "Astor..."

"Thought you didn't like wearing them?" he mocks.

"I don't, but easy access around you isn't a good idea when I'm supposed to be mad at you." He positions himself in between my legs, lining his cock up with my entrance. I look down in fascination, watching as he runs it through my slickness. He pushes in and whispers into my ear, "No barrier will stop me from fucking you, *malyshka*. Now keep those legs open while I fuck my pussy." When he rams inside of me, I see stars. Fucking stars.

Jesus. Christ.

CHAPTER TWENTY-EIGHT
ASTOR

"So, that should be the last of it. The caterers are booked for the rehearsal and the wedding. Your fathers wanted the open bar for the rehearsal and the dinner, are you two ok with that?" I side eye Alessia and she shrugs.

"Sure, Mom," she tells her.

"Are you two going to take a honeymoon?" Eleanor asks.

"Yes," I spit out before Alessia can answer, because she's crazy if she thinks we're not. I already have a honeymoon in the Maldives planned. She keeps saying it's not a real wedding or a real marriage, but she's going to see just how real it is.

"Oh?" Alessia asks, crossing her legs and turning to me.

"Don't ask, I'm not telling you." My mother smiles; she's the only one that knows my plan. She helped plan a lot of it, she knows how hard this is for me. She knows how hurt I was when I lost Alessia the first time. How I spiraled and focused on nothing other than the business. Alessia lets her hand drop and eyes me.

I lean over and whisper to her, "You want me to hold your hand, *malyshka*?" I slide my hand into her small one. She squints her eyes at me and I chuckle, leaning back into the chair.

"You two no longer seem to avoid each other," Ander observes as he and my father join us at the table.

"That's what you wanted, right?" Alessia spits back at him. She's been distant from him since we got here. I wish I cared enough, but I don't. Her being distant from him has made her stick to my side like a thorn and I love it. My father bends down and kisses her cheek.

"We want you happy, Alessia," her father says, making her scowl.

"Alright, so now that everyone is here, rehearsal will be Friday at 6:00 p.m. Our children requested it be small and intimate, so no more than thirty people. The venue is letting us in at 7:00 a.m. and the wedding will start at 4:00 p.m. sharp. They'll be married by 4:30 p.m. and the stress we've been putting on our sweet Alessia over this wedding will be over," Eleanor says, patting her hand.

"Woo fucking hoo," she says and I squeeze her hand. She looks at me and chuckles. "Sorry."

"Are you two getting excited? Six days left," my mother says, leaning over the table.

"Mom, it's a wedding you both forced upon us. How excited do you expect us to be?" She looks down at our conjoined hands and smirks.

"Pretty excited," she mumbles as the chefs start to drop by food. I look down at our hands and smirk. It feels so natural even though I hate hand holding. She's the only hand I want to hold. So yes, I guess I am fucking excited.

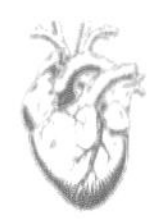

"Astor said Miles is meeting with his father in a week, that's the day after the wedding. They're supposed to leave that night," Ander tells my father.

"We can leave that morning; she doesn't know anything about it, so she won't know it's delayed," I tell Ander as he sits in the chair in front of his desk. We're gathered in his study, discussing how exactly we're planning to exile Miles and his family out of the mafia. He's been poking around, looking for information, and is still trying to buy prominent families to be allies with them.

"He's not going to go out without a fight, Astor. You need to be careful. In his mind, he did nothing wrong," my father says to me, pouring himself his usual.

"What the fuck do you mean, he did *nothing wrong*?"

"He thinks that she was *asking* for it. That's what he told his father. He told him that she was sauntering around the house in her bathing suit and that she left the door to her room open."

I think back to that day and she *was* in her bathing suit—we all were. We were swimming in her pool while our families had a nightcap after the Fourth of July fireworks. I remember her saying she was going up to her room to change, that she was getting cold and was done swimming. I remember her winking at me when she went up the stairs. Miles was behind me and chuckled, I assumed he knew about us. He wasn't oblivious to the fact that we'd been all over each other that entire day. He even caught us kissing in the kitchen that morning. When he said he was going to take a leak, I didn't think anything of it, because I knew I planned on sneaking into Alessia's room in a few minutes, anyway.

My vision starts to turn red when I think about what happened next.

When I went into the house, I heard a scream and something bang against the wall. I knew it was her, I knew her voice. Our parents were trashed after drinking all day, so I knew they either didn't hear it or completely ignored it. When I finally got up the stairs, I saw Miles on top of her, pushing his cock inside of her. I lost it, I ripped him off of her and chucked him down the stairs. I remember climbing on top of him and bashing my fist into his face repeatedly. Then I remember my father stopping me once my hands wrapped around his neck.

"Don't go there, son. Don't think about that day. You have the chance to make her remember. The way her therapist said. You're marrying her, even if she never remembers. You still got her back. She *came back*."

I slump into the seat in front of Ander and he circles his desk, placing his hand on my knee.

"Look, I know we've been at each other the last few weeks, but you know I love you like a son. There is no one else I want my daughter with. That piece of shit may have made her forget what you had before, but he didn't erase you from her memory. Like your father said, she came back. And every day, I know she's closer and closer to finding her true self. But Astor, when she figures out that piece of her life that she lost, she'll need you. She'll hate me for not telling her. She'll hate *you*. But you have to be there, you have to fight for her."

"I will. You have my word," I say, looking straight into his eyes.

Once we say *I do*, that's it. She's mine. Forever.

CHAPTER TWENTY-NINE
ALESSIA

Astor is deafly silent on the drive back to his house. Him and our fathers disappeared for about two hours and it's circling golden hour now. I hadn't planned to be at my parents practically all day, but that's what happened. It felt good to talk about the wedding and not want to kill myself for the first time. Astor seemed more relaxed, too, but when he came back from my father's study, he was quiet. Still touching me, but quiet. It was like I could see the wheels in his head turning. He was figuring a lot of shit out in his head and it was eating me alive not knowing what was torturing him.

I'm debating on questioning him when he pours himself a drink and throws it back before filling another. "Want one?" he asks, grabbing another glass.

"Sure. What are we drinking to?" I ask as I watch him fill it up with an amber liquid.

"To never losing each other again," he says, looking down. I frown and circle the island, standing in front of him.

"Again?" I question, wrapping my arms around his waist.

He still hasn't looked at me. I lean into him and when he finally looks up, his eyes are brimmed red and glossy.

Is he...*crying*?

What the actual living fuck is going on....

"Astor? What's wrong?"

I become panicked. I've never seen him like this.

"You didn't do anything...when you were sixteen, you didn't do anything to me. I just started being mean. Something happened that I couldn't handle. But you didn't do *anything*."

"What happened?"

"I can't tell you that, you have to figure it out on your own. If I tell you, it'll mess everything up." I frown at his words and loosen my grip from his waist. He looks down at my arms and wraps his around mine, hauling me on top of the island to stand between my legs.

"Mess everything up? I don't understand."

"You will, soon. I promise. But right now, just focus on us getting married in six fucking days."

"You didn't seem too upset about it earlier..." I say, leaning into his touch as he runs his hand down my cheek.

"Because I'm not. I never was." I'm shocked, because I remember that day at dinner. I remember him grinding his teeth. I remember how mad he was. I tilt my head to the side and he leans his head against mine.

"But you *were* mad. The sound of your famous teeth grinding is engraved in my head to prove it."

"I was mad because *you* didn't want it. I was mad because *you* honestly thought that there was someone else out there for you. Someone out there who could handle the life we live and love you how you need to be loved."

"And you think you can do all of that?"

"I already am," he says, planting a searing kiss on my lips.

My lips physically feel like they've caught on fire and I don't want to put it out.

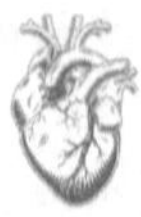

"WHY CAN'T WE HAVE STRIPPERS, AGAIN?" CARO WHINES AS WE PACK up the car.

"Because my fiancé and your boyfriend are batshit crazy, and if they find out some rando is grinding his fucking dick in my face, they'll kill him. Besides, it's my bachelorette party for my forced wedding. It's fine, I'm sure I'll have another." She punches me in my arm and I laugh. "I'm just joking, fuck."

"Look, seriously. I know this isn't what you wanted—I know this isn't what either of you wanted—but you were made for each other, ok? You're so happy. I know you think you're just dealing, but I know you, Les. He makes you happy. You could've been married off to someone way worse."

"I know, I'm going to try. I promise." We climb into the car and head to Xavier's and Astrid's to pick up Elsi.

"Do you know where they're going?" I ask Caro while I search for a song to play. She tilts her sunglasses down and glares at me.

"Bitch, don't be desperate. It's forty-eight hours apart, you'll be fine." I roll my eyes at her and she laughs.

Elsi is standing outside waiting with her bag when we get there. We had to fight Astor and Xavier to let her come to the bachelorette getaway—and it wasn't an easy fight. But we won anyway.

"Let's fucking goooo. I'm ready," she says hopping in the car. I laugh at her and she kisses me on the cheek.

"How many guards are following us?"

"Only two, which is better than the six they originally had." I shake my head as we pull out and head for Bucks County, Connecticut. I made Caroline promise to plan a soothing and calm bachelorette party, because this whole thing has been anything but that.

"I can't wait for a massage; my body is so fucking sore. Justin sure knows his way around it, that's for sure."

"Over fucking sharing Caro," Elsi says. And I laugh, because it's exactly what Astor tells Justin.

These next two days will be exactly what I need before my life *and* my last name changes.

CHAPTER THIRTY

ASTOR

"Take another fucking shot and calm your dick," Justin says, pushing the shot glass in front of me. I quickly drown it and the bartender pours me another. We're in Reno for my bachelor party. Well, our family thinks it's just my bachelor party, but it's also for me and the guys to see if we can sniff out Miles. We've been to every fucking club he owns and he's been nowhere to be found. It's starting to fuck with my head. The last man we tortured said he was hiding out here and wouldn't be back until the weekend—that's two days away. If I could take care of him before then, that'd make the wedding a lot easier.

Not only could I tell Alessia the truth, but I could also show her his head in a bag, too.

"We've been to every spot, where the fuck could he be?"

"Ast, we have forty-eight hours to find him or someone that knows him. Enjoy at least one night of your bachelor party." I let out a gruntled groan as he passes me another shot.

We have our closest friends, Teagan, Mikhail, and Jay with us. All three are just as deep into this mafia shit as we are. We

all go to Redcrest together. Teagan and Mikhail are also seniors, and Jay graduated last year. He's enjoying his year hiatus before his father makes him step up and take his spot in the mafia. Right now, he has a dark headed girl on his lap who's licking the side of his neck as he pays her absolutely no attention. He's scanning the dance floor and his face falls before he locks eyes with someone. He pushes the girl off him and quickly stands to his feet.

I'm to him before he can let out his breath.

"You see him?" I ask. Justin's on my back, waiting for the answer.

"Nah, but I see a bitch that would know him." I follow his gaze and an evil grin spreads across my face when it lands on Miles' best friend. "Wanna turn this club into a bloodbath?" he asks, running his tongue over his teeth as Teagan punches his shoulder.

"Fuck no, Jay. We'll just talk to him." He starts out of the booth and towards Javi. The moment Javi sees Teagan, he tries to run. Mikhail is sitting on the couch watching, zoned in. He never was a man of many words, only with us does he speak.

A moment later, Teagan has Javi by the collar of his shirt, dragging him into our booth.

"Sit the fuck down and don't make me kill you," I say when he fights against Teagan's hold. He glares at me and I push him down onto the couch.

"Well, well, Astor fucking Pavlov. What are you doing here? Wait, actually let me guess. You're looking for Miles." He gives me an evil grin and I look at Mikhail and give him a nod. He yanks him up and we're out the door a moment later. I don't have time for this shit.

Mikhail is a big fucking guy and definitely doesn't look like he's only twenty-four years old. He looks like he benches fucking buildings for fun, if I'm being honest. He shoves Javi into the back of our SUV that's waiting for us at the back of the club.

"Could you be a little gentler? Fuck, you're going to leave bruises on my arm." He yanks his arm out of Mikhail's hold, who withdraws his gun and presses it to Javi's temple.

"How about I just shoot you instead? Stop fucking whining," Mikhail says.

"Both of you, shut the fuck up. Mikhail, put the fucking gun away. It's my bachelor party, no one is dying tonight. Javi, where the fuck is Miles?"

He chuckles and shakes his head. "I don't know, haven't talked to him in two days."

"And where was he when you talked to him?"

"His house that's here."

"Perfect, you're his best minion, you'll take me there. I know you know where it is."

"I'm not taking you—you're fucking crazy. He'd kill you, then kill me for taking you to him."

I let out a sigh. I really didn't want anyone to die tonight. I take my gun out and cock it.

"Two choices, take me to his house or don't take me; I'll shoot you, use your phone, and get to him anyway." I scratch the side of my head with the gun and shrug. "Which one?" I ask him.

"You'll protect me?" Justin chuckles at Javi's question. I side eye him and he pretends that he's coughing instead.

"Get us there. Let us worry about the rest," I spit back at him. He nods and I sit back as he tells Justin the address.

This shit is ending tonight.

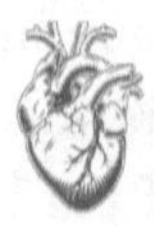

"Let's make this quick and easy. Find him, grab him, and let's go," Teagan says as we inch up the driveway to Miles' house. My phone vibrates and I look down to see a picture from Els. I smile as I'm confronted with a picture of her, Caro, and Alessia. Els has a smile on her face and Alessia is looking off with a wine glass in her hand. Caroline is pointing at something and laughing. They all look happy, but Alessia looks flawless, as always. And that alone makes me want this trip and this mission to be over tonight.

I inwardly roll my eyes as I connect the dots of what's happening in my head.

I fucking *miss* her.

ELSI:

We're having so much fun! So glad you're making her my sister! Love you!

ASTOR:

Be safe. Love you, too.

I chose to ignore the part about me making Alessia her sister. Because if I admit that she fits perfectly into my life, then I admit what I've tried to fight for so long. That I love her. Probably more now than I did six years ago.

"Ast, how do you wanna do this? Walk straight through the front door or quietly?" Mikhail asks.

"Quietly, no need to cause a scene. Kill anyone who tries to stop us from getting to him."

"I thought you said no one dies tonight?" Teagan asks, chuckling. I look down at my phone, glaring at the picture.

"I changed my fucking mind. Let's go."

CHAPTER THIRTY-ONE
ALESSIA

"So, you get married when?" the guy asks as he hovers over the bar and peers at me over his glass. He's become like a gnat that won't go away, regardless of how much we swat him off. He saw us earlier and attached himself like a leach. I don't remember his name, just that he's seriously annoying us.

"Five days," I grumble, looking at Caro in the corner of my eye.

"Are you here alone? Don't you need to get back to your friends or whoever you *came* with?" Elsi asks. He shrugs and looks into his now empty cup.

"They aren't missing me, I'm sure."

"Well, we're heading out. Thanks for the conversation," Caro says, standing and linking her arms through mine and Elsi's.

"Wait, can we exchange numbers?" he asks. I look to Elsi and Caro, unsure of who he's asking. He chuckles and grins. "I'm asking you, Alessia."

"How do you know my name?" I ask, my brows furrowed.

"You told me."

"No, I didn't. Also—what part of getting married in five days don't you understand?"

"Yeah, to a man who can't stomach being around you," he mumbles.

What the fuck.

I hear teeth grinding together and look around for the sound until I realize it indeed is me. I yank away from Caro and saunter up to him.

"Who the fuck are you? How do you know me and why are you here?"

"Someone who can promise that you have no idea who you're marrying. He's hiding so much from you." Then he walks off, the bastard really walks the fuck off. I go to chase him when Caro pulls me back.

"Leave him, maybe call Astor and tell him."

He's hiding so much from you.

"Should we leave?" Elsi asks, looking around. She's scared, I can tell. I give her a small smile.

"We're fine. I'll call your brother." She nods at me, but still looks around.

I pull my phone out and hover over Astor's number.

He's hiding so much from you.

His phone goes straight to voicemail and I can't help the worry that instantly fills my body.

"He didn't answer." I push the phone back into my pocket and decide that I'm not going to let one weird man ruin my last weekend of freedom. "Let's get our massages. I suddenly have an enormous amount of stress that I need to get rid of."

"I agree. That was fucking weird. Let's go," Caro says, laughing as we walk toward the spa.

IT'S BEEN TWO HOURS AND ASTOR STILL HASN'T CALLED ME BACK. THE massage was relaxing, but not enough for me to forget the prick who decided to bombard my space. We're getting ready for dinner when my phone finally rings.

"*Malyshka.*"

"Hi."

"You called? Everything ok?"

"Some random guy came up to tell me that I was not only marrying someone that couldn't stomach the sight of me, but that I was marrying someone who was keeping things from me. Care to explain?"

There's a pause on the other end of the line.

"What did he look like?"

"Uhh, blonde, green eyes, tall. Fucking annoying." Astor is silent and then I hear those fucking teeth grinding, making me laugh.

"Something funny?"

"Just that you're rubbing off on me." He gives an approving hum and Elsi steps out of the bathroom. "Elsi's here, wanna say hi?"

"I'm sure I don't have much of a choice in the matter." Elsi snatches the phone and giggles.

"No, Ast, you don't. Everyone here is obsessed with your girl. They can't keep their eyes off her." I roll my eyes at her as I pull my dress on. She laughs again and I can only imagine what Astor said back to her comment.

I'm choosing to ignore what the man told me about him, because I already know Astor is hiding something from me. He told me himself that it was something I was supposed to figure out myself. I don't like that it's something this mysterious, but it's not a fight I feel is important enough for me to keep fighting.

"Ok, yup. Got it. Love you, bye." She hangs up and throws me my phone.

"Caro, let's go!" I yell out. She steps out of the bathroom and smirks, flipping her hair behind her shoulder.

"Sorry, I needed to have a little peek show time with my man."

"Oversharing."

"Whatever, let's go," she says and we follow behind her.

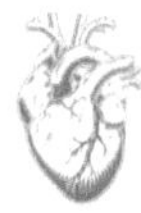

OUR NIGHT WAS GOING PERFECT. CELEBRATING WAS ACTUALLY starting to feel like I had something to truly celebrate. This marriage to Astor wasn't what I asked for, but deep down, I think it was always what I wanted. Zander was right; when we were younger, Astor never gave me the time of day, but I still couldn't keep my eyes off him. He was mean and rude, and instead of avoiding him, I'd find reasons to piss him off more. It was like after a certain time I craved it. I craved the anger I made him feel. I craved it because instead of him being silent and acting like I didn't exist, he showed something. An emotion, a feeling, *something*. I never admitted it to myself, not until Zander said it that day.

"Are you drunk yet, bitch?" Caro says, sliding up next to me with Elsi on the other side of me. Elsi giggles and I shake my head. "I'm not, but she obviously is," I say, tilting my head at Elsi.

"I can't believe you're going to marry my brother," she slurs as I finish off the drink that's in front of me.

"Yeah, me either," I respond. The bartender sits another drink in front of me and I hold my hand up to stop him. "I'm sorry, I didn't order this."

He stops and nods his head to the other side of the bar. When I follow, it lands on the fucking creep from earlier and I groan.

"Is this a fucking joke? Why can't he take the hint?" Elsi asks. I stand and stalk over to him.

"Alessia," he says, raising his drink. "No need to thank—"

"Shut the fuck up, I'm losing my patience. I told you I was getting married in five days, and not only did you blatantly disrespect that, but you also insinuated that I'd willingly give my life over to someone who doesn't want me. It's obvious that you know me, and while I don't know or care as to how, I will say this. Stay the fuck away from me." He opens his mouth to speak, and I swear, I can't help how quickly my fist balled up to haul off and hit him.

"Dominic...leave her." a man says from behind me. I can't help the chills that run down my body at the sound of the voice. I turn around and for some reason, I'm stuck. I don't know who this man is, but what I do know is that the way he's looking at me, he *definitely* knows me.

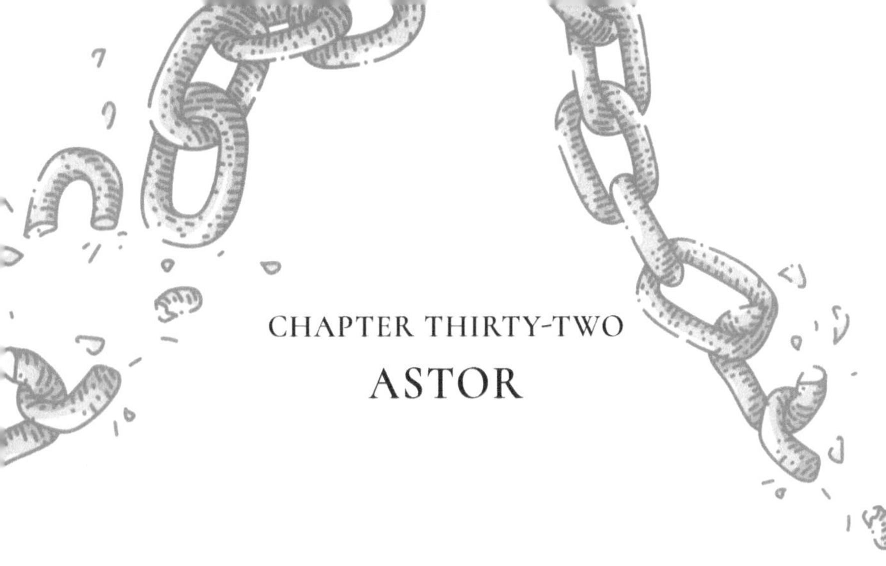

CHAPTER THIRTY-TWO

ASTOR

"Wrap this shit up. He's not here and I'm growing impatient," I tell Mikhail as he stuffs another unconscious guard in a closet. When I walk out of the house, I try my best to contain my anger, but realizing that I'm back at square one with trying to find him makes me want to kill someone.

"What do you want to do?" Justin asks from behind me. I grind my teeth pushing my hands through my hair.

"*Javi.* You said he was here and he's clearly not. So, find out where the fuck your best friend is."

"How am I supposed to do that?" I wrap my hand around his neck and lift until his feet are dangling in the air.

"Fucking figure it out. I'm so close to killing you. You're proving yourself to be incompetent and not worth my fucking time anymore."

"Ok, ok I'll call him. Put me the fuck down, Ast," he coughs out. I drop my hand from his neck and he coughs again, reaching for his phone. I wait patiently as he puts it on speaker phone.

Voicemail.

"Ast, we'll find him. Enjoy the rest of your bachelor party. We have a few more days before his meeting. He can't hide forever," Teagan says, clasping a hand on my shoulder and crawling into the back of the car. The rest of the guys follow except for Javi. He stares at me, his body shaking a bit.

"I don't know where he is, I thought he'd be here. I swear." I tilt my head and spit next to him.

"When he gets back, tell him if the message wasn't clear enough, I'm coming for him for what he did to my wife. And this time, my father won't be there to stop me from ripping his head off his fucking shoulders."

I climb into the truck and Justin pulls off immediately. My fingers tap away on my leg. He should be here, but the fact that there were only six guards at his home makes me truly wonder if he's here at all.

The more I think about him, the more I think about that day. How angry I was at my father for stopping me that day. How mortified Alessia's mother was that she didn't hear her daughter's scream. How fucking devastated her father was that his best friend didn't do what should've been done that day. Miles should have never left that house alive. He should have never been given that freedom. Him being told to disappear wasn't enough. Not for me, not for Alessia's parents, and it damn sure wouldn't be for her when she remembers what the fuck happened to her.

If she figures out what happened to her before I kill him myself, she'll never fucking forgive me. Or worse, she'll go after him herself. And once that side of Alessia is unleashed, *no one* can control her.

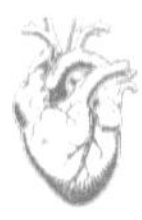

We're at our house rental and my wheels have not stopped turning. I'm on high alert and can't think of anything other than where the fuck Miles could be. The guys are getting shit-faced and playing poker when I step out onto the balcony to call Ander.

"You find him?"

"Fuck no, I didn't. He wasn't there. Something tells me he's not here at all. He only had six guards at his house."

"Goddamn it. Let me make some calls; try to enjoy your bachelor party."

"I don't give a fuck about a party. I want this fucker dead for what he did to her."

"In due time, Astor." I hang up the phone, leaning over the balcony when Teagan brings me a drink.

"Drink it. And fucking chill." I take it from him and down it. He leans against the balcony next to me. "How has she been?"

Teagan and Alessia were close growing up, it was always us and Justin. Our families were all pretty close. He wasn't there that day; his father had a business trip and took him and his mother along. He would've been there if it weren't for that. He never forgave himself for it; he hasn't been able to talk to Alessia for more than ten minutes at a time since the accident.

"She's starting to question shit; things are starting to confuse her. She's starting to wonder why she can't stand a man touching her. I'm losing my ability to keep fucking lying to her."

"Fuck, Ast, you have to tell her before the wedding. You know if she finds out you let her marry you without knowing everything first, she'll leave. And I don't know if you'll get her back."

"T, she'll never get away from me. I let her think for six fucking years that I actually hated her. I'm not letting her get away again. She's marrying me regardless of what she wants."

He chuckles as he pours more whiskey in my glass and into his as well.

"Maybe we'll get lucky and get the *tornado* back," he says, referring to what we used to call Alessia when we were kids.

"You sure you're ready to see her? It's been how long, now?"

"Yeah, and it's been two years. I miss us all being around each other. It would be easier if she fucking knew and then I could just apologize and move on. But it's hard to apologize for something she doesn't remember. She probably thinks I hate her, too."

"She does. She thinks we all hate her and that it was my doing...so the wedding should be...interesting."

"Yeah, to say the least. Speak of the devil and she shall show her face," he says pointing to my glowing phone. Alessia's face pops up and I fight the smile tugging at my lips. Teagan chuckles and looks out over the balcony as I answer the phone call.

"*Malyshka*, having fun?"

"It's Elsi...umm does Alessia have like a fainting problem?"

"A fainting problem? No. Why? What happened?" I ask, straightening up. Teagan turns to me, his eyebrows drawn.

"Well, she fainted. She's taking a shower now, but she said she wants to leave tomorrow."

"She only faints when she's overwhelmed. What happened before she fainted?"

"That's another thing I was calling about...remember the picture of that guy you showed me when we were kids? The one you told me to memorize and run the other way if I ever saw?"

My heart fucking drops.

"Elsi…" I warn.

"He's here…he said something to her and she like froze and fainted. And I was so distracted by his face and what you said that I couldn't get myself to call y—"

I'm moving before she finishes her sentence. I showed her a picture of Miles years ago just in case. I never expected her to actually remember his face, but I guess showing someone the same thing for months stays in their heads.

"We're leaving," I bellow out to the guys. Teagan is on my heels and the rest of the guys start grabbing their shit. I'm grateful for the quickness because the last thing I need to do is pick a fight with them when I know I'll need them.

"Elsi, listen to me, when she gets out of the shower, do not let her out of that room. None of you leave that room without your security. I'm on my way. You stay there. Understand?"

"Who is he?" I swallow and tilt my head back as I gain my composure. Elsi knows that Alessia was hurt growing up, but she was so young she doesn't know the details and I never told her them. The less she knows, the better. Her and Alessia are too close and she'd never be able to keep something so big from her.

"Dangerous. And that's all you need to know. I'm on my way, tell her to call me when she gets out of the shower."

I hang up and we all stuff into the elevator. It's deathly quiet and Jay sighs.

"Will we need a cleanup crew?" he asks, breaking the silence. I grind my teeth and he laughs. "Thought so."

Once we get in the car, I call Ander again, telling him that Miles is in Bucks County.

"Astor, get her home now. Leave him alive and get her away from him. If she figures out who—"

"I know, I'm getting her."

CHAPTER THIRTY-THREE
ALESSIA

When I got out of the shower, Elsi and Caroline were both sitting on the bed, waiting for me. They told me that Astor was on his way here and that we needed to stay put unless we had security with us. Neither of them would tell me why and when I asked if it had anything to do with the man we saw earlier, they both looked away. I didn't badger them because I was nursing a headache from hell and just wanted to sleep. I told them that I wanted to go home first thing in the morning and apologized to them for ruining the trip. They both were so freaked out by my fainting that they told me we could leave tonight if I wanted to.

"So...do you think you know him?" Elsi asks. We're all cuddled in the bed together with some movie on that I truly wasn't paying attention to. I'd been looking at the ceiling for the last fifteen minutes, willing myself to fall asleep.

"I don't know, it felt like I did. The way he was looking at me, like he—"

"Wanted to devour you. It was fucking creepy," Caroline

mumbles, as she scrolls through her phone. She sits up and gasps. "I found him! His name is Miles...Miles Raz."

"Why does that name sound so familiar?" I ask. It bugs me that I know he has something to do with this big secret everyone is keeping from me. I shrug my shoulders. "What time did Astor say he'd be here?"

"I'm not sure, he just said that he was on his way. So, I assume in the next few hours," Elsi says. I peek at the clock.

1:07 a.m.

"Sorry for fainting again..." I mumble and we all bust out in laughter.

"Just don't do that shit on your wedding day," Caro says and I nudge her.

Four days left...

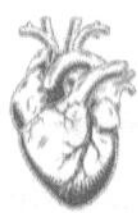

"Wake up, *malyshka*." I jump at Astor's touch and he cradles me against his chest. I push against him and he holds me tighter. "Alessia, little devil, it's me. Open your eyes."

I groan and sink into his hold. "Sorry," I mumble as he kisses my forehead, laying us back against the mattress.

"You fainted."

"I fainted."

"Why?"

"Because he was looking at me like he was undressing me, it creeped me out. I know him, don't I?"

"Alessia..."

"Just tell me, Astor."

"Yes. You know him." I sit up and face him. He's fully dressed despite the fact that the clock says that it's 4:00 a.m. I take in his face and can tell he's tired and hasn't slept. Which means that he got on a plane the second he heard about what happened. I also know that the murmurs I hear outside are way more than the two guards when I went to bed.

"Where's Elsi and Caro?"

"I kicked them out."

"Ast, you can't just kick people out in the middle of the night."

"I can when people come between me being with you. Come here."

I open my mouth to argue and quickly shut it, because for the first time, I have nothing to say. When I woke up from my spell, all I wanted was Astor. I had only fainted twice, but each time he was there. He quickly became my comfort and I needed him, whether I wanted to admit it or not.

I curl into his side and he entwines our fingers, bringing them to his lips to press a gentle kiss on each finger.

There's a light knock on the door and Astor turns the light on before telling them to come in. My breath is taken away when I see Teagan striding in with his hands in his pockets staring at us, a small taint smile hovering his face.

"Teagan...what are you—"

"Security swept this place up and down. If he was here, he's gone. We checked the cameras and it's definitely Miles. But it looks like he left after the...encounter."

I stand up and walk over to him as I stare at him for what feels like an eternity. My mouth is dry; I can't believe it's him. He tucks my hair behind my ear and grins. "Hey, Lessia."

I rush into his arms, hugging him so tight that he grunts. I haven't seen him in two years. He, like Astor, shut me out six years ago, but he still would occasionally speak to me to wish me things like a Happy Birthday, Merry Christmas, and things like that. But then he left. I don't have a clue where he went, but he left two years ago and he stopped reaching out. He was one of my closest friends. He was Astor's friend first, so when he stopped talking to me, I assumed it was just because he was finally given an ultimatum. I knew that he and Astor still saw each other, but never me.

He wraps his arms around me and squeezes, Astor clears his throat and I laugh as Teagan rolls his eyes at him.

"Alright, T, let her go. You've been touching her for a little too long." Teagan flips him the bird and I shake my head at them two.

"Anyway, I'll keep the guards out front of the rooms and the two outside. Your father sent the jet, so it'll be a quick flight back to New York. We can leave whenever you're ready," Teagan says to Astor before he looks back at me.

"When do you want to leave?" Astor asks me.

"He's gone?" I ask, looking between them both. Teagan nods and I let out a sigh. "Well, this is supposed to be our bachelor and bachelorette parties, and we still had another day to celebrate. I think I'd like to stay..." Teagan nods, kisses my cheek, and walks out of the door. I swear I hear Astor growl behind me.

"Are you sure you want to stay, Alessia?" Astor asks, sitting on the bed. I turn to face him and give a small nod.

"Yes. I don't want anyone thinking they have an ounce of power over me."

I push his legs apart and stand between them, wrapping my arms around him. Even with him sitting, he's still taller than me. He runs his hand up and down the back of my bare leg, yanking me closer to him.

"You haven't slept, have you?" I question.

He shakes his head at me and I reach for his shirt, tugging it over his head.

"Do you want to sleep now?" I continue. He shakes his

head again. He watches me as I sink to my knees in front of him, tugging on his pants. He lifts his hips and I yank them down, being sure to take his boxer briefs with them. His cock springs out and I can't help the satisfying groan that comes out of my mouth when I see the head of it already covered with his precum. I run my tongue over it, tasting the saltiness of it before completely covering the tip with my mouth. Our eyes never leave each other's as my head ascends and descends on his cock. I never knew giving head could be so enjoyable, but here I am on my knees, tears streaking my face while Astor brutally fucks my mouth. He's no longer letting me take control. He has his hands in my hair, gripping my roots so tight that I wouldn't be surprised if strands are wrapped in them. He's pushing his cock further and further down my throat with each thrust, but I don't back down; I take it.

"Fuck, *malyshka*. This fucking mouth." I slurp and slurp until I feel his balls tense and jump. I know he's about to come, and I'm so impatient for it that I grab his balls in my hand, tugging them. He lets out a gruntled groan and a second later, my mouth is filled with his cum. I'm overwhelmed with his taste and I swallow every drop of it.

He tucks my hair behind my ear and pulls me up to him, flipping us over onto the bed. He hovers over me and I run my tongue across my bottom lip, moaning at the remaining taste of him.

"Thanks for coming to get me," I say as he lines his cock up with my entrance, sliding himself through my wetness.

"I'll always come after you, little devil. Wrap those pretty fucking legs around me."

CHAPTER THIRTY-FOUR
ASTOR

"She's sleeping. Says she wants to stay," I tell Ander and Eleanor. They've called me three times, but being that I was in the middle of fucking their daughter, answering was the last thing on my mind.

"Astor, I told you to bring her home," her father declares.

"And she doesn't want to yet. I'm not going to make her feel like she has no say so in her fucking life, Ander. I have men surrounding this fucking place, I can protect her. We'll be home tomorrow, as she requested."

I hear Eleanor telling him to calm down and then he curses under his breath.

"Astor, ignore him. He's just on edge. I want her to enjoy herself; distract her. Make sure she has some fun, then get her back here."

"Of course."

"Love you, sweetie. Tell her to call us when she wakes up."

"Love you, too. Will do."

I hang up and lean back against the headboard, looking down at her as she curls into my side. Her breathing is slow and quiet, and I focus on it as it becomes a melody that is soothing enough to almost put me to sleep. *Almost.*

The sun is starting to peek through the curtains and I still can't stop thinking about how close Miles was to her. He could have fucked all of her progress up, she's so close to remembering, and as much as I hope she doesn't remember until after we're married, I'm still glad she's getting there.

I don't like that every time she remembers something she faints, though, and I needed to remember to make her get checked out.

I hear her groan and then a second later feel her soft lips against my bare chest.

"Good morning," she says, looking up at me. "Did you sleep?" she questions. I bend down and plant a kiss on her forehead.

"I'm fine, let's get some breakfast." I go to move her, but she grabs me, keeping me still.

"You have to sleep, Ast."

"I slept." *Lie.* She rolls her eyes and climbs out of the bed to head for the shower. I follow after her shredding my briefs and climbing into the shower.

"The rest of your friends are still coming today?"

"Yes, they should be in within the next hour or so." I wrap my arms around her and she leans back against me. "Excited to celebrate with me?"

"Maybe it was my plan all along. How else can I make sure you don't have strippers at your bachelor party?" I chuckle and begin washing her hair.

"Trust me, little devil, the only woman I want to see naked and grinding on me is you."

"Alright man, what the fuck changed? I mean, I know what happened, but you seem more obsessed than you were six years ago," Teagan says.

"Yeah, you couldn't keep your eyes off her at breakfast... or your hands, for that matter," Jay adds, to which I just shrug.

"Be glad he has someone to keep him in line. Maybe he won't be up our asses as much," Mikhail says. We all laugh and I watch Alessia from the table as she talks with her friends and my sister.

"Who's the redhead?" Jay asks, watching River as she downs a shot. I shake my head and Justin chuckles.

"River. And the one who can't seem to take her eyes off Mikhail is Tess, the one that Teagan is currently eye fucking is Briar." Mikhail looks up from his phone and glances at Tess, making a grunting noise before turning his attention back to his phone.

"What bar we going to tonight?" Jay asks. I shrug as my phone vibrates.

"I don't know, some place Caroline found." I stare down at my phone and grin at the message I read.

ALESSIA:

Stop undressing me with your eyes.

ASTOR:

How about you meet me in the bathroom and I can really undress you?

I watch how she readjusts herself in her seat as she reads the message, her cheeks flush, and River says something that makes her turn even redder. They all look over to the table and Jay waves at them before they bust out in laughter.

Caroline pushes back from the table and the rest of them follow as they walk towards our table. Justin pushes his chair back and Caroline flops down in his lap. He kisses the side of her hair and she leans back into him.

"When the fuck did this happen?" Jay says, leaning forward and eyeing them. Caro shrugs as Alessia appears beside me.

"Lessia, you sure you wanna marry this asshole?" Teagan asks her. He pulls her in for a hug, but I yank her away from him.

"You hugged her this morning. One's enough," I warn him.

"You two give me a migraine. Anyways, I'm being rude," she says, gesturing to her friends as they pull up chairs.

"Everyone, this is River, Tess, and Briar. We go to Redcrest together. You guys know Ast and Justin, but this is Teagan, Jay, and Mikhail."

"Hi! You boys go to Redcrest, too?" River asks as she sits down next to Teagan. Jay nudges him and they swap chairs. River laughs and Jay leans back against his chair.

"I graduated last year; Teagan and Mikhail are seniors," Jay says. River nods and picks up her drink. Tess is quiet, but that's not surprising. She's always quiet. She's the quiet one out of the group, but something tells me she's just as lethal. I know who her family is and there's no way she wasn't trained how Alessia was growing up.

"Excuse me?" Alessia asks. I groan, throwing my head back. She didn't know Teagan was at Redcrest, she thought she was out of state in school. She had no idea how close he'd been the last two years.

"Lessia." She puts her hand up as he begins to talk and I watch as she turns towards him, her eyes full of anger. She was about to let him have it.

"You're fucking telling me you've been at Redcrest this entire time?"

"Maybe we shouldn't talk about this right now?" Caroline suggests. Alessia gives her a death glare and Caroline shakes her head.

"You were one of my best friends and you let me think you were gone for two fucking years?" Teagan stands up and Alessia steps back closer to me.

"You don't understand, I couldn't see you."

"Why?"

He looks at me over her shoulder and she snaps.

"Don't fucking look at him, T, look at me!"

"Alessia...lower your voice," I say, but she ignores me.

"I can't tell you."

"No one can ever tell me *anything*. I'm fucking tired of it. Tell me."

"Lessia, I want to, but I can't."

She throws her hands up and pushes him before storming off. She gets close to the exit when she turns around.

"I don't want you at the wedding. You've avoided me for two years; you don't deserve to be there."

"Lessia," Teagan says, walking towards her, and I see it before anyone else does. Her steps waver and she turns pale. I'm on my feet to get to her before she hits the ground. I catch her in my arms and the rest of them follow behind me.

"Give her space!" I bellow out. They all take a step back as I pick her up and carry her to the car. "Grab a water, T, and tell everyone we'll meet them back at the hotel." He nods and heads back towards them. They all watch in worry as I will Alessia to open her eyes.

This fucking fainting has to stop.

CHAPTER THIRTY-FIVE

ALESSIA

"It's just stress, she's ok. But she needs to stop getting worked up," the doctor says to Astor as he packs his stuff up. I fainted, *again*. It's happening more often, and I know it's because of stress, but I can't help it. I'm so tired of people hiding things from me, about *me*. Hearing that Teagan was not only in the same state, but the same fucking university as I made me so angry. Because what did I do to make him avoid me for two years?

"Make sure she takes it easy, I'm sure the wedding is stressing her out. The fainting spells should dissipate afterwards. If not, call me."

Astor sees the doctor out and turns to me full of rage, but I don't give a shit.

"Don't look at me like that, Astor. You knew he was here, *you knew*, and you didn't tell me."

"It wasn't my place and we weren't the best of friends, Alessia. We didn't talk, and when we did, it was to yell at each other. In what world would we have a conversation about Teagan, or a conversation at all?"

He was right, we didn't talk. We didn't communicate at all until this whole arranged marriage thing. I shake my head and start changing my clothes.

"What are you doing?"

"We're going out, remember?"

"You just fucking fainted. You aren't going out."

"Astor, it was six hours ago. I'm fine and I'm going. You can either come with me or you can call a cleanup crew to be on standby because you'll definitely be killing someone with what Caroline has for me to wear." He stares at me and shakes his head.

"Fuck's sake. We aren't staying long." I shrug and he starts getting dressed. He needs to get used to the fact that his soon to be wife will do whatever the fuck she wants.

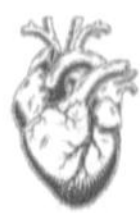

"I'm sorry, you know," Teagan says to me. Astor is ordering us drinks and I'm sitting on Caroline's lap. I want to be angry with him, but most of all, I want to know why. Why did one of my best friends decide to avoid me for two fucking years?

"T, I don't want to talk about it anymore. Until you can tell me why you decided to forget I existed for two years, we have nothing to talk about."

"That's unfair, if I could tell you I would. You have no fucking idea how badly I want to tell you why, but I can't."

"It's the same secret, isn't it?" I say to Astor who's standing behind him. I don't have to be close to him to know he's grinding his teeth. He nods his head and I shake my head, turning back to Caroline.

"This outfit on you is insane, I can't believe he let you out in it." I look down over my short mini skirt and my heels, and grin at her.

"I thought he was going to have an actual heart attack when he saw me. Let's go dance," I say, pulling her by her hand. She leans in and whisper-yells over the music.

"You're really trying to kill him tonight." We brush past him and he grabs my arm.

"Do not bend over. Do you understand?" he growls at me. I shrug out of his hold and saunter onto the dance floor with my best friend. We're quickly joined by the rest of my girls and for the first time since we got here, I'm just enjoying myself.

When the song changes to a fast beat, I feel Astor's eyes on me. It's like no one exists when I find him. He looks like he wants to devour me, I can feel him daring me as my hips sway faster to the beat. He raises his eyebrow and I slowly start to bend over. River gets behind me as my hands hit my knees and my ass starts gyrating.

"You're going to get killed, he's coming this way," she says as I turn back to her. We both laugh when an arm wraps around me and I'm pulled into a body.

I know it's him; his smell is taking over my nostrils and his touch is one I've learned to crave. I push my ass back and he yanks my head back to him, wrapping his hands in my hair.

"I told you not to bend over, little devil."

"What are you going to do about it?"

"Don't test me." I move to bend over again and I'm quickly submerged into the air. I feel his hand covering my ass and I see the crowd parting as we come through. I smile at my friends as we pass them and Astor heads towards the exit with me thrown over his shoulder. I smirk at the valet when he asks Astor for his ticket.

Astor groans as I reach into his back pocket and pluck out the ticket, passing it to the valet. He quickly grabs it and tries to hide his smile. "Thank you, ma'am," he says. His gaze lingers for a second as he passes Astor.

"Keep staring at her and I'll kill you. I really didn't plan on that tonight," he says to the valet. He clears his throat and hurries off towards the cars. I tuck my hands under my chin and rest on Astor's shoulder while we wait.

"I can stand, you know. And I'm pretty sure everyone can see up my skirt."

"I'm covering you. Now shut up." I don't waste my breath responding, instead I wiggle my ass in his hand and adjust my position.

Seconds later, the valet that he just threatened pulls up to the curb with his car. Astor not so gently deposits me into the passenger seat before rounding the car to get in the driver seat.

"You're leaving my friends," I say, looking out the window when he drives off.

"They have the guys there with them, they're fine." I think about how shit keeps happening this week and how honestly, it seems to be because of me.

"Yeah, they're probably safer without me..."

"Don't say that." I shrug and lean forward, looking at the mountain in front of us.

"I wonder what the view is like up there, it's probably gorgeous." Astor grins and grabs my hand in his before turning the wheel.

"How about we find out?"

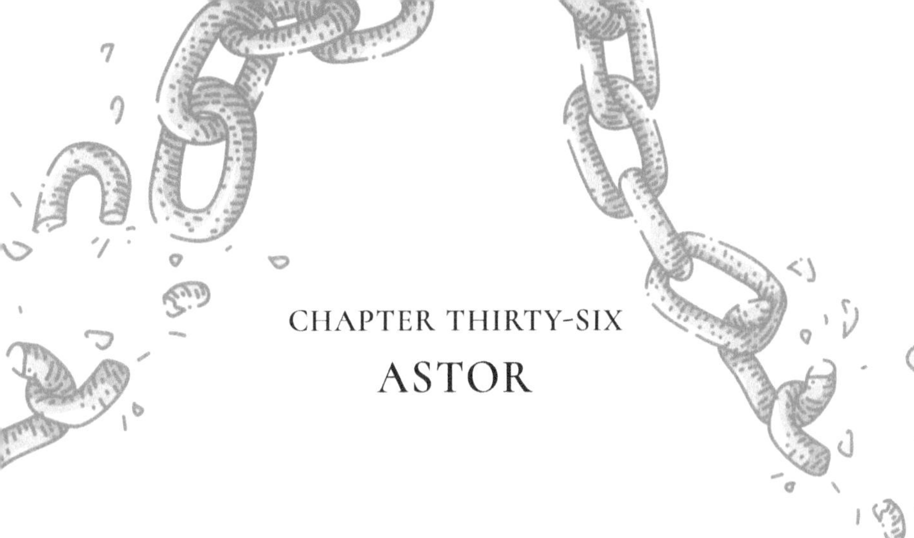

CHAPTER THIRTY-SIX

ASTOR

Once we get to the top of the mountain, I park my car at the edge and Alessia impatiently climbs out.

"Oh my God. This is fucking—"

"*Alessia...*"

"What? This view deserves some curse words..." I shake my head and yank her towards me.

"Remember what I told you would happen if you cursed at me again?" She leans her head back and smirks.

"But I didn't curse *at* you."

"Ehh, semantics." I walk her backwards until the back of her knees touch the car and I push her back on the hood. "Lay back."

"But I thought we came for the view?" she asks as she leans backwards, I lift her leg and I curse under my breath when I get a clear view of her bare pussy.

"You wanted to see the view from up here and I want to see the view down here. Now open those fucking legs." She flinches when I slap her pussy lips and her legs fall to each side of her. "Good girl," I praise before I run my tongue through her folds.

Her back arches as I dig my tongue further into her pussy. I take my hand and push her back flat against the hood of the car. When she moans, I feel the already hard bulge in my pants become rock solid. My dick eager to feel the inside of her. She pushes her hands through my hair and tugs, making me let out a feral groan. I need to get her there and quickly, because I can't take not feeling her much longer. After her little show at the club, I'm stuck between wanting to punish her and wanting to fuck her so hard that she begs me to punish her instead. She knew what she was doing tonight, but I didn't expect anything less.

"Astor, please. I need to come," she says when I pull away from her. I chuckle and hover over her.

"Do you deserve to come?" I slap her pussy again and she throws her head back. "Answer me, little devil. Do you deserve to come?"

"Please," she begs again. I push my finger inside of her and she lets out a gasp. Adding another finger will just send her over the edge, so I refrain from it, even though it's what I need.

"The next time I say not to bend over, you'll listen. The next time I say to stop cursing, you'll stop cursing. Understand?" I whisper into her ear, lining myself up with her entrance.

"Just fuck—" I slam myself into her before she can finish her sentence.

"That fucking mouth on you," I say as I push my way in and out of her, faster and harder. She wraps her legs around me and I feel her hands under my shirt then her nails in my back. "Taming you will never happen, huh?"

"I don't need to be tamed," she moans as I thrust in and out of her.

"Mmm, I beg to differ."

"I need to be loved; exactly how I am." I increase my speed, pulling out of her long enough to stand us up and bend her over the hood of the car.

I kick her legs open and slap her ass, yanking her back by her hair.

"Just fuck me, Astor. Please." My dick slides in and I wrap my hands around her throat as she meets me thrust for thrust.

"What if I don't want to fuck you, what if I want to love you?" She stills and I turn her around to face me, sitting her on the hood of the car and inserting my dick back into her. She tries to avoid my gaze, but I grasp her chin between my fingers and force her to meet my stare. "It's inevitable, I don't want to fight it. You shouldn't, either." She glances down at where my dick meets her pussy and her lip tips up a fraction.

"Fuck it," she groans as I lift her up, fucking her into her orgasm.

Fuck it is right. She's mine. I love her. And I need to make sure she knows that before her secret blows up in our face.

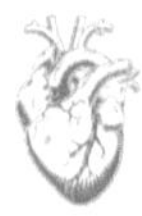

WE'RE BACK IN NEW YORK BEFORE WE KNOW IT. ALESSIA HASN'T addressed what happened last night on the mountain and neither have I. We've barely had time to ourselves since we landed in New York. Her parents and mine have been hovering us, her father is growing increasingly worried that she'll remember something before the wedding.

"Sweetheart, are you feeling ok?" Eleanor asks Alessia. She smiles at her mom and nods.

"I'm fine. It was nothing."

"You've fainted a few times, are you that stressed? Is it the wedding?"

"I don't know, maybe. I guess we'll find out in three days," she says, smirking. I bend down and kiss her forehead. Our mothers smile at each other and start reviewing, for what feels like the twentieth time today, each detail of the wedding. I find my father and Ander in the den; they both have a drink in their hand and I'm not one bit surprised when Ander turns to me and launches his fist at my face.

CHAPTER THIRTY-SEVEN

ALESSIA

"Are you ready for this, *figlia*?" my mom asks when Astor is out of earshot. Astrid excused herself to the restroom and my mom made it very obvious that she could not wait to be alone with me.

"Mom, honestly; does it matter?"

"It does. I know you think it doesn't, but your happiness is the most important thing to me, Alessia. And it's him, he makes you happy, he always has."

I sigh because she's right, everyone around me knows it. It's not something I can ignore anymore; this is the man that has had my fucking heart since I was old enough to know what that meant.

"I know, Mom, I know."

"*Malyshka*, we're leaving," Astor says. The side of his face is red and I jump to my feet when I see it.

"What happened to your—"

"Alessia, now," he says, grabbing my arm. I hear our fathers coming towards us with my father heading straight for Astor.

"She's not going anywhere with you," he says. Astor yanks me behind him and I yank out of his hold.

"What the fuck is going on? You hit him?" I yell at my father when he reaches us.

"He had *one job*—to keep you fucking safe. I told him to bring you home. What if something happened to you!"

"I didn't want to leave!"

"He should've made you!" My mother gently pushes my father in his chest, pushing him towards the family room.

"Ander, that's enough. Our daughter is just that—our daughter. If she didn't want to leave, no one would've made her. Apologize right this instant for putting your hands on Astor."

I fold my arms and stand next to Astor, waiting for my father to speak.

"I shouldn't have put my hands on you. But when it comes to my daughter and her safety, I need to know that you have her. I need to fucking know that she'll make it back to her mother and I in one goddamn piece." Astor steps closer to my father and I shrink a bit when he starts speaking.

"You got one pass and you just used it. Don't ever question whether or not I'm going to protect her. Don't question whether or not I have *her*. And lastly, you need to understand that in three days, it's not about *my wife* coming back to you or Eleanor, it's *me*. See you at the wedding."

He reaches his hand behind him and I take it as he practically drags me out of the house, quickly depositing me in the car.

"Ast, what happened?"

"It doesn't matter. You know I'll protect you, right?"

"Yes."

"And you know that I've always got you, right?"

"Yes. But Ast..."

"What?" he says, pushing a piece of my hair out of my face, his calloused hands running down it.

"I'm not your wife yet," I say, smirking. He kisses my nose and drives us home.

He holds my hand the entire drive, brushing the pad of his thumb across my hand. I smile inside, completely in awe of how he's reacting. I haven't talked to him about saying he just wants to love me. Mainly because I'm still waiting for the other shoe to drop. There's no way we've hit a turning point when I've spent the last few years thinking he hated me.

I don't know how I went from him ignoring my complete and utter existence, to him calling me his wife. Now, we're a few days shy of a wedding that I was so against. I was sure I planned on packing a bag and standing him up on wedding day. Now, I'm finding myself willing the time to wind down so that I can start my life as his wife. It's hard for me to accept the fact that even when he hated me, I never stopped loving him. I always felt pathetic for never having the ability to fully hate him even when he treated me like I had a disease. Zander was right; I always made myself known when Astor was around. I really tried with Zander. I laughed at things that weren't funny, I hugged into him a little tighter, even though his touch made me sick. I smiled at him, even when I wanted to simply tell him to fuck off because his presence made me angry.

"Little devil, what are you thinking about over there?" I blink a few times and look out the window, realizing that the short distance to our house was completely eaten up by my daydreaming.

"Oh nothing, just remembering how much of a fool you made me look like when you couldn't stand being near me." He chuckles as he rounds the car to help me out, kissing the side of my head as he ushers me into the house.

"I'm the fool, baby. Don't forget that." He smacks my ass and I chuckle.

"I need to take a nap," I say, letting out a yawn and pulling my sweatshirt off. We headed straight to my parents' house when we landed back in New York. They insisted on going over the details of the wedding again. Caroline is growing increasingly impatient, specifically for the reception where she swears that she'll catch the bouquet. I can't remember a time she was ever this excited over a wedding or anything, for that matter, that didn't involve hitting someone.

I turn for the stairs, slugging myself up them. My body is exhausted after Astor fucked me last night. He took me back to our room and did another three rounds. We finally closed our eyes to sleep around 3:00 a.m., only to wake up at 5:00 a.m. to catch our 6:00 a.m. flight. Our friends were all still drunk and loud on the flight home, so sleeping was out of the question.

"You coming?" I ask over my shoulder as he watches me. He nods, pushing himself off the counter. He hovers behind me as I reach for the door to his bedroom. I smile to myself, realizing that I don't even bother going into the guest room anymore.

He plants a kiss on my shoulder and I take a deep breath, leaning back into him.

"Did you mean what you said yesterday?" I whisper, willingly myself to push the door open. He nudges me inside, shutting the door behind him.

There's a gift bag sitting on the bed. I turn around and raise my eyebrow at him.

"That for me?" I ask.

He nods. "It is." I saunter over to the bag, peeking inside and slowly opening. He chuckles at me when I hit it to see if anything will pop out. "Stop it, just open it."

I laugh and open the bag, my heart warming when I see a

replica of my favorite t-shirt and hoodie of his that I wear. I pull it out and smirk at him, lifting it up to my nose and inhaling. I frown a bit when it smells new. The whole reason I liked wearing them was because they smelled like him. He walks up to me and pulls it out of my hand.

"What?" he asks, inspecting them. I shake my head. "Nothing, it just...it doesn't smell like you," I say, tucking my lip in the side of my mouth.

"Hmm, I see," he says. I kiss his cheek, taking the shirt from his hand.

CHAPTER THIRTY-EIGHT

ASTOR

S he's been sleeping for the last four hours and I've been doing everything I can in this fucking shirt and hoodie since she closed her eyes.

It doesn't smell like you.

It's been going through my head on repeat since she said it. She's just as obsessed as I am. You'd think I'd tell her that I love her before the wedding, but no. I'm too much of a pussy to let the words come out of my mouth. I can hear water running in the bathroom and I shoot upstairs, yanking the shirt and hoodie off and putting it back in the drawer where she put it. I know she'll grab it when she gets out of the shower.

Justin and Caroline are supposed to be coming over soon, so I need to have my fix of her before they do.

"Ast? That you?" she says when I enter the bathroom. I start to remove my shirt and shorts before climbing in the shower behind her. I pull her to me, wrapping my hand around her hair and yanking her eyes into view.

"You expecting it to be someone else, little devil?" A flash of amusement is hiding in them, but the rest is complete want

and need. The side of my mouth tilts up a fraction and I quickly bend her over without another word. "Fast and hard, so hold on," I warn before sinking violently in her, her moans so loud they echo through the shower walls.

Her hands fly out against the wall and I increase my speed when she moans out my name. It gets me every fucking time— my name on her lips exactly where it should be.

I watch in awe as my dick slides in and out of her, the water trickling down her back over the cusp of her ass. I can't help it when my hand comes down on her ass. She screeches, but pushes back against me. I do it again and again until finally, her pussy is suffocating around my length.

"Fuck, fuck, Ast, stop. I can't," she pleads as I fuck her through it. I bite down on her shoulder as my own climax rips through me. My cum fills her as I pump in and out in a short, staccato rhythm.

"You really are going to ruin me for anyone else, aren't you?" she asks as I lather her body in soap while she catches her breath.

"There is no one else for you, Alessia. But if you choose to figure that out the hard way, then yes. I plan to ruin you."

"Hmph, you already have."

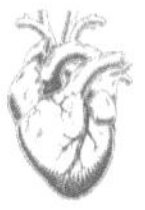

"Chinese or Thai?" Alessia asks us. Justin and Caroline are here and we decided to spend the night in for dinner and a movie. Alessia is still tired and just wanted to feel safe. I'd be lying if I said that knowing my—no, *our*—home makes her feel safe isn't doing some freaky weird shit to me.

Caroline jumps up and snatches the menus out of Alessia's hand before they both look at each other and laugh.

"Thai," they say in unison before ducking off into the kitchen. I can hear them ordering food when I turn to Justin.

"I fucked up," he says before I can speak. I tilt my head and he sighs. "She knows who Miles is. Her, Elsi, and Alessia know his name, but when I got to Caroline's, she wouldn't stop with the questions."

I take a deep breath, because now it makes sense why Caroline has been so sweet to Alessia. Why there hasn't been any name calling or passive aggressive comments.

"She wouldn't leave it alone, Ast, I tried. I told her to leave it alone. I told her to stop asking, fuck, I even tied her up and spanked the fuck out of her."

"Justin. Over—"

"*Sharing*, yeah, I know. But I'm fucking sorry, man. She knows you're trying to find him, that we're trying to make it right."

"What'd she say?"

"That you need to tell Alessia before the wedding and let them both in our planned activities. She said that Alessia is her best friend, and if she asks her if she knows anything, she's not going to lie to her, but she won't say anything unless that happens." I grunt and lean back into the seat, because every day we get closer to this wedding, a strand of my strength to keep this from her breaks. And I'm pretty fucking sure I'm all out of strands.

"Food will be here in thirty minutes. Now, suspense or comedy?" Alessia asks, snuggling up next to me. I kiss her forehead and peek up at Caroline; she's staring at Alessia, her eyes look watery and I clear my throat. She gives a small nod and turns towards the TV as Justin wraps his arm around her waist.

"Suspense," I reply. She puts on *John Wick*, and it makes me laugh on the inside, because she has no idea the shitshow that's about to take over our lives.

CHAPTER THIRTY-NINE
ALESSIA

I t's the day before my wedding and we've been running around nonstop since 7:00 a.m. Justin and Caro stayed over last night and that made me happy. Us all together made me feel like my relationship was a normal one, was a real one. But no matter how happy I feel right now, this all is only happening because our parents made it happen.

We sat with our attorneys this morning who insisted on us signing a prenup, making Astor threaten his life if he suggested it again. We both signed the contract stating that in two months, if I weren't happy, I could leave. We also signed a contract saying that we wouldn't file for divorce until we'd been married for a year. Ever since then, Astor has been silent. He hasn't touched me or even acknowledged me. I signed because he did. If he had put up any ounce of a fight, I wouldn't have signed.

Because we're different. We're different from that night at the family dinner and we're different from how we have been over the last six years. We're happy and I feel like us again.

Our parents are sampling the appetizers for tomorrow,

something of which I truly do not care about. I care about getting to the bottom of why my soon to be husband feels miles away from me on the eve of our wedding. I sigh and push away from the table, walking out onto the balcony the restaurant has. It's a beautiful view that shows you almost all of New York.

How do I tell him that it's just a paper? That we didn't have to sign it and we can get rid of it?

"*Figlia*, everything ok?" I look up and see my father approaching me. I give him a small smile and turn back to the view.

"I think I did something. I feel like I did something, but I don't know what. He's been *off* for the last few days, since the incident at my party. But he was still himself in a sense, but since this morning; he's been cold." My father turns me to him, tucking my hair behind my ear.

"Sweetheart, Astor is battling loving you, and making you do what he says, and loving you, and letting you make decisions on your own. A man who has his amount of power…it's hard to let things just happen. It's hard to let something feel unknown." I'm dumbfounded, because all I can hear coming from my father's mouth is Astor loving me.

"Astor does *not* love me."

Does he?

He chuckles and then full on laughs.

"Alessia, that man loves you so much he'd put himself through emotional and destructive turmoil to keep you happy. Trust me, I was him with your mother; he may not have said it yet, but he loves you. And this two-month trial business is eating him alive."

"Yeah, or it's the secret that you, him, or anyone for that matter, will not bother telling me." He freezes and slowly turns away from me, heading for the door.

"Let me grab you a jacket, its cold out here," he says before ducking in the restaurant and out of the fucking conversation. I fold my arms and lean against the rails again. I am so over this shit. I should go in there and demand they tell me the truth or call off the wedding.

I'm talking myself up, heading for the door, when Astor slides it open and steps out onto the balcony.

He shuts the door and strides over to me, opening his arms for me to step into. I shake my head, but he takes his jacket off and wraps it around me.

"You've been so distant today...did I do something?"

He sighs and leans over the balcony. "Why'd you sign it, Alessia?"

"You signed, too..." I respond, leaning against the wall.

He turns to me and grunts, "We're getting married tomorrow. And the only thing I can think about is the fact that I need to enjoy it while I can, because my wife already doesn't want to be married to me." He goes to walk past me, but I grab his arm, yanking him to me.

"Astor..." I whisper, gathering my courage to make this confession. He needs to hear this and I need to say it. He's going to be my husband in less than twenty-four hours and I need to start acting like it. "I've wanted to marry you since we were kids."

He opens his mouth and I slam my lips against his, silencing him. I don't need him to respond, I just need him to listen. Today was a lot, and instead of spending it being excited, I spent it being scared that I did something to hurt him. I need him to feel how in this I am with him.

"You don't have to say anything, I just wanted you to know. We can call them, we can get rid of the contract, I don't care. I didn't want this at first, but I do now. I'm sorry."

"Fuck, Alessia," he moans into my mouth, pushing his way

in with his tongue. His hands tangle in my hair, our bodies mold together, and the kiss is full of need and reassurance. We're lost in each other so lost that we don't even hear the door when it slides open.

My father clears his throat and Caroline appears behind him, chuckling.

"Came to sweep the bride away, sorry. Say bye, she'll be all yours tomorrow," Caroline says, yanking me away. Astor groans and follows after us. I push away from Caroline and walk backwards to him. He engulfs me in his arms and walks us to her car. Justin and Teagan are there—it's still weird between us. Mainly because I want to understand why he disappeared and he can't tell me. I know him and Astor are close, and as angry as I am, I can't take it away from Astor to not have him at the wedding.

"Go easy on him," Astor whispers in my ear as Teagan walks to me. I give a small smile and nod.

"Lessia," he says, approaching.

"I didn't mean it, you know? Of course, you're still invited to the wedding. I'm still angry with you, but you're important to him." I nod my head upward toward Astor. "So you're important to me." Teagan gives me an appreciative smile before abandoning us and climbing in the car. Astor turns me to him and kisses my forehead.

"Thank you, little devil. See you tomorrow?"

"I don't know…I'm thinking I'll still run," I joke. He grits his teeth and I burst out in laughter. "Just kidding, baby. See you tomorrow."

"You called me *baby*. Don't tell me you're starting to fall in love with me, *malyshka*." I roll my eyes and give him a kiss so quickly he doesn't see it coming.

"Jesus Christ, she needs her beauty sleep. Goodbye," Caro says, stuffing me into the car.

She turns to me, her eyes full of suspicion, and she shakes her head.

"You've went and fell in love with the fucker." I put my head down to hide a smile, because fuck, she's right. I'm in love with the man that'll be my husband in less than twenty-four hours.

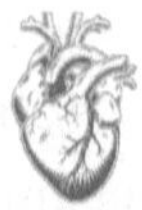

"Where is she?"

"You can't see her, it's bad luck," I hear Caro say to some-one. I step out of the bathroom because I know it has to be Astor.

"Caro, let him in. You know he's not going to leave."

"No, your mom and his would fucking murder me. You get married in four hours."

I nudge her and she throws her hands up before walking out of my room. Astor steps in and I smile at him.

"Hi." I say shyly. I'm in my robe, my hair is done in big, loose curls, and my makeup is perfect and natural.

"You look beautiful." I blush and look down until he tilts my face to his. "Can I kiss you?"

"You can do whatever you want," I reply. He walks closer to me and my feet feel like they are glued to the ground. I don't move an inch as he wraps his hand gently around the back of my neck and pulls me to him. He hovers his mouth over mine before planting a soft kiss on my lips. I moan in the satisfaction of feeling him after spending last night away from him. The whole night I listened to Caro talk about how good her speech was and how she couldn't wait to whoop everyone's ass in the bouquet toss. I missed him. I was so close to sneaking out to go home to him. Again, I don't know when he made me so dependent on him, but it's too late to stop it.

"I came to give you something." He reaches into his pocket and pulls out a small, black, velvet box. When he opens it, my eyes widen, flickering from him to the huge fucking ring staring back at me. "I never gave you an engagement ring." He takes it out and flips his palm out for me. I slide my hand into his as he slides the emerald cut ring onto my finger. I actually think my hand dropped at the weight of the thing; I don't even try to gauge the carats because I know I'd be drastically wrong.

"Astor...this is beautiful." He kisses me again and turns for the door, but I grab him.

"You have to let me leave, because if I don't, I'm going to fuck you over that balcony again."

"Promises, promises."

CHAPTER FORTY

ASTOR

She's challenging me. She knows I'll do it, so I'm not sure why she's pressing to see if I'm bluffing it. I'm on her in a second and I hope to fuck everyone is too busy to notice I'm gone. I had to sneak away when they were toasting to me, I'm sure Justin covered for me. And I'm sure Caroline wasted no time telling him how he failed at his one job of keeping me away from Alessia. A job that even he knew better than to attempt to do.

"Messing with fire, little devil."

"Then burn me," she says, pushing her chin up and walking backwards towards the balcony. I look down and smirk. It'd be impossible not to be seen here, but something tells me that's what my girl wants. These people are paid to unsee the shit they see, including me fucking my girl. I wrap my hand around her throat and she makes quick work of my sweats, pushing them down enough for my cock to spring out. It's cold as fuck outside, but my body feels on fire around her. I lift her and she instinctively wraps her legs around my waist, I take that moment to sink inside of her, causing her to scream

out. I chuckle when she covers her mouth with her hand. I pull out and slam back into her repeatedly as she tries to mask her screams. She fails miserably and lets out a moan so loud that I actually peek around her to see if anyone is watching. I make eye contact with a very pissed off Caroline and I wink at her, then push further into Alessia.

"Better hurry and come, your best friend just caught us and she looks pissed."

"Harder. Go harder," she pleads. And I do just that. Backing us into the room, I turn her to face the wall, bringing my hand down on her ass before fucking her from behind. I snake my hand around, pushing a finger into her pussy to bring her over the edge. She slams her hand against the wall and pushes against my fingers and my cock.

"Astor, Astor."

"Mm, you sound so fucking good screaming my name. Now come on my cock." She comes all over me, my dick soaked in her release when I pull out of her. My cum is leaking down her leg as she wobbles on her feet before I steady her. She tries to hide her smile when the door slings open. I stuff myself back into my sweats and kiss her forehead.

"Are you two fucking kidding me!! Look at your hair! Goddamn it, Alessia!"

I walk towards the door and stop, bending down to Caroline's ear.

"Stop fucking cursing at my wife." I pat her shoulder and make my way back to Ander's office, where the rest of the guys are getting dressed. I check the time.

Three hours before she's mine and eighteen before I kill the man who took her from me in the first place.

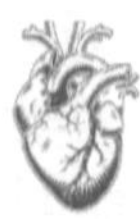

She's fucking beautiful, and at this moment, I feel like my airway is being constricted. I can't breathe, all I see is her. Her dress is perfect for her; it fits her like a glove and showcases every part of her, her tattoo peeking from her shoulder blade and the one on her wrist, but her sleeve is covered. I don't know why that bothers me, but it does. I want the real Alessia up here, tattoos and all. But as she gets closer, those thoughts quickly fade because my God, I thought she couldn't possibly make me fall for her more than I already am. I think of the time where I almost lost her, and I mean truly lost her for good, and I feel weak at that thought. The more I stare at her, the prouder I get seeing how strong she's become. She doesn't have a veil on, and I'm glad she doesn't, because the last thing I want is something covering her face as she walks down the aisle to me. My eyes are burning and my cheeks are wet.

Am I fucking crying?

I feel a hand on my shoulder and then a reassuring squeeze. Justin is next to me, and I realized when he clutches my shoulder again that I've begun to shake.

"Take a breath, here comes your wife." I close my eyes and force myself to breathe. Before I know it, she's standing before me. Ander kisses her on the cheek before handing her over to me.

He stops when I reach for her and leans into me. "Take care of her, Astor; she's yours, now."

She's always been mine. He knows it and I know it. Hell, our entire family knows it.

She slips her small hand in mine as I stare at her.

"You are absolutely breathtaking, *malyshka*." She smiles at me and gives my hand a tug. I look at the officiant and nod. He's talking, but I can't make out any of his words. All I can hear is the sound of Alessia's breath quickening. She's shaking and her eyes are watering. I mindlessly run my thumb over her fingers to calm her. "You ok?" I whisper and she nods her head at me. The officiant clears his throat and we both chuckle.

"Do you Astor, take Alessia to be your wife, in holy matrimony, for as long as you both shall live?"

"I do," I respond. Her breath hitches again and I fight the urge to tense as he reads the same thing out to her. Because in this moment, she could say she doesn't. She could run, she could decide that she wants a different life. She could decide that I'm not worth it, that *this* isn't worth it. I prepare myself for her answer; I prepare myself for the worse. I tell myself that even if she doesn't say yes, she's still mine, anyway.

She opens her mouth and I take a deep breath, willing myself not to close my eyes in fear.

"I do," she says, and I can't stop the tears that escape my eyes. She reaches up and wipes it.

"Astor, repeat after me," he says. I clear my throat taking a deep breath.

"I, Astor, take you, Alessia, to be my wife, to have and to hold, to love and to cherish, to respect and protect, from this day forward, until death do us part."

"I, Alessia, take you, Astor, to be my husband, to have and to hold, to love and to cherish, to respect and protect, from this day forward, until death do us part."

I'm kissing her before he even pronounces us husband and wife. Our family and friends are cheering, but still all I see, all I *feel* is her.

My *wife*.

Alessia is my wife.

CHAPTER FORTY-ONE
ALESSIA

I didn't expect to be as emotional as I was, and I certainly didn't expect Astor to be emotional. When he kissed me, it felt like a restart. It felt like the beginning to my happily ever after that I never knew I'd get. It felt like I was coming home, but it also felt familiar. Like I'd done it a million times before.

"I'm so proud of you, sweetheart. You both are perfect for each other," my mom says, pulling me in for a hug. Astor is talking with his parents and I realize just how big his smile is. It's contagious, because I can't stop smiling myself now. My mom looks at my gaze and smiles. He's walking over to me when he spots me, his smile growing wider, despite how big it already is.

"You were beautiful, Lessia," Teagan says, stepping in front of me. I peek over his shoulder as Astor moves towards me.

"Thank you and thank you for being here; for him." He nods, opening his arms to me for a hug. Before he can hug me, both of our heads snap towards the sudden screams that shriek from behind us. Astor is screaming my name and I feel the cold metal suddenly being pushed in my hand by Teagan. I look down at the gun before I'm being yanked down behind the table Astor and I were sitting at.

"Alessia!" Astor is beside me before I have a moment to wrap my head around the sounds I'm hearing.

"What the fuck is going on?" I scream as the sounds of bullets fly over my head. Astor is covering my head as Teagan peeks from around the table.

"There's five out there, I'll take one and two o'clock, you take five and six, Alessia; take four," he instructs.

I look at Astor and he looks at me with questioning eyes. I know they think I'm *sweet Alessia*. I know they think that the violent side of me is gone. But the truth is, the last few weeks my memory has been coming back with a vengeance. I still haven't put it all together, but what I do know is that my family? They are off fucking limits.

"I'm good!" I yell over the commotion. He nods, cocking his gun back.

"You better be. Teagan, now!" Astor yells. We all stand up and I see these men in suits. They blend in with the guests and I quickly wonder if they've been here the entire time, waiting for the perfect time to cause havoc at my wedding. Teagan shoots his men quickly, Astor following behind. My gun is raised, but it jams as I go to fire. My target notices, but so does Astor and Teagan. I don't panic, I'm surprisingly calm as I run towards the man, swiping a knife off one of the tables as I go. He's shocked; he doesn't expect it. Astor and Teagan are rushing to him from both sides and he freezes, not sure who to go for first.

He reaches out to swing on Astor, then Teagan, but he forgets me. As usual, always doubt the woman.

Big mistake.

I flip the knife around in my hand. When I reach him, Astor

and Teagan back off as I yank him by his head and ram my knee into his nose. My dress is tight, but I still have my range of motion—which Caroline said was a must and I'm glad I listened to her. Blood sprays his face and I ram my fist into his stomach, making him double over. When his knees hit the ground, I yank his head back by the roots of his hair, bending to his ear.

"You're ruining my fucking wedding." Then I ram the knife in the side of his neck; being sure to hit the right spot that'll make him bleed out. He grabs his neck, his hand hovering over the knife as he struggles to pull it out. He drops and I step over him. "Asshole," I grumble, reaching for another knife as we pass a table and head towards the entrance.

I see my father and Xavier telling the guards to keep all the guests in the corridor that's in the backyard.

"Alessia!" my father yells as he rushes up to me. He looks me over and I shrug him off.

"I'm fine, what the hell is going on?" He looks over his shoulder at Astor and I glance between them. "Miles? Right? That's his name? He's here?"

"Find him. Take her to the safe room and fucking find him. Send everyone home, get a body count of who the fuck these animals killed," Astor says to Teagan. I shake my head.

"Fuck that, I'm not running."

"Alessia?" I turn around to see Caroline at the entrance. She's holding her side and there's blood leaking from it.

"Caro!" I rush to her, stopping when I see the man from the bar, the man that apparently holds many secrets of life.

Miles.

"Hi, tornado," he says. My stomach feels sick.

Tornado? Why do I remember that? Why the fuck do I remember him?

Tornado.

"ALESSIA! ALESSIA! OPEN YOUR FUCKING EYES!" I JOLT MY EYES OPEN. I'm on the floor, pictures of Caro rush to my mind and I jump up.

"Caro. She was hurt..."

"She's fine. She's in surgery. You fainted."

"Miles, he was here. He called me..."

"Tornado," Astor says, pushing my hair out of my face. I nod and he lifts me.

"I've got her, secure this fucking place down," he says, walking me to my room. He sits me on my bed and forces my face to his. "You did good, baby girl."

"I did?"

"You did." He kisses me and I expect tears to fall, but instead I feel good. Like I'm on a high, like I never left.

"I need to get to Caroline."

"Justin is with her, he'll call after her surgery is over."

"Did anyone die?" He grinds his teeth and I know the answer before he speaks it.

"Yes, four people. Very important people to the mafia. Bad for Miles, good for us."

My eyebrows furrow and he rubs my hands that look so small in his.

"They want him dead."

"They know it wasn't us?" He nods at me and stands, shedding off his jacket. "You have to leave?"

"Just to your father's office. Come here." I stand, gathering my dress to stand before him. His eyes rake over my body and he pauses on the blood that's welted on my arm. I look down and shrug.

"It's just a scratch." I push my finger in my mouth and go to wipe it off when he grabs my hand. He bends down to my arm and runs his tongue over the clotted blood. It oozes a little and he laps it up again. He presses his lips against it before running his teeth across it. It's sore, but doesn't hurt much. A moan slips from my lips when a knock comes on from the door.

Astor swears under his breath before answering it.

"What?" he asks, yanking the door open to reveal our mothers. "Mom," he says, softening his voice. My mother pushes past him when she sees the blood on my dress and I shake my head before she gets ahead of herself.

"Mama, it's not my blood. I'm fine. Are you ok?"

"Yes, sweetheart. Your father and Xavier put us in the safe room the moment the gunshots went off. I was so worried about you; this is your wedding day, for Christ's sake." She starts crying and I brush the tears away from her face.

"It's ok, the wedding was perfect. They ruined my reception, but they didn't get the satisfaction of claiming my wedding."

"There's a lot of damage control to do. You're ok?" Astrid asks, peeking over at me. I nod and she smiles at me.

"Ellie, let's leave them to it and go clean this disaster up, shall we?" My mom nods and they leave the room. Astor's hand isn't even off the handle before another knock comes.

Fuck's sake.

"Boss, we're all clear. Followed him to an abandoned road, but they lost him. I'll have the report ready in thirty minutes."

"Send it to Ander, we're meeting in there. Make sure no one disturbs me for the next thirty minutes.

"Yes, sir." The door shuts and I watch Astor as he strips off his tie and starts unbuttoning his shirt. I smirk at him, running my tongue over my lips.

"You covered your tattoos," he says, running his eyes down my arm that holds my tattooed sleeve.

"Not all of them, just some. That bother you?"

"Come here, wife." My insides are on fire when he says that, because now it's true. I'm his wife.

"Yes?"

"Yes, what?"

I grin and tilt my chin up higher to face him.

"Yes, husband." He lets out a hmm in satisfaction before wrapping his hand possessively around my neck and yanking me to him.

"Say it again," he growls, nipping at my ear. I let out a moan before obliging and biting my lips.

"Husband."

CHAPTER FORTY-TWO
ASTOR

Husband.

I'm finally her husband. The day didn't end how we thought it would, but I'll be damn if Miles is going to stop me from fucking my wife for the first time.

I reach for the back of her dress, helping her out of it. She's the best thing I've done and I'll be damned if this night ends without me inside of her.

"On your knees, *wife*," I say as she steps out of her dress. She sinks to her knees and pushes my pants down, her eyes zoning in on my cock as it springs to her face. I smirk at her running my finger under her chin, tipping it up to face me.

"Eyes on me while I fuck this pretty face." She smirks as I run my cock across her lips before pushing it into her mouth. She never takes her eyes off me as I fuck her mouth harder and harder. She gags when it hits the back of her throat. I try to pull back, but she holds me there.

"Relax your jaws and take it all."

The moment she does, I force myself further down her throat. Her makeup runs down her face mixed with her salty tears. She cups my balls and I groan, willing myself not to explode so quickly in her mouth.

"Fuuuuuck, little devil, this fucking mouth." I tilt my head back when she takes me completely again. I push myself deeper and deeper, repeatedly. And she takes it, like always, my good fucking girl. I know I'm close, but the only place my cum is going is inside of her.

I yank her up and she gasps at the contact. I need to feel her, but I need to taste her first. I push her onto the bed, placing her legs on my shoulders. Her pussy is on display for me and I don't wait long before I glide my tongue through her folds. She's fucking drenched; it's the fuel I didn't know I needed before I dive in deeper.

"Astor..." she moans, digging her hands in my hair and tugging it. Her back arches as I plaster my face deeper into her pussy. I can't breathe, but I don't give a fuck about it. If this is how I died, I wouldn't give a shit. My wife coming on my face sounds like the way to fucking go.

I look up at her as her back arches more, my hand splayed across her stomach to keep her to my mouth. "Ast, I'm going to come."

"Mmm, good. We're going for three tonight. Let me have the first one, baby." That's all she needed—she's drenches me. The more she covers me in her juices, the more I try to suck it up.

I quickly climb over her and push her legs back, gliding myself inside of her mid-orgasm. She screams out as I fuck her mindlessly. She doesn't bother hiding her moans and I'm glad she doesn't. This wasn't the plan. I wanted to do this in the comfort of our own home. But my father made me promise to stay put until the place was cleared. She wraps her legs around me and I lift her, rushing her against the wall.

She looks down as my dick slides into her, she's just as

mesmerized as I am. Her mouth opens and I smirk at her as I slam into her. She leans her head back against the wall, her eyes closed, and I ram into her with vicious thrusts. I don't care who hears us as I fuck her as hard as I possibly can. She drags her nails down my back and I throw my head back. She's coming again and I silently pat myself on the back for getting her there so quickly.

"Harder. Fuck me harder," she begs.

This fucking woman.

I put her down and push her hands against the wall, palms flat.

"Give me one more."

My hand comes down on her ass and she screams. It comes down again and she groans. After the third slap, her ass turns red and I massage it away before my cock slams into her. She meets me thrust for thrust, taking every inch of me.

"That's right, take it. Take it all. Come on my cock, little devil."

"I can't, it's too much," she groans, but I keep up my pace, wrapping my hand around her to reach her pussy.

"You can and you will. Give me one more, *Mrs. Pavlov.*" The moment my fingers flick through her folds, she caves. I hold her up as her orgasm rips through her. My thrusts become staggered as I fill her with my cum. I run my tongue up her back and she leans into me as she catches her breath.

She turns to me as I slip out of her. I palm her face and kiss her gently. "I love you," I whisper out. She stops, and I mean she completely stops. She steps back and searches my face.

"What?" she asks.

I smirk at her. "I love you, *malyshka.* So much. I have loved you since we were kids. You are it for me. Our parents did something right, pushing us together."

"I love you, too, Astor."

I kiss her nose and she smiles at me.

"I have to meet our fathers, wait for me? Then we can go home."

"I want to get to Caroline, Ast."

"I know, your bag is in the bathroom. Change and I'll take you before we go, ok?"

She nods and I kiss her again, resting my forehead against hers.

"I'm sorry our wedding was ruined, little devil."

She shrugs and smirks. "Would it be us if we didn't have a bit of drama?"

I laugh and head to her father's office.

I need to see what fucking damage this piece of shit did.

CHAPTER FORTY-THREE
ALESSIA

I pick up my phone and call my girlfriends. I didn't get to see them much after I got ready for the wedding. After dinner, they must have thought I didn't see them sneak off with Mikhail and Jay.

"Lessia, are you ok?" River says, answering the phone. "FaceTime her," I hear Tess say in the back. "Hold on, we're FaceTiming."

Moments later, I see their faces.

"Where's Briar?" I ask.

"She stayed with Teagan. They're on the way." I raise my eyebrow and they laugh.

"Any updates on our girl? I'm changing and heading there now."

"It's your wedding night," River reminds me.

"My best friend got shot at my reception. I'll be there in forty-five minutes."

"You looked beautiful. I had my reservations at first, but the way he looks at you, he loves you so much. I'm so happy for you, ok?" she says.

"Riv, don't make me cry, ok? Please?"

"Seriously, bitches, no. Cut it out," Tess says, wiping her eyes. She nods at me as I hang the phone up.

I quickly change my clothes and head to my father's study. The door is closed, but there's still a crack there.

I can hear my father and Astor talking. I stop when I hear the name that clearly holds so many fucking secrets.

"He was here, Ander, at our fucking *wedding*. You said you had security watching every door. How did he get so close to her?"

"Miles is resourceful, I don't know. What's important is that she's safe."

"I'm telling her. You know how badly I've wanted to tell her. You aren't going to make me keep this shit from her. It's eating me alive."

"You won't tell her a goddamn thing," I hear my father say. I peek in and he's in Astor's face. Where the fuck is Xavier? Is this a good time for me to walk in? I decide against it, because I'm done with this.

"You signed a contract, Astor!"

"Fuck you and your contract. I was a fucking kid when I signed that. She's my wife. He fucking raped her! I'm not keeping this away from her!"

Raped. He raped me.

My breathing becomes ragged and I lean over, willing myself to breathe. I refuse to faint when I've finally gotten my answers. I take another deep breath and push the door open.

"That's why I could never stand for a man to touch me..." I whisper, walking in. Astor turns to me and my father freezes.

"Alessia, let me explain," Astor starts. I hold my hand up to him and walk around him, facing my father.

"How long has he wanted to tell me this?" My father

reaches for me, but I push his hands away, my voice getting louder. "Answer me! How fucking long?!"

"Since the moment you lost your memory." I suck in a breath and clutch my stomach. You're fucking kidding me. I can't believe this. This entire time, I've been thinking he just wouldn't tell me. But it was my father—my father was the problem. A *contract* was the problem.

Astor wraps his arm around my waist when the doors open again, and my mother and his parents walk in.

"What is going on?" my mother shrieks, walking towards me. Astor holds out his hand because there's no way I can speak right now.

"Eleanor, she knows. I'm getting her out of this house now," Astor says to her. Tears immediately fill her eyes, and for the first time, I don't give a fuck. I don't care that she's crying. I don't care that my father is white as a ghost. I don't care that Astor signed a contract and couldn't tell me. I just don't fucking care.

I have to get out of here.

"*Figlia*, you don't understand. Your therapist said to let you remember on your own," my mother pleads.

"My therapist?! I'm your fucking daughter!" I push away from Astor and storm out of the door.

I grab the keys to Caroline's car, not looking back when I hear Astor roaring my name throughout the house.

I ignore him, not knowing how to respond to him or how I feel with him in this moment. A hand wraps around my wrist and spins me around. And the moment I lay eyes on him, I know what I feel.

Anger.

"You don't get to touch me," I say to him. He frowns and steps back.

"*Malyshka*, I wanted to tell you. You have no fucking idea how badly I wanted to tell you."

"Then why didn't you? A contract? A fucking contract? We have the best fucking lawyers in New York and you couldn't get out of a fucking contract! He's my father! I could've talked to him!"

"Alessia, please. You don't understand. I was working on it. Trying to find him to bring him to you. I was going to tell you... I had to make sure you were strong enough. You weren't strong enough last time, you don't understand. You tried to....just please." he says, reaching for me again, but I step back.

"I tried to what Astor? Let me guess, more secrets. You could've told me but you didn't, ok? You didn't. I can't be around you right now. Don't follow me, Astor."

"Alessia, it's our wedding night."

"Yeah, and you should thank God that I didn't find this out *before* the wedding." He frowns at my words.

"What does that mean?"

I shake my head at him and I head to the car, ignoring his footsteps behind me.

"What does that mean, Alessia!" I climb into the car and he grabs the door, stopping me.

"Look at me. I love you. I'm sorry; but you aren't leaving this marriage. I will fight you tooth and fucking nail. You aren't going anywhere, do you understand? I'm not losing you again."

"Move. Ast, please." He backs up and I slam the door before pulling out.

I don't know how my wedding day turned from this magical fucking thing to a complete warzone. Fuck this night.

I need to see my best friend.

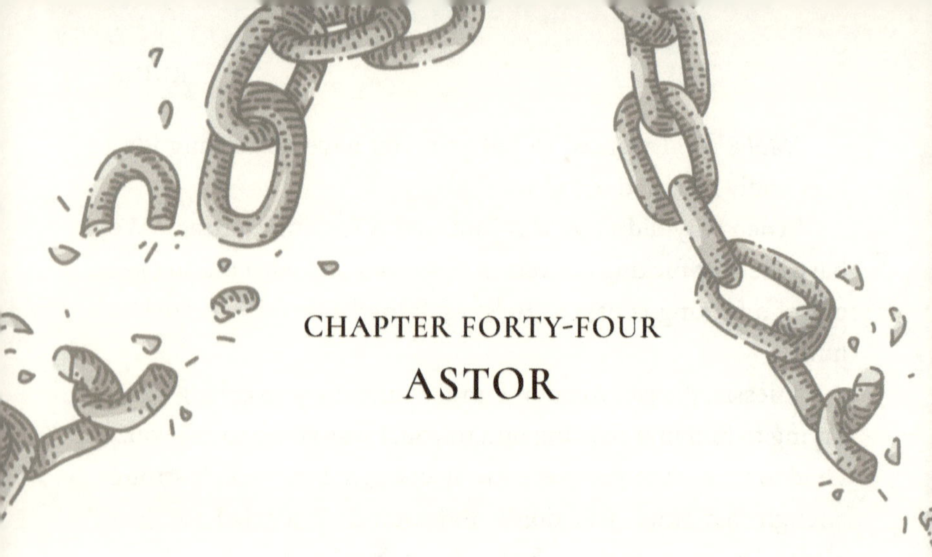

CHAPTER FORTY-FOUR
ASTOR

I'm in my car heading to the hospital when my phone rings.

"Just, she ok? Surgery go well?"

"Yeah, she's been awake for about an hour. That's not why I called." My teeth automatically start grinding and he sighs.

"Alessia is here and she's a mess, man. A fucking mess. The girls are in the room with Caro, but I heard them talking. How the fuck does she know?"

"She overheard her father and I talking. It was a shitshow, a fucking disaster. I'm parking, man, I'll be up in a bit."

He hangs up and I look at myself in the rearview mirror. My eyes are bloodshot red and I'm still in my tux.

I meant what I said to her—she's not leaving this marriage. I'll chain her until she gets over it, but she isn't fucking going anywhere.

I wish on every fucking level that I could've told her before she found out that way.

The waiting room is full of my friends waiting with Justin.

It's a private floor, what we always use when one of us gets hurt. We never use real names and we're never listed in the hospital's computers.

"Ast. What the fuck happened?" Teagan asks me when he spots me. I shake my head and take the seat next to him.

"Her fucking father—that's what happened. It's been a goddamn night. You good, though?"

"Yeah, nothing we couldn't handle. Somehow, though, Mikhail and little Jay here got the girls to *comfort* them." I chuckle and Justin all out laughs when Mikhail curses under his breath. I wish I could say it surprises me, but it doesn't. I knew at some point we all would meet our matches, I just didn't expect it to be my wife's entire friend group.

My wife. My *wife*.

I look up at the door and stand. All of them watch me as I step towards the room.

"Good luck," Jay says before smirking. I give him the finger and take a deep breath. This isn't about us right now; I want to check on Caroline.

When I step into the room, all of the girls cease their conversation.

Briar coughs when Alessia doesn't notice me. She looks at me and shakes her head.

"Caroline, how are you feeling?" I ask, walking to her bed. She smirks at me and nods to the chair next to her.

"Bitches, give us a second." Alessia frowns and looks confused on what to do.

"You, too, Les. I need to talk to him." Alessia shrugs and walks out without giving me a second look.

When the room is clear, she turns to me and I sigh.

"You sure you're ok?"

"Yeah, missed anything vital. We're all clear. I'm getting out of here in a couple of days...So...she knows. And you're still alive. And a contract? Come on, Astor, a goddamn *contract* is what stopped you? Justin didn't tell me that part."

"Yeah, she knows about the contract. She knows how badly I wanted to tell her, but she's pissed. She insinuated we wouldn't have gotten married if she knew beforehand. That I should be *glad* she didn't know before the wedding."

"I know. But listen to me, the only reason *I've* kept it to myself when Justin told me it is because I knew you wouldn't stand a chance. She won't leave you, but she won't give in easily, either. She doesn't know that I knew before—I don't have the heart to tell her that. But she's pissed, Astor. And sounds like she's going on a rampage."

"What do you mean?"

"She's going after him. And she'll need you. I haven't seen her this way in a long time. She's dark, unforgiving, and fucking angry. Help her. Be there for her, and most of all, fucking fight for her."

Fuck.

I lean over and kiss her forehead.

"I've got her. I promise. Get better soon, Justin is beside himself."

"He's a pussy. Send him in here." She winks at me and I nod as I walk back out to the lobby. Confusion surrounds me when I don't see Alessia.

"Where'd she go?" I ask River. She looks at the ground and I snap at her, "Answer me."

"She left. Said she needed to take care of something."

"Goddamn it!" I punch the wall and head for the stairs, not surprised when I hear my boys following behind me. I turn and stop Justin, pointing to Caroline's room. "She wants you. You stay. I'll call later."

"Fuck that. I'm with you."

"No, you're with *her.*"

We all file into the car quickly. I call Alessia's phone over and over again with no answer. I know if I don't get to her quickly, this won't end well.

At all.

After the eighth unanswered phone call, I call her father, who answers on the first ring.

"Astor."

"She's gone. She left the hospital and she isn't answering her phone."

"You don't have a fucking tracker on her phone? Did we not teach you anything?"

"*I do have one.* Her phone is off and she's not wearing the fucking necklace yet."

"Why not?"

"It was a goddamn wedding present! If you aren't going to help, get off my fucking line, Ander." I hang the phone up and call Justin.

"Just, you have a tracker on Caroline's car?"

"Of course I do. Alessia in it?"

"Yes, where the fuck is she?"

"Hold on." I hear him pressing buttons on his phone, and a moment later, he chuckles. "Ast, she's home."

Home. You're fucking kidding me.

CHAPTER FORTY-FIVE

ALESSIA

As angry as I am, I know I can't go after anyone until I remember everything. My mother's words are replaying in my head, of her saying my therapist said to let me remember on my own. But the harder I think, the more I start to believe that the memories never left. That I buried them and made them think I'd forgotten. I remember being this *tornado* as Miles called me. I remember Teagan and Astor calling me that, too. I remember them saying that anytime something happened, especially to our families, that I destroyed anything in my path. I remember being violent and not knowing boundaries. I lacked self-control, the ability to stop myself when it was over. I remember Astor being the one to always reel me back in. I was a loose canon and I was only sixteen. I was on a level of self-destruction. I'm not going after anyone until I can control that.

I'm getting out of the shower when I hear the front door shut and voices. I know it's Astor, but I'm not sure who it is with him. I throw on a pair of sleeping shorts and a tank top, instead of one of Astor's shirts. I don't want to smell him. I won't be able to help myself if I'm in his shirt.

I walk downstairs to grab a bottle of water and Mikhail spots me first. He glances at Astor while Jay elbows Teagan.

I ignore them, every last one of them. I grab my water and head back for the stairs. Astor is on my heels immediately.

I walk past our room and head towards the guest room when he places his hands on my shoulders, guiding me back to our room instead.

"The boys are staying here tonight. You no longer sleep anywhere but next to me."

I ignore him, stepping inside the bedroom. He shuts the door and leans against it, running his hand up and down his tux pants.

"Do you need something?" I inquire, flipping the cover to the comforter back.

"You came home."

"It's twelve in the morning, where else would I go?" I mumble. He walks towards me and I hold my hand out. "Don't. Just please, don't. I don't want to see you, Ast. I don't want to talk to you."

"Alessia, look. You're pissed, I get it. I'd be pissed, too. You were robbed of memories. You were violated. I can't imagine what you are thinking right now. I want to kill him. I truly want to kill him, but don't run from me. Let me fight this with you. Let me help you."

"I bled. I don't understand. How did he rape me if I bled when we..." I shake my head and crawl into the bed. He kneels in front of me, his eyes filled with unshed tears.

"The doctor said it's possible your hymen wasn't broken. I got there quickly the moment I heard you scream.."

"I want to sleep. Let me, please." My head is spinning at

what he's saying, I feel dizzy and just want it to stop. I close my eyes, only opening them when I hear the door shut.

Sleep, Alessia. Sleep. Don't think about the fucking phone call you got just a few minutes ago.

From your rapist.

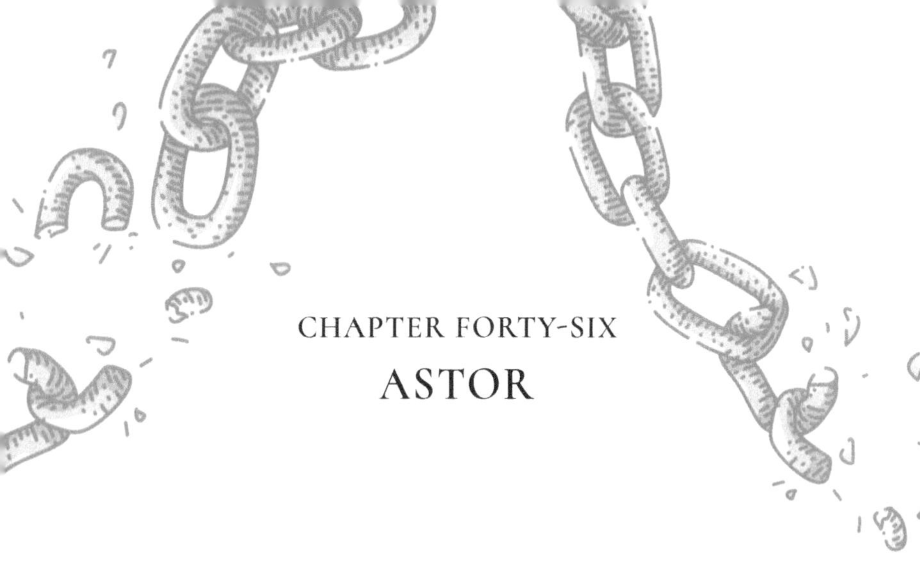

CHAPTER FORTY-SIX

ASTOR

I roll over to see Alessia sitting up, her hair in a bun on top of her head. When I finally calmed myself enough to sleep, it was around 3:00 a.m. The guys and I planned on how we were going to help her get this piece of shit. There was no way I was losing my wife to that waste of fucking space.

"*Malyshka*?" I whisper, sitting up next to her. "What are you doing?"

"It was the Fourth of July...I left my door open for you." My head spins as she tells me word for word what happened that day.

"He told me choosing you was wrong, that he was the better guy. That we fit better. I fought him, but he was stronger...I screamed. I knew you'd hear me." She pauses and turns to me, her eyes dazed. It's like she's not here. Like she's an empty tomb of herself.

"You almost killed him, but someone stopped you. Who stopped you?"

I sigh and run my hands through my hair.

"My father. He stopped me."

"We were together, I was yours. And I forgot...I forgot you. I forgot us," she whispers. "That's what you meant, when you said you couldn't lose me again..."

"Yes."

"I'm...sorry," she says in a rush. She rubs her eyes and throws the covers back before climbing out and heading to the bathroom. I hop up to follow, but she closes the door in my face. I slide down the door and wait there, my arms resting on my knees.

She remembers. She finally fucking remembers.

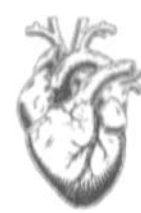

ALESSIA HAS BEEN COLD, ABSENT. IT'S LIKE SHE DOESN'T SEE ME OR doesn't care to see me. She won't let me touch her and she won't talk to me. She's been ignoring her parents' phone calls for the last three days and ignoring everyone's texts except for her girlfriends.

I thought the night she got her memories back she'd talk to me. She'd forgive me for not telling her. But the next day, she completely disappeared, spending the entire day at the hospital with Caroline. When she came home that night, she ignored me and went straight to bed. The next day she did the same thing; helped Caroline get settled, came home at 2:00 a.m., and went to sleep, again, as if I didn't exist.

Well tonight, I'm pressing buttons. I don't give a shit; she's going to see me. She's going to talk to me. And the only way I know how to do that is to get her mad.

So here I am, in the kitchen with Anna standing in front of me in a flimsy, red dress that displays her breasts on full effect.

She leans over the counter, her hand out to touch me when the door opens.

Alessia steps in the door, her face stone. Anna yanks her hand back and quickly straightens, rounding the island to stand behind me. I cringe at how close she is and take a half step back.

Alessia stops and tilts her head at us, eyeing Anna. I expect her to lose her shit, I expect her to react. What I don't expect is her rounding the island, pulling open the fridge, grabbing a water, and walking up the stairs as if she truly doesn't care.

Fuck.

Anna perks up and turns to me, running her hand down my arm.

I snap.

I wrap my hand around her neck and drag her to the door. "Go home."

"But Astor," she pleads, confused.

I slam the door in her face, locking it and calling security.

"Get her the fuck off my property and never let her come back."

I quickly fix myself a drink, hoping the amber liquid will do the trick.

It doesn't.

I sling the glass across the island, watching the shards of glass spread everywhere.

I push my hands through my hair and count to ten, calming myself down.

"Alessia!" I bellow as I climb the stairs. When I push open the door, she's in our bed with her phone in her hand. She looks up at me as I walk in.

I'm angry. Too fucking angry.

"Girlfriend gone already?" she asks, looking back down at her phone. I push my hands through my hair as I walk to her and yank her phone out of her hands. She stares at me, her face blank, but her eyes dark. I pull her up and throw her against the wall.

"I don't have a girlfriend; I have a fucking *wife*. Stop this shit. *Three days*, Alessia. You haven't talked to me in three goddamn days. Not a look, not even a fucking glance. I've been doing everything I can to find this asshole so you can do *whatever* you feel is needed. I could do that better if I knew we were ok. I could do it better if you communicated with me. If you'd answer my fucking texts and phone calls throughout the day."

"I don't want to talk to anyone."

"I'm not anyone. I'm your fucking husband!" I slam my fist into the wall next to her and she watches my movements as I pace our bedroom floor. Only then do I see the bag that's by the door. I stop when I see it and look at her. "You aren't leaving."

"Nope. You are," she says, pushing her hair back. "I can't think when I'm around you. I can't process my feelings, my fucking emotions. I just found out I was raped and everyone around me hid it from me for six years. Including you! And you know what I thought about? How will that make *Astor* feel, how will *Astor* move on, how will *Astor* see me now that I know. It wasn't about me. It wasn't about getting revenge. It was about YOU!"

"*Malyshka*...I'll sleep in another room, but the chances of me leaving you in this house alone is slim to fucking none. Get that thought out of that gorgeous head of yours. And let me answer that for you: I lived it. I *never* forgot it. I pushed you away because I couldn't stomach being around you knowing I didn't get there in time. It was pure fucking torture being around you. I couldn't deal with him still being alive. I couldn't fucking deal with you not remembering us! I couldn't fucking deal with it; I didn't know how to! That fucking day replayed in my head every day for as long as I can remember. It made me hate that our relationship wasn't strong enough for you to remember us, to remember me fighting for you that day. It's always been about you."

"Ast, I'm still angry with you. I'm sorry, but don't rush me. I didn't run from you, I didn't leave you. I stayed when all I wanted to do was block everyone out."

I walk up to her and she inhales as I run my thumb across her cheek. I lean down and kiss her forehead.

"I'm here, ok? I'm here. Be angry, just be angry and talk to me."

CHAPTER FORTY-SEVEN
ALESSIA

Now that my memories are back, it's all I see every time I close my eyes. I see Miles and then I see Astor. I can't figure out why I'm so focused on Astor from that day. I also can't figure out why I'm so pissed, but every day that passes, it's not at him. It's at my parents and myself. Myself because for the last six years, I let myself believe that it was in my head. I let myself believe that I wasn't missing anything. I always knew something was wrong, that pieces were missing. Of my life. Of whom I was. I'm pissed at my parents because they honestly thought keeping this away from me was a smart thing to do.

When I wake up today, I feel better. My mind feels clearer and I feel ready to get the answers I want. Starting with the list of people who are going to pay for letting this asshole get away with this.

I slept more last night than I had the last couple of nights. Talking to Astor did help, but I still hate how my body chooses to react to him.

When he slammed against the wall, I wanted to tear his

clothes off him. I wanted him to fuck me so hard that I forgot about the shitty past week I'd had.

Before I realize it, my hand is mindlessly traveling under the covers to my pussy. I dip a finger in, gasping when it's soaked. Shaking my head at myself, I yank it away and flip the covers back.

The shower wakes me up. I take a little longer than normal to wash my hair and let myself have a moment.

Again, that day flashes in front of me.

Astor can't handle you, tornado.
I saw you two together, you looked unsatisfied.
I knew you wanted me, that why this door is open?

I already know he's going to die. The moment I found out what he did to me I had already made that decision. But I want it to be calculated. I want my mind to be clear. I want him to know I'm coming and that there's nothing he can do about it.

And I know just how to do that and just who to help me do it.

My husband.

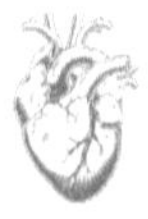

When my bare feet reach the bottom of the staircase, I can hear the TV on. I peek over on the couch and see Astor still sleeping. I watch him for a moment, taking in his face. He looks tired, stressed. There's a furrow in his brow and his hands are in fists on either side of him. He shivers a bit and I grab the blanket off the back of the couch, gently covering him. I know I'm putting him through the wringer, I know he's worried about me, but I need to take it at my own pace. I need to let him back in at my own pace.

I push his hair out of his face and his eyes jerk open in a startle, grabbing my hand.

"It's just me. Go back to sleep," I mutter to him. He entwines our fingers and his breathing slows again. I look down at our conjoined hands and sigh when I look back at him. He's sound asleep again.

I slowly untangle my hand from his, grabbing my jacket and the keys as I leave to head to Caroline's.

My phone rings almost immediately. When I look down, I see it's my mother. I sigh to myself, deciding today everyone gets their one chance to explain to me why the fuck they hide the last six years from me.

"Hello?" I answer.

"Alessia, you answered," she responds quickly.

"I did. What is it?"

"I...I wanted to check on you. It's been a few days and I couldn't get in touch with you."

"I didn't want to talk, Mom."

"Can I tell you my side?" I sigh, but stay silent as she starts to speak. "You were sixteen. You had just finished your training with your father and everyone was starting to notice you. Men, of all ages. It was hard for me, hard for me to protect you from everyone. You and Astor had been close. We always knew it'd be you two together, but Miles' father had become close with Ander and Xavier. And with that, Miles started coming around, too. You were closed off, usually. Your training made you *dark*. Ruthless, even, but for some reason, you allowed Miles in your friend circle. That day, I felt off around him. I kept seeing him look at you when he thought no one was looking, so I stayed close. Your father and the others were in his office drinking and I had stepped out for a second, taking a phone call. A damn phone call. I didn't hear you scream. I failed you that day. I felt something was off and I didn't say anything. My little girl was taken from me that day because I didn't say what I knew. That he was always after you. I can't apologize enough. I got you in therapy immediately and I wanted to tell you, but when I started to tell you scraps of that day, you'd relapse and stop talking again. We tried letting Astor tell you, but it was worse. Your therapist thought it's because he saw you in that moment. So, she told us it would be best to let you remember on your own. She said that when you were strong enough to handle it, that you'd remember. But we wanted to tell you, ok? I fought and fought with your father for making them sign those contracts. I hated him for so long for it."

"How'd you stop? Hating him, I mean."

"*Figlia*, he carried the guilt every day. And every day that passed, I saw how much it haunted him even more. I decided he was hating himself enough for all of us. I let it go and I chose to try the therapist's way. Even when I saw how you reacted if you were touched by any boyfriend or date you'd have. This secret has been over our heads for six years. I know you're blaming Astor for not telling you, and I know you're upset with your father and me for that matter, but he's your husband. You need him and he needs you. Stay mad at us, if that's what you need to do, but don't make him suffer. He stopped by last night and it's tearing him apart."

I swipe at the tear that slides down my face, gathering my thoughts together. Because that part of my memory was still missing. I kept wondering where my parents were. How'd no one notice me missing? How'd no one see him following me.

"Alessia, you still there?"

"I'm here, I'm sorry. I don't want you to think it was your

fault. It wasn't. If he was truly after me, it would've happened another day, if not that day. I forgive you, Mama, I do. But I can't forgive Dad. He made Astor sign a contract. He made me believe he *hated* me for six years."

"He's your father...you have to try. For me, please try."

"I'll try, but I'm not ready to see him."

"And Astor?"

"He's my husband, Mom. And besides, I can't leave him, anyway. I signed a contract, remember?"

"You love him?"

"It's the only reason I'm still there, Mom."

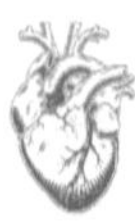

WHEN I GET TO CAROLINE'S, I FEEL….GOOD. MY MOM GAVE ME THE last piece I needed. I can't forgive my father so soon and I'm still not ready to see him. But I can begin to put the pieces back together.

I pull up next to Justin's car and use my key to let me into Caroline's place. It's quiet, so I guess they're still sleeping, but that's about to change.

I push the door open to her room and they're both sleeping. I chuckle and round to Caro's side.

"Bitch, slide over and let me in." She cracks her eye open and groans before sliding over. "How are you feeling?"

"Alessia? Why are you in this bed?" Justin asks, sitting up on his elbows. I look over at him and shrug.

"Get out, Justin. I need my best friend. How about you go be with yours?"

"Don't you have three others that you can climb into bed with? Preferably not the one that is healing from being shot?"

"Justin, go. Take Ast some breakfast or something," Caroline says. He shakes his head and laughs, giving her a kiss and flipping me off as he climbs out of bed. Caroline turns to face me and raises her eyebrows.

"Now, seriously, why are you in my bed this early?"

"I almost masturbated this morning," I say, turning over onto my back and looking up at her ceiling. She makes a gagging noise and I scowl her. "You overshare all the time," I remind her.

"Why does it matter if you did or not?" she asks.

"Because it was to Astor."

"So? He's your husband."

"But I'm mad at him."

"And you fucked him when you so called *hated* him. Who cares? Also, you're not mad at *him*. You're just mad."

"Actually, I don't think I am anymore. I woke up feeling better. I talked to my mom, got some clarity." My phone rings and I pull it out of my pocket to see Astor's name on the screen. I look at Caro and she nudges me. "Come on, you were gonna use him for pleasure this morning, at least answer." She laughs as she rolls over to her side, groaning in pain a little.

"Hi," I say. He clears his throat and I can tell when he responds that he's just woken up. His voice is raspy and still sounds tired.

"You were gone when I woke up."

"I'm at Caro's." There's silence on the other end and I know what he wants to ask, but I also know he's trying to give me the space I need. "I'm coming back, just wanted to see her."

"Can we have lunch today?" Caro says, nudging in the conversation. I give her a major side eye and she shrugs, snatching the phone out of my hand and putting it on speaker. "Astor! Yoohoo, it's me, the person that got shot at your wedding. I want to have lunch today. Bring me the best or don't come at all. You can get your wife back after."

"Caroline, you sound well," he says, chuckling.

"I'm as well as I can be." She slowly throws her legs over the side of the bed and I jump up to help her up. She swats me away and sticks her tongue out at me. "I'm going for a shower; Justin is still here. He'll help." She winks at me and I gently shove her as she laughs. I pick up the phone and put it to my ear.

"Sorry about that."

"Are you ok with lunch?" I roll my lips together and sigh.

"Yes, I'm ok with it." He sighs and the line is quiet.

"I..." He stops again and clears his throat before speaking, "I love you, *malyshka*."

"See you soon, Ast," I say, hanging the phone up with a sly smile.

"He ok?" Justin asks, stuffing his arms into a hoodie.

"Yeah. I guess so?"

"Lessia, you have to talk to him. Last night was...rough."

At this point, I'm intrigued.

"What happened last night?"

"He searched for Miles for hours, he was fucking ruthless. We were with him; we couldn't stop him. He wasn't in control, and we know if there's one thing Astor always has, it's his control. He went to your parents and let your father have it. They assumed he was drunk, he wasn't. He didn't have a drop of alcohol last night. He didn't want to miss anything. He refused to go home because you weren't talking to him. Because you wouldn't let him touch you. Something about you saying you need space. You know, this isn't my place at all, but Alessia, if I were in his shoes and it was Caroline, I don't know how I'd handle it alone. This shit with Caro just started, and if I'm murderous over someone I've been with for a brief time, how the fuck do you think he feels over someone he's been in love with since he was kid?"

I sigh, grabbing my coat and keys.

"And check his hand."

"His hand?" I ask, glancing at Justin.

He nods. "He...had an eventful night."

I shake my head and kiss his cheek. "Tell Caro I'll see her at lunch. I guess you, too."

CHAPTER FORTY-EIGHT

ASTOR

A shower is exactly what I need. Last night took a toll on me. I'm losing my footing here and I feel like I'm still losing her. Three bodies last night and still no information about where Miles is. He's radio silent, *again*.

I'm about to shower when the front door opens and Alessia walks in. Her face is hard to read and I don't like it. I can always read her, even when she hides it from everyone else.

"Let me see your hand," she says, stalking up to me. I frown and she yanks it, staring down at the cut. "What'd you do?"

"I'm fine."

"Astor...what did you do!"

"I'm trying to find him for you...it just got out of hand, one of his guys cut me. I'm fine."

"You need stitches, I'm sure." I smirk and she shakes her head. "No."

"Why? It was a part of our training, you know how." She sighs and throws her bag down, raising her eyebrows at me.

"Where's the stuff?" she questions. I walk into the kitchen and pull out the emergency medical bag.

She grabs it and starts setting up on the kitchen table. She grabs my hand and inspects it. The cut is deep, I knew that, but I wasn't going to say anything. I got it to stop bleeding, so it's probably not a big deal, but I'll take any reason at this point for Alessia to touch me.

"It's going to hurt. I'm not sorry about it," she says, smirking. She starts cleaning it and it stings, but I show no reaction. I watch her and I know by her tongue dashing out that she's zoned in. She preps the needle and string, getting to work.

"You know, if you're going to go after my rapist, you could've taken me," she says after finishing up the first stitch. I will myself to breathe when she sticks the needle back into my punctured skin. "Ok?" she says, stopping and peeking up at me.

I nod. "I didn't want to bother you. I had to find him first."

"Did you?"

"Not yet." She ties off another stitch and starts the last few.

"Good, we'll find him together." I raise my eyebrow and she quickly finishes off the stitches. "And everyone else who helped cover this disgusting fucking secret."

"As you wish, little devil," I say, pulling my hand back and grabbing the gauze. She stops me and wraps it around.

"Be careful next time, ok?" She stands, leaving me to clean the mess up as she retreats upstairs.

I quickly clean it all up when my phone rings.

"You told her about my hand?" I ask.

"She fix it up for you?" I shake my head at his logic, he was trying to help. He was worried last night. I told him he didn't need to leave Caroline to come with us. I had the guys; Mikhail and Jay were there. Teagan was more worried about Alessia and took watch on the house.

"Fucking stupid. What do you want?"

"I think we found him. PI said they thought they saw him at his father's office around 4:00 a.m."

"We checked there," I tell him as I walk up the stairs. Alessia is shedding her shirt, making eye contact with me when I walk in. I tilt my head at her, taking her in, and she rolls her eyes.

"Apparently, there's multiples."

When I walk towards the bathroom, she holds her finger up to me. I stop and sit on the side of the bed. I put the phone on speaker and sit it next to me, muting it.

She goes to close the door and I chuckle.

"Alessia, do not close that door. Finish undressing."

"You don't get to see me."

"You're my wife. Yes, I do."

"True enough, but you definitely don't get to touch."

"Then I won't. But I will watch you touch yourself. Look in the mirror, now." She shakes her head and I raise my eyebrow.

"Now, Alessia." Justin is talking about something. I don't know what it is, but I truly don't care either. Because when Alessia hooks her hand in her panties and yanks them down, I groan. "Bra, off."

She stutters for a moment, fighting with herself on whether she should listen or not. But after a few moments, she snakes her hand backwards and unclasps her bra. I stand and walk over to the door, thinking she would stop me again. But when she doesn't, I stand behind her and direct her to the mirror.

"I don't have to touch you for you to get off, little devil." Justin is still on the phone, and at this point, I'm tempted to just hang up because I haven't heard a thing he's said in the last few minutes, anyway.

Alessia stares at us through the mirror and I put her hand on her chest, gliding it down and back up. She yanks her fingers away from my grip and goes back to tug on her nipple, causing herself to groan. My cock is at attention already, but I know she's still too angry or confused to actually let me touch her.

"Play with yourself and do exactly as I tell you. Understand?" I whisper in her ear. She nods relentlessly as I step back and lean against the wall to watch my masterpiece make herself fall apart. Her gaze follows me to the wall and I shake my head.

"Watch yourself. Not me. I'm not here, just use my voice." Her eyes slam back to the mirror and her cheeks flush when she watches herself. She's never done this before and I'm glad. She and I watch as her hands travel and caress over her body. Her head tilts back and her lips part as she holds back a moan. "Stick your fingers in your mouth and soak them."

She pops her fingers in and when they come out, they are shining with her saliva. "Show me," I grit out and she holds her fingers up for me to see. "Now, show me how wet you are." She slips a finger through her pussy folds and moans, before showing me again. "Do it again, but with two fingers. Push them deep inside." She does what she's told and my hands are moving before my brain can catch up. I pull my cock out and slide my hand over my length as I watch her. "That's right, little devil, push them in and out. Be a good girl and add a third finger. You can take it, I know you can." She's panting as she pushes a third finger inside of herself, working her pussy slowly. "Fuck yourself faster. Isn't that how you like me to do it? Fast?" She moans loudly when her speed picks up; just like I knew she would. My girl likes it fast; she likes it rough. I'm jerking my cock harder and harder as she milks herself.

When her eyes close and her fingers started stuttering, I force myself to keep my load down.

"Don't you fucking come yet. We aren't done. Take your fingers out."

"Astor...please. Let me," she begs. Her fingers are still buried deep inside of her, but her movements have stopped.

"You come when I say *come*, understand?"

"Yes, tell me to keep going. Please, I need to keep going." She's panting and I give in.

"Keep going, fast and hard. Don't hold back." Her fingers work eagerly, she's chasing her orgasm like I've been chasing her. I'm so close to coming from watching her that I truly think my dick will fall off with how hard I'm squeezing it. Her arms start shaking first and she tucks her lip. "Watch yourself come. Watch what my voice does to you. Then I want you to turn around and watch what watching you does to me."

Her face turns red and she explodes all over her hand. She's drenched. Her orgasm rips through her so hard that she starts skipping breaths. The moment she's done, her eyes snap to mine as I pump my cock harder and harder. Her stare intensifies and that makes me go harder. This is what she does to me. She's the only one that I'll let make me resort to jacking myself off like a fucking teenager.

Her gaze never changes as my load drops all over my hand. I grunt as my release doubles me over. Her lip tips up a fraction and then she steps into the shower, leaving me there covered in my own fucking cum.

She looks over her shoulder and smirks at me.

"Justin, I'll call you back."

CHAPTER FORTY-NINE

ALESSIA

I guess Caroline was right, I can use Astor to get myself off. And my God, did he get me off. I still hate that he has that power over me. I hate that even his voice can take me there. Watching myself was something I never thought I'd do; it was fucking hot. I looked fucking hot, and when I saw him with his cock in his hand, I thought I'd come all over again. Who knew watching a man jack himself off could be so arousing?

I know he expected me to invite him into the shower, but when he started stripping out of his clothes, I shook my head at him and he groaned.

His eyes were on me so hard when I got out of the shower that I struggled to hold my smirk back.

Alessia: 1

Astor: 0

I check the clock as I yawn, grabbing one of his shirts out of habit. I stop and shake my head before putting it back in the drawer and grabbing one of my own. Smelling him is not a good idea right now. I'm still not ready to let him know that

I'm not mad at him. Seeing him so attentive and on edge is making me feel more powerful than I should. That sounds so fucked up, but I feel more empowered when he's mopping around for my forgiveness and attention.

I decided when I spoke to my mother that she's right—if she can forgive my father, I can forgive Astor for keeping a secret that he felt he had no choice but to keep. I can choose to respect the fact that he wanted to tell me and just couldn't. But when I do finally put him out of his misery, he needs to understand that if he keeps anything else from me, we're done. I don't care what his intentions were or why he kept it from me, but we won't live our lives keeping secrets from each other.

I'm about to lay my head down when I hear the front gate buzzer. Usually, I ignore it; because if they're allowed in, then the guards push them through. But when I hear it go off for a fourth time, I decide to pull the live feed up on my screen and see what the issue was.

I smirk. Not *what* the issue is but *who* the issue is. I hover over the green light on my phone, pressing it and watching the car drive in.

"It's fine. I'll handle it," I tell the guard through the speaker. It's the one I hit in the dick. Terrible way to be remembered, but it works.

I peek into the bathroom and Astor is still showering. This is the perfect time for me to test my limits. The perfect time for me to see if I have the control I want and need before going after Miles.

I look down at myself and change into one of Astor's shirts, because why the fuck not? With what I'm planning to do, I need to make every rule clear. Every boundary understood.

I'm happy with myself by the time I open the front door to let my guest in. I'm happy with myself when my guest's smile drops the moment their eyes land on me. I'm happy with myself when I draw my fist back and slam it into their face. And I'm especially happy with myself when I don't use the knife laying on the counter to slit their fucking throat.

"Hi, Anna. I was hoping you'd come back to visit," I say, getting eye level with her.

"You crazy bitch, you broke my nose! Do you have any goddamn idea how much this cost?"

"Ahh, tsk tsk. I don't give a fuck. What I *do* give a fuck about is why, after I clearly told you to stay away from Astor, you decided to come back. I also care about the fact that you touched him, *again*. And my personal favorite that I care about, is how you even came back when he kick you the fuck out and told you not to show your face here again."

"You don't know him; you'll never make him happy." I look down at my hand, suddenly upset that I took my ring off on our wedding night. I was so upset that I abandoned it. I laid it on the counter and saw his face when he picked it up later that night. I never asked for it back, just watched where he put it for when I was ready for it. But in this moment, I feel naked, like I left him. Like I let him down. All of the emotions hit me at once. But I don't dare show it on my face. Instead, I swipe the blade off the kitchen counter, grab one of the kitchen stools, and slam her in it before dropping in front of her and grabbing her hand. I look down at her infamous red nails and grin at the idea in my head.

"This will hurt," I warn before yanking one of her nails off. She tries to scream, but I quickly cover her mouth with my hand. The last thing I need is Astor seeing me do this. He'll think I'm over the edge when really, I'm just testing my limits before I fry my bigger fish.

"Now, I'm deciding to be nice. I'm going to simply cut off one finger, *just one*, to remind you never to fucking touch him again." She struggles against my hand as she furiously shakes her head. "Sorry, this isn't optional. I can't have women walking around here thinking it's ok to touch what doesn't belong to them; especially after they've been warned. Hold your hand still for me, please. I don't want to accidentally take two off." The fear in her eyes kick up a notch when I lower the knife to her skin. Her eyes clam shut and I hover over her skin for a little longer. When she opens her eyes, I smirk and in one swift motion, I slice through her finger, tightening my grip over her mouth to silence her pain-filled screams. The satisfaction that comes from me seeing her bleed is enough to make me wonder if something is seriously wrong with me. The thought quickly dissipates when I see her pale. I slap against her face and sigh in frustration.

"Oh, come on! Don't faint, that's no fun!" Not even a second later, she's out and I'm annoyed. I grab a bag, fill it with ice, and stuff her finger inside before picking up the phone to call Todd.

"Mrs. Pavlov, everything ok?"

"Could you come to the kitchen for a second, please? I'm in need of help with..." I glance at Anna as she starts to groan. "... something."

"Right away."

I yank her up, forcing her eyes to open and stare at me. When she looks down at her bloody hand, she gags and I tilt my lip up in disgust.

"If you vomit on me, I'll be so pissed."

"Mrs. Pavlov, you needed help?" Todd asks, stepping into the kitchen. He takes in the scene in front of him and looks from Anna to me. I hold up the bag with her finger in it and smirk.

"Todd, oh so great Todd, would you be so kind as to drive Anna here to our hospital? I'm afraid she won't be able to stay conscious long enough to get herself there. It'd be a shame if she isn't able to get this finger stitched back on."

I'm surprised when I see Todd's mouth tip up a fraction before he reaches and takes my place, holding Anna up.

"Of course, Mrs. Pavlov." Anna frowns at him and turns to me. She tries to speak, but Todd is practically dragging her to the door.

"Wait, *Mrs*?" she croaks out.

I chuckle. "Yup. He's my husband. Bye bye, now!" I slam the door shut and sag against the door, suddenly filled with so much pride. I did it. I didn't kill her when I really fucking wanted to.

CHAPTER FIFTY

ASTOR

"Wanna tell me what you're cleaning?" I ask Alessia when I walk downstairs. She's on her hands and knees, cleaning what looks an awful like blood. I was in the shower for maybe twenty minutes, mainly because I had to fucking jerk myself off again at the thought of her.

"Oh! Um, hi!" she stammers, quickly standing up. I squint my eyes in curiosity when she hides the rag behind her back. I walk up to her and grab her hand, staring at the blood filled rag.

"Whose blood is that, little devil?"

"Umm...no one's."

"You have until the count of four to tell me."

"Well, I'm not scared of you. So here, I'll help you count. Ready?" Fucking *brat*. I step closer to her, fully expecting her to step back, but she doesn't. She doesn't move a fucking inch. Instead, she tilts her head up and stares at me.

"The only reason I've been so nice is because you've been so distant from me, so angry with me. But my patience is

running thin. I haven't touched you since our wedding night. I haven't kissed you. I haven't talked to you. I've jerked myself off more than I thought humanly possible. I am so close to losing my fucking mind over everything that's going on, that the thought of you causing pain to anyone without me makes me furious. It's the only way I've been able to cope with this shit. So, I'll ask again. Whose blood is that and why the fuck wasn't I in on it?"

"Anna's…" she finally admits.

I blink once, twice, and then a third time. "Excuse me?"

She rolls her eyes and steps back, cleaning up the last bit of blood from the floor. I grab my phone out of my back pocket and pull up the cameras. I have to sit the fuck down at what I see staring back at me.

Alessia, cutting her fucking finger off. *At least it wasn't the whole hand.* But why? I turn the volume up and Alessia stands, trying to take the phone out of my hand when she hears her voice.

"Turn it off."

"No. Either tell me why you did it or I'll just listen to why you did it."

"You're an asshole."

"What's the rules about cursing at me?"

"Except rules don't fucking exist right now. Like the fact that you will not be touching me for a very long time."

"Yeah, we'll see about that." I press play on the video and she tries to take it again, finally giving up when she realizes she's just too fucking small. I frown at what I hear come out of Alessia's mouth. She was jealous, territorial. I have to admit, I got a sliver of happiness out of knowing that. That even though she's being so cold towards me, she still cares. When the video is over, I yank her to me and she fights against me.

"Stop fighting me." She continues for a few more seconds,

finally settling when tears stream down her face. I wipe them from her face, palming her cheeks in my hands. "*Malyshka*, I've got you. Ok? I'll always have you. It doesn't matter how angry you are with me. It doesn't matter how long you ignore me. It doesn't matter how long I go without touching you. None of it matters. I've got you. Always. But just this once, let me love you. Please."

"I don't know what I'm supposed to do anymore. I don't know how to feel anymore. Six years of me walking in oblivion. Six years of you acting like you couldn't stand me. Six years of not feeling anything other than confusion. I want to be mad at you, but honestly, I was more upset when I came home and saw her touching you again than I was at you hiding the last six years. That's when I knew it wasn't you I was angry at. But I didn't know how to not be mad after days of shutting you out."

"Wait, you've been angry with me because of *Anna*?" I lean back to look at her face and she shrugs. "I did it to piss you off."

"I know, she lost a finger because of it." I can't help it, I laugh. I full blown laugh and she joins me. "At least I put it on ice for her."

"I love you, little devil."

She sighs and tucks her lip in, wiping the last of her tears from her face.

Come on, Alessia, cave. Just fucking cave.

"I love you, too," she says back, *finally*. I smile at her and lean in, intentionally stopping halfway. She's going to meet me there whether she wants to or not. She scowls at me, but leans in the rest of the way, making our lips brush against each other's.

We stay there for a moment, her wrapped in my arms. It's quiet and I just take in the moment with her. I take in her being this close to me after days of her being so far away.

"Don't shut me out again..."

"Don't give me a reason to. And don't think you're off the hook for that Anna shit. You aren't."

"I tell you what, I'm dying to touch you. So how about you do whatever you need to do to get your anger out? Your anger about Miles, your anger about Anna. Fuck, I don't care, even your anger about your dad. Take it all out on me. Do whatever the fuck you want to me, just fucking touch me. Please."

"I've never…" she hesitates.

"Me either, but we're going to." I grab her hand and direct her up the stairs. I'm not a switch kind of man. I'm not the kind of man that gets told what to do, but I'm finding myself doing things I'd never do.

Except for her.

"What time is lunch?" she asks when I sit on the bed. I quickly check my watch.

"Three hours, why? Hungry?"

"No, just wondering how much time I have."

"Time for what?"

"For you to be on your knees." I raise my eyebrow and she cocks her hip out, placing her hand on it. "Now."

I drop to my knees quicker than someone can take their next breath. She walks over to me, bends down, and fucking whispers in my ear, "Good boy."

Good boy? Why *the fuck* is that a turn on?

"You want me to touch you?" she asks.

"Yes," I grunt. She runs her hand over my chest, and the next thing I know, she has a blade in her hand, dragging it down my shirt and cutting it open. You'd think I'd flinch, that'd I'd be scared, but instead I'm intrigued. I hope she takes my word for it and does what I said.

I think I need it just as much as she does.

CHAPTER FIFTY-ONE
ALESSIA

I don't know how I'm doing this; I don't know where this dominance is coming from. Maybe it's always been there. Or maybe I truly am so angry that it's bringing this side of me out. Whatever it is, I'm embracing it now before I lose my nerves.

I don't know what I expect, but it definitely isn't what I'm seeing right now.

This alpha man, a mafia prince, a man that has an entire city afraid of him, is on his knees, waiting for me to give him the next command. The problem is, I don't know what's next and my nerves are starting to deteriorate. I take a deep breath as I walk around him, pushing my shoulders back. I bend down and yank his head back, gripping his hair tightly.

"How far are you willing to go? How far are you willing to go for us to go back to normal?"

"Do your worst, little devil." I laugh. Because what I'm thinking of doing is probably the furthest thought away from his mind.

"Take your clothes off." He moves with swiftness as I walk

to my side of the bed. I reach into the drawer and pull out my dildo. I'm doing it, there's no need in holding back. I pick up the lube that's next to it and head over to him.

"I'm going to blindfold you." He tenses a bit as I grab the blindfold that's next to the lube. I tuck the lube in my pocket and tie the blindfold over his eyes. I bend down and kiss the side of his neck. He's still tense even as I run my tongue up and down his neck.

"Relax, Astor. I won't hurt you, I promise." I smile inwardly at myself and my self-control. I get down on my knees in front of him and remove my shirt and bra. I wrap my hand around the back of his neck. "Open your mouth."

He does and I stuff my breast into his mouth. He groans on contact and wraps his lips tightly around my nipple, tugging.

I moan and tilt my head back. His hand comes around me and he yanks me closer as he switches to the other side.

Well, fuck. He clearly doesn't need his eyes to touch me, because I feel his fingers slipping into my pants.

"Take them off," he says as a groan slips from my lips.

"I thought I was in charge here?" I tease.

"You are, but be in charge without your clothes. Preferably." I roll my eyes and he runs his tongue over his lip. But, I listen anyway and take my pants off, pushing him backwards onto the floor.

"Turn over," I say. He rolls over onto his stomach and I run my hand down his back. "Good boy. Fuck, you're a good boy." I truly don't understand what's coming out of my mouth, but I go with it. I go with it because it's making me feel empowered. It's making me feel like I have so much fucking power.

I decide against using the dildo on him. I don't know why, but it feels like it's too much. *Maybe another day.* Instead, I run my finger over his anus. He tenses and I counteract with my other hand. I can't reach his cock and I need to. I need to feel it in my hand. "Slide up on your knees, Astor."

When he slides up, I wrap my hand around his cock and yank. He pushes back and it forces my finger inside of his ass. The animalistic growl that comes out of his mouth is gritty and filled with what sounds like want. So, I press further into him and yank off his blind off. When I push my finger in and out of him, further and further, I expect him to push away. Instead, he pushes back on me, so I add a finger. I've never done this, but fuck, why is it so goddamn hot?

"Alessia…" he groans as I pick up my speed. I jack him off as fast as I can with my fingers in his ass. He's taking all of it, just to stop me from being angry with him.

But based off the sounds his making, I think he's enjoying it. It fuels my fire, making me squeeze his cock harder.

"Fuck, Alessia. Stop."

"No, not until you come."

"Goddamn Alessia, *stop*."

"You want me to stop? You need to come. Now." He practically screams. It's a sound I've never heard. It's a side of him I've never seen when he doubles over and spurts his cum out everywhere. I pull my finger out and he curses under his breath, dropping flat onto his stomach.

I quickly stand and flop onto the bed, grabbing the dildo from earlier. I spread my legs and the moment I turn it on, Astor whips his head in my direction.

"What *the fuck* are you doing?"

"It's my turn. And you're going to watch."

"Like fuck I am. You just had fingers in my ass. You just made me come all over my self. I'm fucking you. Whether it's now or after you make yourself come is up to you. You had your fun; you get one more request. You either tell me to fuck you now or fuck you after. But *malyshka...*" he says, crawling towards me, pushing my knees apart. "I will be fucking you."

My breathing hitches as I look up at him. I tuck my lip into the side of my mouth and drag the dildo down my stomach, laying it on my pussy folds. He raises his eyebrow and leans backwards on the heels of his feet to watch me. My eyes close as the vibration of it tears through me. I push it inside of my pussy and silently thank myself for getting the vibrating one. I snap my eyes open and watch as Astor fists his cock, watching me. And just like last time, it's like his stare fuels me, it fuels my body. I dig the vibrator deeper, making my back arch. "Look at you, fighting your orgasm. Let me see it. Let me see how you make yourself come."

My body folds and I scream, I scream because his voice sends me over the edge.

"Good fucking girl. You're so soaked."

I sit up after what feels like a century of what it took me to get myself together.

"Now fuck me. And hard. Because you haven't touched me in too long and I know it's my fault, and I know I should've talked to you more, and I know I shouldn't have pushed you away, and I know I shouldn't have been so mean to you, and..." My eyes fill with tears and I brace myself. "Just fuck me, Astor, because if you don't fuck me, I'll cry. And I don't want to fucking cry anymore. I want to hurt people. I want to hurt the people that fucking hurt me."

He sits between my legs and a tilts my face to his.

"Oh, baby, we're going to do more than hurt them...we're going to kill them. All of them. Now lay back. I missed *my* pussy and I need my fucking fill of you."

He pushes my hair out of my face, tucking it behind my ear as I lay back.

"I'm sorry. I'm so sorry," I say as he kisses me.

"Don't be, little devil. You're going to make it up to me. For the next..." He peeks over me to the clock and smirks. "Two hours...you're mine."

I smirk at him and he growls at me, bending to my ear. "Open those fucking legs, little devil."

Fuck.

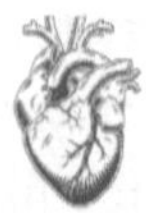

My pussy is sore when I roll over to sit up in bed so I move a tad slower. I guess that's what happens when you avoid you husband for three day. Astor sits up next to me and I lean my head on his shoulder.

"Ok?" he asks. I nod and as I run my hands down my cold thighs, my naked hand catches my attention. I get up and walk over to the draw he tucked my ring in. He watches me as I open it and grab it out and slide it back onto my finger.

I hold my hand out and tilt my head as I take it in.

"Don't ever take that off again, *malyshka*," he says wrapping his arms around me and kissing my cheek.

"I won't, I promise."

And I mean it.

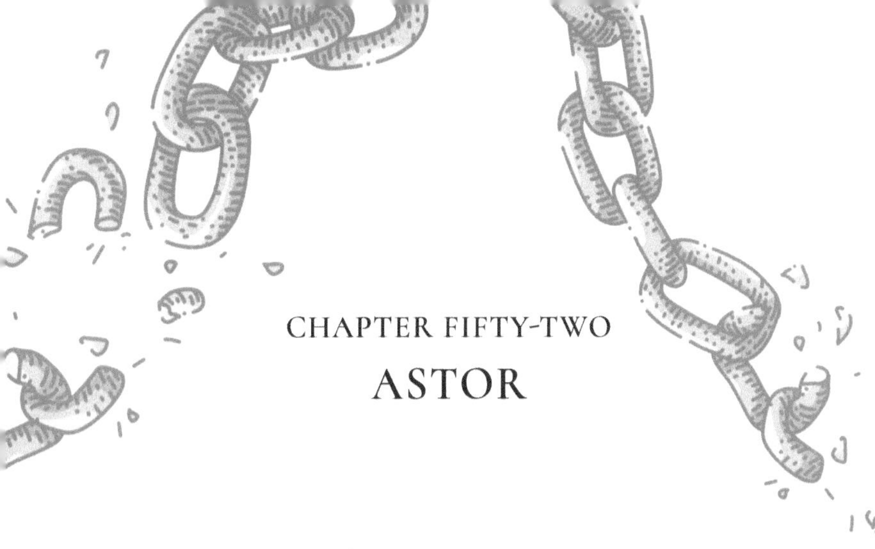

She felt like home. The moment my cock slid inside of her, she felt like coming home. I don't know how or why I enjoyed her finger fucking me, but I did. I even fucking moaned, *moaned*, and I don't know how to take that. But I do know that her hand in mine right now is enough for me to fucking do it again if it means her never putting me through the pain of her not speaking to me again. The pain of her not letting me touch her again.

We laid in bed for as long as we could before having to leave for lunch with Caroline and Justin. When we get into the car, Alessia looks more at peace.

I squeeze her hand and she smiles at me before looking out of the window.

"Are you alright?" I ask.

"I want to go after his father…"

"His father?"

"Yes…his father and then the rest of his family. He has a brother who helped him cover it up. And he has a friend, Javi…I know you went after him; but he lied to you. He knew he wasn't home. He knew he was here when you went after him."

"How do you know that?"

"He called me…" I slam on the breaks and pull the car to the side of the road.

"*Who called you?!*" I bark out.

She swallows and turns to face me. "He called me…three days ago. His voice was weird, but I know it was him. It was when we weren't…we weren't talking. He told me that he could've killed me. He told me the whole time Javi had you where he needed you."

"You're fucking kidding me. Baby, you tell me these things. I could've had the call traced…"

"I'm sorry." I grab her hands in mine and take a deep breath. I know she was probably going through a lot of emotions when she answered that phone call.

"It ok, but you need to hear me, ok?" She nods and leans her head against mine. "We're going to have lunch with our best friends and then we're going to do what you want: kill every fucking person that crossed you. But we aren't starting with his father."

"Who are we starting with?"

"Javi…he knows everything."

"Ok." I kiss her forehead and plan exactly how to track down that piece of shit, because tonight, he's fucking dying.

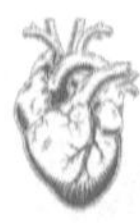

I'M WATCHING HER AS SHE CUDDLES NEXT TO CARO AS THEY SMILE AND laugh. It feels insane that this is the same woman who was in the car telling me her fucking hit list. Now she's curled up next to her best friend, laughing. She's strong. She's doing the best she can and that's all I can ask of her. But I hope she's ready for this, because tonight she's going to see a completely different side. A different side of me and a different side of her.

"So, what's the plan?" Justin asks.

"Mikhail is looking for him. We find him we find the rest of them. She wants to go after his father, then the brother. She remembers him helping Miles hide him. She's hardcore, Just. She may not remember how she was, but I do. We called her the *tornado*, because that's what she was. I was the only one that could bring her back. The only one that could stop her wrath when she started."

"I'm coming tonight." I shake my head and chuckle, because I didn't expect anything less.

"I know. We're leaving at midnight."

"I'll be there."

"Hey…" I hear before I feel small arms wrapping around me. Caroline appears next to Justin and he looks down at her before pulling her into his side. It's weird to see us with people. Or rather, it's weird for me to finally have the one I fought so long to make myself believe I didn't need.

I look down at Alessia and kiss her forehead when her phone rings. She reaches in her pocket and answers it.

"Hello?" she says. I feel her tense next to me and I frown. "Ah, Miles. I didn't say anything when you called the first time, but you should enjoy your last few days. Because I'm going to kill you. But not before I torture you first, just like you tortured me." I watch her as she handles herself. She doesn't flinch when I snatch the phone out of her hand and put it on speaker.

"Ah, I see tornado is back." His voice cuts through the phone and it feels like lightening is surging through my body. I feel like I'm on fire. I'm fucking burning with the urge of wanting my hands around his neck. For what he did to her, for what he did to us. We lost six fucking years. I had to deal with seeing her everyday, knowing she didn't fucking remember me or remember what we had.

She looks at me and grabs my hand. It's at that moment that I know I'm grinding my teeth and loudly.

"Listen here, you piece of shit. The only thing that stopped me from killing you the first time was my father. But hear me, you better hope to God my wife gets to you before I do. Because if *I* do, you're fucked. Don't call her again. We'll see you soon."

"Indeed, you will. Bye, tornado," he says before hanging up. She grips her phone and I look at her.

"I'm fine," she says, reading my mind. I look away and take a deep breath before she yanks on my shirt. "Ast...I am fine, I promise. We'll get him, ok?"

"We sure will. Fucking dickhead," Caro says, throwing back her pain medication. "When are we leaving? There's no fucking way I'm missing you kill this fucker," she continues.

"You aren't going," Justin says, glaring at her.

"She's my best friend, I'm going."

"No the fuck you are not," Justin says. Alessia rounds and grabs Caro, turning her to face her.

"I know you think you're superwoman and I know you want to protect me."

"No, I want to support you."

"Caro, you are supporting me by waiting here. We've got this." Caroline sighs and nods, their foreheads resting against each other's.

"Make him suffer," she says.

"I plan to." I smirk at Justin and he raises his eyebrow.

"Goddamn right," I say.

Game fucking on.

CHAPTER FIFTY-THREE

ALESSIA

W e're all sitting around the table at Astor's parents' house. We're having dinner and River keeps making jokes, calling it the last dinner before *doomsday*.

"He's expecting us to hit him first, he won't expect us to go after his family. Or anyone other than him," Mikhail says. I shove a piece of steak in my mouth and I feel a squeeze on my knee. I look down at Astor's hand hovering over my knee.

"We'll enter his house from the side, the roof, and the front fucking door. He'll have nowhere to go," Jay says, spreading a map over the table. He and Teagan took all day finding a blueprint of the house Javi has been staying in since he got here on our wedding day. Turns out, he flew in right after Astor and the boys left to come check on me. He's been in on it the whole time and Astor is pissed. It's not often that someone can psych him out. It's not often that someone can out-think him. And I know it's getting under his skin.

"Whatever you do, just bring him to me," Astor says. He's grinding his teeth when I nudge his shoulder.

"You're going to give yourself a headache, baby. Eat and relax. You're more worked up than I am," I say, smirking. He raises his eyebrow, but shoves a piece of steak in his mouth. I lean in and whisper low enough for him to hear me, "Good boy."

He practically chokes on his food and I tap his back before throwing my drink back to hide my laugh. He growls and yanks me by my nape. "I hope you enjoyed that, because it'll never happen again."

I giggle and Caroline leans in next to me. "Bitch, did you call him a *good boy*?" I kick her under the table to keep her quiet.

"So, if we can't go, then what are we supposed to do while y'all are all acting like GI Jane and Joe with their little minions?" Briar asks. I open my mouth to respond, but Teagan leans forward and glares at her before responding.

"You're going to go to your friend's to sit there and wait."

My eyes grow big and I fight the smirk on my face.

"Again, Teagan, you are not the boss of me. Shut up."

"You're a goddamn brat."

"Ok, you two. Honestly, you'd give everyone so much relief if you just fucked. If you need the table, we'll leave. For bloody sakes," River chimes and Mikhail grunts.

"Oh, everyone quiet. I think the big guy has something to say," Tess teases. I freeze, because these two are so weird. You never know how he'll respond, at all.

"You're a goddamn brat, too. You might want to be quiet... *princess*." Astor chuckles under his breath and I raise my eyebrow to him. This is a dinner that I truly could do every day. Despite the wrath I'm going to give tonight, I feel light. We're laughing and joking, and I feel like I'm with the people that truly care about me.

"Well, keep playing your cards right and I'll be *your* goddamn brat, *big guy*." I can't help it—I laugh. I laugh *loudly*. She winks at him and I shake my head.

God, I love these people.

"I'm glad this has been so entertaining for you all, but are we ready?" Astor asks.

I look at him and he kisses the side of my hair. I'm about to ask him if we can sneak away before we go, but then the door swings open. I want to vomit when our parents walk through the door.

"I want to leave."

"No. I've got you. Ok?" I roll my eyes, and the next thing I know, I'm grinding my teeth.

Damn it.

"Looks like I've rubbed off on you more than you'd like to admit, little devil."

I smack his arm and he smirks.

"Shut up, you're annoying."

"Alessia."

My head spins towards the sound of my father's voice and I feel angry. I stand up and Astor, along with all of our friends, watch as I walk towards my father. I stop an arm's length away. I look him straight in his face.

And walk past him.

As much as I wish I could talk to him, tonight is not the night to hash anything out with him. My mother stands behind him and I stop to kiss her on the cheek.

"Hi, Mama."

"Be safe, *figlia*." She hugs me tight and I walk out of the door, turning my head to the table as I look at Astor.

"I'll be outside." He nods his head and my girlfriends follow after me.

"You ok?" River says, hovering behind me.

"I'm fine, don't worry about it."

"Are you going to ever talk to him again?"

"Yeah, but not tonight."

"*Malyshka...*" Astor says, approaching me. He wraps his arms around my waist and the rest of the men file out of the house.

"Ready?"

"I am. Are you?"

I look over myself and back at him. "Actually, I want to go home and change."

"Meet you at the spot at midnight," he tells the guys as he deposits me into the car.

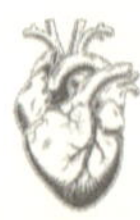

I QUICKLY CHANGE INTO ALL BLACK. I FIGURED IT'D FIT THE OCCASION, someone is dying tonight. And I can't wait. I can't wait to put every single last one of them through what they put me through.

Knowing that I have the support from Astor helps me. It makes me feel more ready, like I can do anything. I was strong enough not to kill Anna when I really fucking wanted to. Now I'm going to test myself again to see if I'm strong enough to torture the fuck out of Javi and whoever else is there to try and protect his miserable fucking life.

"I got you something," Astor says as I pull my black combat boots on. I look up at him and smirk.

"Oh yeah? What is it?" He pulls out a folded blade and tosses it to me. It's smooth under my hand and I run my finger over the engravement on it.

Pavlov

"Nice touch, husband." He pulls me to him and shoves his tongue in my mouth, his hand running over and gripping my ass tightly. I groan into his mouth and tuck his lip in my mouth before gently biting down.

"Ready to cause some ruins?" *Oh baby, I am.*

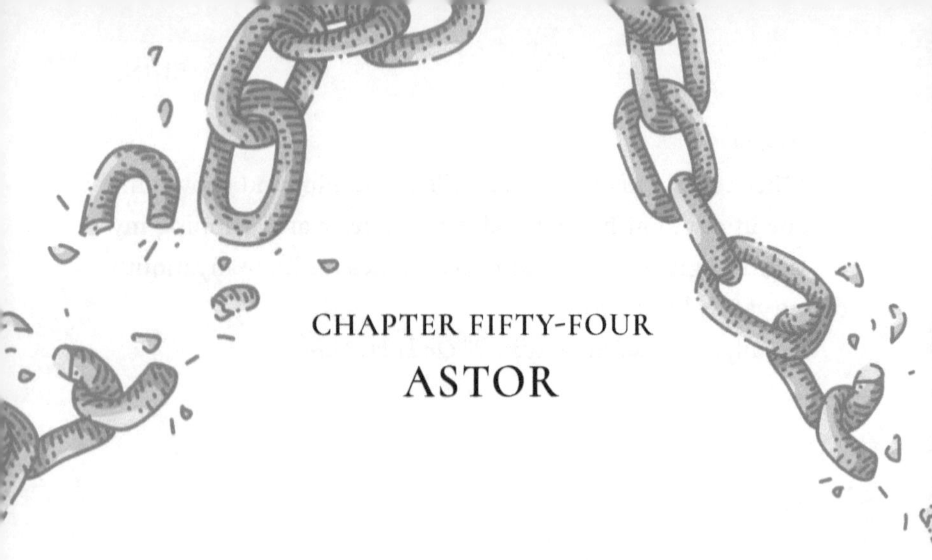

CHAPTER FIFTY-FOUR
ASTOR

She looks like a force to be reckoned with. She's sitting quietly, turning her new knife around and round in her hand while she stares out of the window. She's been quiet since we got in the car to go to the meeting location. I know she's going over what she'll do in her head. Tonight will be the first time I see her lose herself in revenge in six years. I didn't get to see her lose her shit on Anna in person, and from what I saw on the video, Javi is in a world of fucking shit—Regardless of who reaches him first. I rest my hand on her thigh, giving her a tight squeeze to bring her out of her daze.

"I'm ok," she says before I can speak. I nod at her and turn my gaze back to the road. "Do we know where he's hiding?"

"His bedroom is the top floor, double doors. I'm sure the fucker thinks he's safe tonight."

"Yeah, well, I'm pretty sure I thought I was safe in my own house, too. But I wasn't," she whispers. I run my hands through her hair.

"I've got you."

"I know. How much further?"

"Five minutes. Load my guns for me?" She reaches for the gun and magazine that's laying in my lap. She caresses my cock as she does and I growl at her. "Better stop, we don't have the time."

"Hmm, I guess you're right. I need a gun, by the way."

I nod towards the glove department and she reaches in to grab the gun. She pulls back, checking the chamber. The amount of pride that surges through me is insane. This woman is my wife. This woman who wreaks havoc on anyone that threatens her family or crosses her. I haven't seen this side of this woman in too fucking long. I just hope that when shit hits the fan, I still have the ability to reign her back in when I need to.

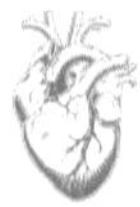

WHEN WE PULL INTO ONE OF THE WAREHOUSES MY FAMILY OWNS, Mikhail, Jay, Teagan, and Justin arrive right behind us. Alessia's father and mine were supposed to be here, but I'm guessing the reunion between them two at my father's wasn't the reunion he was expecting. She's still pissed with him, or she's not, which is even worse, because it means she's done with him. I wish I could be on his side, but right now the only side I want to be on is Alessia's.

Jay knocks on the window and I roll it down.

"Ready?" he asks, handing me two earpieces. I pass one to Alessia and she sticks it inside her tiny ears. Her face is like stone and I know she's ready to cause destruction. I know she's ready to get the justice she deserves.

She starts fidgeting with her fingers when we get out of the car and head towards the SUV the guys are in. I entwin our fingers together and bring them to my lips.

"Cause hell, baby." She smirks at me and climbs in the SUV.

We drive in almost complete silence until Justin breaks it.

"Bet $100 that he'll piss himself when he sees us," he says.

Mikhail sighs and shrugs his shoulders. "$200 says he'll faint before Ast even gets to him," Mikhail says, making me chuckle.

"$500 says that he'll run when he sees Lessia," Teagan says, peeking over his shoulder and glancing at her.

"We're about to find out....we're here. House is three floors; everyone take a floor. Find him. He's here somewhere. Thermal shows there's five moving bodies in the house, which means four should be dead when we leave. His bedroom is the top floor, but remember he could be anywhere in the house," I say, stuffing a gun in the back of my waist band. I take the gun out of Alessia's hand and stash it in the strap that's around her thigh.

"Stay behind me, ok?" I tell her as the SUV slows. "We're going to go through the forest, you ok with walking?"

"Ast, I'm fine. If I need you to carry me," she leans closer to me and kisses my cheek before gently biting it, "I'll let you know."

I shake my head as we all climb out to find all of the guys checking their weapons. Mikhail cracks his neck and Jay laughs.

"Big fucker," he says, as we start our half a mile walk to the house Javi is staying at.

"Tiny man syndrome," Mikhail says back to him. Teagan is behind Alessia while I'm in front of her. She's quiet and her head is on a swivel. I haven't seen her so focused before. She's ready for this, and as morbid as it sounds, I can't wait to see her ruin this fucker's entire life.

The walk is quick and everyone seems to know their job, which makes me feel like Alessia is safer, more protected. I put my hand on the door, knowing that it's unlocked because he's too naïve to think anyone would come after him. He thinks he's irrelevant. As expected, the door opens right up and we all go to split up. Alessia heads for the stairs and I grab her hand. She stops and looks down at my hand and smiles.

"I love that you're a caring husband, but I'm ok. If I need you, I'll...I don't know, scream." I smirk at her and let her hand go. I stop on the second floor and watch her tip toe to the third. I know she's strong enough for this. I know she needs to trust that she's got this, so I force myself not to follow her.

I fully expected her to head straight for his bedroom. I clear my mind and focus on clearing this floor.

"Remember there are five other guards here," I say into the ear piece as a reminder.

"Why does he have guards? He's not important," Jay says. I open my mouth to respond when Justin beats me to it.

"They aren't guarding him...they're Miles' guards."

"Ooo, maybe I'll get a two for one. I see one of the guards. Time to have some fun, boys," Alessia says, whispering into her ear piece. I freeze when I hear a thump above my head and a grunt. I will my body to stay still, to let her handle herself.

You know she can.

Moments go by and finally I hear her breathing through my ears.

"One down," she says to us.

"Two, I just got one," Justin says. "First floor is clear."

"Three down, basement clear," Jay says as I spot one standing the end of the hall. I bend down, walking slowly. He doesn't see me until it's too late, but he reaches for his gun, anyway. I ram my foot into the back of his leg, making him fall to the floor. I grab his wrist and twist it until I hear the sound of the gun hit the ground. Then I wrap my arms around his neck and squeeze, crushing his air supply. Everyone in this fucking house is dying tonight, messages need to be sent. And they need to be clear.

We're coming for you.

He fights me, grappling at my hands, but I tighten my hold around him until he finally lets go. I gently lay him to the ground and step over him.

"Four down. Alessia, I'm on my way to you, he must be in that room. All of the other floors are clear."

She doesn't respond. The others must notice, too, because I see them all behind me, taking the stairs two at a time.

My movements are quick. Why the fuck isn't she answering me?

Then I see the blood and my fucking heart drops.

Why is there so much goddamn blood?

CHAPTER FIFTY-FIVE
ALESSIA

I'm doing it. I'm doing it again. I'm not losing myself. I'm pacing myself. At least, that's what I'm telling myself.

I didn't lose my shit when I saw him in bed sleeping. I didn't take my knife and drive it into his jugular. I didn't slit his throat. I didn't make a scene. I simply tapped him on his shoulder with the tip of my knife and told him to wake the fuck up.

I thought he'd scream, but instead, Teagan was right. Even though I was right next to him, the asshole still tried to run. Which just pissed me off, so I shot him in his knee and now there's blood everywhere. Annoying, because I wanted to see how clean I could keep this.

Astor and the rest of the guys are standing at the door, watching me attempt to drag Javi into the seat that's sitting at a desk in the corner. I blow the fly away piece of hair out of my face and grunt. Staring at all of the eyes looking at me, I glare.

"Feel free to help at any goddamn time," I huff out.

"Who shot him?" Jay asks, looking around.

"Do you see anyone else around here?" I snap.

Astor glances at the gun wrapped around my thigh and I smirk. I used a silencer. Teagan steps forward and chuckles, saying as he walks pass me, "Tornado is definitely back."

Goddamn right, she is. And she's ready for fucking revenge.

CHAPTER FIFTY-SIX

ASTOR

Teagan is right. Tornado is back and I've never been happier to see her than now. Whether she wants to admit it or not, she was in a dark place. She's still in a dark place. She's not sleeping, and when she does, she's tossing and turning all night. I've ignored it, pretended not to know it's happening. But after I would hear her fall asleep in our room, I'd sneak in and watch her, calming her down enough to push through the dreams. I did this every day that we slept apart. Now that she's letting me back in, I hope that she'll be ok now. Especially since she's starting her revenge plan.

"Where do you want him?" Mikhail asks, stepping over top of him and glancing at her.

She looks to me and I know she's asking me to keep him here. I know she's silently begging me not to make her wait to get her revenge.

"Downstairs. Basement," I order. The guys grab him and I grab her hand as they slug him downstairs, his groans getting louder. "You've got this. Breathe through it and don't let him

get to you. This is about control, right?" She nods at my question. "Then show him who's in control, little devil."

I pull her to me by the nape of her neck and kiss her, I kiss her hard. For two reasons; one, being that I haven't been able to freely kiss her in too fucking long and for two, she needs my strength and support. This kiss is the only way I can show that's she's got it.

She pushes her shoulders back and marches downstairs towards the basement.

When we step in, the guys are roping him into a chair. He's gagged and his face is bloody, so he must've pissed one of them off. Alessia takes a deep breath and stops before him, bending over. Her ass is perched up and I can't help but look. I remind myself that this is not the fucking time, but my dick can't seem to give a fuck. I readjust myself, my teeth grinding when she tilts his face to meet hers with the pad of her thumb.

"Javi, is it?" He yanks forward, but she doesn't budge she stares him down, her hand never moving and her voice never wavering. "Let's have some fun, shall we?"

She stands and unwraps her thigh strap, passing it to me. I grab it, but not before she grabs her knife out of it. Javi continues to thrash and turn as she takes the gag out of his mouth.

"You stupid bitc—" I'm in front of him before he can finish his sentence, my fist slamming against his cheek.

"Don't fucking talk to my wife like that. First and final warning," I growl in his face. Jay chuckles behind me and Justin whistles.

"He's clearly not being as nice as he was the last time we were together," Justin says. As always, Mikhail is silent; waiting to be released to wreak havoc when needed.

"Be nice. I really would hate for him to kill you before I get to have my fun, considering you helped your shitty best friend get away with raping me," Alessia says. She rips his shirt open and slowly, but deeply, drags her knife across his chest. He screams out, and his head drops from the pain, she jabs her knee into his face.

"I didn't have a fucking choice! He didn't tell me why he had to leave!" he whimpers. She shrugs as she circles around him. She grabs his hair by the roots and yanks him backwards, pressing the knife to his cheek before twisting it into him. His screams fill the room, but no one flinches. Torture isn't new to us. We've all done this before, too many times to count. I just wonder how long this one will last. How long *she* will last.

"Alessia!" he screams out desperately.

She bends down to his ear and whispers, "You don't ever get to say my name." She runs the knife across his throat. It's not deep enough to kill him, though. When she looks up and stares me in my eyes, I know she kept him alive for me. "I hope you rot in fucking hell for the monster you helped. I don't believe for a second that you didn't know what happened. Your piece of shit friend is a bragger." He shakes his head as best he can, but she rolls her eyes.

"I...I couldn't go against him." She holds her hand up to silence him.

"Save it." She slings her fist across his face, and *fuck*, I didn't know someone so small could pack such a lethal punch.

"As much as I'd love to kill you myself, you've managed to piss off a very dangerous man. So, if I were you, I'd say sorry and mayyybee even beg for forgiveness? I might be able to convince him," she says. His head drops and she yanks his ear. "I'm speaking to you. Hold your fucking head up." He ignores her, blood dripping from his neck. She yanks his ear again, and before I can comprehend what she's doing, Javi's fucking ear is on the floor.

"Did you...cut his ear off?" Teagan says, holding back his

laugh. She shrugs, holding her hand over his mouth, covering his screams.

"Well, he obviously didn't need it. He's not listening, anyway."

Mikhail grunts and I just shake my head at my wife. She wipes his blood on his shirt and tucks her knife safely back into her thigh holster.

She walks over to me, gets on her tippy toes, and kisses me.

"Make it hurt. I'm tapped out. And really want him dead."

"I'll do my worse, baby." She smiles and walks out of the basement door. I turn to Mikhail and Justin.

I bend down to his face to see he's passed out. I figured it wouldn't be long before the pain was too much. He's losing a lot of blood and probably won't last much longer. I smack the side of his face and he groans. I want him to wake up. If he doesn't, it won't be nearly as fun.

"Why'd you lie to me?" I ask. He doesn't respond, just groans again. I press my finger into his now severed off ear and he screams out.

"Answer me, you piece of shit. You helped hide a rapist, a rapist who raped *my* fucking wife. You better have a damn good reason for doing so. Now fucking speak." I press my finger deeper into his wound for good measure.

"He told me she wanted it!" His words are slurred, but I hear them. I'm fucking fuming from it. My fist lands so hard into his face that the chair falls backwards with a thrash. I'm on top of him, sending blow after blow to his face. Blood is everywhere and all I see is that day again. Justin and Mikhail yank me off him and I push away to get to him again.

"Ast! Chill! The point is to torture him before death!" Justin says. I yank away from him, pushing my hair back.

"She's my fucking wife!"

"Calm the fuck down!" Mikhail says. I look at Javi on the

floor who looks like he's an inch away from death. I force myself to calm down.

"Pliers. Take off every fingernail then every finger. And cut his fucking tongue out for being a lying piece of shit."

"You not staying?" Justin asks. I shake my head and look towards the door Alessia just walked out of.

"No, I'm going to find Alessia. String his body up afterwards, make it known that we're coming after Miles and his pathetic fucking posse."

"Goddamn it," Mikhail says under his breath. Jay laughs as he pulls out a twenty with Justin following. They drop the money into Teagan's hand and I shake my head.

"Fuck all of you. Make this quick. We'll be in the truck."

"Air that bitch out before we get back in there," Justin says. I smirk, leaving them to handle the piece of shit.

Before I leave, I hear Teagan chuckle.

"Told you he'd lose his shit the moment she left."

I don't care that he was right.

I just want my wife.

CHAPTER FIFTY-SEVEN
ALESSIA

My head is hanging between my legs as I force myself to breathe.

Breathe, Alessia.

Breathe.

Just fucking breathe.

"Hey, in through your nose out through your mouth." I look up and Astor is there, rubbing my shoulders. I didn't even realize that it was him I heard telling me to breathe. I follow his commands, and slowly but surely, my breathing evens out.

"Good girl, come back to me. Tell me what happened," he says, running his fingers through my hair.

"I heard what he said..." I croaked. I was standing by the door. I wanted to see what they were going to do to him, but when he said that Miles said I *wanted* it, I fled. I felt sick, disgusted, and confused.

"*Malyshka.*" I shake my head at him, stopping him before he can continue.

"Why does he keep saying that? Is my memory wrong? I

wanted *you*, I flirted with *you*, I hinted at *you*. Not him. It was never him. Could he have gotten it wrong?"

"He saw us kissing that day. He knew we were together. You did nothing wrong," he reassures me.

"Why do I feel like this is my fault, then? Why do I feel so worthless? And fucking angry. I don't know where I belong anymore, what I was made for. I don't know who I am anymore. I feel robbed, I feel like pieces of me are dying. Like it'd be better if I were dead."

The words are rushing out of my mouth. They're fast and mushed together almost.

"Alessia, you were made for me and only me. You aren't worthless, you are the strongest person I know. Don't ever say it'd be better if you were dead, because if you go, *I go*. My world wouldn't be better without you. No one's world would ever be better without you." My eyes are watery and I'm fighting every ounce of my being to hold it together. Astor leans in, resting his forehead against mine, his hand mindlessly running through my hair. "You are mine, Alessia. Mine. He will pay for this. I promise, but don't ever think it'd be better without you, do you understand?"

I nod and he tilts my face up to his to look at him, his breathing is becoming a bit erratic, and his eyes look dark and pinpointed. He squeezes me and I jolt at the force.

"Tell me that'll never come out of your mouth again," he begs as I wipe my tears.

"I'm sorry."

"You're mine."

"I'm yours." I plant my lips against his when a scream breaks out. My head whips towards the basement and Astor grabs my hand.

"Let's go, we'll wait for them at the SUV." I nod and follow him, my hand in his.

The walk back to the SUV was quick and quiet. He never let's go of my hand. His grip tightens when I adjust my hand.

"I'm not going anywhere, silly man." He faults for a second, glaring at me and I can't help the feeling of guilt that washes over me when I see his face. He quickly gathers himself and smirks at me.

He turns around and pushes me against a tree that the SUV is behind.

"Of course, you aren't. I'm going to make sure of it." His eyes rake over my body and I can't help how my body reacts to his stare.

"Yeah? How?"

"That's for me to worry about it." He dips his head down and smashes his lips against mine. "You did so good today, little devil. I'd be lying if I said it didn't turn me on."

"Seeing me cut a man's ear off turned you on?"

"Seeing you be *strong* turned me on....and now I'm going to fuck you." I look around and he smirks. "Nothing you say is getting you out of this."

"What if they come back?"

He shrugs as he pulls my pants down and yanks my leg up. I gasp at the sound of my panties ripping.

"Then I guess they'll get the chance to see me fuck my wife before I gouge their eyes out for looking. By the way, I liked it better when you didn't like wearing panties. Go back to that, it gave me much easier access." His pants are down before I can respond and he slams into me. My head hits the back of the tree, but I don't care; I welcome the pain.

I welcome it because I need it. I need it to remind me that this is real life, that I'm not in a bad dream that'll end soon. I need the pain to remind me that I'm here and not off in my mind. Most of all, I need to keep myself from wanting to end it all, and the only way to do that would be to eliminate the stress factor: *Me.*

"Get those thoughts out of your mind, *malyshka.* You aren't leaving me. Ever."

He nibbles my ear before plunging deeper into me again. My groans get louder and soon I'm submerged in nothing but my screams of pleasure. I'm no longer thinking about how fucked up my life is. I'm only thinking about this man who's fucking me so hard against this tree that I'm sure I'll have pieces left in my skin.

He reaches down and grabs the knife from my thigh holster and holds it against my neck. I know right then what I need him to do, what I need to do to feel like I've relived the worse time of my life. I ran away. Not physically, but mentally—and I didn't get to feel the pain the rest of them did. The guilt my parents carried, the resentment Astor carried. I didn't get to feel it because I ran. But I can now, I can make someone I trust put me through that pain. It may not be the same, but it's as close as I can get.

I wrap my hand around his and push it into my neck. He frowns and stares me in the eyes as he loosens his hold on the knife. I watch as he understands. He shakes his head and pulls out of me, dropping the knife on the ground.

"Please, I need to feel what you felt that day."

"Not here, Alessia."

"Then at least finish fucking me." He glares at me, and at this point, I'm willing to drop to my knees and do whatever the fuck I have to do for him to fuck me. My pussy is throbbing and I'm sure that if he runs his finger through it, he'll curse.

Not even a second later, he's back on me, and just like I predicted, he mumbles, *"Fuck,"* under his breath the moment his fingers touch my clit. I moan, letting my head fall back as his cock invades my wetness.

It's always so good when he first slides inside of me; that feeling is untouchable. I wish I could watch as he throttles me, in and out, but it's so dark all I can see is the silhouette of him.

"Goddamn, your pussy is always ready to welcome me home, isn't it?" he growls into my ear. He lifts my leg and pulls out, teasing the tip of his cock against my entrance. I let out an annoyed huff and he chuckles. "Needy for your *good boy's* cock?"

I gulp, and by the tell of his face, he hears it. But I don't care. Hearing him call himself my good boy when he's clearly in control is enough to make me come on spot.

"I asked you a question. Don't get shy on me now."

"Yes...yes, be a good boy and fuck me. Then take me home and show me how much I tortured you all those years."

The sound that comes from him is animalistic, I can't help but to make one myself. Especially when he flips me around, places my hand on the rough tree trunk, kicks my legs open wider, and fucks me so hard that the sound is echoing throughout the woods. I feel euphoric. My body is moving on its own accord, chasing the rhythm that he fucks me in. His hand is wrapped tightly around my high ponytail, and when he yanks me back to kiss me, my legs shiver. Fuck, my entire body shivers.

"You're taking my cock like such a good girl."

"Mmm, don't stop; not yet." I'm so close that I can practically taste myself on my lips.

"Not a chance, baby. I'm not stopping until cum coats my cock like its apart of my fucking skin."

He digs his fingers into my neck and thrusts forward. The extra sensation with the pain sends me over. He's relentless with his thrusts, they've become brutal and fast. I can feel him in my stomach and he doesn't let up, even though I'm screaming from an orgasm so intense, I know at the end if he isn't there to catch me, I'll fall.

The back of my neck is wet.

Am I sweating?

I look up and his face is full of tears and rage. And I realize that Astor is fucking me brutally because he's trying to show me his pain. Just like I asked, but it's still not enough.

"Ast…"

"Shut up and take it, Alessia," he says as he reaches around and slaps my pussy lips. I bellow out and he covers my mouth with his hand. "You wanna know how painful it was? It was like I was suffocating." He tightens his hand that's over my mouth and I soon realize it's over my nose, too.

He's suffocating me.

His cock is slamming in and out of me and his words are becoming disoriented. They're becoming harder and harder to understand. But I try my hardest to hear him, to understand him.

"I couldn't fucking breathe around you, Alessia. I wanted to fuck the memory of me, of *us,* back into you. I wanted to fuck you so hard in your room, on that bed, in that exact position, so that you'd remember me and not him."

I'm becoming dizzy. Suddenly all I can hear is *thrust, thrust, thrust.*

I feel the warmth, but it still hasn't hit me that it's his cum. His hand releases from my face and wraps around my throat. He unloads in me and I try my best to gasp for air. I stay calm, because even though I'm an inch from death, I know he won't let me go. *He'll never let me go.*

Astor goes still inside of me, his hand tightening when my eyes start to droop. They slowly pop back open and I feel him at my ear. "It felt like my fucking heart was going to stop, and then the moment I thought I could move on…" He yanks and lets go right as the house goes up in flames behind us. "*Boom*, I had to marry you." I look up and I see Javi's body being strung up in the tree that's in front of what I'm sure is now ashes of a house.

I grab my throat and cough, putting myself in the tripod position to catch my breath. He stuffs himself back in his pants and slowly pulls my panties back into place, stopping right above my pussy and giving it a slow, torturous lick.

He slaps my ass and yanks me to him, looking me over.

"If you killed yourself, how could I torture you?"

"I won't do that," I say. And as I say the words, I realize that I truly mean it. I'm not doing that to my family, to my husband. They don't get to go through any more pain because of me.

"Good girl. Now get in the SUV so I can take you home and fuck that tight cunt again."

I start for the SUV, but stop and turn to him. I square my shoulders and make myself sound as strong as I can, even though what I'm saying shows how vulnerable I am right now.

"Tell me you love me first..."

He slowly walks to me; I can hear the footsteps of the others crunching on the ground. But I don't care, and Astor shows no indication that he does, either.

"Tell me you won't leave me," he counters. He needs this just as much as I do.

"I won't leave you." He runs his finger down my cheek and sighs.

"I love you, *malyshka*." A tear slides down my face, and as quickly as it's there, it's gone, replaced by the feeling of his lips.

"I love you, too." He kisses the tip of my nose and nudges his head toward the SUV.

"Time to go home, lovebirds," Justin says as all of the guys pile in. I smile to myself.

Home. Time to go home.

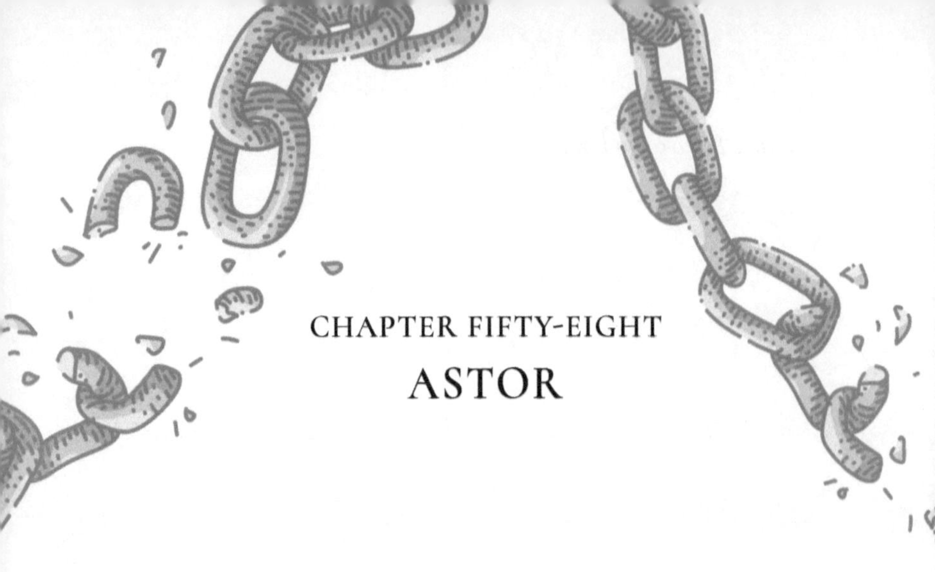

ASTOR

She's wrapped around me the entire way home. Teagan is next to us and keeps glancing at her. They still haven't talked. I know he is trying his best to give her the space he thinks she needs. The problem is, everything is coming to a head and it's best they address it and move on before she no longer cares enough to do it. We were all so close and I know that it does bother her that she can't come to her friend right now. If he knew that she said it'd be better if she were dead, he'd lose it just as much as I did.

I glance at him and he turns away. When I look down at Alessia, her eyes are closed.

"She ok?" he asks.

I nod. "As ok as she can be. Talk to her, you both need it."

"I don't want to overwhelm her. She's getting on her feet again; I'll talk to her after we get this bastard." I nod and run my hands over her head as she tucks herself deeper into my embrace. I kiss the top of her head and stare out the window.

"I'm fucking starving. Your cook home?" Justin asks.

"My cook hasn't been there since Alessia moved in." She

hasn't. I told her that she could take a much-needed vacation. Now that I think about it, it's something I probably should tell my wife. The last thing I need is for her to wake up and see a random woman in my kitchen.

"I'm going through a drive thru," Justin groans. I lean up and smack him in the back of his head.

"You can do that shit after you take me home." He chuckles, but doesn't stop the car until he's in front of my house.

I nudge Alessia and she whimpers before jumping and grabbing me so tightly, even I flinch.

"Hey, we're home." She peers up at me and her eyes settle before she sits up and reaches for the door handle. She turns around and looks at everyone.

"Thanks for tonight, guys. For having my back."

Nods and sounds of acknowledgements go all around. She climbs out and rounds the car, and I watch her in confusion as she pulls Teagan's door open.

She nods her head, signaling him to step out. He quickly glances at me and I raise my eyebrows at him.

"Keep your hands to yourself," I warn as he slides out. Mikhail's phone rings and he groans, throwing his head back against the seat.

"What?" Jay asks. Mikhail tilts his phone, showing Tess' name across his phone.

"You like her, what's the problem?" I ask as he fully turns his body to me.

"The problem is she's a fucking brat that I can't control. She too unpredictable, she doesn't stop fucking talking, and I could have sworn she was supposed to be the fucking *quiet* friend." I throw my hands up and step out of the car, chuckling.

"We'll meet tomorrow. I want this shit ended by the end of the week."

I'm standing at the head of the car, waiting on Alessia.

When I look over, she hugs Teagan, and for the first time ever, I see him emotional. She wipes his tears and then playfully pushes him. I wander over, because I can't help the jealousy that seeps from me.

"Glad you two made up. Now if you'll excuse us, Teagan, I'd like to enjoy the rest of the night with my wife."

"Jealous fuck," he mutters as he climbs into the SUV. I chuckle and lead Alessia into the house.

When the door closes, she leans against it and watches me as I take off my jacket. She clears her throat when I hang it up and smirks at me as she holds her hand out to me. I walk over to her, hovering over top of her.

"Hi, baby," she says. I take it in because she doesn't call me that often. As much as I'm not a mushy person, I'd began to realize hearing her call me that made me feel so good.

"Hi, wife." She stands on her tiptoes and kisses me, making me moan into her mouth.

"Ready to show me that pain?" The pain she's asking me to do is fucking crazy. She's asking me to cut her, and even though I know she'll still get pleasure from it, there's no way I could get her to feel the pain I felt.

But I'd try. For her, I'd fucking try. And I'll just hope I can stop when it's too much for her.

"Go upstairs," I order her. She pulls her fingers and nods. I let out a deep breath and remind myself that this is what she wants. She's strong and I know she can take it. If she can't, she'll tell me.

She's waiting for me on the bed, her hands are on her lap as she pulls at her fingers.

"Don't be nervous. Tell me what you want me to do."

She slowly unwraps the thigh strap and removes her new blade. She stares down at it for a second and then extends it out to me. "Make me feel how you felt that day."

"That's not possible, Alessia."

"Try. Please."

"When you want it to stop, say *tornado*." She gives me fraction of a smile and nods as I swipe the blade from her hands. I consider where I'll cut her. Classes start in a few weeks and Christmas is in a couple of days. I can't let anyone see cuts or scars; I need to do this where only she will know they exist.

"Tonight was hard for me," I admit as I walk closer to her. I spin the knife around in my hand and she gulps. "It was hard to see you touch him even though I knew you wanted to hurt him. It was hard not to kill him the moment I saw him, even though I knew I'd get to kill him soon enough. I don't know how I'll control myself when it's Miles. I don't know *if* I'll be able to control myself for what he caused and what he ruined."

"What did he cause?" she asks when I place the knife at the top of her shirt.

"Heartache." I yank the knife down and her shirt splits in two. She doesn't flinch. She stays put and watches me. Not the knife, just me.

"And what did he ruin?"

My teeth start grinding the moment she asks, because he ruined so much that it'd be impossible to tell her everything. So, I take the knife and slide it across her chest. It's deep enough to make her bleed, but superficial enough to already begin clotting when I move to her stomach.

"Me, little devil. He ruined me." I slowly slide the knife across her stomach and she hisses at the pain. When the blood starts trickling down her flat abdomen, I run my tongue up it.

"More, I can take it."

"I know you can," I say before slicing again in the same spot. This one is much deeper, but should heal perfectly fine. She screams out when I make the same incision on the opposite side of her stomach. I step back and watch as she's covered in blood, her breathing erratic. She looks like a work of art. It doesn't make me want to stop, it makes me want to join.

I flip the knife around and hand it out to her.

"No," she gasps as I push it into her hand. "Astor…"

"Mark me. Just like I did you."

"Why?"

"Because what you feel, *I feel.*" She briefly closes her eyes, but pulls me down onto the bed as she hovers over top of my body. She starts with my stomach, slicing in the same exact spot as I did her moments ago. I don't scream, I don't flinch. Because this is nothing compared to what I felt that day she was taken from me.

Then she does the other side, and when she smirks at me, I know exactly what she's about to do. She bends down and runs her tongue up my stomach, gliding the knife over my chest while she does it.

When she leans back on her heels, she tilts her head and watches me.

"It's still not enough," she says. I yank her to me, our bloodied bodies molded together. I hold her tight and she cries into my shoulder because now we can't get any closer. We can't be anymore bonded than we are right now at this moment.

"Tighter, hold me tighter," she begs.

And I do. So tight that I think I'll suffocate her.

"I've got you. Always, little devil." When the words leave my mouth, I physically feel every ounce of stress leave her body. I feel the weight lifted from her. She needed this; she needed the pain, she needed the blood. She needed it—and she needed it from me. And I finally know what I wanted to know the moment she found out all of the shit we'd been hiding from her.

She's going to be ok.

CHAPTER FIFTY-NINE

ALESSIA

My eyes force themselves open when I feel hands running over my body. Usually I'd freak out, usually I'd jump by this point. But I didn't. I know the hands that are touching me. Whatever he's rubbing over my body is cool and soothing, and my body craves it. I'm sore, but I don't protest when he turns me over on my back.

"These need cleaning and cream," he says, running a washcloth over my cuts. I lean up and watch him as he tends to me. I rake my eyes over his and he catches me. "I did mine already, let me take care of you. Ok?"

"Let me guess, aftercare is your thing?" I ask. The tip of his lip tilts up a fraction.

"It didn't used to be. Guess it's you." He kisses my wounds before rubbing the cool cream over them. "Let those air out for a bit. Let's feed you."

I let out a yawn and he helps me out of bed. I head for the bathroom to brush my teeth and he wraps his arms around my waist.

"How are you?" I know he's asking me about yesterday,

about Javi. I told him I was tapped out and I was. I felt myself becoming overwhelmed with rage.

"I'm ok...with Christmas coming and classes starting in a couple of weeks, I want this over with as soon as possible."

He kisses my shoulder and watches me in the mirror.

"I've been thinking, though, that I want him wondering when he's next. And I want him to feel like he has to hide every second of his life," I say before I shove the toothbrush in my mouth.

"You want to keep him alive..." he concludes. He waits for me to finish and I turn to him. I can feel his anger. He wants him dead and I do, too. But I'm no longer in a rush to do it.

"I want him dead, too...trust me. But I want him to watch us ruin everything he has that means something to him first. We took Javi and that's a start. But I want him to feel how you felt, how my parents felt when I left all of you that day. His family is important to him, right?"

"Yes."

"Then I want them dead first. Then I want him dead." He sighs and rakes his hands through his hair before turning to me.

"Ok, but know, it'll start a war. Most of the mafia is on our side, but some of them aren't. We have to be prepared for anything. Miles' family is a bit crazy; that's why our parents' befriended them."

"Aren't we just as a crazy?" I ask, smiling at him as we walk down the stairs.

"Indeed, we are."

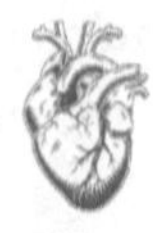

I STARE AT THE PICTURE OF MY FATHER AND ME LIGHTING UP MY phone. Astor and I have been Christmas shopping all day and we're about to have dinner. This is the second time he's called. Each time I've told myself I'd answer, but never do. I gather my strength and accept the call.

"Hello?" I answer.

"*Figlia*." His voice sounds different, he sounds...*broken*.

"Hi, Papa."

He clears his throat and a few moments pass before he speaks.

"I'm sorry...That you found out the way you did. That I made him keep it from you. I just didn't want to lose you again...I didn't want *him* to lose you again."

Tears well up in my eyes and Astor's hand grips around my thighs. I quickly wipe my face and rest my hand over his before responding to my father.

"It's ok, Papa. We're ok. You don't need to apologize."

"Like hell he doesn't," Astor mumbles. I pinch his hand and he shrugs his shoulders.

"I know you're getting revenge; I heard about Javi this morning. You can't do it on your own, you have to let us help."

"Papa..."

"Alessia, you are a mafia princess. I know you hated it for a long time, hated the endless training and security everywhere, but that means that you have people who will die for you. People that are paid to die for you. Utilize them. You can take out his entire family without moving a finger."

"I know, Papa, and I will, but we're laying low for a little. I want to enjoy Christmas. How about we talk about it later? We're about to grab dinner."

"Sure thing, princess. Love you."

"Love you, Papa." I hang up the phone and pull at my fingers. Astor grabs them and holds them still.

"Stop doing that, you'll hurt yourself."

"Can we still take a honeymoon?"

"We can," he says, pulling up to the valet.

My eyes widen in surprise. "Really?"

"Yes, really." He climbs out and rounds the car to help me out. I slide my hand into the cusp of his arm as he walks me into his father's restaurant.

I look at him and he winks.

"When?"

"Whenever you want, wife." I can't help the shade my face changes to, because I'm always going to be affected by Astor calling me his fucking wife.

"Mr. Pavlov, your table is ready for you. Right this way."

We're led to a private table with an amazing view of New York. There's champagne being chilled on the table and a bouquet of red roses on the table. Astor steps in front of me and grabs them, handing it to me.

"You got me roses?"

"I did...sit." He pulls the chair out and I kiss his cheek before sitting.

The waiter pops open the bottle of champagne and pours Astor and I a glass.

"Thank you," I say, taking it from him. He opens his mouth, but then looks at Astor and nods instead, before scurrying off in the opposite direction.

What's his problem?

Then it clicks.

"Let me guess, you told the staff that they weren't allowed to speak to me?"

"I did no such thing, *malyshka*."

"Liar."

"So, you and your father?"

"He apologized...I'm tired of being mad at everyone. He told me to use the *family* at my disposal."

"He isn't wrong."

"I know, I will. But right now, Miles isn't my focus," I speak.

I lean in and he meets me, running his finger over my cheek.

"Yeah? Then what is?"

"My last semester of classes," I tease before chuckling and sitting back into my chair.

"Funny. I'm glad you bought school up. No more dipping out on your fucking driver. *I'm* your driver from now on."

"That's insane, I have a car. And I carpool with the girls sometimes."

"The days you don't carpool, you'll ride in with me. Not up for discussion." I roll my eyes and he cocks his eyebrow up.

"This is stupid." I shove a piece of bread in my mouth as he downs his glass of champagne.

"Ahh be nice, little devil. It's for your safety."

"Ahh be a good boy, Astor." He shakes his head and smirks at me.

"Jesus Christ, woman."

<h1 style="text-align:center">CHAPTER SIXTY
ASTOR</h1>

You truly never know what you need until it's wiped away from you. At least that's what they say, except the problem with that is I did know. I knew what Alessia meant, I knew she was mine to protect. I didn't need a wakeup call; I didn't need a reminder. I just needed her and she was taken from me. Ripped from me the moment we decided to stop fucking around and just be together. That won't happen again. I fought how badly I wanted her for so long and now she's my wife.

My fucking wife.

That I'll protect until my last breath.

"My love...what's going on in that head of yours?" she says, elbowing me. We're surrounded around our friends for our families' annual Christmas Eve party.

"You called me a new name?" I tease. She rolls her eyes and leans into my arm that's draped over the back of her shoulder.

"Lessia, will you tell Mikhail that I'm so much fun?" Tess asks, batting her eyes.

"Mikhail, Tess here is so much fun," she says with a fake smile on her face.

"See! Told ya!" She smacks his arm and plops herself in his lap before he groans and pushes her off. "Big dickhead!" she says, rubbing her hands over what I'm sure is a sore ass.

"Ah don't be such a grump, Mikhail. She likes you," Caro says.

He turns his furrowed stare to her.

"She doesn't know me," he responds before getting up and walking out of the family room.

"Come on, guys. It's Christmas, leave the man alone," Briar speaks up. River nods in agreeance.

"Yeah, don't poke the bear," she says.

"Blah blah blah, I'm going after him. Maybe I can piss him off enough for him to snap at me." Tess winks as she chases after Mikhail like a lost puppy. It's weird, her being so openly into him. Honestly, it seems that all of my wife's girlfriends think I'm either stupid or oblivious to their crushes on my friends. Briar is staring at Teagan every time they're in the same room and River drools over every goddamn sound Jay makes.

Alessia leans up to whisper into my ear. "I wonder which one will fuck first."

I snicker and lean in before responding, "Definitely Mikhail and Tess."

"Eh, my money is on Teagan and Briar."

"Wanna shake on it?"

"I wanna do more than shake on it."

"My bedroom. Now."

"Astor, this house is full of our family and friends. Absolutely not."

"Fine, but later, little devil."

Caroline comes and sits next to Alessia, leaning her head on her shoulder.

"Our boyfriends are about to leave us for some secret mission."

"What are you talking about?"

"Ask him," she says pointing to me. I raise my eyebrow and Alessia frowns at me.

"What's she talking about?"

"Mafia wants to meet tonight with updates on the Miles' situation."

She gently pushes Caroline off and stands, walking away. I follow after her, knowing she's probably pissed. We take the stairs to my old room, shutting the door when I walk in behind her.

"You didn't think I should know about that?" she asks.

"It was going to be quick. They just want an update."

"It's my revenge, it should be my update."

"Alessia..."

"No, you weren't going to tell me."

"Stop."

"*You stop*. This last week you've been treating me like I'm going to break at any fucking second. You haven't talked to me about Miles', you haven't asked me what I want to do anymore. Ever since that night, you've walked on eggshells around me. You won't even take phone calls in front of me anymore. I'm not weak, Astor..."

I start to pace back the floors and she watches me closely.

"I know you aren't weak."

"They why are you treating like I am?"

I grow quiet because she still doesn't remember. I thought she remembered everything, but clearly, she doesn't.

She shakes her head at my silence before heading for the door.

"Because you were going to kill yourself."

She stops in her tracks.

She turns slowly to me and my eyes are fucking filled with tears. I swear you'd never catch me fucking crying, because I don't do it. Now in the last month, it's all I seem to fucking do.

"What?"

"You were going to kill yourself."

"No, I wasn't." She's so confused.

"Yes, Alessia, you were. After he raped you...there was a few hours before you forgot everything. You were hysterical. No one could get you to calm down, including me. You said you were *tainted* and that I shouldn't want you. That your parents deserved a girl who was stronger. You took your father's gun and put it inside of your mouth."

Her head is shaking back and forth. And the more she shakes, the more I sense her memories peer through.

"You told me that if I didn't leave out of the room, you'd pull the trigger. And I told you that if you pulled the trigger, you'd be robbing us of our life together. You told me—"

"—That if you loved me to start hating me, because it'd be easier that way. I made you promise to leave me."

"Yeah...you did."

She runs to me and I gather her in my arms, shushing her as her cries grow louder.

"You avoided me because I made you promise to, I made you promise to leave."

"But I didn't leave. I didn't promise that part."

"But I left...and I forgot. I forgot you. I forgot *us*." When she looks up at me, my heart is broken. Because she finally understands the pain, she finally understands the depth of what I had to go through for her to be able to survive and find herself again. Even though she wanted to do it without me. I wipe her face and plant a kiss on her forehead. "That's why you reacted that way when I said it'd be better if I weren't..." She can't even finish her sentence. I feel sick to my stomach at the words.

"I'm stronger, I promise. He's not taking anything else from me. I'm coming to this meeting."

"Ok. I'm sure your father will like seeing you there. You always refused to go to them."

I smirk at the memory of her refusing to be eye candy for the sons who would be at the meetings. Now though, I know she has no problem going because she knows she's with someone who has no problem carving their eyes out of their skulls if they don't keep them off of her.

CHAPTER SIXTY-ONE

ALESSIA

"*Figlia*, you both can ride in with us," my father says as we grab our coats.

I look at Astor and he nods. "Sure, Papa."

"Let me get security straightened out here and then we'll leave."

"You doubled it?"

"Tripled. Your mom and Astrid have been getting some texts. I'm sure from Miles. Just taking the precautions." I frown at him and he glances at a tooth-grinding Astor.

"Did you know?" I ask in a whisper. He shakes his head and turns for the front door.

"Ast..."

"Give me a second, Lessia. Give me a fucking second." He pulls open the door and slams it shut, causing me to jump at the sound.

"What's his problem?" Teagan asks Mikhail. Jay and Justin's attention are on the door and I know it's only a few minutes before they all file out after him.

"Miles has been threatening our moms, he didn't know."

"Mothers are off limits, those are the rules," Teagan says.

"I guess he doesn't follow them. I don't know." I look at the door and sigh. "I'll go check on him." He grabs my hand and shakes his head.

"Give him a second. Let us go, we got him." I give a small smile and nod, heading over to my girlfriends.

"Ok, so we're going to this meeting. Then you can have your men back until the New Year party."

"*Our men?* I'm the only one in actual relationship with a man. They're all just crushing," Caroline says. I laugh and Tess rolls her eyes.

"Whatever. Mikhail will cave soon, I can feel it."

"I think you're confusing *hate* with him actually *liking* you," Elsi says. I smile at her finally joining the conversation. She'd been missing a lot of the night. I know she's been battling with how to be around me since I figured everything out.

"You'll see." She winks and we all burst out in laughter. The door swings open and Astor appears, standing in the doorway as he watches me.

"Is he just going to stare at you?" Briar asks.

Caroline rolls her eyes. "It's like his thing...he just stares at her."

"Justin does it to you, too, bitch," I remind her.

"Aww, does he really?" I smack her and she laughs.

"Love you, I'll text later." I give each of them kisses on their cheeks before walking over to my eye candy of a husband.

"It should be illegal for you to stare at me like that in public." His stare doesn't change. If anything, it intensifies.

"And it should be illegal for you to look as delicious as you do in public, little devil."

He dips down and plants a soft, quick kiss on my lips.

"Son, Alessia, you all set?" Xavier asks. I nod and Astor signals his friends as we all head towards the car.

The entire drive there, I force myself not to pull my fingers. I force myself not to show how nervous I am. I want to show them my strength, that I can handle this life.

Finding out that Miles' been texting my mother fuels me even more. It's clear that he's becoming desperate if he's willing to go against rules the mafia has set. Mothers are off limits. It's a rule they enforce years ago when one of the mafia's boss' wives were murdered and left two small children.

Astor is next to me and I know he can feel how anxious I am, but I'm grateful that he doesn't make it obvious. Instead, he places my hand in his and mindlessly runs his thumb across my hand until we reach the house where the meeting will be.

"There won't be many women there, the ones who are there are powerful. But you're one of those, so walk in there and own your shit. You're a fucking Pavlov, top of the food chain. They worship at your feet. Don't forget that," Xavier turns around and says to me. Astor looks down and smirks.

"I'm ready."

"Good, we're here."

WHEN WE WALK IN, IT'S EXACTLY HOW THEY SAID. THERE AREN'T many women, but the ones who are there are well known mafia queens and princesses who don't fuck around. But yet, they all still stare at me. No one's eyes have left mine since the doors opened and I stepped in with the men behind me. I feel empowered, I feel protected, and I feel in charge.

"Alessia, or should I say, Mrs. Pavlov. So glad you made it to this one. It's pertinent that you hear this information," the man says as I go to take my seat. He's sitting at the head of the table, and I can't for the life of me remember his name.

"That's Russ," Astor whispers into my ear as he sits next to me. I nod, and as he starts to speak, the room goes quiet as they all turn their attention to Russ.

"First and foremost, congratulations to Astor and Alessia on their recent nuptials. A Pavlov and Ballerini married is a lethal formation. We all wish you both the best."

I smile and Astor gives a nod of gratitude.

"With that being said, in light of the unfortunate information that has come out regarding the Raz family, I've given the Ballerini and Pavlov family all resources needed to get rid of this issue quietly." He turns to me and clears his throat. "I assume the friend—Javi, I believe—was your doing?"

"Yes, sir, it was."

"Very well, I'd like you to put your plans on hold for after New Years."

"I can't do that." I feel all eyes turn to me, but I refuse to back down. I hold my head up high and wait as he watches me. My father and Xavier are both staring at me, but it's not in shock, it's with pride. I don't break my eye contact, but I know Astor is probably staring at Russ, too.

"I'm sorry? Explain, please."

"I'm going after his entire family, I don't give a fuck that it's the holidays. I'll save any plans for him until you tell me it's ok. But his family I can't wait on. I want him to experience the first of something without them, just like he made my family do after he raped me."

He tilts his head at me, his finger tapping, and I can tell he's thinking. But the truth of the matter is, it truly doesn't matter what he says. My classes start and I plan on going to them without the fact that I have to kill an entire family on my mind.

"His mother?" he questions.

"He's been sending threatening messages to our mothers. He leaves them alone; I'll leave his alone."

He turns to my father. "Ander, you ok with this? It'll start a war." Astor clears his throat and leans up, placing his elbows on the table.

"With all due respect, Russ, she's my wife and what Ander is ok with is fucking irrelevant. She wants his family gone? Then his family is gone. End of discussion."

Ander nods at Russ who smirks.

"How are you planning to do this? My only request is you do it quietly. The police obviously protect us, but I'd hate for the others to know there's a war happening between us. My suggestion is a gas leak."

"Not as bloody as I'd like, but I'll oblige."

Russ laughs, and I mean full on *laughs*.

"You are definitely living up to the Pavlov/Ballerini name. The establishment is at your disposal. You tell me when and we'll have you the teams you need should things go left."

"Thank you, sir."

"Please, call me Russ. We're friends, after all. You're no longer little, sweet Alessia and I don't ever want to be on your bad side."

"No, Russ, you don't," I say as I stand up and we all file out of the building.

WITH THE BLESSING OF THE ESTABLISHMENT TO EXILE MILES AND HIS entire family, I feel relieved. And when I become relieved, I realize how tired I am. I've been going nonstop, my brain constantly going to figure out who's next and when. But with the gas leak idea from Russ, I can take them all out together. Miles isn't stupid enough to stay in a house with his family when all of this shit is happening. But the trick will be making sure he's mother isn't exposed. I make myself forget about it as Astor drives us into the gate of our house. He rounds the car, opening my door and scooping me into his arms.

"Baby, I can walk," I mumble as he kisses my cheek.

"I want to carry you." I snuggle into his arms, inhaling his scent. I love his scent; it's something that I could smell every day. He carries me effortlessly into the house and up the stairs.

The way he takes care of me makes me wonder how I could've ever forgotten a time where he loved me openly.

Never again.

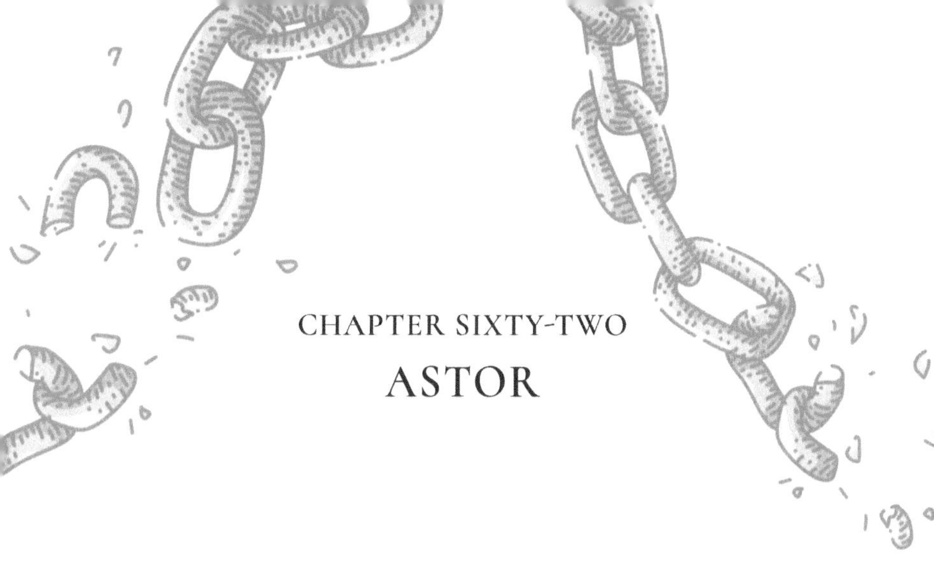

CHAPTER SIXTY-TWO

ASTOR

It's Christmas morning and I'm waking up to the present I've wanted my whole fucking life. Her hair is a mess on top of her head and she has a tiny snore coming from her slightly parted lips. I slip out of bed to grab her gifts. We didn't do a Christmas tree, which I know probably bothered her. She loves Christmas, she always has.

When I get downstairs, I'm hit with the scent of apple cinnamon and the sight of white, sparkling lights. I look around and I'm dumbfounded when I see the nine-foot tall Christmas tree in the corner of our living room. There are presents around it and Christmas decor everywhere. I shake my head and smile, knowing it was Alessia. I slept like a rock last night, because I didn't feel her get up nor did I hear anything. I grab her gifts and place them under the tree before retreating back up the stairs to climb back into bed with her. I wrap her in my arms and kiss the back of her head. Today will be a good day for her. She'll get the present she wanted this morning and the revenge she wants tonight. Russ called my father last night and told him that we were free to take our revenge tonight, but to leave Miles alive until told otherwise. Russ is the only person above our families in the establishment, so unfortunately, unless Miles makes it his business to get himself killed before we're given the ok to do so, we can't budge. I'm surprised at that little stunt Alessia pulled at the meeting, but I felt proud, too. It showed Russ that she was strong and wasn't taking anymore shit from anyone; especially where Miles was concerned.

I look at the clock. It's only 5:00 a.m., so when the fuck did she have time to do a Christmas tree and decorations? I pull her into me and she turns, snuggling into my neck and planting a kiss on it.

"Fuck me," she says into my neck as I run my fingers through her hair.

"Excuse me?"

"Be a good boy and fuck me so I can go back to sleep before our family bombards us."

"Family?"

"Fuck now, questions later."

Bossy.

I slowly slide the covers down, exposing her body. I kiss her shoulder blade and work my way down to her stomach. She arches when my tongue dashes across her stomach and my fingers slide down her bare pussy.

"Mm, finally back to no panties," I groan before pushing my finger inside of her pussy. I curse when I find it slick and dripping. I slide further, placing my face in front of it. My tongue slides up and down her folds and she moans out my name.

The sound of her moaning on top of it being *my name* that's coming out of it gives me a boost of confidence I didn't know I needed.

My hand slaps across her pussy and I dive in for more, holding her stomach down to prevent movement.

"Astor…"

"Stay still, Alessia, I'm enjoying my first Christmas gift."

"I won't last."

"Good, you can give me two then." I push two fingers on her g-spot and circle my tongue around her pussy. Her body starts to shake and I know I've got less than a minute before my face is covered with her juices. Knowing that just makes me eat her viciously. I crave that taste, it's the best fucking taste in the world, and when it hits my tongue, I lap up every drop she pushes out.

Just when she thinks she's recovered from her first orgasm, I climb behind her and my cock slams inside of her. She throws her head back and her arms wrap around my neck as I hook my wrist under her knees and pull them to her chest. This angle makes me so deep inside of her that she's trying her hardest to scream, but nothing is coming out.

My head sinks backwards at the contact, knowing this is what I get to feel for the rest of my life. It makes me want to beat my chest at the top of a mountain to let everyone know I won.

I power drive into her; her cunt so tight it's suffocating me.

"Goddamn it, little devil. You're so tight. So perfect. So mine."

"Yours," she agrees.

"Goddamn right." I pick up my speed and push her legs tighter against her. I'm so deep now that I can feel every movement she makes. Every time she moans, it squeezes me tighter. Flipping her around, I bend down and yank her to me by the nape of her neck and push my tongue in her mouth. She bites down on it and takes over the kiss as I plunge in and out of her.

"I love you."

"I know, now give me another." She wraps her arms around me as I drive her home to the next orgasm. Her screams fill the room and a bead of sweat has formed in between her eyebrows. I run my tongue over it and kiss her nose after unloading my seed inside of her.

"Good girl."

She falls asleep quickly and I wrap myself around her, falling right behind her.

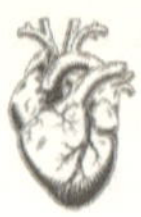

"MERRY CHRISTMAS, BABY," I HEAR IN MY EAR. I SLOWLY OPEN MY eyes and Alessia is laying on my chest, smiling at me.

"Merry Christmas, little devil."

The morning is usually the time I spend watching her sleep. Her hair is always all over her head and she just looks at peace, finally.

"I have a secret..." she says, running her hand up my chest. I let out a yawn, throwing my head back down onto the pillow.

"Yeah? What?"

"You know how I was talking about families bombarding us...well, that's because I told them we'd host Christmas *here*." I lean up and eye her, but I can't say I'm too surprised.

"And when did you tell them this, little devil?"

"Ehh maybe two days ago, but it'll be perfect. We're great hosts. "

"Are we now..."

She smiles at me and nods before putting her head on my chest. The only hosting we've done is our friends, and that's barely considered *hosting* since we shoot from the hip the moment they arrive. A sigh escapes her lips and I run my hands up and down her back. We're both silent for a what feels like eternity. But silence with my wife isn't bad, it's a time where I take her in and remember she's mine again.

"Don't fall asleep, you have presents to open, wife." She quickly hops up and runs downstairs like an absolute child and I bellow out in laughter. I follow her and stop when I'm hit with the scent of food.

Fuck.

I race downstairs, not caring that I'm just in my boxers. My cook is older; she's been with me for years. Seeing me in my boxers isn't a big deal, but when I get downstairs, what is a big deal is when I see Alessia hugging her.

"Ahh, you send me away on vacation so you can get married? How rude, my love." Maria circles around Alessia and pulls me into a hug. "I'm so proud of you," she whispers as I hug her back.

"How'd you…" I say over her shoulder to Alessia who is smiling at me.

"I know everything about you, Astor…you're my husband," she says, passing by me and walking towards the Christmas tree.

"Maria, it's Christmas. Go be with your family," I tell her as she turns back to the kitchen.

"I'm leaving right after I finish."

"I already tried; she wouldn't listen," Alessia says. "Is this a shirt?" She holds up a box and shakes it. "Yeah, definitely a shirt."

I shake my head at her and walk over next to her.

"Just open it before you find something fragile and break it."

Her eyes widen and she squints at me in suspicion. "Does

that mean there's something fragile amongst these gifts, husband?"

"Maybe."

She laughs and hands me a gift. I smirk at her and take it. It doesn't surprise me that she wrapped it perfectly.

"What time did you wake up to do all of this?"

"Caro came over and helped me. You were exhausted, almost like you were drugged or something..." I stop unwrapping the gift and glare at her. When her lip tips up a fraction, I lunge for her. She jumps up and tries to run, but I catch her quickly.

"Did you *drug me*, little devil?"

"I did no such thing. How would I have known that you'd drink the water on my side of the bed last night?" I bite her neck and she squeals, fighting against my hold.

"My love, what are you doing to that sweet girl?" Maria asks, her hands shooting to her hips as she rounds the corner.

"She drugged me last night to *decorate our house*."

Maria waves her hands dismissively at me.

"You look perfectly fine to me." She winks at Alessia and I throw her down on the couch.

"You're in trouble, I hope you know," I say, crawling overtop of her. She leans her head up, looking behind her. "She's in the kitchen, and that wouldn't stop me anyway," I continue as I hook my fingers in her shorts and yank at them.

"But our families will be here soon, we don't have time."

"Guess you better come quickly then, unless you want an audience...again."

"But you didn't finish opening your presents..."

"Excuses, excuses, *malyshka*."

I run my tongue over my lips and the moment they meet hers, my ears are cursed with the sound of my fucking friends clearing their throats.

"We can come back," Mikhail says. Teagan is leaning against the wall and Jay plops down directly in front of us.

"No, it's fine! Sit down. Ast was just being a caveman," Alessia says, quickly pulling her shorts up. I groan and readjust my painfully hard cock.

This is going to be a long day.

CHAPTER SIXTY-THREE

ALESSIA

O ur friends and family are all opening presents while I sit on Astor's lap. I lean into him, pushing my hand into his.

"This is chaos," he whispers in my ear. He's looking around the house and there's wrapping paper everywhere with trash cans are overfilling.

"Don't worry, I'll clean it up, baby. I know the OCD in you is freaking out."

He pinches my side and I laugh. I bend over and grab a wrapped present that's beside me. I don't know why I'm so nervous to give it to him, but I am.

"Here, I know we didn't open ours yet, but I want you to open this one."

He eyes me in curiosity and quickly opens the small, wrapped box, revealing his new wedding band. I'm mindlessly pulling my fingers when he turns it over and reads the engravement.

Always yours.

The jeweler finished it in a day because of who we are. It was an idea I thought of right after killing Javi. Seeing how I destroyed him, how he was so worried about me that he let his friends have the revenge he wanted for himself, I knew then that I wanted to give him something that showed him how I was in this, too.

"Alessia..."

"I wanted to get you a new one, one that means something." I take his left hand and slide the other one off. I picked the first ring I saw, or at least that's what I told myself. In reality, I still picked a ring that suited him, a ring that showed off power.

"I love you and I appreciate it, but this isn't the ring you promised me forever with."

"Then how about I do that." I smirk at him and continue. "I promise to never leave you. I promise to love you even when I want to hate you. I promise to listen and understand you. I promise to be your calmness and your headache. And most of all, I promise to always be your little devil."

He leans his head on mine, running his hand up across my cheek before kissing me. I'm lost in his lips, in his touch. So lost that I don't even notice that the entire room went silent. When we break apart, they're all staring at us.

"What?" I ask, shrugging. Briar has her hand over her chest and Caroline is smirking at me.

"Mind your fucking business," Astor grumbles before pulling me back in for another kiss. Everyone laughs, but does what he says, turning back to their conversations.

"I have one I want you to open, too." He reaches into his pocket and pulls out a long envelope.

I rip it open and a smile spreads across my face. It's pictures of a house that's surrounded around water that's so blue, it looks like the water was dyed that way.

"That's beautiful." I turn it over and frown when I see a new passport. "What's this?"

"Your updated passport."

"I have one...ahh, not with my new name. What do I need it for?" Then realization hits me. "Are we going on a trip?"

He nods at me, looking down at his ringing phone.

"Russ, Merry Christmas," he says. I lean in to listen to the conversation, but Astor gently pushes me off his lap and stands, retreating upstairs to our room. I fight the urge to follow him. I know he'll tell me what the phone call is about. I know he'll keep me in the loop, but I can't stop staring up the stairs.

"Everything ok?" Briar asks, sitting next to me.

I lean my head on her shoulder. "Yes. I'm glad you're all here."

"Any excuse to stay away from my family, especially during the holidays." Briar isn't the biggest fan of her family, and definitely doesn't like being around them for extended amounts of time. I pull her in for a hug and I'm instantly met with Teagan's eyes on her. I raise my eyebrow when he realizes he's been caught. He shrugs his shoulders and smirks before turning back to his conversation with Justin and Caro.

"So, what's going on with you and Teagan?"

"Umm, nothing. Why did he say something?" she asks. Her hands shoot to her hair and she oddly wraps it around and drags it across her mouth.

"No, but you kinda just did. You do that god awful thing of playing with your hair when you get nervous. You like him, so what? Do something about it, I know you two were together after the wedding."

"I just stayed behind to see if he needed any help..."

"Right, *help*." I pat her shoulder and move to take the seat in between Astor and I's parents.

"I'm so glad you both decided to host this year," Astrid says. Every time I see Astor's mother, it's like she gets more beautiful. She nor my mom age, they look the exact same as they did over twenty years ago.

"I'm glad we did, too."

She looks around and frowns.

"He's on a phone call, I'm sure he'll be back any moment," I say.

My father wraps his arm around me and kisses my forehead.

"I never got the chance to tell you, but I'm so proud of you, *figlia*. How you handled yourself at the meeting. How you stood up for what you wanted. You are so strong."

"Thank you, Papa."

"I take it things have been going well?" Xavier says.

I nod as my mother smiles at me and starts fixing my hair. I'm sure it doesn't need it, but it's always been her thing. I lean into her, letting her do it; I wonder if it's a self-soothing thing for her.

"Yes. Things have been great."

"Did you open the present yet?" Astrid asks, leaning forward with a bright smile.

I nod. "For the trip? Yes, I did, although I still don't know where we're going."

"Ahh, I'll let him tell you. But you'll love it. Absolutely breathtaking."

"I'm so jealous I can't go," Elsi says, plopping down next to her mom.

"You, sweet girl, can stay right here and enjoy the company of your mother." She rolls her eyes and smirks at me.

"He told you?" I ask.

"Told me? Oh, honey, he's been planning this since we told him you two had to marry."

When she says that, my eyes flicker to the stairs in time to see him descending from them. He searches the room, quickly finding me and striding over.

"Hi, honey, everything ok?" Astrid asks.

"Everything is fine. Ander, Dad, if you're planning to join us tonight, Russ just called and said he has everything we need and a team to do it when we're ready."

"I'll be there, son," Xavier says as my father nods. Astor reaches his hand out to me and I take it.

"Well, we've taken up the whole day. It's been a magical Christmas. If these two are going out tonight, we're going to head out and enjoy them a little while longer," my mom says as she kisses my cheek and Astor's.

"Thank you for coming, Mama."

"See you at Sunday brunch?"

"Of course."

Soon enough, our place is clear except for our friends. I finish cleaning and join them in the living room.

"Kitchen is clean, no one go in there unless you want me to slit your throat," I say, pulling my feet up and placing them on Astor's legs.

"What is it with you and slitting throats?" Caroline asks.

I shrug. "You like your toys and I like mine."

"And what exactly is her toy of choice?" Justin asks, making me laugh.

"I hope you never have to find out," I tell him honestly. Because if he does, he'll probably run for the hills.

"Briar, you cold?" Teagan asks, grabbing a blanket. She tries to hide her smile as he wraps it around her shoulders.

"It *is* pretty cold in here, isn't it?" Tess asks, looking at Mikhail. He glares at her and lets out a loud huff before yanking a blanket from the blanket holder and chucking it at her.

"You all are fucking insane," Jay says as River sits beside him. He opens his arm and she slips in as we all turn our heads to them in confusion.

"What? It just sort of happened," Jay says. River turns bright red and tries to hide her face when Caroline lets out a excited scream.

"River! We're your best—what do you call it?—*mates*! We're your *best mates* and you didn't tell us! Bloody hell!"

"Stop with the British lingo, Caro. It really did just sort of happened, like maybe a week ago."

"A WEEK! You wanker!" We all burst out in laughter and Caro starts spitting out every British saying she can possibly think of.

There's some Christmas horror movie on, but I can't focus. All I can focus on is knowing that in a few hours my revenge plan will start.

Russ told Astor that we didn't need to be there, that it'd be quiet and he'd get Miles' mom somewhere safe, but there's no way I'm missing anything. I need to watch Miles' life blow up in his face, knowing the reason for it all is him.

I'm wrapped in warmth and it pulls me out of my own head. Astor kisses my cheek and wraps his arms around my waist, tugging me in between his legs.

"I want them to leave, I want to fuck my wife," he whispers in my ear. My legs automatically clench together because all it takes is his voice to make me wet, apparently.

"Too bad, they're staying." They are all staying the night. We think it's funny because we're too fucking old for sleep-overs, but all of us have been drinking heavily today and it's nice to hang out before classes start and everyone gets busy again. Elsi is the only one who's missing. She was voluntold that she had to tag along with our mothers for Christmas night movies and dinner.

He pulls at the seam of my waistband, shoving his hand inside. I adjust myself and thank God that we're sitting in the back, behind everyone. Well, everyone besides Mikhail. I glance over at him and he's buried into the movie.

"Better be quiet," Astor says as he slides his finger into my folds. My back arches slightly and I bite my lip to hold the moan that almost escapes my mouth. My head is resting on his chest and he's so close to my ear that I feel like we're sharing our next breath. "I wish I could fuck you all day," he whispers as he bites my ear. I groan, not caring if anyone else hears it, because when he pushes his fingers in deeper, I feel like I'm going to explode. I move my body with his, digging my feet into the couch when he adds another digit. His cock is hard against my back and I want so badly to embed myself on him. He's teasing me. He knows that it's impossible for me to be quiet and knows I'm not going to. He wants to play? We'll play.

When he starts milking me, I let out a moan and it alerts Caro. She looks over her shoulder and winks at me. He slides his fingers out and yanks the covers off me.

"Kitchen…now," he growls in my ear. I stare at him as he pushes me up off of him.

"If you're going to moan, make it count! Don't be shy!" Caro yells as we head towards the kitchen.

"Shut up, Caro!" I yell as Astor lifts me, throwing me over his shoulder when I stop in front of him.

He quickly gets me in the kitchen and slams me against the fridge, yanking my pants down.

"Bare pussy, ready to be fucked. Just like I like it. Open your legs."

"Be a good boy and make me," I say, leaning my head against the cool surface. His eyes get dark and I know I've unlocked exactly what I want. "Either make me or go back in there with your fri—"

He's on me before I can get the last word out. "Don't try me, little devil. You'll be moaning so fucking loud this wall won't hide what we're doing in here."

"I didn't say I wanted it to." I brace myself for what will happen to me. I'm playing with fire, but I don't care. With his cock in hand, he yanks my leg up and slams into me without warning. I try to fight him, but he takes his hand and squeezes my thigh, pushing it out further.

"You said be a good boy and make you. Stop fighting me." My legs relax and he grins before plunging inside of me. The fridge shakes and I scream out.

"Fuck, Astor...more."

"Louder."

"We're going to get..." I'm out of breath, but I force the answer out, "caught..."

"This is my house, I don't give a fuck. Louder," he groans. His strokes become brutal and he lifts my leg so high that I'm practically on my tiptoes. He leans me over the kitchen island and his hand comes down on my ass, loudly. I groan and his hand wraps around my neck. I look up and see River and Jay are there. I know Astor knows and I know he doesn't care. I know it fuels him to fuck me harder, to fuck me deeper. Jay has his hand on River's back and squeezes, making a small moan slip from her lips. She leans against him and his hand slips in her pants as they watch Astor continue his assault on my pussy. His hand tightens around my neck and he flips me to face him.

"Eyes on me. They aren't here. I am, only me."

"Only you," I moan as his mouth attacks mine. His tongue slips in and out of me and I gasp for air when his hand is around my neck again.

"Come," he growls, his eyes never leaving mine. I push my hips against him and I hear River moan again. My eyes wander and he squeezes my neck again. "Eyes here, little devil. Come, *now*. Then get on your knees and swallow every drop of me." That sends me over the edge because I love tasting him; I'm always eager to taste him. My body shivers and I come with force. He slides out of me and pushes my shoulders until I'm on my knees.

"Watch your friend bring mine to his fucking knees from her mouth, ribbon." I hear Jay's voice followed by a gasp coming from River.

My mouth wraps around the tip of his cock. It's covered in my juices and I run my tongue over his shaft.

"That goddamn mouth, *malyshka*." When he says that, I know I'm doing exactly what I need to do. I do my best to take his length in my mouth as he wraps his hand around my head and fucks my mouth. I hear the bathroom door shut and it doesn't take me long to know that Jay and River and gone. I continue my work, grasping his balls as my head moves in a rhythmic motion. "Fuck, I'm going to come. And you'll swallow it all, won't you?"

I groan around his cock, and not even a moment later, my mouth is full of his cum. I swallow it down as it hits the back of my throat and I can't wait to drink him.

He leans his head against the cabinet and I lean on the back of my heels, wiping my mouth. He helps me up and kisses me. "Go change, we'll leave soon."

I nod and head for the stairs. "I got an email with my classes, check yours," Briar says, staring at her phone.

"Ehh, I'll look later. We're about to head out," I say. Caro slides next to Briar and stares at her phone, I assume looking at her schedule.

"What are we looking at?" I jump at the sound of River's voice, turning my face to her. She tries to hold back her laugh and plays it off as a cough, sitting next to them.

"Schedules are out. I think all of us have a break at the same time," Caro says and I raise my eyebrow. She looks at me and shrugs. "What? You should change your password." I laugh and head upstairs to change for the night I have ahead of me.

Time to end this.

CHAPTER SIXTY-FOUR

ASTOR

"I didn't see anything, was too busy watching my girl unravel from watching you two go at it," Jay says.

I nod and wait by the door for Alessia. "Jay, I don't give a fuck who watches me fuck my wife. She's *my* wife." He chuckles and Alessia appears in front of me. Our fathers should just about be here and we're the only ones going.

"You're sure you don't want us to come as backup?" Justin asks.

I nod. "It'll be quick, we'll take his mother out of the house, the gas will leak, house goes up in flames. Be back within an hour."

"What are you doing with his mother?" Caroline asks.

"Leaving her there. Mothers are off limits, as you know."

"Then why the fuck has he been texting both of yours? I say kill her," she says, her face heating up. Justin rubs her back and she looks at him.

"Go to bed, twink, wait for me there. I'll be there soon." It looks like the other girls are in bed, too, because I only see the guys out in the kitchen and the living room is oddly quiet. The house feels weird being this full, but I know Alessia loves it.

"We'll be back, don't fuck our house up," Alessia says with her hand on the doorknob. I look at them and smirk.

"You heard the wife, don't fuck the house up."

My father's driver is pulling into the driveway when we step outside. I deposit Alessia inside and we head to the Raz's holiday family home they all stay at every year. Everyone except Miles, because he's so on edge that he's staying elsewhere. He's made no contact except the threats to our mothers. He's being a coward and hiding. Ever since the news came out about Javi, he's been radio silent; probably calculating how he can get us back.

"*Figlia*, you still want to do it this way?" Ander asks her.

"Yes, Papa, what other way is there? Russ requested we be silent."

"And you requested more blood. We have silencers. You want blood, we can get you blood, sweetheart," my father interjects. I look at her and watch her battle with her choice. I put my hand over hers and give it a gentle tug.

"It's whatever you want," I tell her.

"Pull his father and mother out of the house. Blindfold her, but bring him to me. He'll be the blood and everyone else can burn in hell," she says, looking out of the window, and I can't help the chill that runs over me when she says it.

Her father nods and my father picks up his phone to tell our team the plan.

Moments later, we're pulling up to the gate of the Raz's holiday home. Our tech guy bypasses the security alarm and lets us in before killing the lights in their home. We stand on the lawn and wait as the team storms the house.

"Remember, if it becomes too much, you tell me," I remind

Alessia. She looks up briefly at me and turns her eyes back to the door.

"What if he's here? Russ told me to leave him alive. If he's here, Ast, I won't—I can't leave him alive."

"If he's here, he's not leaving alive. I don't give a fuck what Russ said." I crack my neck and watch as our fathers screw silencers on their guns.

"Xavier, you take east and I'll go west. Make sure no one is trying to get out of the house." My father nods and they both take off, not giving us a second glance. It's funny, seeing them in action, because they very rarely ever have to get their hands dirty. They have men waiting to be chosen to do their dirty work, but it's nice to see that they still have fight in them.

A moment later, I can see flashes of light from the gun going off. Alessia switches her weight back and forth in feet.

"Relax, *malyshka*. No one is getting past us." A moment later, the front door sling open, and Miles' father, Donnie, stumbles out. Alessia is moving before I am and I watch her. I know she can handle him; I don't want her feeling like I'm undermining her strength and abilities to handle herself.

"Going somewhere, Mr. Donnie?" she says as she draws her foot back and clocks him in the face with it. He hits the ground and she stands over top of him, squeezing his face until his eyes find hers.

"Your son raped me and you did nothing about it. You didn't report him to the establishment. You didn't check in to see how my family was. You didn't even apologize. You helped him, helped him out of the country, helped him stay unnoticed. You're just as bad as he is, and now you're dead."

She walks away from him and heads towards me as the team rushes out of the house. One guard is holding his wife, she's blindfolded and placed on her knees in front of the house.

Our fathers round the corner and we walk away from the house.

"What about Donnie?" my father asks, right when Alessia turns around, not bothering with applying a silencer. She points the gun and fires, putting a bullet directly through Donnie's head. Miles' mother screams, frantically looking around despite being blindfolded.

"That's my girl," her father says, patting her back. "Let's get you back home. You've had quite the day."

I watch as Donnie hits the ground, but I'm still not satisfied.

"Baby?" Alessia asks, her hand reaching out to grab my arm.

"I'm not leaving until the house is up in flames. Tell them to blow it."

My father says something into his phone, and a second later, the house combusts and Miles' mother screams again. We'll leave her there, Miles will come eventually or maybe she'll break out of the binds and set herself free. Either way, we kept the rule and didn't harm her.

"Now we can go home," I say, kissing her forehead.

Phase two, complete.

It's been three days since the *accident* of the Raz holiday home going up in flames. Magically, the texts to our mothers stopped. Does it surprise me? Not at all. He saw that we had the opportunity to kill his and we didn't. I guess some of his morals are still in there somewhere. Alessia has been acting more and more like her normal self. Every morning, I wake her up to my cock inside of her and every night she rides me like she owns me.

She does.

She hasn't mentioned Miles since that night and she's hasn't had trouble sleeping in the last few days, either. I'm not naïve enough to believe that she's over it, but I think she feels more at peace knowing that Miles is looking over his shoulder, waiting for the other shoe to drop. It's interesting, because that's exactly what will happen when we see fit. As of right now, we're focused on taking our honeymoon before classes start back up in a week.

Alessia doesn't know where we're going; all she knows is that it's around water and that she needs a passport.

"Are you sure I'm packed appropriately?" she asks, looking at her suitcase at the door. I kiss her forehead and pull her into me. She stares up at me and for the first time, I see the Alessia I saw when I was eighteen. The one that was carefree, and strong, and attached to my hip.

"I'm sure, now let's go. We'll miss the flight time."

"Which airline is it?"

I chuckle and she frowns as we walk out of the house.

"What's so funny?"

"*Malyshka*, we're using the private plane. I can't fuck my wife on a commercial flight."

She swats my arm and climbs into the back of the car. "You're addicted to sex, you know."

"No, I'm addicted to you. Big difference."

"You used to act like you hated me."

"I still like to act like I hate you, little devil."

She slides up next to me and climbs over my lap. She kisses my neck before biting down on it.

"Oh yeah? Well, I hate you, too."

The privacy screen is already up, as always, because I never know when I'll need her. Lately, it's been constant, and right now, it's urgent.

I yank at her pants and she hovers over me so I can pull them down.

No panties. Fuck.

She sinks down onto my cock and groans; I wrap my hand around her neck and yank her to me.

"You don't hate me. You never did," I growl into her ear before pushing into her. She let's out a loud moan and I push my hand into her shirt, cupping her breast. Her body is moving up and down on my cock at a torturous rhythm. I wrap my hand around her waist and take over. I fuck her with a vengeance and watch her as she quickly unravels. It doesn't take much longer before I'm pumping her full of my cum. She leans her forehead against mine and tries to slow her breathing down. I push her hair behind her shoulders and rub gently.

"I don't hate you. I love you," she says, and my world stops at the rawness in her voice. I always knew she loved me, but it's like the love has intensified over the years, at least for me. And I never thought she could love me as deeply I loved her; I've never been so happy to be wrong until just now.

"I know, little devil. Don't ever fucking ask me to leave you again."

CHAPTER SIXTY-FIVE
ALESSIA

The Maldives is beautiful. I can't believe Astor got me here without me knowing where we were going. The bungalow is surrounded around water, just like in the picture, and the room is insane. We were welcomed with drinks and an array of food, and while it was nice, I was exhausted from the flight and from Astor deciding to fuck me three more times before we landed. My legs felt like rocks, it felt impossible to move them. Astor didn't miss a beat and carried me to our room. It felt like a private island because our bellhop said there wasn't anyone around for the next five miles.

Once we got settled there, we went out and explored a bit. Astor showed me a few places he owned, or as he says, *we own*, now. We did a wine and food tasting, and I even got him to dance a bit while we were out.

Our room is fully stocked and truly gives us no reason to leave it, and that's the plan for tomorrow. To stay in all day and just enjoy my husband with a view that people would kill for.

I'm wrapped around him like a snake and he's laughing.

Something he's been doing a lot today and it's beautiful. It's a completely breathtaking sound. I kiss his cheek and let out a yawn. He puts me down and looks at my tired eyes until his phone lights up and he peeks at it. We've been leaving our phones here during the day to be in the moment. I told him I didn't think it was smart with everything going on, but he insisted we do it for the first day.

He deposits me in the bed and picks up his phone. "Rest, *malyshka*. I'm going to take care of this," he says looking down over it. His face is lax as he scrolls through the missed notifications. Usually, I'd wonder what it's about, but I'm so tired that I turn over on my side and close my eyes. I'm met immediately with a dream, a dream that I know was once a reality.

I'm sixteen and I'm on my balcony. It's raining and cold, but I'm wrapped in a blanket and it's perfect. My phone is on my lap and I'm staring at it, willing it to go off. I pick it up and hover over his name before putting it down, just to do it again. Finally, I put the phone down and just watch the rain.

"You're going to get sick out here, you know." I jump at the sound of his voice and look over my shoulder at the figure standing behind me. Only one person bothers me when I'm out here. The one person who I always welcome to bother me.

Astor.

"I have a blanket, what are you doing here?"

"So what, you're mad at me now?" he asks, circling around me. He leans against the balcony and rain pours down on him.

"No, I'm not mad at you. Now it's you who's going to get sick. Get out of the rain."

"Then why haven't you texted me back? I told you I liked you and you fucking freaked out."

"I didn't freak out. I was going to call you, but you showed up. Can you please get out of the rain? There's literally a fucking chair

right there." I point to the chair next to me and he ignores me, staring at me, willing me to tell him the truth.

I stand up and march over to him. I keep the blanket wrapped around me and hold onto it like it's the shield I need to gain the strength to tell him this. My true feelings.

"Alessia, don't fucking curse at me." He hates that, and I love egging him on, but tonight isn't the night to do it, because he's right.

"Ok, I freaked, but it's not why you think."

"Then why?"

"Because I...I don't like you..."

"Ok, whatever...That's fine, we're still frien—"

"I don't like you because I love you, idiot. I've loved you since we were kids. I loved you the moment I figured out what it was. And you never noticed..." He puts his head down and chuckles.

"Why is that funny?" I'm getting angry and that's the last thing he wants. He knows when I get angry I'm what they love to call the tornado.

"I did notice, but you didn't notice that I felt the same way." He yanks me to him, and I freeze. I'm dumbfounded. I don't see it coming, but when it does, my body relaxes, and my mind is clear. There's no nervousness or second thoughts.

His lips settle on mine and he kisses me gently before pulling back and staring at me.

"By the way, I love you, too, tornado."

I smirk as my wet hair sticks to my face. He tucks it back behind my ear and kisses me again.

"I don't want to be your friend anymore, Ast."

"You aren't...now you're mine."

"Haven't I always been?" He kisses my nose before pulling me into a hug. The rain is beating on us and my door opens. We both look towards the door and Astor pulls me tighter into him.

"Dinner when you're done," my mother says to us. She smiles

and shuts the door, leaving us to have a moment that seems like everyone knew we needed to have. Except us.

My eyes fly open and I'm staring at Astor's tattooed back. He's changing his shirt when I tiptoe over to him and wrap my arms around him.

"Guess what?" I ask, kissing his back. He turns to me and engulfs me in his arms.

"What's that, *malyshka*?"

I look up at him and smirk. "I remembered something…"

"Yeah?"

"I remember that night on the balcony, in the rain. When I told you I loved you."

"Mmm, that was a good night."

"It was…"

"Not a lot has changed since then, except now I love you more and you have my last name. You're still mine, you're still a tornado." I lean my head back and laugh as he kisses my neck.

"Thank you for this…I really wanted to get away with you. Take a break from the mafia life and just enjoy us."

"I know, it's almost over. Then we can go back to you only having to remember you're this badass mafia princess when we have our once-a-month meetings."

"Ahh, the luxury, I can't wait."

"Let's go for a swim," he says. It's nightfall and it's the perfect temperature outside. Our pool is heated and it's right outside of our room. I watch him strip and take in his naked body. I run my tongue across my lips as he swims out further. I quickly shed my clothes when his phone rings.

"Your phone is ringing!" I scream out to him.

He shrugs. "Answer it.'

I pick it up and place it to my ear. "Hello?"

"Ah, Mrs. Pavlov, how is your honeymoon?"

"Oh! Hi, Russ, it's lovely. How are things there? You calling to tell me I can kill my rapist?"

He chuckles on the other end and I wait patiently.

"Funny girl. No, I'm calling to tell you and your husband that Miles hasn't been doing too well. Seems like he's scouting people out to help bring you both down. I've been told he isn't having too much luck in the department, but still figured you should know."

"Yeah, not too worried about it."

"I didn't think you would be. You are free to take him out as you see fit, when you see fit."

"Thank you, sir."

"Enjoy the Maldives."

The call ends quickly and I swim out to Astor.

"Who was it?"

"Russ...apparently Miles has been trying to get people on his side to get to us. He's not having much luck. Russ said we can take him out when we're ready."

"Yeah? And when will that be?" I shrug and swim up closer to him. I look out into the darkness.

"When he pisses me off again. Until then, he can live."

"Fair enough, come here."

"Keep your dick away from her, she's sore."

"Good. What's a little more pain, hm? Turn around. It'll be fast and hard, baby."

And my God was it.

It's our last night here in the Maldives and I'm sad. We'd been in such a bubble the last six days. When we get back, classes will be starting and we'll have to learn our new normal. Which is married college students.

I also have to get used to the fact that my name is no longer Alessia Catalina Ballerini, it's now Pavlov.

"I don't want to leave tomorrow," I pout as I throw the last bit back into my suitcase.

"We can come back during spring break," he says, pulling me to him. My body is sore from the constant sex and I truly do not think I'm capable of handling anymore.

We're going into the town today and I can't wait.

"Boat should be here in a few."

"Ok," I say, pushing my hands through his hair. We got massages earlier and it was so relaxing that we both fell asleep during them. When we woke up, there was a platter of food spread out for us and a movie date set up.

It was the perfect morning to end our trip.

When we get to the town, our dinner is in a building that sits right on the water. Our table has a perfect view and the food deserves a Michelin star.

"Have you enjoyed it here?" he asks me.

I smile. "Yes, best honeymoon ever." The stare he gives me reminds me of the stare he gave me at that bar, the night he fucked me in the bathroom. And even though I'm sore, I can't help how wet my pussy gets from the flashback of that night.

"Head out of the gutter, my little slut. I know what you're thinking."

"And what's that, good boy?"

"I tell you what, how about tonight I'll be your good boy again and you can boss me around as much as you want?"

I tilt my head at him and raise my eyebrow. I pucker my lips to him and he leans in to kiss me. I stop for a brief second and tease, "Good boy." Then I quickly kiss him, laughing to myself.

"You, my perfect wife, are lucky we have an audience tonight. Otherwise, I'd bend you over this table, spank that ass red, and then fuck that sweet pussy raw."

"Hmm maybe an audience is just what we need, then. It's our last night here, let's get a little crazy."

I know this island has sex clubs and I know he knows where they are. I also know he probably owns one or knows who does. He raises his eyebrow at me and his lip tips up a fraction.

He gets the attention of the waitress and pays the bill, then holds his hand out to me.

I slowly take it, knowing this is my consent to a crazy fucking night; but I want it. And I want it with him.

"Well, let's go get a little crazy then, *wife*."

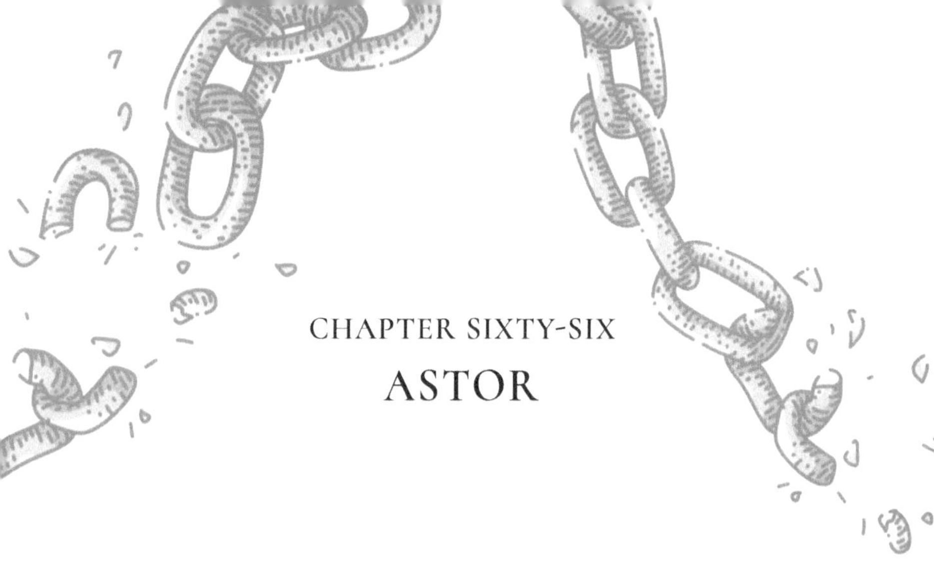

CHAPTER SIXTY-SIX

ASTOR

I've never cared about someone watching me fuck before Alessia. I did it all the time. They meant nothing and it gave sex a little more interest with someone so uninteresting, I never remembered their names. When Alessia erased us from her memory, she also erased that guy. The guy who did the right thing, the guy who only lost his shit when it came to Alessia. Then before I knew it, I was the guy who lost his shit over nothing. The guy who didn't give a shit about anything. I became the man my father needed me to be when I took over, except it was way sooner than he wanted. I became lethal way sooner than I needed to and I became something who everyone was afraid of.

I still protected Alessia, like I was raised to do. But I did it the worst way. I ran off every boyfriend and I made her hate herself, because she made me hate being around her. I didn't care about her feelings because if I did, that meant I had to care about her again. I fought so hard, for six fucking years, to make her remember. I wanted her to remember because if she didn't, then I'd never get myself back. I was tired of being angry. I was tired of making her pay for something she didn't know happened. I was tired of fighting with everyone about how I was. I was tired of my sister mourning the relationship Alessia and I had. She didn't know what happened, just that Alessia was *gone*.

So, she held onto everything she could. The dinners were the only time she saw us together. And seeing us together and arguing was always better than us avoiding each other to her.

When Alessia found out...I hate to admit it, but I felt relief. I felt fucking relief, relief that she knew. Relief that the pieces would start falling into place for her, for us. Even if I didn't get her back, I knew she'd remember us at some point. So having her here now, having her here with me, having her as my *wife*. Seeing how much she's overcome. Seeing how much our love grew from the moment we found out we had to be married. It's everything.

When she said she wanted an audience, I said yes because I'm not going to deny her what she wants. But this club that we're going to, they're used to people sharing. They're used to touching, so I texted my friend who owns the club and reserved a watch room. Because if anyone touches her, I'll kill them and she knows it. When we walk into the club, she's right next to me, our hands are conjoined, and she has a black wristband on her arm signaling not to touch her.

"Ast, good to see you, man! What are you doing in Maldives?"

"Brandon, good to see you. We're on our honeymoon." Alessia steps out from behind me and Brandon smirks.

"Finally got her, huh?"

"Indeed, I did." He looks her over and his eyes land on the black wristband. He chuckles and nods his head to follow after him.

"I knew you weren't the sharing type."

"With her? Fuck no, I'm not."

I've known Brandon for years. We've shared women count-less times, so I'm glad he knows this is different. I'd hate to kill a friend because he didn't know how to keep his dick in his pants.

He walks us pass the open room, which is a room for any and everyone who wants to participate and share. Then he leads us behind the red rope and into our room.

He points to a room in the middle and we walk into it. There's a huge window and a couple behind it. The man is on his knees with his hands tied behind his back and there's a woman circling around him with a whip in her hand. She takes the whip and slams it across his back. Alessia pauses, her full attention now on them. I watch her as she watches them. Brandon stops and raises his eyebrow at me.

I wave him off and lean against the wall as she watches the woman sling the whip again. She grabs the man by his hair and yanks him backwards, steps in front him, and plants her pussy on his face. Alessia's breathing quickens. We're the only ones back here, which is unusual. I step behind her and move her hair to the side, kissing her neck.

"Does watching them turn you on?"

She clears her throat and runs her hand over her neck. She opens her mouth and I immediately know it'll be a lie.

"Don't lie, little devil. Tell me the truth. You like watching them, you like what she's doing to him."

"She's so good at it, strong."

"You are, too. If you told me to drop to my knees and eat your pussy, I'd do it...I'd do whatever you told me to do."

She groans when I wrap my hand around her neck and push her against the window.

"Don't make noises like that or I'll have to fuck you right here."

"Then do it."

"Is that what you want?"

"Yes..."

"Say it. Say exactly what you want, baby."

"I want you to fuck me, right here. So be a good boy and do it. Get me off right here, while anyone can walk by and see."

I yank her dress up and waste no time sinking inside of her. When I look up, the woman is being fucked by the man. He has her arms bonded tightly now and she's begging for more.

Ah, they're switches.

Alessia's hand slams against the glass, catching their attention. It defrosts the window to where they can see us, as well. A smile spreads across the woman's face as she watches me fuck Alessia harder and harder. My hand slaps against her ass once. Twice. Thrice, until she screams out.

"More," she grunts out, making me smirk. I flip her around and throw her against the glass.

"Feeling like my little slut tonight?

"Yes."

"Good, I'm going to fuck you like you are."

I turn her around and yank her breasts out, stuffing them into my mouth. The door opens and the couple who was behind the glass are now in front of us.

"I have rope, if you want it," the man offers. I stop and stare at Alessia, and she nods. I reach out and grab it, tying her hand behind her back before I take her into the room. Usually, it has to be cleaned first, but they didn't use what I want to use on her.

I bend her over the bench that's cornered in the room and thrust inside of her. She jolts forward and I catch her before driving back into her. I can see more people at the window watching. When her pussy clenches around me, I rip my cock out of her.

"You don't get to come yet. Sluts don't get to come yet. You wait until I tell you to come. Do you understand?" She nods and I wrap my hand around her neck, cutting off her air supply. "Ahh, little devil. Tell me you understand."

"I understand," she croaks out. I bite down on her shoulder, hard enough for her to groan.

"Of course you do, baby."

I pull her up and untie the rope to find there's already marks around her wrist. I walk her over to the Saint Andrew's cross. She looks over it and then looks to me. "I'll strap you in and make you have the best orgasm of your life. If it becomes too much, say yellow and I'll slow down. If you want to stop, say *tornado* and it's over."

I quickly strap her in and grab a flogger that's hung up on the wall. She watches me intensely, her body writhing around.

I run the flogger over my hand before taking it and slamming it across her stomach. She gasps and I do it again. She's so out of breath by the third time that I think she may faint.

I bend down to run my tongue through her soaking wet pussy folds and she screams out my name.

"You can be a good girl and cum on my face." I devour her, eating her like she's my last meal. She's trying her best to thrash around, but she's bond to tight.

"Fuck, I'm coming!" she moans as I smile into her pussy. *Good.* That's what I wanted. She covers my face with her juices and I unstrap her. She walks me over to the untouched bed and takes my pants and briefs off in one swift motion. She pushes me down on the bed and climbs on top of me. My cock in her fist, she spits on it and covers me with her mouth. That fucking mouth will be the death of me—I just know it. Her head bobs up and down and I push my hands into her hair as I fuck her mouth. I push my cock to the back of her throat and tears leak down her face, but she takes it.

She takes all of it. She doesn't gag, she just lets me fuck her face.

"You look fucking perfect with a mouth full of your husband's cock." When she looks up at me, I'm so close to coming that I yank her up by her hair. "Now climb up here and fuck me."

She quickly hovers over me and slams down on my cock. I can't help the moan that escapes my mouth. She rises and drops down again. I open my mouth, but she covers it. "I didn't tell you to speak," she says, her mouth tipping up a fraction when I remain silent. She's only done this once to me, only calling me a good boy at times. But today, she's trying and I'm going to let her.

"Let me be your good slut and make you come, but you don't speak until I tell you to talk. Understand?" I look at her and raise my eyebrow. She lifts up and hovers over my cock. "Answer me."

"Yes, I under—" She cuts me off and slams down on my cock, I tuck my lip in to hold back my moans. She feels so fucking good, she fits me like glove. There's no need in saying she's made me for me, because that's already a given. She fucks me to the point of me feeling like if I don't explode now, I'm going to lose it. I need to come, but I can't tell her that yet because I'm not allowed to fucking speak.

When she lifts her leg around and fucks me harder, I break. "Alessia, fuuuck."

She bounces up and down, faster and faster. "Be my good boy, pull my hair. Wrap it around your hand and pull it."

I do as she says and her pussy tightens around me.

"Let me come, Alessia. I need to fucking come."

"Then shut your fucking mouth," she moans. She moves her hips in circles and I pull her hair so fucking tight, that I know I'm pulling some of it out. "Fuck, fuck, fuck, *come*. Fill me with your cum, baby."

My body shakes, it's never fucking done that before, and it's met with her cum. Her pussy is snaked around me so tightly that it's physically impossible for me to pull out of her. I feel like I've been coming forever, like it'll never end. And when she flips back around, I grasp her hips to keep her there.

"Stop fucking moving, little devil." She freezes and it's like my breath completely leaves my body. "Fuck you feel good."

I slide out of her and she lays beside me. I look up and the voyeurs are started to disperse.

"That was...amazing," she says. I kiss her forehead before grabbing our clothes.

"It was. Get dressed, time to go back to reality, *malyshka*."

Reality isn't so bad anymore.

CHAPTER SIXTY-SEVEN
ALESSIA

When we get home, I feel alive. I feel like myself for the first time since I heard about all this shit. I feel happy, even. Our honeymoon was exactly what I needed. It was what we needed.

We spent the day at home, entwined with each other. There was no talk about school starting back up, there was no talk about revenge plans. It was just an extra day of us loving each other. It felt like we were still on our honeymoon, except we were enjoying it at our own home.

So, when we wake up the next day, I'm not upset that we have to go back to normal life. Instead, I roll out of bed, get dressed, and head to my car.

"Hey, we drive together. You know the rules."

"But I carpool with the girls, too."

"Not today, *malyshka*. Justin is driving Caro. Let's go."

He holds out his hand and I place mine in his.

Time to take on Redcrest University as Mrs. Pavlov.

WHEN WE GET TO CAMPUS, PER USUAL, ALL EYES ARE ON ME. IT NEVER surprised me before, but now it seems they aren't even trying to hide their stares.

"Everyone is staring at us," I whisper to him.

He shrugs and entwines our fingers together. Caroline and Justin spot us. "Lessia!"

She engulfs me in her arms and hugs me tight.

"Hey, Caro."

"How was your honeymoon?" she asks. I smirk at her and she raises her eyebrow. "Ok, so you were a slut for your husband. Love that life for you." Astor turns his head towards me and I wave my hands in innocence.

"I told her nothing," I say. He throws his arm around me and we laugh as we walk to class. I don't how we all got the same senior seminar class, but we did, Teagan included.

"Fuckers!" We all turn around and see Jay walking towards us, behind him is Teagan and Mikhail.

"Where's the girls? I thought you were bringing River?" I ask Caro.

She shrugs. "She's at the coffee shop with Briar and Tess, I'm about to head out." I look at the coffee shop and nod. "See you in class? I'm going to wait for them," I say to Astor. He nods and they walk ahead of us.

"I'm surprised he said yes..." Caro whispers.

"Yeah. Me too, honestly," I say back to Caro. She laughs and we walk into the coffee shop where the rest of the girls are.

"You bitches get us anything?" Caro asks. They all squeal in excitement when they see me.

"Ahh! You're back! How was the Maldives?" River asks.

"Yeah, you lucky bitch, how was it?" Tess asks. Briar smiles at me and orders Caro and I our usual.

"It was amazing, we…had a lot of fun."

"Why the fuck am I the only one who didn't get senior seminar with everyone?" Briar asks with a shrug.

"Maybe that's a good thing. We aren't going to do anything besides distract each other, anyway," Caro says, taking her coffee from Briar. She hands me mine and I kiss her cheek.

"My hero, I totally skipped coffee this morning," I say, taking a sip of the latte. It's warm and makes me feel cozy as we walk towards our class.

Briar breaks off and heads to hers while we walk into our class.

The boys have a row and I drop into the seat next to Astor. He kisses my cheek and I push my coffee towards him.

"Want some?" I offer. He shakes his head and pulls out his phone. His arm is thrown around the back of my seat as we wait for our professor to get here. I know that whatever is on Astor's phone is pissing him off, because he's grinding his teeth.

"What is it?" I ask, frowning. He ignores me at first, but I elbow him in his side. "Answer me."

"No matter what, you stay in this fucking seat. Do you understand?"

"What? Why would I get up?"

"Alessia, enough questions. Do not lose your cool. Do not flip the switch and wreck everything in your path."

"Ok, what the fuck are you talking about?"

"Don't curse at me." I roll my eyes and sit back in my seat. I don't know what he's talking about, but it seems like all of the guys do because they are suddenly on high alert. And when the door opens and someone steps in, I suddenly know why I was told to stay in my seat.

Miles.

I lurch forward a bit, but am stopped by Astor's hand. I look up at him and he shakes his head.

"Not here," he says, never taking his eyes off Miles.

"What the fuck is he doing here?" I growl. I'm calmer than I expect, which makes me feel strong. I'm staring my rapist in the face and I haven't thrown my knife at his throat yet. When he walks past us, Astor tucks me in his side and we watch him as he watches me. I scowl him and his lip tips up in a smile.

When he looks at me, I mouth to him slow and clear, so he won't miss a fucking beat.

I will kill you.

For a split second, he showed his fear. Anyone else would've missed it, but I didn't. He turns around and deposits himself into the seat two rows in front of us.

"Lessia, you good?" Caro asks, leaning into me.

I look at her and nod. "I'm ok. I promise."

When our professor gets here, he starts calling off names for attendance. Too bad for Miles, he won't make it past the first week of class. I'm so distracted that I don't hear the professor call my name, my *new* name.

"Alessia Pavlov?"

Astor gently shakes me and I blink twice, coming back to realm.

"Yes, sorry, right here."

"New name to get used to, no worries. Congratulations on your marriage," he says. I smile and nod at the professor.

When class starts, my phone goes off.

CARO:

So, does he like go here now?

BRIAR:

Who?

RIVER:

Alessia's rapist...he's literally sitting two rows in front of her.

BRIAR:

What the fuck...Lessia you ok?

TESS:

No, she has murder in her eyes.

TESS:

She hasn't stopped staring at him.

CARO:

And Astor hasn't stopped staring at her.

ALESSIA:

I'm fine.

CARO:

She's totally not fine, she's pulling her fingers.

RIVER:

Bloody hell.

ELSI:

When did I make it to this group chat? Fuck yeah. Sis, give him hell.

BRIAR:

Get her out of there, she's going to lose it. He fucking raped her.

BRIAR:

Wait...is Astor like, ok?

CARO:

Currently grinding his fucking teeth so hard I can hardly focus. And Justin won't stop leaning over to look at him. Seriously, the bromance is next level with this group.

ELSI:

If he's grinding, he's about to lose it. I'd clear out if I were you all.

ALESSIA LEFT THE GROUP CHAT

CARO ADDED ALESSIA BACK TO GROUP CHAT
CARO:

No you don't, bitch. Tell us what you're thinking.

ALESSIA:

No, it'll make you all accessories to murder.

ELSI:

Well, hello, mafia princess.

RIVER:

Oh fuck. I'm starting to see why they call you tornado.

CARO:

Oooo, this is gonna be fun. Whatever you're planning, count me in!

I sigh and put my phone back into my pocket. I watch the clock as time ticks by. When class is over, I hope he's ready because he's about to see just how out of control I can get.

CHAPTER SIXTY-EIGHT
ASTOR

I know she's spiraling. And I know her well enough to know that she is not letting him leave this campus without getting to him. So, I'm on edge the entire class as I watch her from the corner of my eye. When class is over, I've never jumped up so fast. But she doesn't move. She watches Miles as he stands, but when he looks over his shoulder at her and smiles, she's up in a split second.

"Hey!" she yells at him. He ignores her and takes off out of the door. She pushes away from me and chases after him.

"Alessia!" I yell behind her. She stops and turns to me. Her eyes are clear and I know she's got this. I nod at her and she continues her rampage.

We're all outside, back in front of the coffee shop area. She doesn't care that campus is full, she doesn't care that there are innocent people around when she screams his name. He freezes and turns towards her as she marches up to him, glaring at his face.

All of her friends are staring at her, Briar included. I'm

guessing they all were texting in class. The guys are standing by Mikhail, waiting as usual.

I walk up behind Alessia. Her fist is bawled and I know she's going to hit him before she even does it.

"Why the fuck are you here?" she grits through her teeth. She's trying not to cause a scene. I can tell by the level of her voice, but anything can set her off.

He opens his mouth to respond, but she hauls off. Her fist flies straight to his nose and blood spurts immediately. She shakes her hand out and rams her knee into his stomach. When he drops to his knees, she grabs his head and rams her knee into his face.

People who were passing by have fully stopped now. There are murmurs everywhere, but not a cellphone in sight. They know who she is, and they know if they recorded her, they'd be next. The campus knows she's a mafia princess, so naturally, there's a fear.

She steps over him and presses her black, knee-high boots on his throat.

"Alessia," I warn, but she ignores me.

"I want you to know that the girl you raped that night is gone. So, when I finally get to kill you, don't look for any mercy." She releases her foot and walks away, leaving him on the sidewalk with a bloody smile on his face. She walks past me, and I barely notice because I'm so enraged with the sight of him. I walk up to him and drag him by his shirt towards the bathroom. The guys follow me as everyone makes a path. No one dares to say anything.

I push open the stall and dunk his face in it, holding him down until he's thrashing for air.

When I yank him up, I take his face and slam it into the mirror.

"Don't fucking come back."

"You killed my family," he spits out as he catches his breath. I grab him by his shirt and slam him against the wall.

"You raped my fucking wife...and make no fucking mistake, the only reason you aren't dead right now is because I promised her she could kill you herself. And trust me, she's going to kill you."

I look up at Mikhail. "Call Jay. I don't want this piece of shit out of our sight until Alessia's ready to have her revenge. I doubt she'll be waiting much longer." I throw him to the ground and walk out of the bathroom, Teagan and Justin on my heels.

I don't see Alessia when I come out. I pick up my phone and it goes straight to voicemail.

"Call Caro, find them," I tell Justin.

He nods and picks up his phone. "Where are you?" he barks into the phone. He puts it on speaker and I listen as Caroline curses at him.

"Don't fucking call me with that tone."

"*Caroline*...where are you?"

"I'm going to my next class."

"Where's Alessia?" I say, taking the phone.

"She's in her class, I dropped her off myself." I hand Justin the phone and head to Alessia's next class.

I have to make sure she's alright.

When I get to the class the professor is already teaching, but I don't give a fuck. No one on this campus in their right mind would correct me, including the professors.

"Mr. Pavlov, do you need something?" the professor says.

"I do, I need to see Mrs. Pavlov, ma'am." She nods and Alessia gets up.

When she gets out of the class, I grab her hand and walk into a supply closet that's close by.

I grab her hand and she winces in pain. It's bruised and

already beginning to swell. I shake my head and cup her face in my hands. "You good?"

"I am. Hand hurts, but I'm fine."

"That was quite the show you gave."

"Ehh, memorable last first day, right?" I kiss her and she sighs into my mouth. "Did you kill him?" she asks.

I chuckle. "No, little devil. I told you that was your revenge to take. But I did bang him up a bit."

"Yeah?"

I nod and she smirks at me. "You sure you're ok?"

She removes my hand off her face and kisses it. "I'm ok, I'm in a different space. I still hate him, I'm still enraged, but I can control myself. I promise, you don't have to worry."

"Meet you after class?" She nods and kisses me on the cheek before walking out of the closet back to her class. Fuck's sake, what a first day back.

Redcrest, you never cease to amaze me.

I open the door to the Dean's office, not bothering to knock.

"Mr. Pavlov, what are yo—"

"Tell me, Dean, why there was a face in senior seminar today that I personally told you was never allowed on this fucking campus. Tell me why my wife almost committed murder in front of half of your students. Tell me and tell me quickly."

"I'm not sure what you're talking about."

"Miles Raz. Why is he a student at Redcrest University?" He leans forward in his chair and types on his computer.

"It-it wasn't me. I didn't enroll him!" he says quickly. I hop up and circle his desk with my gun in my hand.

"Then who the fuck did?"

"The professor! It was the senior seminar professor!"

"Hope you have someone to fill the position, because Mr...." I look at the name, because I didn't care enough to listen to it in class. "Bello will be resigning; effective immediately."

He nods quickly and throws his hands up. My vibrating phone alerts me to a message that makes me see nothing but fucking red even more.

MIKHAIL:

He got away, we can't fucking find him.

ASTOR:

You're fucking kidding me.

JUSTIN:

He wouldn't have gotten away if you left his measly ass with me.

MIKHAIL:

Whatever helps you sleep better at night, Princess Justin.

ASTOR:

Just fucking find him.

JAY:

We will.

TEAGAN:

Where is Lessia?

ASTOR:

Class. I'm going now. Find him.

"Of course, Astor, of course." I nod and exit his office.

Time to pay Mr. Bello a little visit.

Class is in fucking session.

CHAPTER SIXTY-NINE

ALESSIA

I'm standing at Astor's car, waiting for him. I check the time again. He's ten minutes late. I pick up my phone and call him. When it goes to voicemail, I will myself to calm down. I call again and he answers almost immediately.

"Little devil, I'm sorry."

"Where are you? Are you ok?"

"I'm fine, meet me at senior seminar class." I frown at his request. *Why do I need to meet him there?*

"Ok…I'll be there in a few minutes."

I look around with the feeling of being watched, but quickly ignore it when my phone rings again.

I answer it, knowing it's probably Astor because I'm not there yet.

"Baby, I'm coming. Just give me second, I'll be right there."

"Calling me baby after the scene you made today?" the male voice says.

My blood goes cold and I stop in my tracks.

"Why *the fuck* are you calling me?"

"Just to tell you that the next time I see you, you'll be

underneath me again. I'll be so deep inside of you that you won't have a choice but to like it," Miles purrs to me.

"Oh, don't we love a rapist raving about being a rapist. I truly can't wait...because the next time I see you, you'll be underneath me. *Dead.* With my knife so far into your jugular it becomes a part of you. I can't wait to see you choking in your blood. You're going to pay for what you did to me."

"You wanted it, whether you want to admit it or not. You wanted it. You wanted me. And you still do, tornado."

"No, I wanted Astor. Only Astor. And it will only ever be Astor." I hang the phone up and walk into the building, heading the senior seminar class. Fuck, I can't wait to kill this bastard.

When I walk in the classroom, Astor is sitting on the desk with his gun over his lap as Professor Bello sits behind his desk with fear in his eyes.

"Ast...what is going on?"

"Bello here is going to tell you how Miles got enrolled in this class."

I frown and stand next to Astor, looking at the professor. He visibly swallows and I raise my eyebrow.

"I added him..." he admits with a whisper.

"Why?"

"He's...he's my nephew. His mom is my sister, you killed his entire family."

"He raped me. And as of a few minutes ago, he called to personally tell me he planned to do it again." Astor shoots me a look.

"I-I—" Professor Bello stutters.

I hold my hand up, stopping him. "You don't matter. You're going to resign and never stick your nose in business that doesn't concern you again. If you do, I'm sure my husband has no problem taking care of a lose end."

He nods his head vigorously and I look to Astor.

"Can we go now? I have a shit ton of homework."

Astor looks at the professor and grunts, tucking his gun away before holding his hand out for me to take.

We're almost at the car when Astor stops me and turns me to face him.

"What did you mean, he said he was going to do it again?"

"He called. It's nothing. It's not going to happen."

"Alessia..."

I sigh and bite the inside of my lip.

"Promise you won't haul off and call a team to take him out if I tell you? He's mine to take care of."

"I won't promise that," he says.

"Figures. He told me that the next time I saw him, I'd be underneath him. That I'd like it. He said I wanted it then and I'll want it again." His teeth start grinding and I run my hand up and down his arm. "It's fine. I'm fine."

He turns away and hits the unlock button on his key fob when suddenly the car goes up in flames. The explosion knocks us back and Astor covers me with his body.

"Alessia!" I'm disoriented, my vision is blurry, and my ears are ringing. There's smoke all around Astor and I can see the car in flames in the distance behind him. He's snapping his fingers in my face and his lips are moving, but I can't make out the words or hear them. I force myself to focus, to hear him.

"Are you hurt? Hey! Talk to me, *malyshka*. Are you hurt?" I shake my head and he looks me over.

"I'm ok," I cough out. The smoke is getting inside of my lungs and I'm beginning to feel like I can't breathe and I'm dizzy. "Ast...Ast...I can't breathe."

I can hear sirens blaring in the back, but who called them? Astor has his shirt over my nose, but it's not helping. My lungs are burning and I feel like I'm drowning. I see Caroline and Justin running towards us. What the fuck is happening?

"We need to move away from this smoke, hold onto me." But the moment he stands me up, I collapse. The last thing I can hear is Astor yelling my name.

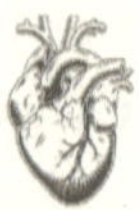

"I WANT HIM FUCKING DEAD. TONIGHT. I DON'T GIVE A FUCK WHAT you or your men have to do. My wife is in a goddamn hospital bed!" I can hear Astor yelling at someone, but I can't get my eyes to open yet.

"Ander, you have to do something. What if they were in that car when it exploded? Our little girl would be dead."

"Eleanor, don't worry. Russ is already getting a team ready for us. It will be handled."

"I'm not waiting around for Russ or his team. I'm going after him," Astor says.

"You can't leave, when she wakes up, she'll want you, " a voice reminds him.

Caroline.

I let out a groan, but no one hears me. Soon after comes a cough and that gets Astor's attention. I see him barreling through the doors and at my bedside a moment later, my hand in his.

"Hi," I say. He sighs, kissing my hand.

"Hi, little devil."

"What happened?"

"Too much smoke for those lungs of yours. You can go home in a hour or so."

"We aren't going home, we're going to find Miles. And I'm fine. Who called 911?"

"Alessia, you're going home. You're going to rest and you're going to let me handle this. And Caroline called, she was waiting for you outside of your class to walk with you. She wanted to make sure you were ok." I nod, turning my attention back to the bigger problem.

"You are not doing this without me, so if I have to rest, then I guess you're going to have to rest, too."

He shakes his head and picks up his phone before putting it to his ear.

"If you catch him, tie him up and take him to the warehouse. Water and that's it. No food, no bathroom breaks, nothing...and Jay, take Mikhail with you; he's been itching to rearrange his face." He hangs up and tilts his head at me. "Happy?"

"Ecstatic, now get me out of here."

"Lessia, I'm glad you're ok," Elsi says, hugging me. I smile at her and she hands me my coat. The doctor didn't think it was wise for me to leave, but I told Astor that I was either being discharged or I was breaking out. I wasn't staying here, that's for sure.

"You've been MIA these last few days. Everything ok?" I haven't talked to her since Christmas.

"I know, I know. Mom is making me restart my training. Says that it's getting dangerous and she doesn't like that I stopped. So, I've been literally fucking fighting for my life."

I laugh and wrap my arm around her, "Aren't we all? Let's get your grumpy brother home before he kills someone."

CHAPTER SEVENTY

ASTOR

O ur friends and my sister have been over since Alessia got home and I'd be lying if I said I didn't want them to fucking leave.

I watch as they all stuff their faces with the takeout Italian we ordered, but I need Alessia to rest so that we can put an end to this bullshit and move on with our lives.

"Hey, you're grinding. Do you want them to leave?" Alessia asks, leaning into me. I wrap her tightly in my arms and kiss her. "I want you to rest."

"I *am* resting, I told you I'm ok. I had barely eaten that entire day, so the explosion was just the icing on the cake."

"Well, Maria comes back tomorrow. No more skipping meals."

"Ok, sir."

I raise my eyebrow at her and she full out laughs. I lean into her ear and give it a soft bite. "I think I prefer good boy."

"Ok everyone, we have classes tomorrow and torturing to do!" Alessia says, her voice cracking. Elsi looks at her through suspicious eyes and laughs.

"In other words, my brother wants to fuck his wife. Ok, got it. We're going."

I shake my head at my sister and she shrugs her shoulders as she grabs her coat.

"Can I come to the torturing?" she asks, making me shake my head.

"Absolutely the fuck not." I give her a hug and she hugs Alessia. "See you Sunday, love you," I tell her.

"Yeah, yeah. Love you."

Caroline waltzs up to Alessia, her hands on her hips, and Alessia laughs.

"Yes, Princess Caro?"

"Justin is on shithead duty, so I'm staying here. Don't worry, I'll pick the guestroom on the other side of the house. Honestly, how aren't you pregnant yet?" Alessia's eyes double in size and Caro laughs as she heads towards the guestroom.

Jay and Mikhail got Miles pretty easily, it was almost like he wasn't even hiding anymore. They took him to the abandoned warehouse we own and Justin has first watch of him. I don't know what we're going to do with him or when we're going to do it. But I want Alessia to know that she's safe until she decides that she's ready.

I guide her upstairs as everyone leaves, stripping her out of her clothes and throwing one of my t-shirts over her head.

"So, he's at the warehouse?"

"He is."

She nods and flips the blanket back on the bed and slides under it.

"He's alive?"

"He is."

"Will he stay that way?"

"He will, until you tell me otherwise."

"Thank you."

"For what?"

"I know it's hard for you to see him and not kill him."

"Oh, baby, I haven't seen him. Because if I do...I will kill him."

I climb in bed next to her and pull her into me. She lays her head on my chest and traces the part of my tattoo that snakes around the front of my chest.

"I want him dead, but I want him to suffer."

"Malyshka, I'll do whatever you want me to do. If you want him living in fear, then we'll hurt him so bad that he never wants to step foot here again."

"Yeah?"

"Whatever you want, this is about you."

"I'm glad you have my back, but even if I'm too weak to do it, I want him dead." She's losing her confidence, that spark she had. I pull her up to face me and I see her slipping.

"You got this. I know who you thought you were isn't who you really turned out to be, but that's ok. Because to me and your friends, you were never the sweet, innocent Alessia. You've always been our tornado, you've always been our head-strong, opinionated firecracker who takes no shit from anyone. Be that person, because that person is who I fell in love with when we were kids."

"What if I can't go through with it? What if I get to him and freeze? What if I dissociate again..."

"Then I'll be there to bring you back again." I kiss her and lay her down next to me. "I'll always bring you back."

When she's sound asleep, I slip out of the bed and down to the kitchen. The boys are meeting me here for an update. When I get downstairs, they are all waiting, drinking a beer. Justin throws one at me and I catch it, popping it open and gulping it down.

"The revenge she wants is...different," I say.

That piques their interest.

"Explain," Mikhail says. I knew he'd be the one with questions.

"She wants to torture him, but it sounds like she wants him tortured by us all. I think she wants to test her limits."

"So, we get to have some fun?" Jay asks.

I nod. Teagan is quiet and I look at him and he shakes his head.

"She needs to kill him. She should have killed him the moment she saw him. You should have made her."

"She's making the rules here, T."

"How are you ok with this shit? He fucking rap—" I cut him off and slam the beer bottle against the wall.

"I fucking know that! I was there! Not you, me! *I* had to walk in on her being fucking violated. *I* had to see her being fucked by someone other than me. So don't fucking question me. I'm hanging on by a goddamn thread. Don't push me, Teagan."

He throws his hands up and sits down at the barstool.

"Is everything ok?" We all turn to see Alessia at the bottom of the stairs, staring between me and the broken beer bottle.

"I'm sorry, everything's fine. Go back to bed," I say, as I start picking up the broken glass.

"No. It's not," Teagan says.

I'm on him in a second. "Fucking leave it!" Justin and Jay and yank me off him and Alessia has a wretched look across her face.

"Say it, Teagan. You think I'm stupid for letting him live."

"Teagan, if you open your fucking mouth," I spit at him, pushing against Jay and Justin.

"Astor, shut up. I want to hear it," she says, silencing me.

Teagan looks at her. "I don't think you're stupid, I think you'll regret it. Because what if you and Ast were in the car when it blew up? What if the opportunity never comes again and when he gets away, you'll never find him again? What if you lost track of him?"

"See, Teagan, that's where you're wrong. I'm not going to think about the what ifs. Because we weren't in the car, we didn't lose track of him, and the opportunity definitely has presented itself again. He'll be dead soon enough. Anymore concerns?"

He shakes his head and she nods before heading back up the stairs, shutting the door.

He looks at me and drops his head. "I'm sorry, I just hate that the fucker is still breathing for what he did to her."

You and me both.

CHAPTER SEVENTY-ONE
ALESSIA

Apparently, no one expected me to be in classes today. All of my professors seemed surprised to see me today. Once again, everyone is staring and it seems like every day it's for a new reason. But today, I don't know if it's because I beat the shit out of someone in front of everyone or if it's because Astor's car exploded in the parking lot. It doesn't matter, honestly. It doesn't matter because Redcrest University is crawling with people who do bad shit and get it covered. It's crawling with students who do nothing but drugs all day and party all night. It's the place for fuck ups; except it's the most poised fuck ups you'll ever meet. So they can stare. I'm sure what I've done isn't nearly as bad as what they have.

When my class ends, I head out to the common area outside. I spot Caroline first and head towards her.

"Hey, bitch," she greets, hugging me. Astor yanks her by her hair and she squeals. I swat at him and he wraps his arm around my shoulder.

"I told you not to call her that," he says as I shake my head in amusement.

"And I told you that I'm a part of the mafia, too." She rams her fist into his stomach and he hunches over before she bursts out in laughter. "Oh, come on. It wasn't even that hard of a punch."

"Caro, keep your hands to yourself. You too, Astor." He flips her off and she smirks.

"You about ready to go?" We're going to the warehouse tonight and I feel good about it. I know what I want to do and I have Astor's support with it.

"Yup. I'm all set." I turn to our friends and wave to them. "See you all tomorrow!"

Astor deposits me into the car and we're zipping off towards the warehouse.

"How was classes today?" he asks, his hand resting firmly on my thigh.

"It was fine, people stared as usual, but it was fine. You?"

"Same. But we're almost done with this chapter of our lives."

"That's true."

"Then we can start the other part," he says, never taking his eyes off the road.

"And what part is that?" I ask.

He glances at me and adjusts himself in the driver seat. "The happy part. Where we're a normal married couple that travels, handles business together, and fucks every chance we get."

"Aren't we doing that now?" I look behind us and see there's no cars on the road besides us. "Speaking of fucking anywhere...think we can spare time before we go to the warehouse?"

He glares at me and yanks the car off the road into a dirt road. Not even a moment later, the car is in park and he's pulling me over the seat onto his lap.

"If you think there's ever a time that I'll turn down fucking you, you're crazy."

I unbuckle my pants and shove them off, watching as he pulls his down.

He wraps his hand around my neck and I hover over top of him, lining his cock up with my pussy.

"Good," I say, slamming down on him. We both moan into each other's face. "You always feel so good," I say as I start to move myself back and forth on his cock, faster and faster. He grips my hips and holds me there. "Don't chase it, let me come to you. Stay still."

I stay where I am and let him take control. And when he does, I feel free. I feel lightweight. He's fucking me slow and deep, and I can feel him everywhere. The window is starting to fog, but I could careless. My body is tingling and his cock is penetrating me from my pussy to my throat. The more he thrusts, the deeper he goes. And I can't help but to moan in pleasure.

"I need to come, Ast."

"Mm, ask me nicely," he growls in my ear as he plumets my pussy.

"Please, please, baby. Let me come. I need to come."

"Then give it to me, come all over my cock. Mark me." It's instant. The moment those words leave his mouth, I cover him. He doesn't stop pumping in and out of me until I feel his warmth shoot inside of me. I lean my head against the cool glass and he jerks inside of me, his hand wrapped tightly around my nape.

"Fuuuck, Alessia. Fuck."

He pulls me into his arms and runs his hand down my back.

"Ready to go cause havoc?"

"Damn right, I am."

"Good girl. Buckle up."

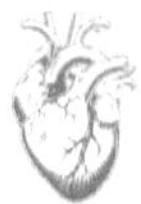

The abandoned warehouse has a few rooms in it, but for the most part, it's a big, empty floor plan. Miles is tied up and has chains that are connected to the wall. When he hears the door open, he looks up and his face looks deformed. His eye is split open and there's a gash on the side of his face that probably needs at least fifteen stitches. I walk up to him and tap the side of his face. When he looks me in my eyes, I see evil. This man doesn't care what he did. He doesn't care that he took six years of my life. He only cares about himself.

"I'm disappointed, Miles, I must say. I could've sworn that the last time we talked, you threatened to rape me again." Astor is sitting in a chair watching me, his eyes strictly on me. I'm sure that if he looks at him, he'll snap. So watching me is good for now. I just hope he doesn't tell me no to my plan to teach Miles a lesson, because it involves him in every way.

I take my knife out of my thigh holster and twirl it around. "I did want to ask you something. Why'd you think I wanted it so badly? Did I say something to you? Did I do something to you?"

He ignores me and looks off. I take my knife and jab it into his side, causing him to scream out.

"She asked you a question. Answer it," Astor says, his voice lethal.

"You pranced around in that fucking bathing suit. You acted like you wanted Astor, but always laughed and smiled at me. Always hugging me goodbye, kissing my cheek hello. You wanted me, not him!"

I'm completely shocked, because he truly believes this.

"You can't be fucking serious. It's called being polite, being a friend. And trust me, the bathing suit? It wasn't for you. It was for the one you walked in on me kissing that day, or did you think I didn't know? Astor saw you in the kitchen, he knew you caught us kissing."

"He'll never have you the way I did. You liked it so much you couldn't even speak. But I loved your screams, I replay them in my head all the time. I loved every moment with you even though I guess I was too late on the virginity aspect. You didn't even bleed."

This time, it's Astor who inflicts the pain. He takes a drill that's laying on the table and drills into his pants, right where his cock is.

"She didn't bleed because your dick was too fucking small to break her hymen...but guess what? Mine wasn't and she bled so fucking pretty for me, Miles." He drives the drill deeper and the crotch of his pants are covered in blood in an instant. "And she does speak, especially when she begs for my cock."

Something sparkles in Miles' eyes. "So I was the first to take her virgin pussy, then?" He looks at me. "No matter what you do, even if you kill me, you can never take that away from me, tornado."

Something in Astor snaps. He takes his fist and plunges it into Miles' face. I block out his taunting because Astor is my one and only. I sit on the table and watch in awe at the man I married beat the ever-loving shit out of a boy who's so delusional that he thought raping me was the way to get me.

Astor shakes his hand out and looks at me. He's out of breath and he looks murderous. The next thing I know, he has the gun out and to Miles' head.

That's not my plan.

"Don't kill him, Ast," I say, walking closer to him. He won't look at me and I know that if he doesn't, then this battle is over. I step in front of the gun. "Ast, don't. It's not your fight to fight anymore."

"Not only did he rape you, but he wanted you."

"Never gonna happen, baby."

"You belong to me."

"Show him that, then. Show him how I like to be fucked, how I'm not quiet unless you make me quiet. Show him how much of a slut I am for your cock and your cock only."

It takes him a few moments, but he drops the gun and pulls me to him as his tongue pushes into my mouth. I let him take control because it's about showing him that he's the one I belong to.

"Miles, sorry about this. But it can't wait, I need to fuck my husband. But please, keep those eyes open so you can see just how good he does it."

"You bitch!" he grunts out. Astor tries to turn towards him, but I stop him.

"No, fuck me."

"On your knees, I'm going to fuck that mouth of yours," he says as he pushes me down. The floor is cold and a shiver surges through me, but I open my mouth just in time for the first thrust. My jaw is lax as he pushes his cock in and out. I gather my spit and cover the head of his cock before shoving it to the back of my throat. His balls are in my hands, and when I tug on them, he groans out and pulls my hair by the roots. Giving Astor head is easily one of my favorite things to do, but having him fuck my mouth? That's top fucking notch.

"Goddamn it, little devil. You take it so well. Tears streaking your face while you choke on my cock. Fucking sight to see," he says, wipes them as he continues to fuck my mouth.

He pulls me to my feet a second later and drags me to the table that's in front of Miles.

"I can't wait another fucking second; I need to be inside of you." He throws me on the table and rips my jeans and boots off. He dips his finger inside of me and brings it up to his nose. "Fuck, Miles, she smells so good." He plunges inside of me and I scream out. "But she feels so much better." I wrap my legs around him as his cock moves in and out of me. My screams fill the warehouse and I almost come on the spot when I feel his thumb hovering over my asshole.

His hand is around my neck when I try to scream again. "Shut up and take it," he says as he draws his cock completely out and slams into me again, bottoming himself out in me.

"Ast! Fuck, more."

"More? My slut wants more?" he taunts.

He turns me over and pulls me up on my hands and knees. His hand comes down on my ass and the moment my back arches, he wraps he hand around my hair and yanks me back onto his cock. I'm not going to last much longer, and when he snakes his hand around and plunges two fingers inside of me, my body shakes.

"I think she's coming, Miles. Her pussy is wrapped so tight around my cock that I can feel every pulse, every tremble, every fucking move she makes." He adds a third finger and it sends me over the edge. I'm coming and moaning, or screaming at this point, I don't know. I just know that I feel euphoric.

"Give it to me, baby. Give me all of it," he whispers in my ear. And I do. His pace is slowing down and his thrusts are beginning to stagger. "I'm going to fill this perfect fucking cunt up with my cum."

Seconds later, warmth spreads across my stomach and I'm kissing my husband like my life depends on it.

"I fucking love you," he grits out, sliding out of me. I run my hand down the side of his face. "I love you," I respond.

Once we catch our breath, I get myself together again. Miles is glaring at me and I smirk at him.

"See, the only person I'll ever be underneath—is my husband." I unzip his pants and yank them down, revealing his bloodied cock.

"Alessia…" Astor says. I look over my shoulder and smirk. I twirl the blade around and slice through his dick. He screams out and I watch it as it falls onto the floor.

"Can you sit him up, please?" Astor yanks him up and I grab his balls and ram the knife through them both. He starts gagging and I squeeze his face so hard that when the vomit comes, he starts choking on it.

"Don't fucking throw up on me, that's rude." I take the knife and jam it into his stomach.

"You know, I'm thinking back to that day and how your hands were wrapped around my neck so tight I had your hand print on me for days." I look at Astor and his eyes go dark.

"I have this thing I'm really good at, it's cutting off fingers. Wanna see?"

Miles groans and I pick up one of his fingers when the door to the warehouse flies open. The guys step in and Jay pouts his way over.

"He's going to be dead before we get a turn, Lessia," he says. I laugh and toss him the knife.

"I was just going to cut his fingers off. You can do the honors, if you do it painfully." He rolls up the sleeves to his shirt and has a sinister smile on his face. Teagan replaces Astor and keeps Miles still as Jay slowly cuts through his fingers.

"Cauterize those wounds or he'll bleed out before I get my turn," Mikhail says standing in the back. "Justin grabs a blow torch and runs the flame over the cut on his stomach, the sizzled skin closing as Miles screams. Then he runs them over his balls.

"Well his dick is gone, soooo there's no saving that. Pretty sure that stomach cut is deeper because the fucker is bleeding again. Might want to do what you want now," Justin tells Mikhail.

Astor pulls me on his lap and sits in the chair as we watch his friends rip Miles apart.

And I mean actually rip him apart.

Mikhail fires up the chainsaw and starts with his arm, his screams are so loud that it echoes around the warehouse. I'm overwhelmed with the amount of anger I see seeping from Astor's friends. They're this angry for me, for what happened to *me*. That shows me that they are there for me. Whatever I need, they'll be there. I matter to Astor and I matter to them.

Mikhail looks to me and I raise my eyebrows. All the guys are all covered in blood and I wish my friends were here to see their men in action. It's fucking hot.

"Wanna do his head?" he asks. I turn to Astor and don't realize that I'm pulling my fingers until he cups them in his.

"You got this. Breathe, ok?" I take a deep breath and stand up, walking over to Mikhail, grabbing the chainsaw from him. Miles is basically dead, his arms are severed off and his right leg is gone. There is blood everywhere and when I kick him, all he does is groan. The groan is so quiet that I know he's seconds away from death.

"You don't get to die until I kill you," I spit at him. Then I take the chainsaw and slice it through his neck. His head falls on the floor and I began to shake profusely. Mikhail quickly snatches the chainsaw and my knees hit the floor.

Tears begin to cover my face and I feel free. I feel strong. I feel like *me*.

Astor's arms are around me not even a second later. He pushes my bloody hair back and kisses my forehead.

"You did good, *malyshka*. You did so good. It's over, he can never hurt you again."

He wipes the tears from my face and stands me up. I turn to the guys and gather myself, looking at Miles' head on the ground.

"Thank you, all of you. Truly," I tell them. Justin walks up to me and lays his hand on my shoulder.

"You're one of us, Lessia. We got you, always."

"They fuck with you, they fuck with us," Jay says as Mikhail nods his head.

"I'm ready to leave now," I say, turning to Astor. He nods and look to the guys.

"Clean up crew will be here in a hour. No need to stay. I'm sure the girls are at home waiting up. Let's fucking go." They all file out after us, and when we get outside, I stop and look up at the sky as I release a breath and smile.

I finally feel free.

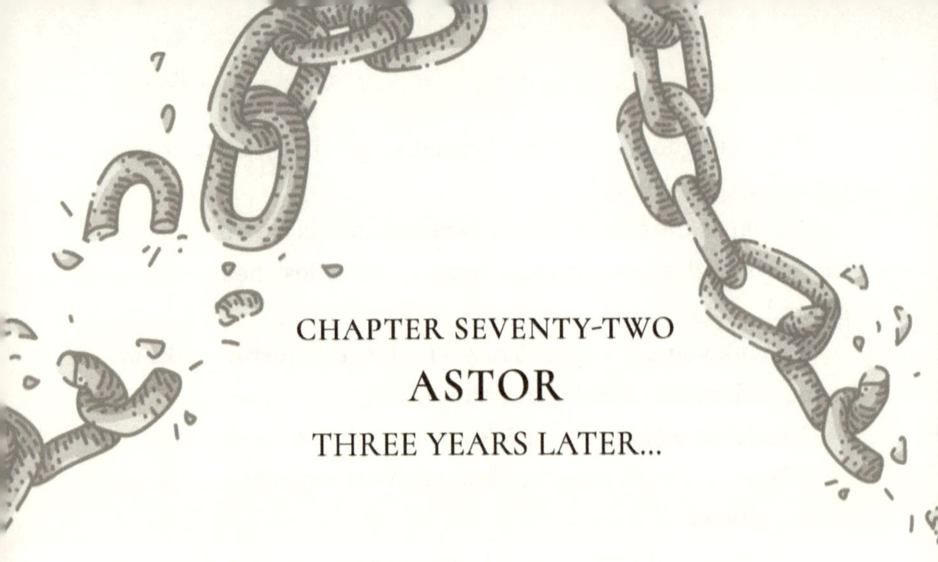

CHAPTER SEVENTY-TWO

ASTOR

THREE YEARS LATER...

"Who do you think will have the slutty wedding sex?" Alessia asks, leaning into me as we watch the wedding reception unfold.

"I hope us," I say back as she laughs. She's so full of life. Three years ago was the end to who she used to be and the beginning of who she wants to be. She's strong and resilient. And fuck, my girl is badass. I sure as fuck wouldn't cross her.

"Dance with me?" she asks. I pull her up and twirl her into my arms. We're swaying back and forth when Caroline comes up and kisses her cheek.

"You two are so having the slutty wedding sex tonight," she says. I can't help but to laugh at her, but secretly hope that she's right.

"Alright, Mrs. Pavlov, I've had enough of sharing you tonight. Let me take you home."

"Ahh, I have a better place in mind." She winks at me and pulls a black bracelet out of her clutch.

"Oh, you want to play tonight, little devil?"

"I rented the watch room and playroom." I pull her into me and kiss her mindlessly.

"Then let's go play, wife."

Going to the sex club has become something we do often. We're twenty-five and twenty-seven-years-old, and we're doing exactly what we want to do.

Everyone keeps asking her how's she's doing, like they're expecting her to collapse at any second. But the truth is, the night Miles died, Alessia truly and fully came back to me. And if he had to die all over again, then so be it. My wife is my purpose, my wife is my everything. And if I play my cards right, then my wife will be pregnant by the end of this night.

1 YEAR LATER...
ALESSIA

"Why do I have to stay here?" I pout. Astor hands me my cup of tea and kisses my forehead.

"Your friends will be here soon."

"But I'm perfectly capable of attending the meeting. I'm pregnant, not cripple."

"Can you just stay still and focus on growing my tiny human?"

"*Our* tiny human."

"The meeting will be a quick one there's no need in you cancelling your girls' night. I'll be home in less than two hours and I'll bring the calvary. That way, Teagan can start harassing you about being the godfather and give me a fucking break."

"Can you at least fuck me first?" He leans his head back and runs his tongue across his lip.

"Hands and knees, little devil. Fast and hard."

I silently thank God, because he hasn't done fast in hard in weeks. He's been so gentle with me. I'm only fifteen weeks pregnant, but he's acting like I'm about to go into labor. I strip out of my clothes in record time, because I know my friends will be here soon.

He yanks me by my ponytail and impales himself inside of me, letting out a groan.

"Fuck, you're so tight. Relax and let me in." I take a deep breath and he buries himself inside of me before fucking me so hard that I feel faint. I come so hard that he has to hold me up as he fills me with his load shortly after.

We barely have time to get our clothes back on before the front door opens and our people flow in.

"Where's my favorite bitch?" Caroline yells. I laugh as Astor groans.

"Be nice, it's a friendly bitch," I tell him as I walk into the kitchen to meet her. She's glowing, but I guess being knocked up will do that. How we managed to get pregnant at the same time, I'll never know, but I'm glad my baby will have a built-in bestie from the start.

Elsi hugs me and pulls out her laptop. I quickly shut it and shake my head. "No homework tonight! It's girls' night." She's a junior at Redcrest now and she's pledging, so hasn't had much time with us.

"Yeah, until we get back. Then it's time to whoop your ass in game night," Justin says. He leans down and kisses Caro's belly and then heads for the door.

"Ok, fuck me, then. I'm just the one carrying the baby." He stops and grins before pulling her in for a kiss. I shake my head as Astor wraps his arms around me. It's been three years and Mikhail and Tess are still acting like they don't want each other. It's funny because they can't seem to stay away from each other. When she started dating some guy, Mikhail stopped coming around if he was there. Or he'd do things to piss Tess off, instead. Teagan isn't much better, following Briar around like a puppy. She leaves to go traveling through Spain soon and he's been in a pissy mood since she announced it.

But even as dysfunctional as we are, they were all there for me. None of them judged me. None of them disowned me when I didn't know who the fuck I was anymore. Four years is a long time to grow. It's a long time to reflect on the person you want to be.

And even though I'm going to be a mom, I'm going to be true to myself, too. I'm a badass woman who doesn't take shit and isn't afraid to cause ruins to someone's life if they cross me. I'm going to be the best mom I can be while also remembering that I was *Alessia* before I was a mom. My mom always seemed so wrapped up in me. And knowing what happened to me, I understand why, but I saw her over these last four year become herself again. And that's what I want. I want to take trips and travel around the world. I want my husband to fuck me in cars on back roads. I want the rush of causing chaos. I want to feel like me. Most of all, I want my baby to grow and look at me and think, *my mom is a badass.*

And you know what? That sounds like pretty badass Mama to me.

ACKNOWLEDGMENTS

First I want to thank every person that has been with me from the beginning. You all are the reason I keep writing and I can't thank you enough. If you are a new reader, I truly hope you enjoyed this ride. To my editor, Hannah, girl I tell you; you are the apple of my eye and make this so much easier to do. You made this process so much easier, I can't wait for our next adventure. To my PA, Olivia, I hate that you're leaving me soon; but I love how much we've accomplished together. Thank you for keeping me straight and boosting me when I really wanted to doubt myself. To my alpha team, THANK YOU. Thank you for the feedback, the encouragement and the laughs. To Shay (Disturbed Valkyrie Designs), I am obsessed with you and your work; so I hope you're ready for some fun!

I am in such awe of this being my third book, and I have no intent on slowing down. I hope you all loved this, I put my heart and soul into this and can't wait to give you guys more! Stay tuned for 2025 updates!

Love you all,
    Alaina T. Lee

ABOUT THE AUTHOR

Hi, my new friends! I'm a country girl who loves writing and reading in my free time. I currently live in Oklahoma (Boomer Sooner!) where I work as an RN in the Emergency room. I love traveling and making memories with my friends and family. Food is seriously the way to my heart. I can be a bit of a firecracker sometimes, especially if I'm hangry, but can't we all? I love baseball, good beer, and great vibes!

I started writing when I was about 15 years old; my imagination should have gotten me in trouble long ago. I have so many ideas for different books, and I truly cannot wait for you all to experience them with me!

Thank you for trusting me to give you the book fill you need!

You can connect with me on:
Instagram: @alainatlee_author
Facebook: @Alaina T. Lee Author
Facebook group: Alaina's Dark and Twisty Favs
TikTok: @alainatlee_author

ALSO BY ALAINA LEE

Whew! So many thoughts, so many books to write! If you haven't read my spicy billionaire romance series, the title of both is below. Follow my readers group, and socials to stay in the loop of new book releases coming in 2025! Thank you for being on this journey with me.

Xoxo,

Alaina

Tantalized and Insatiable available on KU and Amazon

www.ingramcontent.com/pod-product-compliance
Lightning Source LLC
Chambersburg PA
CBHW020348010826

48973CB00005B/1319